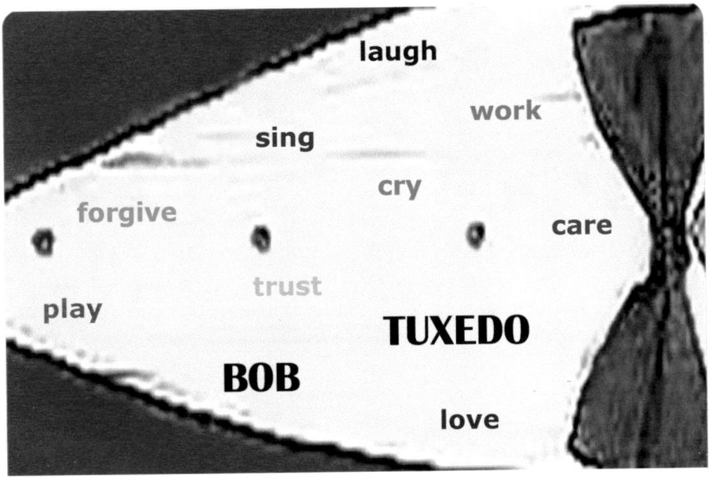


"Popularity is rarely based on merit."

Orville Fledsper 1960

John—
Be forever Happy!

6/12

TUXEDO BOB

# TUXEDO BOB

Rob & Susan Hegel

ISBN: 1-4033-3223-1 (e-book)
ISBN: 1-4033-3224-X (Paperback)
ISBN: 1-4033-3225-8 (Hardcover/Dustjacket)

Library of Congress Control Number: 2002092085

This book is printed on acid free paper.

Printed in the United States of America
Bloomington, IN

1stBooks - rev. 09/12/02

This book is a work of fiction.
All names, characters, places, and incidents
were formed from the authors' whimsy.
Any resemblance to actual occurrences
(other than historical events) or persons living or dead
(other than historical figures) is entirely coincidental
no matter what you may have heard to the contrary.

Appreciation to EMI Blackwood Music, Inc.,
for giving the authors permission to reprint the lyrics of Rob's songs.

THE SANITARIUM SONG
MY LONG ISLAND COMA GIRL
I JUST LOVE TO COMPLAIN
OUT OF MY MIND
DISPLAYS
YOU DO IT FOR MONEY
RUMORS
ANYTHING TO WIN


Appreciation to Famous Music Corporation
for giving the authors permission to reprint the lyrics of Rob's songs.

BAD MAN
I DON'T WANNA BE IN ANYBODY'S DREAMS
SAY YOU LOVE ME
A LITTLE BIT OF LOVE
DON'T FORGET ME
SHE'S GONE
WHISPER IN THE WIND
WE GIVE THE BEST WE'VE GOT
I JUST WANT YOU TO BE HERE


Gratitude again to EMI Blackwood Music, Inc.
for permission to reprint Amanda George and Rob's lyrics of the song

I JUST GOT THE BUSINESS FROM THE BUSINESS

Dedicated with love and gratitude to our parents

Orville Eugene (Gene) Hegel
Eileene Hegel
John Florian Wagner
Margaret Jane Wagner

We're proud to be your children.

We sincerely thank:

Our families and friends for giving us their kind words of support and encouragement whenever we needed them;

Ruth Wagner for inspiring Margaret's letter to her son;

Our good friend, Stephen Pino, who provided the "tuttedo ony!" photograph of Tuxedo Bob;

Jim (JR) Reeves (www.reevesaudio.com) for his amazing production expertise transforming Tuxedo Bob's songs into presentable demonstration recordings;

For facts and information that were crucial to the book's historical accuracy: Rabbi Reuven Lauffer at Ohr Somayach Institutions, Ann McDonald at Boston College Law Library, The Coca-Cola Bottling Company, The New Orleans Visitors and Convention Bureau, and www.mapquest.com;

Christina Rust at Famous Music Corporation, Jennifer Siracusa, Richard Aurigema, and Glenn Goldstein at EMI Blackwood Music, Inc., and Julie McDowell at Hal Leonard Corporation for processing the paperwork allowing us to reprint the song lyrics.

A Personal Note From Susan

Thanks to Professor Catherine Hearn of The College of St. Catherine who taught me the art of criticism and encouraged me to continue writing, and the late Mrs. Gallia McKinney for teaching me to play the piano. Thanks also to my first co-author, Kate McCarthy. The Twins Motor Inn opus that we created planted the seed that I wanted to write a book.

A Personal Note From Rob

Many people have supported my creative endeavors in various ways over the years. Among them are Chuck Dembrak, Amanda George, Wally Gold, Chris Jones, Bob Kalina, Don Kirshner, Jim Knippenberg, Howard Lindeman, Chuck (Fred K.) Morgan, Charlotte Patton, Stephen Pino, Ed Polcer, Jim (JR) Reeves, David St. James, Warren Schatz, Jay Siegel, Dick Wagner, and Irene (A.H.) Wagner. I thank you all. And I thank my dad, Gene Hegel, who told me that if I was patient I would find a wonderful book hidden in the alphabet.

# Overture

"No person has ever been hurt by a kind word."

Orville Fledsper

# solo

I am wearing my last clean tuxedo. My other five "After Six" ensembles are packed inside the road worn Samsonite suitcase that is also providing additional service as a chair. Sitting atop my dependable traveling companion I only need to perform an occasional adjustment to the placement of my feet to prevent myself from tipping over. The bouncing motions of the train might make my journey less comfortable than most traditional means of transportation — even the slightest bump gets emphatically announced within the walls of this baggage car — but I'm forever happy.

Part of my happiness comes from remembering, "Any situation in life is better when experienced in formal attire." My father (God rest his soul, and pass the potatoes) used to say that. He was a tuxedo dealer, and he used to say a lot of things. Many years ago, at the funeral of my piano teacher, he told me that if I remembered something about a person who had passed away, then that person would always be alive inside me. As I ride the rails in the direction of Schulberg, North Dakota, a number of hearts are beating among the musical notes in my mind.

Schulberg is the town where I was born, and where my twenty-three year career in the music business started. I know I have a modest bank account waiting there, but since I have no hard currency on my person — other than a quarter that I'll never spend — traveling in a boxcar is a necessity. Had it not been for a guitar player named Deke (God rest his soul, and may I have another napkin, please?) I wouldn't have known of this economical conveyance, and instead I'd be walking or hitchhiking my way across the northwestern states of America. Neither option is black-patent-leather-shoes-friendly.

While I bounce on my possessions a concerto for flute and violins begins to play in the part of my mind that composes music. The percussive quality of a properly tongued flute is a pleasant accompaniment to the rhythm of the rails. A soaring swell of strings adds lightness and breath to my cramped accommodations. For a moment a baggage car filled with crates and boxes and me becomes a symphony hall. It is in this moment that I notice the wooden coffin directly to my left, and my mental music yields to thoughts of my mother (God rest her soul, and can I get you another canapé?)

My mother was a mortician, and she taught me a lot about coffins. This one looks to be on the higher end of the pine family, and some of those can be quite plush on the inside. I don't know who's in there, but I'm certain he or she is much more comfortable than I presently am.

My mother's career choice was the reverse of her initial desire to be a doctor, but as my father used to say, "Someone has to take care of the dead." It was indeed her calling. I once remarked to her that she seemed to love her job so passionately that, had she actually become a doctor, she probably would have killed her patients for the sheer joy of preparing them for burial. Much to my surprise she found this observation profoundly unfunny, and out of respect I never repeated the remark. My father, however, used variations of the line on several occasions in mixed company. "Margaret's spending so much time with Mr. Norton, I'm beginning to wonder if he's really dead," was one of my favorites. Her usual response to his teasing was a curt but loving, "That'll be just about enough now, Orville!" Everyone knew when Margaret said, "just about enough," she meant, "far more than necessary."

During their first year of marriage, Margaret developed an allergy to precious metals. This made her sad because she could no longer wear her gold wedding band. She wrapped it in the piece of paper Orville had given her as a first anniversary present, and put it away with her keepsakes. After that, my father made sure his gifts were both useful and hypoallergenic. A cotton dress was presented the second year, followed by a leather coat, and then a dozen yellow roses. He broke away from standard tradition the fifth year; I was in my twenties before I learned that the correct order of anniversary gifts for the first five years of marriage was not: Paper, Cotton, Leather, Flowers, Funeral Home.

Orville spent seven months constructing a red and brown brick building adjacent to the house, and invited the whole town to witness the surprise presentation of his gift to Margaret. I was born in 1946 — between anniversaries nine and ten — so I missed the pageantry of the ribbon-cutting ceremony, but I know his gift of "Margaret Fledsper's Funeral Home" was appreciated.

Appreciated, but certainly not much of a surprise. My mother was the inquisitive type, and I'm sure she was aware of the abundance of sawing and hammering. I can't imagine her accepting, "Nothing, honey, go back to your knitting," as a sufficient answer to her inquiry, "What are you doing out there, Orville?"

Orville and Margaret's relationship began during the depression. He was an enthusiastic soda pop salesman with a tuxedo rental business on the side; she was a levelheaded college student. To hear them tell it, one glance was all it took. They courted, and after she graduated as a licensed mortician, they got married and bought a house in Schulberg. Margaret became the town's undertaker; Orville left the soft drink trade, and developed his side business into the most popular formal wear rental company in seventeen counties.

During their sixth year of marriage, Orville suggested they kill two birds with one stone and perform their respective occupations together in the anniversary structure. "Fledsper's Funeral Home and Tuxedo Shop" flourished, and its one-stop shopping convenience was most appreciated by the customers requiring both services.

Margaret became an accomplished artist who used the dearly departed as her canvas. Many times I overheard the relatives of a deceased loved one say to her, "You made her look so loving," or "He never looked so good," or my personal favorite, "He seems perfectly happy now." I wasn't sure if love, good, or happy, entered into the experience of the departed, but I knew they were the best ways to live.

I used to love watching my mother tinker with a corpse. I could view the proceedings from various locations in her workroom, but my position of choice was to prop myself up among the waves of puffy-soft vanilla-cream satin that lined the shiny brass Blessed Victory - Model 1000. This was the creme-de-la-creme of coffins, and while most women would choose a lower priced model as the final destination for their husbands, my mother sold quite a few of these Cadillacs to Schulberg's indecisive widowers. "I'm sure your wife will thank you for all eternity interred in this one," was all she had to say and another Blessed Victory - Model 1000 would be hidden under the finely manicured lawn of Faraway Meadows Cemetery.

Mother's workroom was always marble-cool, and the Blessed Victory - Model 1000 was exceptionally comfortable. However, nothing ever created by mankind is more comfortable than a standard weight, black "After Six" tuxedo ensemble. Lying in that casket while wearing an "After Six" was heaven on earth to me.

I would lie in the grandeur of that elegant coffin — eyes closed, hands folded over my heart — for hours on end, waiting for the opportunity to watch my mother perform her magic. She thought that my pretending to be dead was precocious.

"You'll never amount to anything lazing about like that," she would say.

I wasn't certain what she meant, but I did know it was an important thing for a parent to say to a child. However, as long as she didn't say that she'd "had just about enough," I wouldn't respond. Playing dead meant no talking.

I apologize to my mother's memory for the times my playful tamperings were in opposition to the respect she and others had for her handiwork. One time I added a curl to the hairdo of a deceased eighty-year-old woman to make her appear younger. I put an Oreo cookie into the palm of one of my father's friends because he used to see me eating them, and would always say, "I'll have to try one of those one of these days." Another time I wasn't caught making a change to my mother's finished product occurred in the winter of 1955 when the Fledsper home became a haven of refuge for eighty-nine of our neighbors.

Schulberg's winter season of 1955 was abnormally brutal. Warnings of an approaching major storm system had circulated among the town's residents. A weather forecast predicting fifteen feet of snow falling within a two day period had the town divided between the skeptics and the believers. Some, fearing the apocalypse, decided that the milder climate of the south would be more suitable, so they moved to South Dakota. Others, like Margaret and Orville, bought up every available non-perishable food item they could find within fifty miles.

"It's a lot of bull-hooey!" shouted Jake Simpler. An impromptu town meeting was being held in Carper's General Store where my parents and I had gone to purchase two more hearse-loads of canned goods. Jake was modestly intelligent, and the most vocal member of the contingent who didn't believe a storm carrying fifteen feet of snow was fast approaching. He wasn't aware that my mother considered the use of the term "bull-hooey" to be swearing.

"Watch your language, Mr. Simpler! There's a child in the room!" She added one of her searing parental glares to the admonishment.

"Oh, I didn't mean nothin' by it." His manner was like that of a slapped dog, and his apology was accepted.

"That's all right, Mr. Simpler," I said. "You were just stating your opinion that the probability of fifteen feet of snow falling on our town is highly unlikely."

He thanked me for my insight with an affirmative, "Yeah, that's what I meant."

It was the last time I ever saw him. The storm arrived, and twenty-seven feet of snow covered most of the town and all of Mr. Simpler. Since the Fledsper house was atop a forty-foot hill at the northern end of town, elevation and strong westerly winds prevented it from becoming part of the Schulberg snow bank. Looking south, across our new virgin-white lawn, the only visible reminder of the town was the steeple of the First Baptist Church; it's jagged gothic spire stuck out of the snow like the point of a dagger. Even as a nine-year-old, I could appreciate symbolism.

Our hearses of food were kept in the garage, and though they seemed odd storage containers, there was simply no room for all of that food in the house. There was no room because the house, and its adjacent anniversary structure, had become the shelters-of-choice for eighty-nine of my parent's closest friends. Given the fact that there were only three bathrooms on the property the word "closest" was defined most literally.

Petty bickering, jealousy, a shoving match over bathroom privileges, an affair, and various disagreements about the best way to disguise canned meat products all contributed to the disharmony that altered the lives of the remaining residents of our once peaceful community. There was no place on earth, with the possible exception of Hollywood, California, where the saying "familiarity breeds contempt" became more evident than at my house.

The Conners family, consisting of two adults and six children, staked a claim at the east end of the living room immediately upon their arrival. I believe they did this because of the location of the television set. Though gruff and disagreeable, Mr. Conners had a surprising fondness for the comedic talents of Milton Berle. "I'll be damned if I miss a show," was how he put it. I accepted his connection between eternal damnation and television, but I doubted the punishment fit the crime.

Mr. Conners had served his country as a master sergeant in W.W.II, and enjoyed his recognition in the community as a decorated war hero. Because he had medals for killing a large number of Japanese people, there was no resistance to his appropriation of the entertainment capital of the Fledsper home.

The attic became the home of the Eberly, Moore, Bartlett, Harrison, Anderson, and Hogan families. They had started a marathon Yahtzee tournament, so the top floor became a communal Siberian outpost into which no other resident of the house would dare venture. Their twenty-three children also made the upstairs bathroom a place to avoid.

By the grace and sense of humor of God, my hometown was now wholly contained within my house. It had become mini-Schulberg, and the community focused on one dream, one vision, one truth; snow eventually melts. Forty-five days is a long time to wait for the temperature to rise above thirty-two degrees, especially in the company of eighty-nine people trying to watch "The Honeymooners." I kept myself entertained by listening to my roommates argue over programming choices, or complain about their lack of privacy, or bemoan their limited wardrobe options. "Thank you for letting me stay in your home," was the phrase forgotten.

Obviously, father's tuxedo rental business had taken a dizzying downward spiral during those days of despair. There were no special occasions planned that required the participants to arrive in formal attire, so as Thanksgiving approached I tried my best to convince the men of the house to rent a tuxedo to celebrate the holiday. I thought it would be nice, but given the circumstances, no one felt like dressing up.

Thanksgiving's tradition of fine-china place settings with roast turkey and all the trimmings was replaced by a cold buffet on paper plates. Our dining room table was covered with Tupperware bowls of canned tuna mixed with mayonnaise, little bites of marshmallows suspended in fruit flavored Jell-O, miniature hot dogs from Vienna, and bottles of grape pop. Everyone ate, and even though they were thankful for the hearse-held food supplies, no one called it Thanksgiving. A vote was taken during dinner, and an overwhelming majority officially canceled the holiday. The political climate was ripe for an annulment of the entire Christmas season.

The Fledsper generator provided ample electricity, but it would have been imprudent to use any of its power on our annual holiday displays. There would be no rooftop display of eight reindeer pulling Santa's sleigh this year. We wouldn't be stringing yards of twinkling colored lights around the branches of the oak tree, and there was no need to unfold and set up the cardboard nativity scene in the front yard. In spite of the loss of these traditional and festive accoutrements I believed Christmas had a chance of surviving a close vote. Someone would certainly mention that with so many of Schulberg's children in one place Santa's job couldn't be easier. Besides, Christmas was four weeks away. A lot can happen in four weeks.

Hushed-toned conversations among the adults concerning Mrs. Bartlett's secret affair with Mr. Anderson occupied the first three weeks of December. No one could figure out how it had been consummated in the sardine environment of Hotel Fledsper, but its discovery caused Mrs. Bartlett to take her three children and move in with the four families who occupied the funeral home/tuxedo shop. Mrs. Anderson said she was so humiliated by her husband's dalliance that she refused to continue as his partner in the Yahtzee tournament. I still don't understand the link between Yahtzee and sex, but even at nine years of age I could see there were hurt feelings. Years later, a New York actress showed me the link between hurt feelings and sex.

On the Thursday before Christmas, Mr. Conners was electrocuted by our television set. Although Mr. Eberly said that anyone who punches the screen of a defenseless piece of electronic equipment should anticipate something in return, the look on Mr. Conners' face seemed to indicate unexpected shock. Mrs. Hogan defined the event as poetic justice. She said Mr. Conners' demise was the direct result of his decision to control the pleasure center of Hotel Fledsper. The general consensus was that death was nearly instantaneous, and only briefly painful.

Just prior to his fatal encounter with the power of electricity, Mr. Conners had taken offense to someone singing the song "Sh-Boom" on the popular show, "Your Hit Parade."

"What does it mean? Life could be a dream, sh-boom?" Mr. Conners asked no one in particular.

He continued talking in a manner that suggested his thoughts were running into each other and he could only speak in sentence fragments, but I remember hearing the words "jungle-music gibberish" and "communist plot." His view on the evils of the world seemed a bit extreme, and under normal circumstances I would have left the room, but the veins on his forehead fascinated me. They looked like the big night crawlers my father used for fishing.

"Mr. Conners, sh-boom is slang for 'what do you think'," I said with a hint of playfulness so he wouldn't get offended. "Life could be a dream, sh-boom." I perceived he was forming a thoughtful response. "What do you think, Mr. Conners?" I was cautiously polite, but not overly deferential. "In your opinion, is life, or is life not, a dream?"

"What do I think?" He looked down at me, and hissed his rhetorical question again through clenched teeth. "What do I think?"

No one would ever know because he put his fist through the front of a high voltage, top-of-the-line Philco black-and-white console television set. I perceived the incident as divine intervention. Since the town's usual holiday functions had been obliterated by the storm, and there were no weddings on the immediate horizon, a funeral was the only occasion that could provide both of my parents with a source of income. Merry Christmas, Orville and Margaret Fledsper.

Mr. Conners had died in the living room, and since it had been his home for twenty-nine days, it seemed appropriate to my mother to give his widow the family discount rate on the funeral expenses. Mrs. Conners looked over my mother's casket inventory, and chose a slightly scratched floor model for her husband's remains.

"I'll take this one," she stated while wiping away a tear.

Mr. Conners would be buried in a Pleasant Dreams - Model 55N2P. The N2P is code for "number two pine" which means it's cheaper than N1P. Mrs. Conners' logic behind her selection was evident when she paid my mother, and said, "No one's gonna see it after it's in the ground, anyway."

It was now my father's turn to take Mrs. Conners by the hand, and offer his condolences and services. After showing her how much money she had saved on the coffin purchase, he sold her a top-of-the-line gray morning coat ensemble. Mr. Conners looked very dashing dressed in the expensive going-away gift from his devoted wife.

In honor of the Conners family, public viewing was held in their east-end encampment. Since no one had foreseen the need to pack a suit when the snowstorm began, and everyone wanted to be respectful of their departed housemate, forty-eight of the remaining eighty-eight residents wore tuxedos rented from Orville Fledsper.

The funeral service was brief, and no one noticed the word "sh-boom" on the middle finger of Mr. Conners' left hand that had been written with one of my mother's eyebrow pencils. When the lid of the Pleasant Dreams - Model 55N2P was closed, Mr. Conners and my playful tampering were locked away for all eternity.

The food portion of the funeral was much like the "it's not really Thanksgiving" buffet. The quantity of canned goods my parents had obtained from Carper's General Store was massive, but the assortment was limited. Once again there was tuna on crackers, the little hot dogs with ketchup, pork and beans, and marshmallow infused Jell-O. However, there was one delightful culinary addition to our menu; Mrs. Culver's mashed canned potatoes. Mrs. Culver, a sweet old spinster who was living comfortably and quietly in the linen closet, mixed some canned Irish potatoes with dry milk and water, and whipped them to a fluffy consistency. They were delicious. If Mr. Conners received a star in Heaven, he shares it with Mrs. Culver's mashed canned potatoes.

Instead of the usual solemn occasion, this funeral turned into a party; the first and only party we had for the entire forty-five days. There was respect for the dead, but interspersed among the "He's got his wings" statements, I heard "Please pass the potatoes." Paired with the obligatory, "I'm sorry for your loss, Mrs. Conners" was the seemingly inappropriate question, "Can I have another canapé?" Even I followed my "God rest his soul" statement with "May I have another napkin, please?"

• • •

There is no food service in a baggage car, and I'm at least five hours from my destination. "May God rest your soul, whoever you are, and I'd sure like some of mother's tuna salad right about now." The words I speak at the stranger's coffin go unheard and unheeded.

I'm sitting on my packed suitcase. The stranger is packed in a suitcase. The metaphor momentarily presents itself as a lyric for a song yet to be written, but the idea will have to rest among the other unfinished symphonies. My thoughts are focused elsewhere.

I'm sure it's the coffin, and the faint medicinal smell of formaldehyde that's stirring my memories. For some it's the smell of bay laurel in a simmering stew that activates a longing for mom's home cooking. For others it's the fragrance of a certain fabric softener that brings a memory of their mother hanging laundry. For me it's formaldehyde. When it drifts into my nostrils it reminds me of lavender toilet water and yellow roses, peppermints and boxes of chocolates. It always makes me think of my mother.

## duet

There are a number of services available to the modern day train traveler that are not offered in baggage class. Seating, food, beverages, bathroom facilities, other people, and a view of the passing countryside add to the comfort and pleasure of the ticketed passenger's journey. The most critical amenity I find lacking in my surroundings is the accessibility of a toilet.

Nature's call requires an answer. It would be easy to respond in one of the car's corners, but doing so would seriously downgrade my personal standards. Since "holding it" has lost its tenure as an option, I decide to push open the large sliding door, and cast my fate away from the wind. Arriving at this resolution, however, is easier than its accomplishment.

As I pull back the handle I feel the rusted resistance of old metal rubbing against older metal, and I wonder if this door is only operable from the other side. After all, the presence of a handle doesn't guarantee performance, it merely suggests potential. I continue to push and pull with no appreciable result.

Nature is still on the phone, and if I don't answer soon my body's operator will put the call through anyway. Crossing my legs helps alleviate the urgency, but provides no balance or leverage to my door-opening dilemma. So I uncross them, and discover it's the right thing to do. The door squeaks open about a foot, which is more than enough room for the task at hand.

The clean grassy smell of late summer in Montana hangs in the air as I carefully position myself in the slightly open doorway and unzip my trousers. I begin the process of relieving myself onto the great outdoors, and take a moment to appreciate the meaning of the word, "Ah!" I don't want to lose my balance or my euphoria, so I use the utmost caution while delicately directing the stream downwind. At seventy miles per hour it is prudent to avoid both the back splash and the potentially nasty tumble.

My father comes to mind, not because he was the main supporting character during my toilet training, but due to his particular definition of proper behavior. He believed the rules of etiquette could be condensed into one concise standard, "What if everyone did it?" He used that slogan whenever he felt the need to illustrate the fragile boundary that separates civilization from chaos. My guess is he would not have bestowed his seal of approval on my present action because I have personally observed only one other person doing it.

Mr. Hobo was much more adept at the procedure. He had great balance, and stood with his arms at his sides even when the train jerked from side to side or negotiated a sharp curve. Since I am obliged to hold on to both the doorframe and myself, his technique was quite impressive.

I don't remember Mr. Hobo's actual name. He jumped on board a New Orleans bound train somewhere in west Texas, and quickly expressed his individuality by sitting alone and avoiding eye contact with me and the members of my band. Everyone respected his privacy, but when he got up to relieve himself I saw the words, “Don’t even try it!” tattooed on his lower back in crude black lettering. Curiosity compelled me to ask what was implied by the inscribed motto.

“I got it in prison.” His answer was certainly direct, but lacked my requested definition.

I repeated the question to the back of his head. “What does it mean?”

“What do you think?” His voice was surly.

I was hesitant to reply in case I came up with an unsatisfactory answer. “It could be anything.” My response was sly, and skirted around any possibility of being taken the wrong way.

“Hey, pal, it means back off!” He turned around, and his harsh demeanor melted into a smile of recognition. “Hey, I know you! Yer that guy who’s always in a tuxedo.”

“Yes, sir.” There was no use denying his incisive perception. My attire was a dead giveaway.

“Yeah, I seen you perform in Vegas. I was a security guard at The Sands before I got busted for drugs. Got two years just because my boss had a thing about me getting high on the job. You know, me carrying a gun and all.” He snarled as if it was absurd his boss had a problem partnering drugs with gun, but then his voice took on the sound of a child asking for a piece of candy. “Could I have yer autograph, mister? You can sign my back. Just put yer John Hancock right next to my tattoo. I even got a pen.”

He pulled a disposable pen from a pocket of his oil-stained blue jeans, and handed it to me. As he turned around and bent over, the true meaning of his tattooed inscription crossed my mind. I was hesitant to add my signature.

"I don't feel comfortable signing my name to something I didn't write."

"It don't matter. The guy who done it's dead." His matter of fact statement did nothing to ease my predicament until he added, "If it'd make you feel better, write somethin'!"

He had given me the perfect solution. I quickly composed a three verse lyric complete with chorus and bridge titled, "Don't Even Try It!" I printed it on an angle from the top of his left shoulder blade down to his right kidney. I finished by signing my name just above the inspirational tattoo.

Mr. Hobo jumped off the train at the Louisiana border. To this day I can't recall the lyrics I wrote. I didn't think to make a copy of that creative moment, but if Mr. Hobo hasn't bathed in nineteen years, "Don't Even Try It!" still exists.

• • •

The fields of Montana roll by as I continue my response to nature's call. I'm filled with a sense of freedom, but this feeling is only partially due to urination. The feel of the air and sunlight reminds me of being back in Schulberg on a Sunday at the end of church service. There was no freedom on earth quite like that which was granted when the giant doors of The First Baptist Church of North Dakota, swung open after a fatiguing hour and a half of worship.

Preacher Dave Adamian was full of the devil's fire and brimstone, and he never tired of combining the glories of God with the horrors of Hell. He was a man possessed with demons, which he attempted to exorcise with each and every sermon. In his mind everyone in town was a sinner sentenced to eternal damnation regardless of their race, color, creed, wealth, occupation, eating habits, or personal dress code. His voice had the quality of fingernails on a blackboard. His demeanor was sour, his posture was poor, and he wore a toupee that always looked like it was on backwards. Aside from those factors, he was a perfect gentleman.

The last time I saw Preacher Dave was on a Sunday, naturally, after an exceptionally brutal sermon on his favorite topic, "You Are All Going To Hell!" He was lurking near the open doors, issuing his usual admonitions to the departing defeated congregation filing from the nave through the narthex toward the nirvana that waited outside. The money was in the collection plate, so a compulsory smile and handshake were all that was necessary to gain another week of freedom. Last stop, Preacher Dave. Praise the Lord!

"What are you going to do with your life, son?"

His flaccid handshake always felt like one of the sunfish my father caught, and I had no idea how to answer his question.

"Will you be ready when the Lord calls? Do you hear the Lord when he speaks to you, son? Are you ready to carry out the plan God has for your life?"

He was persistent with his questions, and I suspected he would continue asking them in order to elicit further discussion.

"Well, sir, I'm only ten years old. I'm not presently aware of God's plan for me, but I'm certain I'll be wearing a tuxedo when He lets me in on it." I thought my response would conclude the need for my presence in line, but I underestimated the length to this line of questioning.

"It's never too early for a sinner to know the path God has chosen for him."

He called me a sinner in front of God and my parents.

"I'm sure you're right, Preacher Dave, sir," I replied, "but even a sinner is smart enough to let God handle all the details."

I've answered God's most recent call from the open doorway of this baggage car. I'm still dressed in a tuxedo, and still waiting for His long-term plan to unfold in case I'm not already living it. God's plan for Preacher Dave, however, unfolded quickly.

Preacher Dave had been the town's minister of doom for less than a year when his personal call from the Lord arrived on a perfectly sunny November Sunday. His sermon commemorating the one-year anniversary of the big snowstorm had ended. In the gospel according to Dave, Schulberg had been in God's doghouse, and the storm was God's apt punishment. Most of my fellow parishioners appeared uncomfortable at the bellowed suggestion that our small town had displeased God to such an extent that He delivered twenty-seven feet of snow from the heavens as a divine lesson. As it turned out, Preacher Dave got a lesson on the danger of combining yelling with brain aneurysm.

"Are you prepared to," were Preacher Dave's last words. Doctor Brigner tried, but could not revive him after he collapsed on the front steps of The First Baptist Church of North Dakota in mid-handshake.

I remember the promise I made the day Preacher Dave was called away on eternal assignment. Whenever I encountered a disagreeable person who I felt was in need of censure, I would defer to God's judgment because there's no limit to His methods of problem management. I have always had the utmost respect for true creative genius.

Prior to the storm of '55, Paul Peters had been our pastor. He was a kind man with twinkling eyes and a ready smile. Since both my parents were orphans, he was the perfect replacement for the grandfathers I never knew. His voice was as soft as the fuzz on a peach, and he had a kind, jovial nature that always made a person feel at ease. His sermons painted a picture of Heaven that invoked thoughts of pearly gates, golden streets, and choirs of angels. He made Heaven sound like the ultimate vacation destination.

It is because of my relationship with Pastor Peters during my formative years that I believe in God. I find it comforting to know there is a higher authority keeping an eye on everything. Whatever happens in life is God's will, and since He's God, I never argue with the circumstance, and I rarely disagree with the result. Sadly, Pastor Peters perished in the storm of '55, and was replaced with Preacher Dave. I still question God's choice in that particular matter, but God does as He sees fit regardless of other opinions.

• • •

My wandering mind has been a useful accessory, but random thought occasionally hinders my ability to pay attention to current events. This truth is directly represented by the presence of a train conductor who has entered the baggage car, and is walking toward me. I tuck in my personal belonging, and zip up my pants to diminish the embarrassment of discovery.

I fear the worst. The worst being that he will exhibit no civility, and I will be swiftly hurled from a moving train. However, I embrace my optimism in the hope he will simply inform me that my trip is ending at the next scheduled stop. Whichever is my fate, I look to the heavens for a sign from God. There is none evident, but appreciating His sense of humor, I step away from the open door as a preemptive maneuver.

"I'm sorry for your loss," the conductor says in a solemn tone with his head bowed toward the coffin.

It's an honest mistake. To most people a tuxedo is not a stand-alone item; it must relate to something in order to justify its presence. In life, death, and baggage car the artful blend of tuxedo and coffin are beyond reproach or question. As he leaves me to what he supposes is my grief, I murmur respectfully, "May I have another napkin, please?"

# triad

I was a normal boy with a normal childhood. I collected frogs, liked/disliked girls, played baseball, took piano lessons, skipped stones, ran, jumped, got into mischief, and refused to eat jellied consommé. I was good at math and grammar, not so good at science, and I had a mild crush on my fifth grade teacher, Miss Throckmorton.

I grew up doing what any child would or could do in Schulberg, and though my choice of attire elicited some teasing, I always reacted to taunts with a smile. I viewed my tuxedo as everyday wear, like others would view a T-shirt and blue jeans. As I got older, I began to sense there was something greater to life than Cub Scouts, sports, and the 4-H Club. I knew there was an entirely different world waiting beyond the borders of Schulberg, North Dakota, and I wanted to see it.

I became infected with an extreme case of wanderlust. Other children caught colds or got the measles, but I contracted an ailment whose symptoms included intense longings and profound intrigue. I had to see where the rising sun came from, and where the setting sun went. I pinned my curiosity on the edge of the horizon.

I made some attempts to humor my affliction by cutting pictures of skyscrapers and bustling crowded street scenes from magazines. My bedroom walls and ceiling were covered with collages of big cities, and I would lie in bed gazing at the wonder of it all. I wanted to know why some of the buildings had names and others just numbers. Did the air smell different? Who were all those people, and did they know someone was taking their photograph?

During my fifth year at Colonel Clement H. Lounsberry Elementary School I started planning my escape. Leaving would come as no small blow to my parents for I was, after all, their only child, but I knew they would not want me to follow in either of their footsteps if it didn't make me happy. Undertaker or bright city lights? The tuxedo trade or the great unknown? The choice seemed clear to me, but I was a bit fuzzy about what I would pursue once I got to wherever I would go.

There were two distinct patterns in my life. I had a passion for tuxedos, and I always had a melody playing in my head. I didn't equate this symphonic phenomenon with a mental disorder because I thought everyone had music strolling through their brains as a source of personal entertainment. Years later I would discover that few people possessed a built-in stereo, and of those who did, some were institutionalized.

I wrote my first actual song because of a homework assignment. Each child in Miss Throckmorton's class was asked to write a story about something he or she saw on the way home from school. A large black crow provided my inspiration, and I wrote the following lyrics that I sang in front of the class the next day.

"Caw, Caw, Crow.
Caw, Caw, Crow.
You said caw, not tweet,
when you flew over the wheat.
Now you don't make a sound.
You just lie on the ground.
There's no caw from the beak on your head.
You can't fly.
You can't speak.
You're dead.
Caw, Caw, Crow.
Caw, Caw, Crow."

It was the first public performance by Tuxedo Bob. The melody was suitable for Ethel Merman, and copying her style I drew out the last line for dramatic effect. I received career supporting applause from my classmates, and a B plus from Miss Throckmorton whose two cents included the opinion my song should have been in a minor key since it was about death. I told her I had purposely avoided making the obvious melodic choice.

"CAW, CAW, CROW," albeit a neophyte effort, gave me a direction. I was a songwriter. Over the next few years, while growing from a boy's size 8 to a 37 regular, I wrote a number of romantic ballads and up-tempo tunes that included my thoughts about the sky, wheat, hospitals, grasshoppers, church, tuxedos, and preparing the dead for burial. I judiciously surmised that if I was going to continue to write songs I would need to seek inspiration in greener pastures.

I deposited every penny of the money I earned mowing lawns, shoveling snow, and delivering papers into my account at Schulberg Savings and Loan. By my eighteenth birthday I had saved three thousand dollars. I asked my parents for permission to travel to a city where I could see buildings that were bigger than the one-story structures that lined Main Street of downtown Schulberg, and they gave their approval. I immediately bought a black Samsonite suitcase, and packed it with six "After Six" tuxedos and a few required toiletries. The bank exchanged my dollars for traveler's checks, and I headed for the bus depot. I was an excited, blue-eyed, brown-haired, slender young man on his way to Chicago, Illinois, but the unpredictability of my future made it seem prudent to ask the Greyhound agent for a round-trip ticket.

There was a short ceremony at the corner where the Greyhound bus would come to whisk me away. My father shook my hand, and asked me to keep up the weekly payments on the six tuxedo rentals. He added the enigmatic phrase, "Don't take any wooden nickels," which I believe is something fathers say to their sons when nothing else comes to mind. I assured him I wouldn't unless wood turned out to be the money used in Chicago. A tear dripped from my mother's left eye as she made me promise not to talk to strangers. Though anyone I would meet outside Schulberg's city limits would fall into the "someone I didn't know" category, I agreed to her request out of respect.

The bus trip was long, and mostly uneventful except for the discovery that there was a limit to my curiosity. Someone I didn't know who sat in the seat across from me mumbled to himself whenever he wasn't asleep. He didn't sleep much, so consequently neither did I, and that's how we got into a conversation. I think his name was Gus McNulty. It may have been MacNaltree. Whatever his name, he had a long, yellowed fang tooth that hung down over the left side of his lower lip and made most of what he said unintelligible. I listened politely in case he was armed.

As he talked I watched his tooth, wondering why he still had it. Its loss would not provide a vast cosmetic improvement, but it might allow his lower lip to do something other than make flapping sounds. I mustered up the courage to ask him about it.

"Can I ask you something about your tooth, sir?" I phrased it in a way that he could decline my request if the subject made him uncomfortable.

"Sure." His reply contained a few other words that I think were supposed to be, "If you've a mind to," though they sounded like, "Foova myta."

Since he had given me the go-ahead, I asked him why he hadn't removed a tooth that was obviously developed beyond its capacity to serve a useful purpose. Somewhere in his response I gleaned that he had a friend who liked the way it felt. I paused for a moment to ponder the distinction between acquiring too much information and unrestrained curiosity. I decided there were some things I didn't need to know.

"That's nice," I said with a smile. "Oh, look, Chicago!" It was convenient to be able to end the trip and the conversation simultaneously.

Sixty seconds on the streets of Chicago, and I was aware of the primary difference between a big city and a little city. In a big city everything happens at the same time. I knew Chicago would be more vibrant than Schulberg, but I was not fully prepared for the decibel level. I admired the residents for their ability to put up with the cacophony.

The museum of art and a large gothic library were the only quiet places I found during my dizzying first day. When night fell I walked along the concrete and rock shores of Lake Michigan, and slept in a park that was named for President Lincoln or a car. A policeman woke me around three in the morning to inform me I couldn't sleep where I was sleeping. I wanted to tell him I was performing the feat just fine, but thought better of stepping on the wrong side of the laws' sense of humor.

I gathered my belongings, bid the officer goodnight, and found an all-night diner that advertised "Authentic Home-Style Pie" in red, white and blue neon. Cardboard crust filled with applesauce, though not the authentic style in my home, didn't taste half bad at 3:17 A.M. My father used to say, "Something that is not half bad is not necessarily half good."

Passing the time reading an informative brochure from a "Free - Take One!" display, I discovered Chicago had two nicknames: The Windy City, and Second City. That was enough for me. Chicago was no windier than a Schulberg wheat field in November. I went back to the bus depot, and exchanged the remaining portion of my round-trip ticket for one-way passage to New York, New York.

Two days later I emerged from the Port Authority Bus Terminal onto Eighth Avenue and Forty-second Street at one in the afternoon. What a sight! There were buildings and people everywhere. I watched as people went in and out of the huge skyscrapers, and I wondered where they were headed and what they were doing. Some carried briefcases, some dragged luggage; many had cameras dangling from their necks. People were delivering packages, waiting in limousines, lugging over-sized shopping bags, spitting on the sidewalk, asking for donations to charities of which I had never heard, and jockeying for position to attract the attention of taxi drivers. Everywhere I looked there were people of all conceivable shapes, sizes, colors, nationalities, dress codes and hairstyle preferences, and they all seemed to have someplace to go, something to do, and not enough time in which to do it.

Every square inch of available audio space was taken up with the sounds of rumbling subways, whining black-smoke-spitting buses, and honking automobiles. People chattered at each other, or to no one in particular, in every known language, and in tongues yet to be discovered. My magazine cutouts had come to life. As I watched and listened I knew I had found a loud, but fertile environment for song ideas.

Much to my surprise no one asked me if I was going to a prom or if I was running for governor. No one even acknowledged my existence. God bless the streets of New York where a man dressed in a tuxedo can be just another face to ignore in the crowd.

I located a YMCA with the help of a phone book, and got a room for three dollars a night. If I had no other expenses I could afford to stay there for almost three years, but after deducting the cost of essentials like food and toothpaste, I figured I would have to find some type of employment within six to eight months to remain on the safe side of dire straights. As it turned out I would not have to wait that long. My ship would arrive on the morning after the evening of the second day.

• • •

The second day started out like any other normal day in Manhattan. A resounding chorus from the "Concerto For Jackhammer And Police Siren in D Major" made it impossible for me to sleep past 7 A.M. I showered, shaved, dressed, and walked down the block to purchase a grapefruit from a corner fruit stand. I noted that fruit was one of four items available every fifty-nine steps. The other three were newspaper, cup of coffee, and hot dog.

I spent the day strolling through museums and art galleries, and discovered there was a huge difference between being outdoors and indoors. No one paid attention to me outdoors. Indoors I found myself repeating, "I'm sorry, but I don't work here," to numerous inquiries from strangers.

When I happened to actually know the answer to a particular question I soon learned not to be forthright with the information. This was due to the strange custom (possibly native only to New York City) where a person with any knowledge at all attracts a crowd. The custom is followed by an assumption that if someone knows one thing he knows everything. It's a fragile theory, and when disproved creates downright unpleasantness.

<u>Introduction to Fragile Theories: The Museum of Modern Art.</u>

It began quite innocently right after a matronly woman wearing severe makeup reprimanded me for pronouncing the museum's monogram, MOMA, with a short 'o' instead of the accepted long 'o'.

"A person as well dressed as you should know better," she said with a drop of disdain.

I apologized and humbly moved away to view a peaceful painting by Cézanne.

"Pardon me, but where's the restroom?"

The old man's question was innocent enough, and I had just passed a door labeled, MEN. "It's just around that corner, sir." My answer was straight to the point, and as he left I returned to the painting on the wall; my privacy was short lived.

"What bus do I take to Coney Island?" The woman who was asking had a small fussy child suspended from each arm.

"I'm sorry, but I don't work here, ma'am." It was the safe and true answer.

"I didn't ask you if you worked here. I asked about the bus to Coney Island."

She was obviously collapsing under the pressure of caring for two self-absorbed children and wanted to get to the island of Coney, but I couldn't help her. "I don't know, ma'am." It was the last clear statement for the remainder of our conversation that soon included at least seventeen other people.

The woman with the two children had made the incorrect assumption that since I had told the older gentleman where the restroom was located, surely I could give her the assistance she required. It is hard to remember all that was said over the next few minutes. A number of people in the gathering crowd wanted to know why I wouldn't tell her the number of the bus, and one irate gentleman in particular called me a Nazi bastard. Somewhere in all the commotion I know I said, "You're standing on my foot," "Why are you yelling at me?" and, "No, I don't know which painting is Marilyn Monroe's favorite."

I escaped from this lesson in big city manners with the help of a security guard who escorted me to the street, and asked that I consider the consequences if I should decide to return and create another commotion. I assured him I had no such agenda, thanked him for the rescue, and walked off in search of something to eat. I was hungry, and not at all prepared for destiny to show her hand.

I found a little restaurant with an Italian name on the corner of Madison and Fifty-third. This establishment was the catalyst to two important events in my life: my entrance into the music industry, and the loss of my virginity. Both could be classified as the shedding of innocence, and both events would take place over the next otherwise uneventful twenty-four hours.

The restaurant's extremely handsome dining room was dimly lit, and soft music played from the ceiling. There were lovely paintings on the walls, and the tables were dressed in lace tablecloths with linen napkins, elegant white candles, and freshly cut red roses.

I waited next to the unattended dark walnut podium that appeared to be the guest registry. A man, dressed in a Dior tuxedo, approached and asked if I would have three bottles of the finest champagne sent over to his table. Before I could respond, "I'm sorry, but I don't work here," he put a twenty-dollar bill in the palm of my hand, and returned to his seat. It struck me as odd that asking someone to do a favor required an exchange of money, but this was not yet my town, and I wasn't up to speed on all the local customs.

As I was putting the bill behind the travelers' checks in my wallet, another man, dressed in a tuxedo of unknown origin, greeted me with a warm smile, and welcomed me to Il Milano de Grazie. When he asked if he could help me, I retrieved the twenty-dollar bill, and, using the surreptitious handshake method I had learned from the first gentleman, asked if he could deliver the three bottles of champagne. He was more than adequately delighted to fulfill my request, and inquired where I was seated. I said I wasn't seated yet.

"Do you have a reservation?"

Had I been armed with the knowledge I was to gain in the next hour and a half my answer would have been quite different. However, "No, sir, I do not have a reservation," is what I said.

He escorted me into the dining room and proudly offered, "Your table, sir." He then asked me if Dom Perignon would do.

"Would do what, sir?" I was pleasant, but cautious.

"The champagne for your friend. Dom Perignon is the finest." As he spoke his eyebrows moved up and down, suggesting we were sharing some mysterious secret. I sat down in the chair he offered, and told him Mr. Perignon would do just fine.

"Very good, sir." He sauntered away quite pleased with himself; I was gratified to have played a part in his happiness.

I was gazing at the red leather bound menu filled with words I could neither pronounce nor understand when a waiter excused himself.

"Pardon me, Signor. Would you care for some wine?"

My previous dining experiences had all taken place in fast food or family-style restaurants, and though no counter or waitperson had ever asked me if I cared for something, I was certain this inquiry referred to purchasing something. Naive, yes, but dumb I was not.

I had never had wine before, and felt this would be the proper occasion, so I proudly stated, "Yes, thank you. I would care for some wine."

"Certainly, sir. What would you prefer?"

"What do you offer?" It was his turn.

"Would you like red or white?"

"Which one do you prefer?"

His smiling reaction to my question caused me to think, mistakenly as it turned out, that I was on to something.

"We have some fine selections in our wine cellar, sir. I'm sure we have something you will appreciate. Have you looked at the wine list?"

The menu was difficult enough, and I had no inclination to view additional reading material.

"Red, please." My snap decision was based on the probability there was a fifty-fifty chance of making the correct choice, but I wanted to leave no room for doubt. "And I leave the choice to you, sir."

"Excellent, sir, excellent. You will not be disappointed."

He was right. Disappointed would not be the word to describe the events of that evening.

Before I had a chance to catch my breath, a second waiter approached to inform me of the evening's special items not listed on the menu. Thankfully this list was mostly in English, and each one was "absolutely fantastico" according to him. I chose the Carne con Porcini e Tartufo from the menu because he said it was beef, and a side of Crostini di Polenta because he said I should try it, since I had stated a preference for corn.

The first waiter came back and held a bottle labeled "Chateau Margaux" in Old English lettering in front of my face. The significance of his proud gesture eluded me.

"Nineteen fifty-five, an excellent year, sir."

He was so satisfied with his selection that I decided not to mention the Schulberg snowstorm. I nodded my approval, and he proceeded to remove the cork from the bottle with a metal screw. Then he removed the cork from the metal screw, and set the cork on the table. A moment passed before I realized he wanted me to have the cork.

"Thank you. It's a very nice cork," I said as I moved it to the opposite side of my plate.

"Yes, sir. Nineteen fifty-five," he repeated as he poured a small amount of wine into my glass. "I think you will find it most enjoyable."

I figured he stopped pouring because he was anxious to hear my opinion. I took a sip, and though I thought it was a touch bitter, I smiled and congratulated his expertise. He bowed, poured more wine in my glass, and thanked me for my good taste.

The wine started to taste better after a few minutes, and I began to appreciate the good nose, excellent body and round finish that the waiter had mentioned. The medium-rare steak with foreign mushrooms, and the cornmeal toast were also excellent.

"Thank you very much. You didn't have to do that." The gentleman in the Dior tuxedo was far more grateful for my assistance with his champagne request than I thought necessary.

"You're quite welcome, sir." After checking for the absence of any additional embarrassing compensation, I stood up to shake his hand. "I was glad to do it."

"What's your name?" He was the first person since I left Schulberg to ask me that question, and I was ready with my response.

"I'm Tuxedo Bob, and I'm a songwriter." The words rang true.

"Well, Tuxedo Bob, the songwriter, you've got a lot of class."

"Thank you, sir." It seemed appropriate to return his compliment, so I added, "That's quite a handsome tuxedo."

His sophisticated manners became even more apparent when he turned to his friends to include them in our conversation. "You hear that? He likes my tuxedo." His companions laughed, and though I missed the joke I smiled amiably.

"You're a good, kid." His accent and demeanor reminded me of Edward G. Robinson. "Here's my card. You come see me tomorrow, and show me what you've got, okay?"

"Yes, sir. I'll do that." I wanted to read his business card immediately, but I thought that might be ill mannered and insinuate mistrust, so I put it in my pocket.

Exuding confidence, I shook his hand again. After advising me to call his secretary in the morning he left with his friends in tow. I was excited, sated, and a bit tipsy. I basked in the delight of this heady trio of feelings, and treated myself to dessert.

When I had finished the tiny cup of powerful coffee, a thin piece of lemon skin, and a chocolate-covered ice cream concoction (prophetically called a "bomb") the first waiter brought my bill. I have yet to find the word to describe how I felt opening that check presentation folder.

Total - $965.56

I stared at the amount, and then moved my eyes slowly up the column. Three bottles of Dom Perignon - $450.00, one bottle of Margaux '55 - $380.00. Dinner was reasonably priced by comparison. I didn't blame my mother for failing to include the words "because it can be expensive" to her warning about talking to strangers.

Doris Simmons, the waitress with the tallest beehive hairdo at Trucker's Haven just north of Schulberg off U.S. Route 85, had given me a lesson on proper gratuity etiquette the week before I left home. The required fifteen percent of the total before tax raised the cost of dinner-for-one to just over eleven hundred dollars — roughly the equivalent of one year's room rental at the YMCA with breakfast included. I paid the bill with almost half my travelers' checks, and exited to a chorus of good wishes, come back anytime, and it was nice to have me. It most certainly was.

# forte

I filled my lungs with crisp fall air, and exhaled a relaxed sigh. Acquiring my first contact in the music business made all the other activities of the day inconsequential. The sneak attack on my financial well-being had caused a minor wound, not a major catastrophe. I still had fifteen hundred dollars, but I decided it would be best to be conservative with my remaining funds and let my feet take me back to the YMCA.

I stopped at a corner newsstand where the light was more suited for reading, and took the business card from my pocket. The raised lettering of the words “Pavilion Music Publishing” and “Arnold B. Grimstein, President” was impressive, and gave the card a professional look.

“Electricity ain’t free, you know.”

I returned the card to the safety of my pocket, thanked the vendor for his financial insight, and continued on my way; completely unaware that destiny was not through with me for the evening.

I was busily humming along to a new melody in my head (a raucous tune I was certain would ultimately include the word "restaurant") when I noticed a small crowd engrossed in a playing-card version of the shell game. Since I had so easily found the nickel hidden under one of three cups at the North Dakota State Fair a number of times, I stopped to view the proceedings.

"Find the red lady!" The young Negro croupier was referring to the queen of hearts, one of three cards lying facedown on his cardboard box presentation table.

The contestants enjoyed his cajoling, and games were played at a furious pace; each game ended with the exposure of the queen of hearts. The dealer seemed genuinely sorry collecting the twenty-dollar bets from the losers, and was happy paying the two men who were winning more often than not.

I carefully watched the movements of the dealer's skilled hands. The queen, king of spades, and jack of clubs were presented for identification purposes, and placed facedown on the table in a tidy row. The cards' positions were switched around in a series of rapid maneuvers that included exposing the queen a few times for the benefit of the players. When his hands stopped the game began.

"Find the red lady!" Ten games in a row I picked her from the concealed line-up.

"Find the red lady!" His prodding was having an effect. Here was an easy and harmless way to recoup some of my dwindling funds.

"Try your luck! Find the red lady!" His discourse was clear and concise. "Hey, Tuxedo Boy! Win twenty dollars! Find the red lady!"

I accepted his invitation, set my twenty on the table, and confidently made my selection.

“King of spades! Try again, Tuxedo Boy!”

Knowing I would be ahead by $180.00 had I started betting eleven rounds ago, I confidently withdrew another twenty dollar bill.

“My name’s Tuxedo Bob, sir.” Anticipating the resumption of my winning streak I felt it would be polite to properly introduce myself.

“And I’m Martin Luther King. Introduce yourself to the red lady, Tuxedo Bob.”

I met the king of spades again, and twice more for good measure. What was happening? My recoupment plan was pushing me farther down the road to certain poverty, and I was out of twenties.

“Do you take travelers’ checks?”

Before I received an answer, Mr. King, and the two men who had been winning, abruptly ran off. I realized it had something to do with the policeman rounding the near corner.

“Save your money, son. You can’t win that game.”

He ran after the King party before I had the chance to explain how I had picked ten winners, and that I had also been quite successful at several State Fairs. As I watched him disappear into the night, I realized that I wanted to tell him he sounded just like my father.

“Never play another man’s game,” was something my father always said about any form of gambling. Those words repeated in my head until they mated with a somber melody. I was in no mood to encourage the wedding, but my mind had a mind of its own. I let the song play on, and during a break in the chorus I reaffirmed my pledge to be more financially frugal.

Sleep was all I wanted now, and sleeping until it was time to call Mr. Grimstein's secretary would be a real money-saver. I focused on that comforting thought while my internal dance band added a string section. My home away from home was only a few more blocks.

Flash bulbs popping from hundreds of cameras abruptly ended my mental opus. Had I been paying attention I would have realized I was walking through a crowd of formally-dressed people near the Waldorf Astoria Hotel. The street was a sea of black stretch limousines, and three large spotlights painted the sky. A somewhat hysterical crowd, held in check by sawhorse barricades, yelled names in my general direction. Their frenzy heightened whenever someone courageously approached them to autograph an offered book or scrap of paper. From the banner across the hotel entrance I ascertained there had been a party for Antoinette Perry, and she was quite popular.

As I attempted a hasty retreat from this pandemonium, which I perceived as potentially harmful, I wasn't watching where I was going, and accidentally bumped into a young woman; actually I knocked her to the ground. I apologized profusely; unaware the impact had been the result of destiny's enthusiasm.

"That's okay." She was polite as she smoothed her tight brown skirt. "I'm fine, really." Her shoulder length strawberry-blonde hair glistened and complemented her dark green eyes. "My name's Judy. Judy Tetter. I'm an actress."

I had never thought to use chimes as a musical introduction, but there they were, a sweet, light ringing in my head.

"Nice to meet you, Miss Tetter. I'm Tuxedo Bob. I'm a songwriter." I stumbled through my introduction. It had been so confident earlier; now it was awkwardly burdened by the sound of infatuation.

"So, did you win?" Her question, although coated by her extremely cute coyness, was odd. Unless she was clairvoyant she couldn't have known about my participation in the quest for the red lady, but I played along to keep the conversation going.

"No, I didn't win. I lost four times."

"Four times? Gosh, you'd think you might have won at least one or two, huh?" She was close to the truth.

"Actually, I thought I couldn't lose, but the king of spades kept turning up."

"I don't know that one, but it doesn't matter who won, right? I mean it's just really great to be here, isn't that what you think?" Even though everything she said ended in a question, the sound of her voice was silk to my ears, her smile was so warm and soft, and those chimes kept ringing.

"Yes," I said. I was becoming more intoxicated by the beauty of her face with each passing second. "I think it's really great to be here."

Discarding every lesson from the previous twelve hours, I decided "Never throw good money after bad" would be another of my father's axioms to ignore. I cashed a travelers' check in the lobby of the Waldorf Astoria, and escorted Judy, at her urging, to a small club on the Upper East Side. Full speed ahead and damn the torpedoes!

Club PJ was small, dark, and crowded; its air a thick cloud of cigarette smoke. Wall-to-wall revelers screamed approval for the rock and roll band at the far end of the room executing an assertive thrashing of what I assumed was a song. The noise momentarily drowned out my chimes, and Judy and I huddled in a booth shouting conversation.

"JUDY TETTER'S NOT MY REAL NAME! IT'S MY STAGE NAME!"

"OH!" My acknowledging response hid the fact that I had no idea what she was talking about.

"WHAT'S YOUR REAL NAME?" I was more pleased she had the manners to ask, than disheartened she had forgotten so soon.

"TUXEDO BOB!"

"I MEAN YOUR REAL NAME! WHAT DO YOUR FRIENDS CALL YOU?"

"TUXEDO BOB! WHAT DO YOUR FRIENDS CALL YOU?" She laughed. I had never been good at chitchat, but I felt comfortable participating on this level.

"THEY CALL ME JUDY! YOU'RE CUTE, TUXEDO BOB! I'M SORRY YOU LOST TONIGHT!" She leaned over, closed her eyes, and gently kissed me on the lips.

The noise of the club suddenly became sweet and unobtrusive. I wanted to tell her that her smile possessed the warmth of a million suns, and that her eyes twinkled with starlight, but "I think you're cute, too," was the extent of my poetic response.

Her face, still so close to mine, presented the unique opportunity to kiss again, but I wasn't sure it would be a proper gesture. Maybe she wouldn't let me. Perhaps one kiss was all that was necessary in a club setting. Did a kiss call for a response, and if so, would another kiss be the correct one? I really wanted to kiss her, but I thought I probably shouldn't kiss her. Shouldn't I at least acknowledge the kiss? I could just say thank you. No, I didn't like the sound of that. What could I do instead? If I did decide to kiss her, and I kissed her, then what? I told myself to shut-up for a second so I could think.

Impulse outvoted hesitation. I closed my eyes, and gave her a quick kiss in exchange for the one I had received. Actually, closing my eyes just prior to the moment of impact screwed up my sense of direction, and I wound up kissing the tip of her nose. But a kiss is still a kiss.

We continued to shout, and exchanged a few more kisses into the wee hours of the morning. When she expressed a desire to go home I ushered her to a cab, and accompanied her on the ride through a large recreational area in the center of Manhattan to her west side apartment. I knew that a gentleman always escorted a lady home after a date, and I was looking forward to the goodnight kiss that might be available at her door. When the anticipated kiss was replaced by an offer to come up and see her place I eagerly accepted the invitation. I couldn't believe my luck. I was going to experience my first glimpse of a New York City apartment.

We climbed the stone staircase, and she unlocked the entrance door. Three steps inside, and we were standing in front of another locked door. While she unlocked this second door, I noticed a row of mailboxes on the wall to my left. I deduced from their presence in a double-locked entryway that the person who owned this building was serious about postal security.

I followed Miss Tetter into the small foyer, and up four flights of creaky wooden stairs, past doors where I imagined a Fred and Ethel or a Ralph and Alice might live. She opened her door, and I entered the one-room home she called a studio.

Everything in the room, chairs, table, bed, walls, ceiling, and floor was cotton-candy pink. As I gazed around this monument to her favorite color she lit some pink candles, and put an album of romantic tributes to the lonely by Frank Sinatra on the turntable of her pink Fisher "hi-fidelity in stereophonic sound" console.

"I think you like pink." The soft light and softer music had made me both sleepy and dim-witted. She noticed as I stifled a yawn.

"Do you want to go to bed?"

That sounded like a good idea. I wanted to be in my bed at the YMCA, but the look in her eyes did not seem to include my immediate departure. She moved closer to me, and I tried to form a sentence with the words, "should be going," "sleep," and "meeting with Mr. Grimstein," but the heady combination of pink, Sinatra, and chimes only produced the reply, "Sounds like a good idea." It was not.

When my head finally hit the pillow of my bed at the YMCA at 5:27 A.M., I was no longer Orville and Margaret's innocent little boy. My father had summarized this embarrassing adult ritual in a short "Wait Until You're Married" speech when I was fourteen, so I had no idea what to expect. I now understood why he left out a number of details.

My confessed lack of experience had amused Miss Tetter, and she teasingly asked if I was certain I wanted to give her something so valuable. The feelings I had being naked with her under the pink sheets of her bed more than compensated for my gift. Though I was a nervous participant, by the time the act was finished I could tell from the melody in my head that it was something I would probably enjoy attempting again in the near future.

The gentle caresses and pleasant conversation that followed the main event ended upon her discovering that the king of spades was not a Broadway show, and that I was not an acquaintance of Antoinette Perry, whom she called Tony. Words that had never been spoken in the Fledsper household flew from her mouth, and I was ordered to leave. I learned an important lesson: Be wary of any date that begins with a knockdown.

The cost of three taxis, added to the club's cover and minimum, plus the required fifteen percent gratuity had depleted my available assets an additional eighty-six dollars. The words "it's only money" came to mind. I didn't recall my father ever using this particular phrase, and I pushed it aside, along with its accompanying melody, to make room for a quick, eye-opening financial computation: If I continued spending at yesterday's hourly rate I would be insolvent by nine that evening.

# quintet

The morning cobwebs, much thicker after a sound night of no sleep, had been washed from my senses by a brisk shower. Twenty YMCA residents showering at the same time had a detrimental effect on the hot water supply, and my arms and legs became covered in tiny goose pimples. When I pointed out this bumpy dermal phenomenon to the other naked men, you could have heard a pin drop if the water hadn't been running.

"Look at all these goose bumps!" There was no tuneful etiquette lesson throwing up a red flag to stop me from speaking, so I blurted it out without thinking. Though some of the men expressed an interest, most just turned their backs.

I was embarrassed, and apologized for making the remark to those who may have found it offensive, adding that I'd never taken a cool shower with twenty naked men before. One man put a friendly hand on my shoulder, and said there was a first time for everything. I appreciated his gesture, and had I not been pressed for time I would have accepted his kind invitation to see the "something" he wanted to show me in his room.

I dressed in world-class time, and ran down the stairs to the pay phone to place my expected call to Mr. Grimstein's secretary. Wanting to make a good first impression, I dialed the number on the card at precisely ten o'clock. Being punctual outweighed any thought of not wanting to seem overly eager.

"Pavilion Music," a woman answered in a clear voice.

I gave my reason for calling, and was connected to Miss Shirley Rownanski. Miss Rownanski told me to bring my tape at eleven for the meeting with Mr. Grimstein. I was polite and business-like when I said I would be there, but she hung up before I could ask what she meant by my tape.

Panic set in. I had less than an hour to get a tape. I was going to have my first meeting, and I didn't have a necessary item. I explained my situation to the kind gentleman at the front desk who had checked me in a few days ago. He solved the mystery, and offered an acceptable solution.

• • •

Prior to analyzing the details of my meeting with Mr. Grimstein I decided a light snack was necessary to calm my churning stomach. I purchased an apple at a delicatessen, and walked to Central Park. Since it was the only abundance of grass, trees and water I'd seen in the city, it was the perfect spot for recess. Thousands of brown bag lunchers, bicyclists, handholding couples, thinkers, tourists, pigeon feeders, chess players, and paddleboat enthusiasts also enjoyed the park's relaxed atmosphere.

I nibbled on the shiny red McIntosh while seated on a wooden bench in the shade of a majestic maple tree. The tree was similar in size to the giant oak that had listened to every one of my piano lessons as they filtered from the living room window of my parent's house in Schulberg.

"Remember to keep your knuckles curved and your palms raised," Mrs. Edwina Bailey would say every time my digits approached the keys. Digit was her word for finger. The first digit of each hand was the thumb, and each finger followed in numerical sequence.

"The fifth digit should be on the sharp, not the natural," was strange language at first, but I got used to it, and became an adequately proficient piano player.

I loved Mrs. Bailey for assisting with my musical development, and I would always be thankful for her time, attention, and teaching technique. She died of old age during my sixth year of lessons, and was buried with a leaf from the Fledsper oak tree that I had delicately placed between her first and second digits.

I re-filed the memory, and tossed the apple core into a refuse container. My stomach was quiet, and it was time to examine the details of the meeting at Pavilion Music. I thought it had gone fairly well.

• • •

At precisely five minutes to eleven I entered 1650 Broadway, took the elevator to the seventh floor, and walked into Suite 700 — the offices of Pavilion Music Publishing. There was a handsome gray-haired woman sitting behind a desk, and when she asked what she could do for me I recognized her voice.

"We spoke on the phone earlier, ma'am. I'm Tuxedo Bob, and I have an appointment to see Mr. Grimstein."

"Have a seat young man. I'll call Miss Rownanski and tell her you're here." She picked up the phone and added, "I must say you're very well dressed."

"Thank you, ma'am. It's After Six." She gave a confused glance at her watch, and laughed when I informed her it was the brand name. Things were going extremely well.

I sat down on one of the two overstuffed deep-green leather sofas, and stared at the framed records made of gold that covered the walls. It was an impressive collection, and though I thought it unwise to display such a fortune, I now understood the presence of the security guard in the lobby of this building.

Ten minutes passed. Then another ten minutes. Mrs. Mintz, the gray-haired receptionist, introduced herself, and told me all about her job. She had worked for Mr. Grimstein for twenty years; it was like a family, and the company was successful and well respected. I appreciated her willingness to make me feel comfortable, and when I mentioned this feeling to her she said I had very nice manners. It was much easier to chat with a stranger when neither kisses nor chimes interrupted the conversation.

At eleven-thirty Miss Rownanski appeared from behind the large oak doors to the right of Mrs. Mintz, and asked me to follow her.

"Did you bring your tape?" She was straight forward, but her clipped manner of speech made her seem a bit annoyed.

I avoided any inclination to inquire if something was the matter; this was a business situation, and prying would have been inappropriate. As we walked down a long hallway with more of the golden records hanging on both sides, I explained what I had brought instead of the tape.

"I brought a record I just made." I was going to add that I hoped this would be an acceptable substitution, but she interrupted.

"So, you're a singer?"

"Yes, ma'am. I sing all the songs I write." I smiled proudly for a second, then realizing I might be acting pompous added, "But I'm only here to see Mr. Grimstein about my writing, ma'am." I didn't want her to think I was trying to alter the agenda.

"Wait here." Miss Rownanski went inside an office. The door had a brass plaque that read "Arnold B. Grimstein — President." She returned as quickly as she had left, and announced, "Mr. Grimstein will see you now."

She stepped aside allowing me to pass, and closed the door as she left. I took a deep breath and swallowed nervously. I tried not to focus on the possibility that the man sitting behind the huge mahogany desk, smoking a big cigar, and staring at me could hold the key to my future.

"So, you're still in a tuxedo?" The words floated toward me in a haze of smoke.

Though Mr. Arnold B. Grimstein was questioning the obvious, I politely answered with a simple, "Yes, sir." There didn't seem to be any need to add I wouldn't be me without it.

"Have a seat, kid. So, did you enjoy your dinner last night?"

Mr. Grimstein's first sentences were designed to put me at ease. Since I had never been in any situation of this kind, I was grateful for his display of professionalism, and sat down on a piano bench.

"Yes, sir. The food and the service were very good. Did you enjoy your meal?" A puff of cigar smoke enveloped my face, but it would have been bad manners to fan it away.

"So, kid, let me hear what you've got." He hadn't answered my question, and I made a mental note that I shouldn't be so presumptuous to ask another one.

I confessed that I didn't have a tape, but had instead brought a recording that I had made at the thirty-five cent machine in an amusement arcade. I said a silent "thank you" to the man at the YMCA desk as I handed the plastic disc to Mr. Grimstein. It was clear from the expression on his face that he had seen more than a few of them.

He placed the disc on his turntable. My palms began to sweat as the needle found the groove, and my song began. I made another mental note: Admonish my hands for their impolite opposition to my confidence.

Four walls around me painted green.
Bars on the windows instead of screens.
Life's very safe in the sanitarium.
I think I'll stay here awhile.
Nurses bring me coffee.
Doctors give me tests.
My family put me in here,
and I can use the rest.
Life's very safe in the sanitarium.
I think I'll stay here awhile.
When I need a vacation,
I walk down the hall to recreation.
There I can string some beads,
or basket

The song ended abruptly because the arcade's machine only made forty-five second recordings, but I was ready to take over at the piano. With digits poised, knuckles curved, and palms raised, I jumped in on cue.

"-weave.
Or play with paper mâché."

My all-of-a-sudden live performance caught Mr. Grimstein off guard. I whistled my way through a short instrumental passage, and politely pretended not to notice his cigar had fallen out of his mouth.

"I have peace and quiet;
when that gets boring I can start a riot.
The nurses know it's all in jest,
and I get blessed with love
from the medicine chest."

I went into the last verse after a modest half-step modulation.

"And then I do not feel worried.
I don't feel pain.
(I don't want to feel too much,
'cause I might go insane)
Life's very safe in the sanitarium.
I think I'll stay here awhile."

I repeated the last line, and ended with a simple triplet of the $D^7$ followed by an arpeggio of the $G^9$. I thought to go directly into another song, but decided to wait through the silence until an invitation was extended.

"You brought me a song about a sanitarium?"

I thought he might be troubled by the incorrect assumption that I had been institutionalized, but before I could reassure him, he informed me the subject matter I had chosen lacked "hit potential." He was "only looking for songs about young love and relationships" because that was what the public was buying. I told him I had a love song about a girl from Williston, North Dakota.

"That sounds more like something in the ballpark, but nobody knows where North Dakota is. The girl has to live in a place with a recognizable name."

He offered some alternative locations, and I selected Long Island since it had the same number of syllables as Williston. I started to sing. He stopped me after the opening line, which was also the song's new title: "MY LONG ISLAND COMA GIRL."

Though Mr. Grimstein said we would not be doing any business, he graciously thanked me for coming, and added that he thought I was uniquely talented. He gave me the business card of a booking agent acquaintance, proclaiming that Sy Silverman might be the right person to help me get my feet wet.

I was getting my feet wet in the cool water of Central Park's duck pond, and looking at the bright orange business card that said: "The Silverman Agency — A Place For Big Talent." Mr. Grimstein had said I should wait a day before calling because he wanted to tell Mr. Silverman about my need for seasoning. The thought of being viewed as a bland casserole amused me, and made me hungry. With socks and shoes in hand I walked back to the YMCA where I would wait until the morning of my third day before embarking on my next adventure.

# major sixth

A soft-spoken Chinese couple who used a French process to clean my tuxedos owned Manhattan Premium Dry Cleaners. This blend of cultures worked well together, and the five ensembles I had left in the care of Mr. and Mrs. Huwang Wong looked perfectly pampered when I picked them up. Mr. Wong appreciated my business, and graciously offered me a volume discount while his wife proudly showed me a picture of her son who was in college in Pennsylvania.

"He write letter every week," she said. I knew her words were not spoken by accident.

I had not written to my parents since I left Schulberg, and probably over-apologized for my thoughtlessness in the first sentence of the letter I wrote immediately upon my return to my room. I gave them an accounting of all that had taken place — from the time I left for Chicago to the take-out Chinese food I had for dinner the previous night — leaving out any experience I felt would be of no interest to them, or potentially embarrassing to me.

My mother would be most concerned with my eating habits, so I emphasized that subject. I wrote about the flavors of ethnic foods, which were quite unique to my taste buds, and how over the last three days I had sampled a slice of New York pizza, a Jewish hot dog, and a Greek salad. The letter continued with a recap of my attempts to eat chunks of chicken with cashew nuts, and steamed white rice from paper cartons with two wooden sticks. I told them how I had tried to master this ancient technique as described in little pictures on the utensil's packet, but since my digits would not cooperate I was grateful for the foresight of China Express for enclosing a plastic fork.

The meal had been quite inexpensive, but I didn't think it was necessary to write how this had helped stop the leak in my monetary supply. Information such as that can cause a parent to worry. I just wrote that Chinese food tasted good when topped with soy sauce, and about the oddly shaped cookie that contained the message, "You Are Forever Happy!" As evidence of my discovery I enclosed it with the letter.

I ended with a p.s. promising to write more often, and a p.p.s. that I would let them know how things went with Mr. Silverman. Even though I didn't include a tuxedo rental payment, I was certain my communication would be appreciated. I only wrote four more times to them. This first letter was also the last I would mail from New York City.

I called Mr. Sy Silverman that afternoon, and when he answered the phone I discovered he talked faster than a machine gun could fire fifty rounds. "I've been waitin' for your call, kid. You think I like to wait? I don't, but Arnie says you're okay. Thinks I should take a look at you. How do you look, kid? You clean-cut? How soon can you get here?"

I went over to his office immediately. Mr. Grimstein had described Mr. Silverman as a "true original," and as I looked at his outfit consisting of a green and pink-checkered jacket, powder blue pants, and bright yellow shirt flattered by an orange ascot, I was certain he was.

"So you're Tuxedo Bob, huh? Arnie tells me you got a different kinda slant on things, and maybe I should give you a shot playin' a gig. You ever play a gig, Bob? Can I call you Bob?"

He talked so fast I hadn't been able to answer his first question, so I gave him all the answers at once. "Yes, I am. Not to my knowledge," and, "I prefer Tuxedo Bob, sir."

"Hey, you call me Sy. If we're gonna do some business we gotta be on a personal level, you know what I mean? By the way, that's a nice tuxedo you got there. First class."

"Thank you, Mr. Silverman."

"Call me Sy, kid."

"Thank you, Sy." I was uncomfortable addressing any adult in an informal manner.

"That's better. Mr. Silverman makes me sound like some kinda mortician."

"My mother's a mortician."

"Hey, that's a good one, kid."

"Her name's Margaret."

"I'm sure it is. Look, kid, play me something funny. Arnie tells me you might be funny. Are you funny, kid? Well, you better be, 'cause if you're funny, you know what that means? It means you're gonna be the opening act for Vince Genoa. Yeah, you heard me right, I said Vince Genoa. You know who Vince Genoa is? He's only my biggest client, that's who he is. Pays my rent; puts food on the table. He's bigger than huge. Women love him, but guys like him too, you know. That's what makes him so gigantic. He's a ladies man, and a man's man all at the same time. Yeah, everybody's crazy about Vince. You like Jerry Vale? Well, forget him. He's back selling fruit from a wagon next to my guy. You don't think I know what I'm talkin' about? Hey, I know a great singer when I hear one, and Vince is the best of the best. Absolutely cream of the crop. You hear what I'm sayin'?"

Mr. Silverman asked questions, but didn't wait for my responses, so I just sat and listened, occasionally nodding my head. I hadn't heard of the superstar he was talking about, but I was enjoying watching his mouth move faster than I could think.

"So, Mr. Tuxedo Bob, impress me, and you're on the next bus to the Catskills for Thanksgiving. What do you think of that? Sound good? Well, you impress Vince, and you're there through the first week of January, but you gotta be funny, you know? People who go there expect to get a few laughs, and I got my reputation to consider. And what's a man without a reputation? He's nothin', that's what. So, let me hear what you got. Make me laugh, kid."

I sat down at his out of tune spinet, and played the complete versions of the two songs Mr. Grimstein had heard along with three other numbers. Mr.

Silverman chuckled throughout my audition, and was effusive with compliments.

"Not bad, kid. A little twisted, but not bad. If you got twenty minutes of material I got a spot for you. Actually, if you're breathing I got a spot for you. I'm in kind of a jam, and I gotta replace a guy who got sick on me, okay? Okay. So, how's, say, seventy-five bucks a week? Three weeks guaranteed, three shows a night, you got Mondays off, and I'll get the club to throw in free room and board. Sound good? Can you start tomorrow? What do you say? We got a deal?"

We had a deal, and I signed my first contract. By the next morning I had packed, checked out of the YMCA, and was on a bus to Pressman's Golf and Ski Resort in Kiamesha Lake, New York. I was scheduled to open for Vince Genoa at Billy's Night Life Lounge that night.

Upon arriving at the hotel I went straight to the rooftop lounge. Mr. Silverman had told me I was to meet the owner there; a man named Sonny, not Billy. Next to its open door I saw a sign with "APPEARING THROUGH THE NEW YEAR — VINCE GENOA" in bold lettering. I entered the lounge slowly with a light-headed feeling of wonder.

There were at least seventy-five tables covering the floor from the long bar on my right to the windows overlooking the lake on my left. The stage, directly in front of me, had a beautiful Steinway baby grand, an upright bass, and a red lacquered set of drums with Vince Genoa's name in blue sparkles on the front.

Mr. Sonny Napoli, a man whose extreme proportions tested the strength of the seams of his shiny shark-skin suit, was seated at one of the tables to the left of the stage with two other men. They got up, and walked away as I approached. I introduced myself, and handed him the two contracts Mr. Silverman and I had signed.

"Dinner shows are eight and ten, third show's at midnight." Mr. Napoli could talk without moving his lips, and he spoke with a guttural rasp. "You do twenty minutes. Sy tell you all that?"

Listening to him made me think of clearing my throat, but I resisted the temptation. "Yes, sir. Mr. Silverman told me that, and I can perform for twenty minutes."

Mr. Napoli took a fountain pen from his jacket, and signed the contracts without reading them. "I'll mail Sy his copy."

"Excuse me, sir, but do you want me to sing the same songs in each show?"

"Look, kid. I don't care if you stand on your head, so long as the crowd spends money. Just do a full twenty minutes. You go over good, you get another twenty. Now get outta here, and be backstage by seven forty-five."

"Yes, sir, Mr. Napoli." As I exited I reminded myself that I was in a business that had little time for my questions. I needed to be patient and gain on-the-job experience.

I proceeded to check into my sparsely furnished free room located on the floor beneath the lobby. All resort employees had rooms on this level, except certain higher paid officials. My mother would have certainly had a few words to say about cleanliness to the previous tenant, and I spent the next few hours cleaning. I scrubbed and scoured every inch with supplies I had borrowed from Mr. Murphy, a gentle Negro janitor of few words, who stood in my doorway watching me as I worked.

"Judging from the condition of this floor, it's probably not very often you've seen someone clean it, isn't that right?" I had picked up the east coast method of ending a sentence with a question.

"Nope."

"I really appreciate that you let me use your mop. Do you have any more bleach?"

"Yep." If there was a sentence with less than one word, Mr. Murphy would have wanted to use it.

He brought me more bleach, and I continued my chores.

"Zatta tuxedo?"

"Yes it is."

It occurred to me he might have never seen one up close, so I showed him the other five hanging in the closet. He seemed to enjoy petting the material, murmuring, "Snice," a few times.

"I'm singing in the lounge tonight. Do you like music?"

"Yep."

I invited him to come to my first show, but he declined with a simple, "Tain't loud." There was a rule prohibiting employees from entering the lounge unless they worked there, and I could tell that Mr. Murphy felt the same way I did about rules. They were not meant to be broken.

My room was spotless, and I still had a few hours before showtime, so I spent them exploring the grounds. Like the sign advertised, seasonal golf, tennis, and skiing were available. While I watched an elderly couple playing tennis, a hotel guest asked me for directions to the indoor swimming pool. I realized I couldn't say, "I'm sorry, but I don't work here," and I escorted the guest to the information desk in the lobby. He was grateful for my assistance, and handed me a dollar. The custom of giving money for kindness was making me wonder if shaking hands was a good idea.

When I sat down to my first experience of free board I met two other employees, Sylvia Aaron, an attractive blonde waitress, and a young Hispanic bus boy named Ernie Santos. My macaroni casserole, green salad topped with thousand-island dressing, and glass of milk looked delicious. I bowed my head to express thanks for the gifts I was about to receive.

Miss Aaron said she was impressed that I said grace before eating, and I replied that in my house grace was considered essential. Ernie informed me that most of the singers he knew didn't drink milk because it coated the throat, so I only took a few sips. Both of my new acquaintances worked in Billy's Lounge, and said they were looking forward to hearing me perform.

I went back to my room, took a long hot shower in my own private bathroom, and laid down to get a few minutes of rest. If Mr. Murphy had not knocked on my door at seven fifteen, I might have slept through my debut.

"Stime, boy," he said as I opened the door in a panic.

I thanked him, and let him touch one of my tuxedos while I hurriedly dressed.

"Do good," he said with a smile. I assured him I would do my best.

I was standing backstage next to the edge of the red velvet curtain when a young man, upset because I had missed my sound check, approached me. He informed me that I could only use the microphone at the piano, and because I had not given anyone my lighting cues all I was going to get was a basic follow spot. I apologized, and tried to reassure him that everything would be fine with the items he had mentioned. I confessed that I had never done this before, and that I appreciated all his efforts. He accepted my statements, and though his inflection on the words, "That explains everything" had a slightly bitter edge, I figured he was just under pressure to do a professional job.

The precise moment my professional career began was just after the house lights dimmed, and a voice over the loudspeakers said, "Ladies and gentleman, Tuxedo Bob." I walked onto the stage, and a light followed me to the piano as promised. There was a smattering of light applause.

"Hello. I'm Tuxedo Bob. Is everyone enjoying dinner?" No one actually responded to my question, but people continued eating, so I assumed dinner was satisfactory.

There were four unlit candles in a candelabra that had been placed in front of the raised lid of the baby grand, and since each table in the room had a lit candle, I thought it would be nice to light mine.

The audience responded to my request for a match by hurling a number of hotel matchbooks in my general vicinity. My comment that I was glad I hadn't asked for a knife induced mild laughter.

After I lit the candles, I sat down and sang my sanitarium song, followed by "I JUST LOVE TO COMPLAIN," and "MY LONG ISLAND COMA GIRL." The spotlight, which no longer had to follow me anywhere, changed from bright white to soft yellow to an even softer blue during my twenty minutes. I closed with a new song I had written during my three-hour bus ride from Manhattan to The Catskills. The audience's lack of my vision of Judy Tetter did not deter them from enjoying "COMPLETELY NUDE." I thanked the audience for listening, and as I left the stage to their applause I spotted Miss Aaron giving me a thumbs-up. I took that as a good sign.

I remained backstage near the red curtain to watch "the best of the best." Mr. Genoa started his show with a finger-snappy "WHEN THE SAINTS GO MARCHING IN," and ended with the crowd-pleasing sing-along "WON'T YOU COME HOME, BILL BAILEY." His blend of old and older favorites brought him a well-deserved standing ovation. I wanted to introduce myself as he passed, but he was in a hurry to speak with the two men I had seen at Mr. Napoli's table earlier that afternoon.

Two duplicate shows later, and my first day as a professional performer ended. The shows had gone well for both myself and Mr. Genoa, and Mr. Napoli proved himself to be a real gentleman when he took the time to shake my hand and tell me he thought I'd done a nice job. I was glad that his hand did not contain money.

Charles Derbin, the bartender, told me that each performer was allowed one free drink at the end of the night. After telling me Chateau Margaux 1955 was not available, he handed me a rum and coke like the one Mr. Genoa was sipping at the other end of the bar. I thought this might be a better time to introduce myself, but Mr. Derbin advised me, "Don't bother Vince when he's in a sour mood, which is usually always."

His comment surprised me. Mr. Genoa's three performances had been quite successful, but I accepted Mr. Derbin's whispered explanation that "Vince picked the incorrect positions of several ponies." I didn't really understand the implications, but I knew most people did not enjoy being wrong.

I finished my free drink, said goodnight, and went back to my free room. I crawled into bed with the knowledge that I had just earned twelve dollars and fifty cents, and went to sleep for the first time in my life as a paid professional.

# diminished seventh

Tiffany Sanson. That's the name written in the contents section of the shipping label atop the coffin. I feel a bond of kinship with the woman inside the item that has sanctioned my continued on-board presence. I've never known anyone named Tiffany until now. When I was growing up children were given a simple biblical or Italian name like Mark, Beth, John, Ruth, Peter, Mary, Frank, Tony or Thomas. Two syllables or less was the common practice.

Each generation has to distinctively time-stamp itself to stand out from previous ones, and the easiest way to do this is by naming its children uniquely. Ezra and Edna certainly walk with the aid of a cane, and are never carded for beer. Biff and Buffy have skateboards, and nothing they say is important. I suppose it is some type of discrimination to think of Gertrude or Hermione as elderly women, and Bambi or April as teenage girls, but that's the popular mind set, even though it is possible someone is visiting their Grandma Bambi at this very moment.

I think it would be more appropriate to just give babies a number at birth, and let them choose their own name when they're conscious enough to do so. That way Female Baby #34293 can ask to be addressed as Sally or Henry or Spring Floral Arrangement, and only have herself to thank.

My christened name is not Tuxedo Bob. Through precocious insistence I coerced my parents into legally changing my name when I was three and a half years old. Robert Fledsper became Tuxedo Bob Fledsper. I had no use for the last name, but even with my explanation that Schulberg was a small town where everyone knew I belonged to Orville and Margaret, the County Clerk of Records would not allow its deletion.

I was still in diapers when my father put me in a tiny tuxedo for a Christmas portrait, and from that moment I wouldn't accept being dressed any other way. My parents endured my tantrums whenever they tried to dress me in something they considered more suitable for a toddler — usually pastel with cartoon animals — but they finally acquiesced to my demand for "Tuttedo ony!" during the eighth exceptionally childish conniption. They figured it couldn't do any harm, and I was free advertising for my father's business.

Many of the townspeople took their time getting used to the sight of a child in a tuxedo. Viewed as a walking billboard for my father, I was commonly referred to as "that weird little Fledsper boy," or "the midget butler," but name calling never bothered me. Since insults need a reaction to be effective, teasing me was quickly deemed a huge waste of time.

After my legal name change I would only speak to someone if I was addressed as Tuxedo Bob. For a while this kept the number of people who engaged me in conversation to a bare minimum. My parents supported my wishes by informing everyone in town that I had good manners, and would speak when spoken to if addressed in the court's decreed terminology minus the cognomen. I'm sure everyone thought it was a phase I would grow out of, but as time passed everyone in town, except Brian Ackerman, grew into it instead.

Mr. Ackerman owned an auto repair shop, and was the person responsible for keeping the family hearses in tip-top working order. Oil changes, transmission and brake fluids, anti-freeze, hoses, belts, and basic engine tune-ups were just a few of his fields of auto expertise. Of anyone in town, he had the most knowledge pertaining to the care of motorized vehicles, and the least amount of common courtesy. In the who's who of Schulberg hierarchy Mr. Brian Ackerman held the positions of chief mechanic and town bully.

"Your mommy likes to play with dead people."

This was just one of the comments Mr. Ackerman enjoyed saying to me under his breath when my father's back was turned. He said he was trying to 'get my goat,' but I didn't own a goat, and consequently just ignored him.

"Hey, I'm talking to you. Are you deaf?"

Though there was no prize to be won by coercing me into a conversation, Mr. Ackerman remained tenaciously unwilling to call me by name. Maybe it was the same force that made him drive his car the fastest, drink beer all day, and use cuss words. I thought to ask his wife, who was always pleasant to me, but I didn't think speaking about any person behind his or her back was appropriate.

Mrs. Ackerman was a sweet, fragile, soft-spoken woman who always had a bruise from falling down or running into a door. Everyone in town said she was unlucky or extremely accident-prone. I took her some flowers from my mother's garden when she was in the hospital with a broken nose she said she got from a fall while hanging her laundry.

Putting up with Mr. Ackerman's attempts at verbal confrontation was easy because I enjoyed watching him work. "You're a weird little boy, you know that?" and "What are you staring at, tuxedo freak?" were examples of his relentless pursuit to get my goat, but his lack of social grace had nothing to do with the fact that he was an expert mechanic. I got to view numerous spark-plug timings, tire rotations, and radiator flushes. I think he knew how much I admired his work, but he was crushed underneath a '58 Ford Country Squire before we ever had a two-way conversation.

No one saw the mishap when he was caught between the concrete floor of his garage and the station wagon that had slipped from its jack. Though she was in a great deal of pain from the ribs she had broken while mopping, Mrs. Ackerman seemed quietly relieved during the funeral. Shortly after receiving a large insurance settlement, she left town with a man she met at Trucker's Haven. Mr. Ackerman remained in Schulberg; buried wearing a tuxedo with a picture of a goat neatly tucked in the breast pocket.

• • •

"Williston!" The train has stopped, and I'm close to my destination. The voice outside yells, "Williston!" again, and I casually detrain. I know I have ridden my last train, and as I watch it pull away, I wave good-bye. The coffin with Tiffany Sanson inside will continue on to Chicago. I will be in Schulberg, North Dakota before midnight.

My life has been on a circuitous path since I left, and by returning to the place of my birth the start and the finish of my journey meet to form a circle. Once a circle is formed it has no beginning or end. There was a ritual used by some North American Indian tribes where an adolescent boy would leave his home to wander in the wilderness for a time before returning as a man. I left Schulberg as a boy. I return as a grown-up.

The smell of the air is familiar as I look around at scenes from my childhood. I wander up the road through the northern end of town, and pass the Piggly-Wiggly market where my parents shopped after the snowstorm of 1955 caused the collapse of Carper's General Store. The limited inventory and resources of Schulberg made it necessary for Orville and Margaret to come to Williston at least once a month to purchase groceries, and other items not readily available from their neighbors and friends.

When I was eleven I rode my bicycle on this same twenty-mile road that connects Williston to Schulberg to buy a birthday present for my mother. Though she appreciated the decorative lead-crystal container of pink rose-scented bubble bath I purchased at the Rexall Drug Store, I got into trouble for not informing my parents of my intention to take the trip. I would have considered my punishment of no dessert for a week to be cruel and unusual had there been chocolate tapioca pudding on the menu, but Margaret did not make my favorite thing in the whole world during the disciplinary period.

Most trips to Williston were family outings. I especially enjoyed the excursions that included ice cream or the acquisition of a new toy. One occasion, when I was taken to the Rialto Theater on my eighth birthday to see "The Wizard Of Oz," was an exceptionally fine experience.

My parents and I sat with our popcorn and soda pop as the lights dimmed. The green velvet curtains opened as a Tom and Jerry cartoon began. I watched with some amusement, and questioned my father as to how a cat could live after being repeatedly struck on the head with a mallet, flattened by an anvil, and blown up by ten sticks of dynamite, but he said it was just a cartoon. Though he hadn't answered my question beyond the obvious, I didn't pursue the subject.

My heart sank when the MGM lion roared in black and white at the start of the main feature. I had black and white television at home, and was feeling a bit disappointed as I watched the story of a farm girl in love with her dog unfold in shades of gray. My spirits lifted a bit when she sang a song about a bluebird infested area located somewhere over a rainbow; no color, but at least there was music.

Well, when Dorothy opened her front door after the neat tornado sequence, I was awestruck. My mouth and eyes were wide open with wonder as she stepped into that garden. I was so utterly impressed I don't believe I moved a muscle throughout the remainder of the film. When it was over I told my parents the experience had been inspiring, and that I would most certainly write a movie musical one day. I remember my mother patted me on the head, and intuitively predicted, "Of course you will, dear."

My return trip home does not include Orville and Margaret anxiously waiting at the door. They no longer live in the house of my childhood. No one in Schulberg knew where I was when my parents were moved to the south end of town, and it wasn't until my fifth letter was returned marked "deceased" that I was aware they were gone forever. I will stop by Faraway Meadows to pay my respects before ending my journey at my old house on the hill now owned by Tom Conners Jr.

In 1955 he was a ten-year old boy playing with a set of toy soldiers in my living room when his father was electrocuted by my television set. Now he lives there with his wife and children. I suppose it's doubly ironic that he is also the town's undertaker.

My father used to say, "The more things change the more they stay the same." I've never been quite sure of this particular axiom. I'm headed home dressed the same as I left, but my eyes have become astigmatic, my voice is a few notes lower, and my pace is not as quick. Twenty-three years, ten thousand performances, thirty-one recordings, one hundred forty-eight tuxedos, and the loss of some close friends separate that boy from this man. But as I walk toward Schulberg under a canopy of familiar stars and faithful moon, and I hum along to a resounding chorus of French horns, I realize, in the grand scheme of things, Orville was probably right.

# octave

My three week guarantee of three shows a night except Mondays in Billy's Night Life Lounge at Pressman's Golf and Ski Resort in Kiamesha Lake went by in a flash, and had it not been for some of the hotel employees dressing as residents of Plymouth Rock I would not have been aware it was Thanksgiving. The Puritan costumes worn by some of the men made me feel as though I was adrift in a sea of prehistoric tuxedos.

A Pilgrim and an Indian greeted the hungry hotel guests who had lined up for the huge buffet that snowy afternoon. Seven hundred people consumed twenty-three roast turkeys, eleven baked hams, eight rounds of beef, and mountains of brown sugar-crusted yams, fluffy mashed potatoes with giblet gravy, chestnut-fig stuffing, squash, corn, green beans, peas, cranberry-orange relish, cole slaw and assorted rolls. They also found room for fifty-nine pumpkin and twenty-seven mincemeat pies.

The usual simple fare of my free board was replaced that day with portions from the same feast, and it was quite delicious with one exception.

I had never heard of minced meat as a dessert item before so I tried a piece. It wasn't meat at all. There were only raisins and little bits of unidentifiable chewy things in it, and though I wished I had asked for pumpkin instead, I ate it in deference to the starving children in China of whom my mother had so often referred.

Mr. Silverman telephoned the next morning to tell me Mr. Napoli was satisfied with my performances, and my contract had been extended through the first week of January.

"You're gonna be big, kid, you know that? Are you listening to me? I said big. They love you up there, but am I surprised? No, and I'll tell you why I'm not surprised. I know talent when I see it, and, kid, you got what it takes, you know that? Anybody who says Sy Silverman can't pick talent is full of it, you know what I mean? Of course, you do. Hey, I got Vince Genoa. I got Tuxedo Bob. Did I die and go to Heaven, or what? You're gonna go places, kid, you know that? You hear what I'm saying?"

He made me dizzy, but I was pleased by his enthusiasm. He promised to come up on Christmas Eve, and asked if I knew what he was saying four more times before hanging up. I had no idea what he would do if I said I didn't.

On the Sunday after Thanksgiving an eight-day celebration began that was new to me. People of the Jewish faith celebrated Hanukkah, which commemorated the rededication of a Middle-Eastern temple won in a battle many centuries ago. This religious observance was so special it had an alternate spelling, Chanukah, and two additional names, Feast of Dedication, and Feast of Lights.

Each evening featured the lighting of a special candelabra, which held nine candles and was called a menorah. The middle candle would be lit, then used to light one candle the first night, two the second night, and continued in sequence until all were lit on the eighth and final night. There were prayers spoken in unison as the candles were lit, and afterwards a Cantor sang songs. I didn't understand any of them because they were all in the Hebrew language, but I could tell Hanukkah was a joyous occasion to be taken seriously.

The children in attendance were given presents. Money and a small spinning top (called a dreidel) were especially cherished gifts. The cantor, who had a rich tenor voice, gave me a gold foil-wrapped chocolate coin each night because he said he appreciated my respectful interest.

Mr. Genoa called it "Jew Christmas," and a number of people who overheard him were offended, saying his comment was uncalled for and inappropriate. When I learned the Jewish faith did not include the birth of Christ on its calendar of events, his remark seemed merely an uneducated contradiction, and I believed he meant no malice. I was still a few years away from discovering that there were people in the world who, like Brian Ackerman, chose to be discourteous on purpose.

During the week of Hanukkah, Miss Aaron told me that because audience reaction was so positive I should think about adding an encore. I informed her of my first conversation with Mr. Napoli about performing for only twenty minutes, but she said I was missing her point. I apologized for not being more agreeable to her suggestion, and explained that by adding a song to please the crowd I would have to break an agreement. My father used to say, "A man's word is his bond," so it was clear I had no other choice in the matter, and would have to adhere to the agreed upon performance schedule.

It was not clear to Miss Aaron, however, and she spoke with Mr. Napoli who gave me his permission to add an encore number whenever audience response demanded one. This idea backfired, and permission was withdrawn after the end of my next eight o'clock performance.

I had finished my closing number, "CHOCOLATE TAPIOCA PUDDING," and was thanking the audience in my usual manner with a gracious bow, when it occurred to me the volume of the applause combined with shouts of "More!" were clues that an encore was in order. I had written a new song called "OUT OF MY MIND" that afternoon, and was eager to try it out, so I sat back down at the piano. When I finished, I got up and bowed again. The clapping and cheering were louder than before. I held up my hands to quiet the diners, explaining that I had performed the complete inventory of my songs, and added that I was gratified they liked my newest number.

No one from any audience had spoken directly to me before, so I was taken by surprise when a woman, sitting alone at one of the front tables, interjected that since I didn't have any more of my own songs, I should sing a song written by someone else. I had been cautioned by Ernie to watch out for hecklers, but since there was such a sweet lilting quality in her southern-belle voice, I took her suggestion as genuine interest. I politely replied that there were so many other songs I wouldn't know which one to choose.

This prompted a flood of requests from the crowd, and I had to raise my hands again to restore order. I turned back to the woman at the front table, and said I thought she should make the selection because it had been her idea. She looked up at me with a warm smile, fluttered her eyelashes, which

I took as an expression of modesty, and replied that “OVER THE RAINBOW” was her favorite song of all time. She blushed when I said it was one of my favorite songs too, and that I would sing it for her even though I wasn’t certain how to play it.

During this exchange Mr. Genoa’s bass player, whose name was Bee-Bop, had quietly come on the stage to set up for the main show. He saved me from any potential embarrassment when he said he had the sheet music, but it would cost me a quarter. The audience laughed at his comment. I was in a bind because I didn’t have any change, so I handed Mr. Bop a dollar. He wasn’t carrying any change either, and said so as he put the bill in his pocket. The laughter continued then turned to applause when I said I would have paid much more for it. He gave me the music, and with a toothy grin said he’d remember that the next time. It was a dollar well spent.

I sat down at the piano again, and quickly scanned the pages to see if they contained any difficult chord combinations that might catch my digits off-guard. As I put my hands on the keys the bright white spotlight quickly changed to a pale pink, and the stage lights dimmed to a halo of blue as if both had been struck by divine intervention.

I sang “OVER THE RAINBOW” as a soft and simple, plaintive ballad, changing the time signature from 4/4 to 3/4 every now and then for effect, and my tenor voice filled the stillness of the room with the sad beauty of the melody. I had never interacted musically with another musician, and was quite honored when Mr. Bop added bass accompaniment during the second verse. When we finished, the room was quiet. Most of the members of the audience had tears in their eyes as I got up and walked from the stage. The moment of silence was more gratifying than the two minute standing ovation that followed.

I don't mean to imply I had disrespect for the ovation. I just never saw it. As it began Mr. Napoli's two associates were rushing me to Mr. Genoa's dressing room. Mr. Genoa was extremely upset because the start of his show had been delayed fifteen minutes. He was the star, and didn't think his audience should be kept waiting while "some little amateur nobody sings stupid little songs."

Mr. Napoli was also in attendance, and remained patient during the tirade. After comforting Mr. Genoa with a declaration that he was indeed the star, I was informed there would be no more encores.

I apologized to both of them for being unprofessional, and promised it would never happen again. I told Mr. Genoa how grateful I was to be a part of his fine show, and assured him that I would work on my vocal and writing skills. His professional advice of, "Yeah, well, you'd better!" ended our discussion, and indicated to me that the problem was resolved.

Two weeks before Christmas my name was added to the announcement at the door. I considered it quite an honor when I saw "with Tuxedo Bob and his off-beat songs" written in small letters of green glitter. I made sure to thank Mr. Napoli, and promised to be more precise with the tempo of my music.

I mailed a Christmas card to my parents, telling them all my good news. I enclosed a picture of my good friend, Mr. Murphy, standing next to the new sign in front of Billy's Night Life Lounge, and a one hundred dollar bill to cover the delinquent tuxedo rental payments. Since I had few expenses, largely due to Mr. Napoli having given me free use of the hotel's dry-cleaning service, I also sent a dozen yellow roses to my mother because they were her favorite flower.

The decor of the lounge changed with the passing of each holiday. The festive Thanksgiving decorations of Indian corn and pumpkins had given way to numerous blue and white-lit Stars of David, and those were replaced with twinkling colored lights and silver garlands of tinsel draped around Christmas trees that had been sprayed with fake snow. The stage was adorned with pots of poinsettias, and a wreath made of pine branches and holly hung from the lid of the baby grand. It was very pretty.

All of the Pressman employees were participating in a secret gift exchange program, and I included myself by writing my name on a slip of paper and dropping it into a gaily-decorated box. I drew the name Sven Ertslof who was a ski instructor I had not met. Miss Aaron found out he was from Sweden and missed his parents, so I gave him a nice box of stationary and some airmail stamps.

One of the hotel maids came to my door with Mr. Murphy on Christmas Eve, and told me she had drawn my name from the box. She spoke in a courteous manner, and sounded embarrassed when she asked if she could clean my room, or do my laundry instead of buying a gift because she did not have a lot of money. Mr. Murphy had obviously shared his knowledge that cleanliness was important to me, and I was quite touched by her desire to give me something so personal. The offer of her talent was a wonderful present, but I hesitated to add to her daily drudgery. However, declining her gesture would have been ungracious, so I agreed to receive her gift of floor vacuuming the next Wednesday afternoon. I extended a twenty-dollar handshake, and asked her to please wish her seven children a very Merry Christmas from Tuxedo Bob.

I wanted to give presents to Mr. Murphy, Miss Aaron, and Ernie because I always sat with one, two, or all of them during the employee meals, and they were my first friends outside of Schulberg. Initially our conversations had been about how we got our jobs and where we were from, but as the days passed each of them disclosed information of a more personal nature.

Ernie Santos said I was easy to talk to because I looked him in the eye. I knew what he meant because eye contact is important. My father used to say, "The eyes are the window to the soul," and I believed him. When someone is respectful enough to call me Tuxedo Bob, I return the honor by looking into their open windows.

Ernie was seventeen years old, from San Juan, Puerto Rico, liked big dogs, sent money to his family back home, wanted to own his own restaurant, and was a homosexual who didn't like the words queer and faggot. He wondered if I liked men the way he did, and after he explained what he meant I said the thought had not occurred to me so I probably didn't.

Miss Aaron liked the fact that I never interrupted her with a personal opinion unless asked. She was candidly honest, had immaculate manners, the face of an angel, and commonly referred to herself as overly emotional. She was twenty, from Boston, Massachusetts, had a peculiar way of pronouncing any word with an "ar" sound, was earning money to continue her law school education, hated her thighs, collected hotel matchbooks, and had a problem with an uncle when she was eight which caused her to avoid having her face too close to any man with liquor on his breath. She cried during the story of her uncle, and I held her hand. I felt sorry for what had happened to her, and said that if I been her friend when she was eight, I would not have waited to be asked before offering my opinion on the matter.

According to Mr. Murphy, his body was fifty but his mind was ten. He was from Arkansas, his first name was Andrew, he had no surviving relatives, had worked at Pressman's for twenty-seven years, loved barbecued ribs and cornbread with hot pepper sauce, dropped out of school in the third grade, and had a problem in his brain that prevented a well constructed thought from becoming a complete sentence. Embarrassment was his reason for using one or two word phrases as often as possible. He said he would rather be thought of as stupid instead of retarded, though in truth he was neither; he was just slower than most.

"You are not like other people." Mr. Murphy carefully formed each word.

I started to thank him for the compliment, but he stopped me in mid-sentence, which was his way when he was attempting to connect a thought to his vocal cords.

"You are very nice, Tuxedo Bob." Over the next few minutes I waited patiently while he struggled to communicate his question about why I didn't treat him the way other people did.

"You are a very good man, Mr. Murphy, and you have a kind heart." I smiled at him and continued, "When you speak to me, I am interested in what you have to say. I'm not concerned with how you speak, or how long it may take for you to finish a sentence. I'm your good friend."

"I'm your good friend too."

He most certainly was, and on that first Christmas Eve away from home I gave him, Miss Aaron and Ernie, a small Santa Claus ornament dressed in a personally hand-painted tuxedo as a gesture of my affection.

I couldn't decide what to give Mr. Genoa for Christmas because I didn't really know much about him. He was not inclined to be entirely cordial to me, but he was the star of the show with many responsibilities, so I could not take his rejections of my attempts at a professional relationship personally.

"First, you pay the dues," was what Mr. Murphy had said was required of any person who was an opening act. If part of my dues was accepting Mr. Genoa's disinterest, then I would happily abide by the rules. I soon discovered that "dues" could be paid directly to the star in the form of unsecured loans.

Mr. Genoa spent most of his time either in the company of the two buxom blonde women who served as his background vocalists or with the two gentlemen who were Mr. Napoli's associates. He worked hard perfecting his show, usually needing one or both of his singers for extra rehearsals in his room, but they didn't seem to mind the additional hours. They were probably nervous he might hire one of the other women often seen going to his dressing room for a late-night audition.

At some point every evening he would speak to Mr. Napoli's associates, and hand them some money. They were an odd threesome. Mr. Genoa with his perfect hair and teeth, dressed in his white suit, talking with replicas of Mutt and Jeff. I didn't know their real names, but that is what Mr. Murphy called them. One was short, fat and quiet, the other was thin, tall, and had a nervous twitch on the left side of his face when he spoke. They were always dressed in dark suits, and wore felt-brimmed hats. The short man reminded me of Jimmy Bartlett, of the Schulberg Bartletts, because he had the same type of chicken pox-scarred complexion.

After every midnight show Mr. Genoa would sit with his background singers, and have a few drinks. Mr. Murphy, like Mr. Derbin the bartender, said Mr. Genoa had some problem with ponies, and though I still didn't understand the equine terminology, I could see he drank a bit excessively. On the few occasions when he spoke to me, he had a habit of beginning the conversation with something other than what was actually on his mind.

"Hey, Bob, can I talk to you a second?"

Of course he could. I no longer stuck to my basic rule of communication because I was learning not to expect everyone to call me Tuxedo Bob in every situation. I was a professional, and he was the star.

"You sounded good tonight. Can I buy you a drink?"

Though performers' drinks were free, I accepted the generosity of his offer, and asked Mr. Derbin for a rum and coke. I knew that Mr. Genoa hadn't yet come forward with what he wanted to ask me.

"So, I know we don't talk a lot, you and me, but we're both in the same boat, right? I mean we're both entertainers, and we have to stick together."

I tried to imagine the lounge as the boat we were sailing in tandem, and how long it would take us to dock at the purpose of his conversation.

"Look, I'll be straight with you. I know I've borrowed a couple of dollars from you a few times, and I'm going to pay you back, you've got my word on that, but I'm coming up a little short for Christmas. I was wondering if you could loan me another fifty just until payday." His eyes darted from side to side as he spoke, and his voice conveyed the type of self-consciousness that forms when truth mingles with fiction.

To date I had given him a total of two hundred dollars. I was aware he used the word "loan" to mean something that would probably not be returned, but I still had almost a thousand dollars, so I saw no reason to deny his request. Money did not mean to me what it meant to others. It was only a unit of exchange, and Mr. Genoa was momentarily happy when I handed him the fifty he desired.

Mr. Silverman arrived as promised to see the Christmas Eve shows, and decided to attend the employee party held afterwards. He said he was satisfied with my performances, and pleased I had remembered him with a belated Hanukkah present. As he put on his new green ascot festooned with penguins in Santa Claus hats, he declared that it blended perfectly with his blue and white-striped jacket, purple slacks, and red shirt.

"Didn't I say you were a natural, kid? Well, I'm not just sayin' it to hear myself talk. The crowd loved you. You're a funny guy. That song about the pudding? Hilarious. Made me hungry. Look, kid. I'll catch up with you later. I gotta say hi to Vince, but I mean it when I say you're a natural. You gonna remember I said that? Well, you'd better. Sy Silverman knows a natural when he sees one, and kid, that's what you are; a natural. Hey, save my seat. I'll be back in a minute, okay?"

He jumped up, and rushed off before I had the chance to ask, "A natural what?" He had to judge the champagne chugging contest at the bar between Mr. Genoa and his background singers, so my question could wait. After all, this was a party, and at a party everyone has a good time laughing, talking, and drinking large quantities of either champagne or eggnog laced with rum.

Mr. Murphy was busy wiping bottles of liquor behind the bar, Ernie was alternately picking up dirty dishes and downing glasses of eggnog, and Miss Aaron was serving drinks and bringing plates of holiday snacks from the kitchen. My friends were still working on Christmas Eve while I was sitting sipping champagne. I felt slightly guilty, but everyone had his or her own job to do, and I had finished mine for the evening.

I had dropped a song from my Christmas Eve shows so I could make room for the addition of "SILENT NIGHT." I wanted to do something seasonal like Mr. Genoa who had a fast-paced medley of Christmas songs in his act complete with his trademark finger snapping. Though I disagreed artistically with his staccato version of "AWAY IN A MANGER," the audience applause was always enthusiastic.

"They ate it up!" is how I overheard him refer to their reaction, which I learned was backstage show business jargon for "the crowd was having a good time." It made sense to me that it was a term best left off the stage. I couldn't imagine Mr. Genoa replacing his frequently repeated audience solicitation, "Is everybody having a good time?" with "Is everybody eating me up?"

"SILENT NIGHT" was my favorite carol, and since it was not included in Mr. Genoa's speedy medley, I felt safe using it to close each of my three Christmas Eve performances. I started at the piano, sang the second verse a cappella, and then invited the audience to sing along with the reprise of the first verse.

During the invitation I played the verse's chords while I spoke of the magic that happens when people sing together, and how it didn't matter if an individual felt his or her voice wasn't of professional quality. While I was talking I realized it was the first time I was asking anyone to sing along with me, and I didn't know the proper procedure to follow if they should decide not to participate.

"The Bible says to make a joyful noise," I reminded them. "So, whether you picture yourself as an angel or a frog, I invite you to contribute your own individually unique noise to my show."

Some people jumped right in, while others held back waiting for inspiration to strike. By the fifth line everyone was singing, and the room transformed from a lounge into the choir loft of a great cathedral.

Even the staff of waitresses, busboys, and bartenders stopped working during the sing-along, and no one seemed to mind because no customer was ordering anything. My good friends, Miss Aaron and Ernie, sang with increased gusto as the evening progressed, and by the third show they joined me on stage along with fifteen enthusiastic members of the audience. The late show crowd demanded that the verse be sung twice, and I hoped Mr. Napoli would not view this as an encore. Fortunately no repercussions came from the four-minute overrun.

This extended performance also included the voice of my good friend, Mr. Murphy, who had learned to create some excuse to clean behind the bar every so often in order to hear me sing. I was glad he had been able to attend some of my shows, but most particularly this one. He made a number of courageous attempts to sing a word at the same time it was being sung by everyone else, and I watched him in admiration. I knew he was singing the entire verse in his head, and to me, his noise was the most joyful of all.

After I thanked the audience for the beautifully sung Christmas present they had given me, I left the stage to the sound of the applause everyone so deservedly gave each other. I wrote my third, and shortest letter to Orville and Margaret that night. I told them I loved and missed them. No other information seemed important.

# dominant ninth

The heavy rains on Christmas Day dampened the moods of most of the people who had planned to ski during their holiday weekend in the Catskills. Miss Aaron, Mr. Murphy, and I got soaking wet on our walk to and from the morning service at the nearby Good Shepherd Methodist Church. Upon our return, and after changing into dry clothes, we warmed ourselves in front of the lobby fireplace with cups of hot cocoa topped with marshmallows. Ernie joined us, but passed on the cocoa because he had a throbbing headache from "mucho mucho eggnog."

I had picked up a few Spanish words from Ernie, and enjoyed the way they sounded coming out of my mouth. My personal favorite phrase was "Vaya con Dios" which Mr. Murphy pronounced, "buy a cone de dose." I had also begun using Miss Aaron's "baah" pronunciation whenever I referred to the lounge, and I could tell from her effervescent giggle that she took it as a sign of my affection.

As the fire crackled, I told my friends what Mr. Silverman had communicated to me earlier in the morning as he was leaving for Manhattan. He was planning to send me out on the road as the opening act for Mr. Vince Genoa after my contract was up with Pressman's. The complete itinerary was still up in the air, but it was going to start sometime in January. Miss Aaron expressed how happy she was that I had been presented with such a great opportunity, and Ernie agreed.

"Muy buenos, amigo. You will be a big star," he said with a smile that quickly turned to a grimace. "Aye, mi cabasa," he groaned, rubbing his forehead.

Mr. Murphy carefully set down his cocoa, and put his hand on my shoulder.

"I miss you," he said.

"And I will miss you too," I responded. Though I knew I had left my home in Schulberg, North Dakota to do exactly what Mr. Silverman was offering, it never occurred to me that there would be sadness involved. It would be hard to leave my friends.

The week between Christmas and New Year's Eve presented two situations that would test both of my father's theories of what it takes to be a man; "a man admits when he's wrong," and "a man walks away from a fight." These notions were firmly implanted in my brain, and I had no reason to doubt their validity.

*The First Situation: S*omeone had hung a sprig of mistletoe above the service area of the bar presumably because it was the perfect place to kiss the waitresses. Miss Aaron let it be known that she felt there was no hard and fast rule requiring her willing compliance to this holiday tradition.

Since I had always believed a kiss was something given, not taken, I agreed with her point of view. After the last show on Christmas night, one of Mr. Napoli's associates presented his opinion on the subject.

The audience had retired to their rooms, most of the staff had completed their duties, and the lounge was almost empty. Mr. Genoa and his background singers sat at their usual table, drinking their usual drinks. Mr. Derbin washed the last of the dirty glasses littering his bar, and was engaged in conversation with the taller of Mr. Napoli's two associates who was mistletoe loitering. Miss Aaron was busy resetting the tables. I was polishing the piano. My father always said a good craftsman takes care of his tools.

"Stop it!" I heard Miss Aaron shout. Her demand seemed clear and to the point. I looked up and saw her pushing Mr. Napoli's associate away from her.

"It's mistletoe. You gotta kiss me," he slurred, and forced his mouth upon hers in a way that did not resemble a token of holiday affection.

As I walked over to intercede on Miss Aaron's behalf, she freed herself from his grasp, and ran into the kitchen crying. Though Mr. Napoli's associate was inebriated and not entirely in control of his actions, I was reminded of something my father used to say: "Intoxication does not excuse bad behavior."

Mr. Derbin set down the glass he had been wiping with a cloth. "Ah, Frankie, why'd you have to go and do that, huh?" he asked rhetorically as he exited to the kitchen.

Mr. Napoli's associate, who Mr. Derbin called Frankie, steadied himself against the bar, and laughed, which intensified the twitch on the left side of his face.

"Excuse me, sir, but I think you owe Miss Aaron an apology." Before I could add that there was no humor in hurting someone's feelings he assumed a threatening pose, and crudely told me to mind my own business. I made an attempt to dilute the volatile atmosphere with an off the cuff remark. "If I minded my own business, sir, I'd never learn anything."

He stopped laughing, and opened his mouth as if to reply, but he merely exhaled heavily in my direction. His breath was quite pungent.

"I'm sorry if I offended you by interjecting my opinion," I offered sincerely, "but Miss Aaron is my friend, and I felt I should say something."

"So you said somethin'. Now buzz off before some little twerp in a tuxedo is real sorry for messing with Frankie The Weasel."

It occurred to me that his surly attitude might be the result of our never having been properly introduced. I extended my hand, and said with a smile, "My name's Tuxedo Bob, Mr. Theweasel. It's a pleasure to meet you."

He pushed my hand away, said he knew who I was, didn't care to meet me, and didn't need another two-bit lounge singer telling him what to do.

I mulled his responses for a moment, and decided it would be best to redirect the focus of our communication to the original reason for my intrusion. "I'm sorry you feel that way, sir, but I still believe you owe Miss Aaron an apology for your behavior."

"Well, I believe you got a smart mouth." This was not spoken in a complimentary fashion as he glared at me while adjusting the tilt of his fedora. "How about me and you go outside, and settle this man to man?"

"This isn't about us, sir. It's about you being a gentleman, and apologizing to Miss Aaron for upsetting her." I spoke softly, and though I exhibited a brand of bravado foreign to my temperament, I was confident he would take the high road and see the error of his ways. I was mistaken.

"I'm not gonna apologize; I'm gonna rearrange your face, you little son of a bitch!"

One of the blonde back-up singers made an attempt to come to my aid by blurting out, "Oh, Frankie, leave the kid alone," but Mr. Genoa wisely advised her to stay out of it.

Although Mr. Theweasel thought he wanted to involve me in a physical altercation, I knew it was just the alcohol talking. However, I was also aware of liquor's ability to be an assertive accomplice to irresponsible behavior, so I had to quickly consider a course of action that would dissuade him from his malicious intent. I noticed he was still positioned under the mistletoe, and since continuing our conversation any further would be counter-productive, I kissed him on his twitching cheek and said, "Merry Christmas, Mr. Theweasel!" This approach proved most effective. He became instantly befuddled, and hurriedly left the room muttering something about being kissed by a queer.

Miss Aaron and Mr. Derbin returned from the kitchen. She wiped her eyes on her shirtsleeve, and apologized for making a scene. Mr. Derbin said she didn't have anything to be sorry about. I added that if anyone should apologize it should be me for my inability to exact a proper request for forgiveness from Mr. Theweasel.

"You are too much," she said giving me a warm hug.

Before I could ask her what she thought I was too much of, she started crying again. Mr. Genoa got up from his seat, and offered her his handkerchief.

"Hey, stop your blubbering. It's over already."

It was the first time I had seen him make an unselfish gesture, and I was gratified viewing this endorsement of my faith in human nature.

Miss Aaron's emotional experience had exhausted her, and she asked to be excused. When Mr. Derbin kindly offered to escort her to her room, Mr. Genoa told his backup singers to leave also because he wanted to speak to me in private. I checked my pocket for the presence of the fifty-dollar bill I always carried for such emergencies.

"That wasn't a smart thing to do, kid. Frankie is not the person you want to be on the bad side of." Mr. Genoa sounded almost fatherly, but dispensing parental advice was not his objective. "Look, I wanted to ask you, if you think I'm good for it, could you float me another fifty? I'll be getting a raise the first of the year, and can pay you the entire three hundred then. What do you say?"

I had already taken the additional loan from my pocket. As I handed it to him I said, "Mr. Genoa, as my Christmas present to you, I release you from your obligation of repayment."

"Hey, there's no need to do that. Vince Genoa always pays his markers." He tapped his index finger on his chest to indicate there was truth in his statement.

"I know that deep down inside you're an honorable man, Mr. Genoa. I would ask that you consider my gesture to be a part of my dues-paying program. I've learned a lot from you, and I'm grateful for that." My statement seemed to surprise him.

"Yeah?" For a second he appeared vulnerable, but the quizzical look on his face quickly reverted back to one of confidence. "I mean, yeah, of course you have. You know there's a lot of guys out there who would jump at the chance to work with me." Filled with self-satisfaction he crossed his arms and relaxed in his chair. "Consider yourself lucky, Bob."

"I do, Mr. Genoa, and I thank you for the opportunity." I leaned toward him. "May I ask you for a favor, sir?"

"What kind of favor? It's nothing weird, is it?" Though Mr. Genoa didn't know me well enough to comprehend he had nothing to fear, he was prudent to be wary of the unknown. "You're not like what Frankie said, are you?"

"The favor I want concerns horse racing."

This piqued his interest. "You want to play the ponies?"

"No, sir."

"So what do you want?"

I knew that Mr. Genoa's attention was hard to keep when he felt a conversation was not centered on him, so I got to the point of my request. "I've heard that you like to bet money on horse races, and that you usually lose."

"Hey, anybody can have a bad day," he said in an attempt to justify his habit. "I'm just on a bad luck streak."

"It appears that way, sir. It's also been an expensive streak."

"Yeah, well, you can't make money if you don't bet money. Get to the favor you want."

"The favor is that you take the fifty dollars, and wager it on the horses you think will lose."

"What?" he interjected incredulously. "That's crazy."

"Not necessarily, sir. The horses you think will lose are the ones doing all the winning."

He looked at me suspiciously for a moment, and then he smiled. "You know something, Bob? That just might work."

It worked.

The next evening Mr. Genoa proudly invited me to his dressing room where I watched Mr. Theweasel and his cohort pay three thousand dollars for the nine losers he had chosen. When I congratulated him on his good fortune, he chided me for letting him off the hook for the loans. I was glad he was so happy.

Mr. Napoli's associates were quite sour during the exchange. When Mr. Genoa informed them that I had been the key component in their monetary liability, their moods deteriorated. I would soon become a participant in an unpleasant situation with both of them during the special eleven o'clock show on New Year's Eve.

*The Second Situation*: The lounge was adorned with hundreds of balloons and crepe-paper streamers. Each table was furnished with a champagne bucket, and each place setting included a packet of confetti, a noisemaker and a festive party hat. I heard that the room had been sold out for eight months, so I realized this would be an audience of serious revelers. Though I would not be on stage for the final countdown into year 1965 (that was the duty of the star) I wanted my last show of 1964 to be my best ever.

I had written a new song for the occasion, and was able to procure the services of Mr. Genoa's background singers and bass player to assist in its inaugural presentation. There had been time for only one rehearsal, but since they were professionals I was sure "THAT'S WHAT I CALL LOVE" would come off without a problem.

I started my show with "COMPLETELY NUDE" because it put the audience in the mood to laugh. Next came "I JUST LOVE TO COMPLAIN" followed by "OUT OF MY MIND," which was the perfect lead in to "THE SANITARIUM SONG." The crowd was laughing and crying at the same time; the standard mixture of emotions my songs evoked. It was time for my new number.

After introducing Miss Sarah Goodard, Miss Pam Barner, and Mr. Bop to the patrons, I gushed gracious thanks to Mr. Genoa for his kind loan of their services. The audience responded with a round of applause that I'm certain he appreciated. I sat down at the piano, and asked Mr. Bop to please start the song with a solo performance. He nodded, and began plucking the repetitive nine-note figure that continued throughout the opening eight bars. I informed the audience that this was my first composition with a walking bass line, and I had written it specifically for Mr. Bop and his talented digits. I added a few chords on the piano in counterpoint to his steady rhythm.

"We're cookin', now!" he said with a wink in my direction.

It was a nice moment of musician camaraderie. Cooking felt good, however, halfway through the second verse a fire started.

From the corner of my eye I had been watching Mr. Murphy in his usual spot, cleaning behind the bar, and I sensed that something was not right. I observed him working at one end of the bar, then walking quickly to the other end to wipe a few glasses, then returning to his first location. He did this a number of times, and since he wasn't one to fidget, I surmised that the simultaneous movements of Mr. Napoli's associates probably had something to do with the situation. Mr. Murphy was trying to do the right thing by walking away from them, but they were persistent.

Ernie, on his way to the kitchen with a tray of dirty dishes, also noticed Mr. Murphy's predicament. He decided to take a less direct route to his intended destination, and crossed the length of the room so he could accidentally step in front of Mr. Theweasel and his friend. There was a loud crash as the tray of dishes and the man Mr. Murphy called Mutt hit the floor. Ernie stood with his arms outstretched as if he couldn't believe what had just happened. Mr. Theweasel stumbled backward in an attempt to avoid falling, and tripped over a table covered with Sterno-heated chafing dishes that were set up for the evening's festivities. The thunderous racket created by this collision diverted what was left of my audience's attention, and as the tablecloths and Mr. Theweasel's fedora united with the flames from the toppled Sterno candles, "THAT'S WHAT I CALL LOVE" abruptly ended.

There was nothing comforting about a fire in an enclosed room filled with hundreds of people. The patrons and workers began panicked dashes toward any exit in the opposite direction from the flames. From my vantage point on the stage, however, danger looked to be impending, but not immediate.

Using my microphone I quickly put Miss Throckmorton's fifth grade fire drill trainings to use. I asked everyone to remain calm, and to please walk toward the exits in an orderly fashion. I did not add the comment, "Now we are really cookin'!" that Mr. Bop made to me as he walked off the stage, though I thought it was humorous.

Mr. Murphy took the most sensible approach to the problem. He went into the kitchen, and brought out a large container of baking soda that he used to smother the flames. By the time the Fire Department arrived, the fire was out. The only casualties were some tablecloths, the food, and a badly scorched fedora.

Under orders from the Fire Marshall the room could not be used until a full inspection was completed. The New Year's Eve audience re-assembled in the hotel lobby, and at thirty minutes after the stroke of midnight the New Year was saluted with free drinks compliments of Mr. Napoli. The festivities ended after a brief performance by a reluctant, albeit professional, Mr. Genoa whose finger snapping pizzazz seemed at odds with the acoustic guitar accompaniment.

In the morning Mr. Napoli called a meeting in his office to sort out what had happened. He arrived at the conclusion that if Mr. Murphy had followed the employee regulation prohibiting non-assigned staff from being in the lounge he would not have been in the bar, and therefore, nothing would have happened. I could not silently protest his finding.

"May I speak to you in private, sir?" I felt that what I had to say was best said between the two of us.

He obliged me by telling Mr. Murphy and Ernie to go to their rooms, and ordering his associates, Frankie (whose nickname I had mistaken for a surname), and Benny (Mutt) to stand outside the door.

When everyone had gone I told Mr. Napoli what I had seen prior to the fire, and of Miss Aaron's mistletoe experience, and that I thought his associates were a bad influence on an otherwise professional environment. In Ernie's defense I stated that his behavior may have been an example of poor judgment, but his motive was honorable. He came to the aid of his friend.

Mr. Napoli leaned back in his big leather chair, and looked at me while tapping his fingers on his desk. I couldn't tell if he was angry from what I had said, but whatever his response would be, I knew I had spoken the truth. My father used to say, "Truth is like a good book. Once you get started you can't put it down." My book had been presented; it was time for a decision.

The silence was broken when Mr. Napoli exhaled, shook his big head, and mumbled, "What's a decent kid like you doing in a business like this?"

"I like to sing, sir." It was the most truthful answer in my good book.

Mr. Napoli imposed no punishment on Ernie. Mr. Murphy was told to abide by the rules, and stay away from the lounge unless he had a very good reason to be there. Messrs. Frankie and Benny were banned from the hotel for a week, and ordered not to bother my friends or me. It felt like justice.

I paid homage to Mr. Napoli by using his words "in a business like this" in my song "ANYTHING TO WIN,"[1] which I wrote after hearing he had been killed in front of a New York City post office.

---

[1] "ANYTHING TO WIN" was written in the spring of 1974, six years after Mr. Napoli's death. It was eventually recorded during the Eclipse Records sessions in Hollywood, California. Although several bootleg tapes have been in circulation, the Eclipse studio version was not available to the general public until its inclusion as a bonus track on "Tuxedo Bob - The Recital" - Bopadest Records - OM 98351.

# tenth verse

Mr. Silverman returned to Pressman's on January eighth to confirm that I would be continuing in my present position as Vince Genoa's opening act.

"I'm putting you on the Vince Genoa Express to fame and fortune, you know that? Do you know how many up-and-comers would jump at the chance you're getting? I'm talking big bang, shooting star, name in lights, brass ring, the whole salami! You hear what I'm saying? Are you listening to me, kid?"

I nodded my head to let him know I was paying attention. I discovered that my new contract and extensive itinerary required my services twice a night over the next four months in ninety-seven cities. Mr. Silverman rapidly added that this tour would get my feet much wetter, and that he would be able to see if I had what it took to keep up with the grueling pace and harsh reality of life on the road. His less than attractive choice of adjectives did not diminish my enthusiasm. Being on a grueling, harsh road trip sounded romantically mysterious; traveling to new cities was the reason

I had begun my journey in the first place. I told Mr. Silverman I appreciated his confidence in my abilities.

"You better appreciate it, kid. Hey, I'm on a limb here sending you out so early. You know that, don't you? I want you to pay attention to Vince because you can learn a lot from him. He's a pro, you know. A real pro. Audiences love him, but why not, huh? He's Vince! You gotta love him, right? Do you hear what I'm saying? You watch; you listen; you learn. Do that, and the sky's the limit. I got a lot riding on you, kid, so don't let me down." He casually withdrew some folded papers and a ballpoint pen from the inside pocket of his orange and yellow-striped jacket, and placed them on the table as he continued his rapid-fire discourse. "Hey, who am I kidding here, huh? You're not gonna let me down. You're a natural! You're gonna do great. I got nothing to worry about. I've got a pro and a natural. It's too good to be true, that's what it is. If I'm dreaming, don't pinch me, kid, 'cause I love this dream. You hear what I'm saying? I'm talking big love here. Oh, by the way, before I forget, you gotta sign this."

My father would have described Mr. Sy Silverman as a person who could "talk the spots off a leopard," but I was not thinking about that when I eagerly signed my name on the dotted line. Rejoicing at perceived good fortune affected my judgment, and I paid no attention to the terms contained in the contract's fine print. I was too excited to consider the consequences of agreeing to stipulations regarding extensions, exclusive service, percentages, and right of assignment.

Mr. Silverman signed his name, and the transaction was complete. I was now legally bound to continue singing in front of strangers at seventy-five dollars per week, but the benefits did not stop there. The arrangement for my free room would continue in the form of a semi-reclining seat on Mr.

Genoa's tour bus, and my free board would be one dinner at each nightclub combined with whatever I cared to purchase with a three-dollar per-day food allowance. I could certainly find a quick dry cleaning service when required, so it seemed to me that everything important was handled.

As happy as I was to be a part of Mr. Silverman's dream, was as sad as I was saying good-bye to my three good friends after the final show in Billy's Night Life Lounge. The Four Musketeers, as Miss Aaron nicknamed our quartet, walked down to the lake where Ernie conducted a ceremony of friendship his father had taught him.

He chose a spot on a small hill by the shore where four pine trees stood close together, and asked each of us to pick up a small stone. When we had made our choices, we simultaneously threw them into the water. Ernie said this was a symbol of our lasting brother and sisterhood, and we were like those little rocks that would always be together in the same big lake. It was a nice moment, and it produced a long teary-eyed group hug. We headed back to the hotel arm-in-arm, knowing that the ceremony of the stones would keep us connected, no matter what lakes we sailed.

I went to my room, and had just gotten into bed when there was a knock on my door. Opening it revealed Miss Aaron who timidly asked to come in. I had wrapped myself in my bed sheet, which she thought was quite funny.

"I've never seen you in anything but a tuxedo. You look rather Roman."

Her giggle was so captivating; I knew I would miss its sound. I waited a moment for her to say why she had come, and when nothing was said I asked if everything was all right. Speaking helped diminish the blush of embarrassment on my face from being dressed in a bed sheet. Miss Aaron did not reply. She just stood in front of me, slightly trembling.

In that moment of nervous silence, I flashed on a memory of something my father used to say. "You can tell what a man's got on his mind by listening to what he isn't saying." As my feelings for her surfaced in the form of teardrops, I figured my father's words must also be true for a woman.

"I care about you, too, Miss Aaron. And I will care about you beyond my last breath."

Tears had been in such great abundance this last day that it seemed appropriate to shed a few more. Mine were running down my cheeks, and a stream of them fell from her beautiful gray-green eyes. She spoke through them, saying her presence in my room at three in the morning should indicate that there was a strong possibility I could suspend formality, and would I please call her Sylvia just once.

"Always addressing a person with respect is a habit of mine, and I'm sorry if I've offended you by never calling you by your first name. Sylvia." The sound of her name was so pleasant as it rolled across my tongue and through my lips that I had to say it again. "Sylvia."

She smiled, and her lower lip curled under her perfect white teeth. "You never offend me. I don't think you could offend anyone." Then she asked me to give her a hug.

When we put our arms around each other I felt very warm and somewhat electrified. That hug was quite different from any I had previously experienced. We laid down on my bed, and I continued to hug her until she fell asleep in my arms. I stroked her soft brown hair, and listened to her breathe until the sun came up. When she woke, she kissed me tenderly on the cheek, and told me I was the kindest and nicest person she had ever met. I thanked her for the compliments, and as she walked out the door I added that it takes one to know one.

I had less than an hour before the scheduled 7:15 AM departure time, and I still had to pack my suitcase and clean my room. It was important to me that the next person to live here arrives to spotless surroundings. I got fresh linens and towels from the supply room, scrubbed the bathroom, dusted the furnishings, washed the walls, and mopped the floor. When I was satisfied all was in order I picked up my suitcase and walked out of room number 110 for the last time.

There were more tears and extra hugs among the Musketeers as we stood next to the loaded and waiting tour bus. We had no idea what the future had in store for us, but we knew our friendships were everlasting. For the present time Ernie and Mr. Murphy would continue working at Pressman's, Sylvia would follow her plan to start classes at Boston University in the spring, and I would be on the road.

"Vaya con Dios, mi amigo." Ernie's warm-hearted farewell flashed like gold in the bright sunlight.

"Buy a coned de dose, Tuxedo Bob. I will miss you." Mr. Murphy shook my hand firmly as he spoke slowly and distinctly.

"You know how I feel." Sylvia averted her tear-filled eyes from me as she spoke, and I respected her privacy.

"I want to give each of you a part of me," I said as I handed one of my bow ties to Ernie, one of my cummerbunds to Mr. Murphy, and a set of my simulated pearl studs to Sylvia. "Each of you will always have a very special place in my heart." I might have said more, but I was interrupted.

"Hey, kid! Are you gonna stand there all day? We gotta get going!" Mr. Genoa did not want a tardy departure, and correctly discerned that a barked command was needed to re-focus my attention.

I got on the bus, and found a seat by a window where I could wave good-bye to my friends until they were no longer in sight. The Vince Genoa Express, with Mr. Genoa, two background singers, Mr. Bop the bass player, a guitarist, a drummer, a pianist, a bus driver, and me rolled toward its first stop in Marienville, Pennsylvania.

Mr. Genoa must have noticed I was less than my typically exuberant self. He put his hand on my shoulder, and offered some professional words of advice.

"There's a lot of fish in the sea, Bob. That's why fishing is fun." He expressed his opinion that forming attachments during the beginning of a career to people outside the business was not smart unless they could be used to an advantage. "Take that cute little waitress, for instance. Now I'm sure she's good for a few rolls in the hay, but you're gonna have more women than you can shake a stick at. Don't complicate your life. Love 'em and leave 'em. That's my motto, kid. Friends are a dime a dozen."

I paid attention to his advice, per Mr. Silverman's request, but I had no interest in adopting his principles. I thanked him for his concern, and leaned back in my seat. Even after applying the Vince Genoa dime-a-dozen value system for friendship, I knew I would still miss my two and a half cents worth of three very special Musketeers.

Marienville, Silver Springs, Hidden Valley, Uniondale, Canton, Xenia, Fort Wayne, Elyria, Grand Rapids, Galesburg, and Ironton. There was either a large resort, or a small club, or a noisy bar, or a barn-style dinner theater waiting to greet us in every town. We would arrive, set up, eat, perform, pack, and leave — day after day after day.

As a newcomer to "the road" it was important to keep my mouth shut and my ears open. I knew that being paid to perform was not the only distinction between a professional and an amateur, and there were lessons to be learned. Both Mr. Genoa and I were comfortable on stage, but I lacked his expert ability to take an audience for granted. Backstage, Mr. Genoa would bemoan the task of enduring "another bunch of inebriated riffraff" yet still go out and give a brisk performance. I figured that I would need a great deal of seasoning before I was no longer fascinated by the endless variety of faces in front of me each night.

I was awed by Mr. Genoa's brand of professionalism, and wondered if I had what it took to be a headliner. His shows were exact clones; every night he would deliver the same well-oiled, rubber-stamped performance to an audience of fifteen or two hundred. It was such an exercise in precision that I could lip-synch his show from start to finish with my eyes closed.

In contrast, my shows were formed by opportunity. I had more songs than I needed to fill my twenty-minute slot, so I had the freedom to choose which ones I would perform. I never knew what choices I would make until after I said hello, thanked the people for coming, and introduced myself (even if an announcer had provided an introduction). If anyone in the audience returned my greeting I would exchange a few pleasantries with that person, and then sit down at the piano and open with a slow number like "MY LONG ISLAND COMA GIRL," or "THE SANITARIUM SONG."

My reasoning was that any audience response indicated a willingness to actively listen, and a song with a story line was the proper choice.

If the audience was passive I would start with an up-tempo number. Quiet crowds were always more lively after hearing either the blunt opening line of "OUT OF MY MIND" — "If I had known you for a day before I met you, I would have shot you on sight" — or the playfully libidinous lyrics of "COMPLETELY NUDE."

My twenty minutes were up after I sang six songs, and following Mr. Genoa's wishes there was never an encore. He also stated that I could not have the assistance of Mr. Bop or Misses Goodard and Barner to perform, "THAT'S WHAT I CALL LOVE." Since that song would not be the same without background vocals and a walking bass line, I decided not to perform it until I had a band of my own. I didn't know it at the time, but the band of my own was currently backing Mr. Genoa.

The only fixed segment of my show was the closing number, "I JUST LOVE TO COMPLAIN." The last verse of this song, about a cantankerous person trying to cope with the aging process, always shifted an audience's laughter to contemplation.

"I pull up closer to the fire.
I'm feeling bitter cold.
The dreams I used to have for us
have all been bought or sold.
I wanted to have everything,
and all I got was old.
But I feel no pain.
I just love to complain."

There was always a stillness that swept the audience as I sang those words. They were probably not used to hearing a song that started out funny and ended on a note of regret and dashed dreams. Some people may have thought I was singing about my parents. Others might have flashed on a thought of their own parents, or of themselves. Whatever the reason, the applause that would follow my exit from the stage, whether polite or heartfelt, was never quite as important to me as that brief moment of silence.

During the third week of the tour we were in Lake Geneva, Wisconsin, and I wrote my fourth letter to Orville and Margaret. I told them how much I was enjoying getting my feet wet, and enclosed my performance schedule. The current itinerary would bring me no closer than nine hundred miles from Schulberg, but at least they would know where I was each night. I thanked them for having given me the greatest gifts a parent can give their child: Acceptance, Tolerance, and Kindness. All are certainly included under the general umbrella of love, but those three expressions of my parent's affection were the one's I wanted to point out as the most gratifying. I was sure they missed me, but I knew they were happy for me.

I had been picking up matchbooks from any hotels near our engagements, and I sent the collection to Sylvia along with a note to her, Ernie and Mr. Murphy. I wanted them to know that they were in my thoughts every day, and in my prayers every night.

Even without the four stones at the bottom of the lake I would always think of Ernie when I put on my bow tie. Whenever I wrapped my cummerbund around my waist I would do it slowly and carefully, thinking of Mr. Murphy. And I cherished my simulated pearl studs, knowing Sylvia had a matching set.

# eleventh chorus

My three-dollar meal per diem was not actually mine to spend. It was my share of the twenty-four dollars per day allocated to the members of the tour. We spent the money on group grocery purchases. Mr. Genoa controlled the funds, but as long as there was a bag of Fig Newtons on board he didn't care what else we bought.

"The Vince Genoa Express Bus To Fame And Fortune" (named by Mr. Genoa) served a standard breakfast of water mixed with dry milk powder poured over cereal; the individual boxes of corn flakes or raisin bran conveniently doubled as bowls. Bananas, apples, oranges, peanut butter crackers, pretzels, cheese doodles, and candy bars were our lunch and snack items. Every so often we would pull into an A&W drive-in for root beer and burgers, or a Stuckey's for bacon and eggs or pecan pancakes. These stops were always enjoyable and appreciated events.

Dinners were as varied as the places we played. The best supper clubs offered thick T-bone steaks with baked potatoes. This meal was by far the most popular with our group, and Mr. Genoa always proclaimed that any place that served a twelve-ounce steak had a lot of class. The buffets at the dinner theaters featured baked ham, roast beef, fried chicken, and a fine assortment of side dishes and desserts. The bars and lounges served casseroles of macaroni or rice with vegetables, spaghetti with tomato sauce, grilled cheese sandwiches and potato chips, or hot dogs and french fries. No one in our band of gypsies was ever in any danger of dying from hunger.

Being "on the road" necessitated washing it off, and when one of the smaller cabarets on our itinerary didn't have shower facilities everyone would contribute to the cost of a motel room. Mr. Genoa always chipped in an extra dime so he could shower first. I was amused that he equated his desire for hot water insurance to the value of a dozen friends. Miss Goodard and Miss Barner would alternate between the second and third positions, the four musicians would flip Mr. Genoa's dime for their turns, and I would shower last, after Mr. Carlton the bus driver.

Every once in a while there would be enough hot water for everyone, but more often than not the shower would become tepid during, or just after, the third person's turn. Mr. Genoa's musicians started betting on who would be bathing when the water turned cold; the surest and safest bet was anytime prior to me.

Traveling from one place to the next was fascinating as there was an ever-changing landscape of big cities, quaint towns, rolling hills, flat fields, dense forests, lakes and rivers. Staring out the windows at the marvelous vistas, taking naps, snacking, and poker were the most popular diversions used to fill the hours between performances.

Misses Goodard and Barner dubbed our tour "one long slumber party," and could usually be found doing their nails on the back bench-seat with most of our pillows. They had a mildly heated discussion with Mr. Genoa about the smell of nail polish remover. His point of view prevailed, and the women agreed to open a window to keep his dislike of the noxious fumes to a minimum. This example of the privileges of rank satisfied everyone because "Performers Asphyxiated In Unlicensed Nail Salon" was not among the newspaper headlines anyone cared to see.

Mr. Genoa generally kept to himself, conserving his energy for the evening's performances. Fig Newtons, a daily newspaper's sports section, and an occasional late night meeting in the back of the bus with one of his singers were his only requirements.

When the four musicians weren't asleep they talked about jazz or rhythm and blues, and played poker. They were sociable, and actively included me in their conversations, but Mr. Bop excluded me from participating in any of their card games because I did not possess the proper face for poker.

"Tee-Bee, you got a face that says, 'Please take my money!'" was the way he phrased his judgment.

Musicians gave nicknames to everything, and "Tee-Bee" was mine. I took it as a sign of their respect and approval. Though they would often call Mr. Genoa "Mr. Vee," Miss Goodard "Fox One," and Miss Barner "Fox Two," I felt more comfortable using their proper names. I did, however, join them in referring to Mr. Carlton, our bus driver, as "Bee-Dee," and (with no disrespect toward Mr. Genoa's nickname for our bus) we called our bus "The Big Limo." The nickname of every town we played was "Paradise."

Delroy "Bee-Bop" Washington was from Harlem, New York. He had three brothers and nine sisters, appreciated any song with a good bass line, and said I hadn't really lived until I'd eaten chitlins, collard greens and fat back. Mr. Washington liked that I had referred to him as "Mr. Bop" prior to learning his real name, and he informed the group he was officially changing his nickname. "Call me Mister Bop, or don't call me," was how he put it, and he would not respond to his fellow musicians if they addressed him in any other way.

"You got some talent, Tee-Bee," Mr. Bop said one afternoon while I watched the poker game. "You won't be Mr. Vee's lap dog for long."

When I asked if "lap dog" was another term for "opening act" everyone laughed, and I was given a quick lesson in the language of the musician.

"Hip" was something currently in fashion. Both "hot" and "cool" were used to express approval. "Bread" was money. "Gig" was a job. "Dig" was to comprehend. "Nailed it" meant a particular performance had been extremely hot and/or cool. "Jive" was any degree of deception. "Groove" was the way something sounded. "Bad" meant good, "chops" were skills, and "soul" was feelings from the heart. Mr. Bop said he thought I had a lot of soul for a white boy from North Dakota.

Joe "Sticks" Dunbar said I had a lot of soul for a kid from anywhere. Sticks was also from Harlem, had played the drums since the age of four, and said he had the hippest chops in the business. He thought anything was cool as long as it contained no jive, and most of his sentences ended with the word "man." He spoke in a gravelly whisper, and with his shifty eyes and fidgety gestures he was the perfect stereotype of a person about to participate in criminal activities. After the gig at The Spotted Deer Lodge in Warsaw, Missouri, Sticks approached me about starting a band.

"Dig it. You gotta get a band, man. You got a hip way of thinkin', and if you're ever lookin' for a smooth groove, remember Sticks can do the trick. You dig what I'm sayin', man?"

"I dig your lack of jive, Sticks," I replied. "It would be hot to play with some really bad musicians." The new words did not fit me as comfortably as my tuxedo.

"Cool." Sticks moved closer to my ear. "Dig it. Bop is hip to the plan, and Pappy and Deke'll swing with whatever we do if the bread is happening, man. No jive." He returned to his seat next to Mr. Bop after telling me to keep my groove on the move, and that he would catch me on the rebound.

Charlie Donovan was called "Pappy" because he was two months older than the other band members. He was born in an area north of Manhattan called the Bronx, and enjoyed reading the sports section of each town's newspaper so he could keep up with his Rangers and Yankees. His expert digits could play a piano, saxophone or clarinet with equal grace. He limited his input to discussions with either "Sounds like a plan" if he was in agreement, or "Won't fly" if his opinion was one of dissent. I thought he was shy, but he was just the quietest member of the animated foursome.

Deacon "Deke" Brown played guitar, banjo and trumpet. He was born in Memphis, Tennessee, and from the age of twelve had been a traveling musician. He and Pappy played together in Manhattan for ten years prior to joining Mr. Genoa's band. He said it was because they needed the bread. His slow southern drawl and composed temperament, distinctly the opposite of Sticks, complemented the manners of Mr. Bop and Pappy. He told me to respect my song writing talent, because the most important thing in his life was expressing someone else's music from his soul.

"If nobody never write nothin', there be nothin' for Deke to play with." Even with a confusing triple negative his point was clear. "You maybe might someday want to learn some guitar, Tee-Bee. If'n you come to that mind, you let Deke know. Deke teach you a chord or two."

Because he always spoke of himself in the third person, I responded in kind. "Deke can teach me whenever Deke has the time."

Late one night during the tenth week of the tour (March 19, 1965 to be exact) I was awakened by the touch of a hand on my shoulder. When I looked up, I saw my father standing over me flipping a coin. I was certain his unexpected appearance on The Big Limo indicated I was dreaming.

"We're proud to call you our son." Orville's lips were moving, but it was my mother's voice I heard.

My attention was momentarily distracted by the drum and horn sections of the marching band that had suddenly begun to parade down the aisle. I wanted to tell them they were blocking my view, but no sound came out of my mouth. When I looked back toward my father, he was gone. I had to find him. I attempted to get up, but my legs wouldn't move. Then I woke up.

I spent the rest of that night writing the fifth and longest letter to my parents. I started by telling them how proud I was to be their son, and nine pages quickly followed with detailed descriptions about my new life, the experiences I was having, and the friends I wanted them to meet. I closed with a promise to come home for a visit at the conclusion of my current tour. In the morning I mailed the promise that would not be kept in the letter that would never be read.

# twelfth dance

I was putting the finishing touches on my letter around 5 A.M. when heavy rain and hail began pelting The Big Limo just outside Evansville, Indiana. The booming thunder, and crackling flashes of lightning woke up my slumbering traveling companions. Though some grumbled at first from having been awakened so abruptly, the power and beauty of this pre-spring storm quickly changed all verbal communications to short exclamations of "Cool!" "Wow!" and "Dig it!"

By seven-thirty the rain had diminished to a drizzle, and we pulled into a truck stop for gas and a hot breakfast. Most of us took the opportunity to freshen up in the restroom before sitting down at the counter in the dining area to feast on buttermilk pancakes or oatmeal.

Mr. Genoa abandoned the group to use an available pay phone. Placing mysterious phone calls had been his habit of late, and speculation about what could have him so preoccupied was the main topic of the band's breakfast conversation.

Most of their questions were directed toward Miss Goodard and Miss Barner because they spent the most time with Mr. Genoa, but both skirted the inquiries with, "I don't have any idea," and "He doesn't tell us what he's doing." Though the mystery piqued my curiosity, I figured his business was his own. If he was betting on horse races he must be using the "pick a loser" strategy because he hadn't asked for a loan since Kiamesha Lake.

Whatever the reason, "This is gonna be great!" was the usual remark Mr. Genoa made to himself after each of his phone calls, and sure enough, when he got back on the bus he said it again. Today it was Deke's turn to press for further clarification.

"What's gonna be great, Mr. Vee?"

No matter who asked, Mr. Genoa would simultaneously snap his fingers, wink, smile and respond, "Nothing at all. Don't worry about it."

Though my father used to say, "A wise man ponders every attempt to divert his attention," I took Mr. Genoa's word on the subject. Whatever was going to be great was making him happy. His personal pleasure increased when he spotted a quarter on the floor next to my seat.

"Finder's keepers," he shouted as he proudly waved the coin in front of my face. "You should be more careful with your money, sonny. Hey, I made a rhyme! I'm a songwriter!"

He was delighted with himself, but when I blurted out that I would pay him a dollar for it, suspicion colored his mood.

"For the quarter or the rhyme?"

It was a fair question because he didn't know about my dream, or how I had awoken in a state of panic.

"It's a lucky quarter my father gave to me." I felt a tightness in my chest. I couldn't tell him he was standing in the exact spot Orville had stood flipping a coin before disappearing amid a marching band. "At least, I think it's the one from my father."

To my utter surprise, he flipped the coin onto my lap. "Here, kid. It's important to hold on to something from your father." It was the most endearing thing he ever said to me.

I held the quarter tightly in my fist; my mind busily engaged composing dark, dense themes derived from the dream, the storm, and my lie about the quarter's origin. I didn't notice Sticks had slid into the seat in front of me until he tapped me on the forehead. It was an abrupt but welcome interruption.

"Dig it, Tee-Bee. Ever wonder why Mr. Vee snaps his fingers so much when he sings?"

I shook my head, and replied that I thought it was simply technique.

"No jive, man, listen. His daddy got him hip to the sound when he was a little boy; keeps him close in his heart. It's soul, my brother. You dig?"

I dug, and put the quarter in my pocket. While Sticks' statement made Mr. Genoa's ability to remain separate from his feelings all the more perplexing, I gained a renewed respect for his artistic style.

By the middle of the next week we were at Betty's Supper Club in Hamilton, Ohio. A young journalism major moonlighting as a reporter for the local newspaper came backstage, and asked for an interview.

"Actually, to be honest, I was supposed to interview Vince Genoa, but he canceled at the last minute." Miss Holly Summer spoke sharply making no attempt to hide her aggravation.

When I asked if she had enjoyed my show, she sheepishly admitted she hadn't seen it, and offered to conduct the interview after my next set. I agreed, and during my second show I introduced her to the audience as an important writer from their local paper whose talents should be appreciated before she was snatched away by The New York Times.

The attention and extended applause pleased Miss Summer. My mention of The New York Times caused Mr. Genoa to reconsider his decision, and he delayed the start of his second show for more than fifteen minutes while he granted her an exclusive interview.

When Mr. Genoa finally went on stage Miss Summer came into my dressing room, and apologized for making me wait. I told her it was no problem at all, and that I was glad she had obtained the interview that she had come for in the first place.

Her questions were the simple "Who are you?" and "Where are you from?" variety. As we spoke I gave her the correct spellings of Schulberg and Fledsper, told her being on tour was fun, and that I had no commitments beyond my current bookings. However, nothing I said to her had the significance of what she told me.

"So, how do you feel about Mr. Genoa's plan to be on Broadway by the end of April?"

The surprised look on my face clearly displayed my ignorance. As she stammered through an apology for opening her "big yap," and letting "the cat out of the bag," I assured her that I would not repeat the information. I asked if she was certain she had heard him correctly because the end of the current tour was not until the second week of May. She was adamant that

Mr. Genoa had been very specific about his date of departure. Other than that bombshell, my first interview went quite well.

I escorted her to her car, and as I watched her drive away I flashed on something my father used to say, "Never assume a secret and the truth are brothers." Recalling this bit of wisdom eased the feeling that I needed to do something with the information that had come into my possession. If it was true that Mr. Genoa had a secret agenda, it was up to him to decide when it should become public knowledge.

The stop in Hamilton was one of the rare occasions we were scheduled to perform for two nights. Rooms were provided for us at the nearby Golden Empress Motel; sleeping in a horizontal position on a real bed was an exciting and comforting prospect. When we arrived at the registration desk we were informed that no rooms were available for Mr. Bop, Sticks, Deke, or Bee-Dee. I offered to let them stay in my room, but the stern-faced motel clerk said that would not be possible, and suggested an establishment on the other side of town that catered to their kind.

Hearing there was a motel for the exclusive use of musicians and bus drivers was as surprising to me as the information I had accidentally discovered about Mr. Genoa. However, an irate Pappy swiftly distracted my astonishment when he cursed, and stomped out of the lobby.

I followed the band and Bee-Dee outside while Mr. Genoa and his singers checked into their rooms.

"Pappy. You and Tee-Bee might be better off staying here tonight," Mr. Bop said. Then he turned to me and added, "It's just the way things are sometimes."

"That don't fly, Bop!" Pappy said as he stepped up into The Big Limo.

I also declined Mr. Bop's invitation, declaring, "We musicians and bus drivers have to stick together."

I sat down in the somber atmosphere of The Big Limo, and listened while a lonely French horn accompanied my contemplation that there was more to the motel situation than I immediately understood. As we pulled onto Interstate 75 for the short trip to the other side of town, Sticks broke the mood with a whisper.

"Dig it, Tee-Bee, your cherry ain't been popped yet. You might believe that love makes the world go round, but you got to know there's a lot of places that don't love no niggers."

Though I had heard the band members use the word "nigger" a number of times, this was the first time I spoke up and said I found it unpleasant. "I think it's demeaning."

"It's just a word, Tee-Bee," Mr. Bop interjected. "Don't mean nothing when any of us say it."

I disagreed. "My father told me the only word that means nothing is 'nothing.'"

"I meant we don't mean it in a derogatory sense when we say it," Mr. Bop responded.

"I understand that, but my father said it's a derogatory word, and anyone who used it was just showing his ignorance. You guys aren't ignorant; you're my friends."

Sticks apologized, and said, "Your father sounds like a cool dude."

Deke chimed in, "Your daddy teach you right, Tee-Bee. Deke sorry, and Deke don't use it no more."

"I still say that words can't be bad or good," Mr. Bop added. "It's a person's intentions that are what's important to me, but I agree to your request. Truth is I don't much care for the word either."

We never slept at the motel on the other side of town that served our kind because we never got there. Deke started talking about an after-hours club in Cincinnati that we should visit. Everyone agreed with Pappy that it sounded like a plan, so Bee-Dee drove past our intended exit, and headed toward a place called The Devil's Den.

During the thirty-five minute drive, Mr. Bop continued to talk to me about the importance of word usage and interpretation, steering the conversation in the direction of my song writing. He thought my lyrics were unique, and he wanted to know what I thought about when I wrote. I asked him for a specific example, and he chose the opening line from "OUT OF MY MIND."

"Why's a young innocent like you writing, 'If I had known you for a day before I met you, I would have shot you on sight'? You really want to kill somebody?"

I laughed. The deep resonance of his voice made my lyrics sound strange, though I was self-consciously pleased he knew them. "No. It's just supposed to be funny."

"And it makes me laugh every time I hear it, but what was your intention? Were you mad? Did a girl break your heart?"

The rest of the band was listening from the seats behind us, and Sticks asked, "Who put the hurt on our altar boy?"

Pappy surprised everyone by saying, "I've wondered whether you wrote that song about someone in particular myself, Tee-Bee." It was a rare and monumental occasion to hear him say anything other than his two standard phrases, and the way we were staring caused him to add, "What? A guy can't speak his mind around here?" This got a big laugh from everyone.

"Deke say you tell 'em, Pappy!"

Even Bee-Dee yelled from the front of The Big Limo, "If that was Pappy talkin' I'm gonna stop this here bus, and get me a tapes recorder so I can hear him for prosper-airity!"

No one had ever asked me why I wrote a particular lyric, and I had never really given it any thought, but if the subject was important enough to elicit a complete sentence from Pappy, I figured I should come up with an answer. My problem was I had no idea how or why I wrote what I wrote.

"I don't actually know." It was an honest answer, but pizzicato violins plucked at my brain insisting I add something more substantial. "I suppose I could have written, 'If I had known you for a day before I met you, my love will last eternity plus one day', but that's such an obvious choice, and obvious choices are heard in songs all the time." A resounding crash of brass and timpani punctuated my arrival at the border of sounding pompous, so I abridged my statement. "I don't try to come up with unusual lyrics, they just always come out that way. I think them, but I don't know why I think them or where they came from."

Mr. Bop grinned and said, "Not knowing is your biggest strength, Tee-Bee."

Deke put his hand on my knee. "Don't never you look for the magic, boy. Just let the magic do the magic."

His comment produced a contemplative moment of quiet that quickly ended when The Big Limo came to a stop.

"We here!" Bee-Dee shouted.

We walked down a flight of stairs to the unmarked entrance of The Devil's Den. As Deke opened the door and we entered, I was immediately struck by the strong odors of liquor and sweat. It took a moment for my eyes to adjust to the dim red lights and blue smoke haze that defined the club's interior. Our group had attracted the attention of the few dozen people in attendance; even the trio performing on the small stage paused momentarily. Everyone's eyes seemed to be focused on me.

Sticks leaned over and whispered in my ear. "Pappy be used to the scene, Tee-Bee. How you dig bein' the minority?"

I was quite accustomed to being the only person dressed in a tuxedo wherever I went, so I had no feeling one way or the other to dig. But before I could reply, an excited gentleman seated at the bar to our right shattered the quiet murmuring in the club.

"Is that you, Deke?" the man yelled. "Well, I'll be a son of a bitch! Deke Brown! Get on over here!"

A sign of recognition was obviously a good thing in The Devil's Den because the activities that had halted when we came through the door recommenced. The trio picked up the beat, the audience went back to their own amusements, and the bartender poured drinks. Deke directed us to an empty table, and then went to speak with his friend.

A cocktail waitress, wearing a uniform of insufficient size to properly cover her private areas, approached and asked what we wanted to drink. When Sticks ordered six beers with double Jack backs she pointed her pencil at me and said, "Drinkin' age is twenty-one. Kid got ID?"

Sticks put a five-dollar bill on her tray. "That's jive, girl. Mr. Lincoln all the ID he need, you dig?"

She accepted this gesture, and left to get our drinks as Deke returned with his friend.

"This man be Deke's friend, Maddog. This here his place."

Mr. Maddog was over six foot four, and weighed at least three hundred pounds. Sticks recognized him.

"Dig it, man. You Maddog Jefferson. Used to play for the Browns."

"That's right. Left tackle; number seventy-four." Mr. Maddog had a friendly smile, and though he spoke proudly, his massive dimensions were contradicted by his thin, squeaky voice that was more befitting a cartoon character than a football player. "Welcome to The Devil's Den. Any friend of Deke is my friend too." He shook everyone's hand, and when we exchanged greetings he asked if I liked football.

"I think football is cool." I added, "I dig your club," but my speaking in musician language was like brown shoes with a tuxedo.

"Tee-Bee new to the scene, my man, but he's no square. You dig?" Sticks' remark in my defense was proof that I was accepted as one of the group no matter how I talked.

When the waitress returned with the drinks, Mr. Maddog informed us the round was on the house. Before our generous host returned to his seat at the bar he told us to have a good time, and said we could jam if we felt like it. As the drinks were passed around, Sticks explained to me that "jam" meant perform, and I added this new word to my list of musician terminology.

Deke was the first to go and jam. He had played with the club's pianist before, and was invited to add his guitar to a song that seemed to have no particular structure other than it was in the key of A Major. Mr. Bop said it was jazz, and that my impression of the meandering nature of the melody line was just the way a musician expresses himself with no constraints. Nonetheless, the music was hard to follow. Some parts were slow and ponderously monotonous, other parts were played at a furious dissonant pace. It seemed to me that jazz allowed each musician to play a different song at the same time.

Bee-Dee thought my evaluation was humorous, and said something about my inability to hear the variations of the theme. "You got the see the differentiality, Tee-Bee. You got to feel inside the heart of the man playin' in order to see where he comin' from."

Mr. Bop turned to Bee-Dee and said, "Only way for Tee-Bee to see is for Tee-Bee to be." With that running rhyme Mr. Bop, Sticks, and Pappy got up and walked onto the stage.

While Pappy moistened the reed of his saxophone, Mr. Bop, Sticks and Deke had a short discussion after which they began whistling and waving for me to join them. I had no idea what contribution I could possibly make in their jam, and I sat frozen in my chair. Everyone's attention was again focused on me, and I wanted to disappear. I think I heard Bee-Dee whisper, "Get on up there, boy," but his actual words were difficult to comprehend because my world was spinning in slow motion.

The only person who was able to move through this rotating molasses at a normal pace was the scantily clad waitress who walked over and defined my predicament. "You got stage fright, Mr. Lincoln?"

It was the jolt I needed. The world returned to standard time, and I got up. The club was quiet except for the sound of patrons shifting their chairs to improve their view as I made my way to the stage. I had no idea what to do, so I offered my standard greeting, and sat down at the piano.

"Hello." The sea of black faces, veiled by dense cigar and cigarette smoke, did not respond.

I didn't hear Mr. Bop's deep voice cut through the haze with, "We're gonna play a little somethin' written by our brother in the tuxedo." As he started to pluck the walking bass line intro to "THAT'S WHAT I CALL LOVE" I remember thinking how glad I was he was playing something I recognized.

Just before Sticks and Deke entered at the top of the verse Pappy leaned over and told me to lay back a minute until the groove was in place. I was a child lost in the woods, so any encouragement to do nothing was most welcome.

I sat and listened, engrossed by how different my song sounded in the hands of these musicians. The only one who had performed the song before was Mr. Bop; his digits adding new notes to the pattern he had played at Pressman's. Deke strummed different variations of the same chord while playing notes from the melody line. Sticks kept the swing-style rhythm in place, but added more punch with interesting accents on the snare and hi-hat.

Pappy leaned over to my ear again, and told me that once he started playing I should add a few eighth-note chords on the downbeats. I was also to watch him for the cue to my vocal entrance. He knew I was nervous, but

I hoped he also knew I was grateful for his willingness to guide me through my first jam.

I wiped the sweat from my palms onto my trousers as Pappy began the verse, and I played an eighth-note chord on a subsequent downbeat. I was very proud of myself, and played a few more. I looked up from the piano and noticed something in each band member's face that I had not seen before. The professional demeanors they exhibited when backing Mr. Genoa were replaced by relaxed looks of contentment and satisfaction. These guys were radiating with joy.

The joyous feeling spilled over to the crowd. Everyone was either moving in their chairs or had risen to their feet to dance to the music. I was so caught up in the experience that I stopped playing my chords, and I missed Pappy's vocal entrance cue. I made certain I nailed it the second time around.

We jammed "THAT'S WHAT I CALL LOVE" for over ten minutes. The band sang the background parts, and each member took a turn at an instrumental solo. When Pappy indicated it was my turn, I played the melody line backed only by Deke's staccato-strummed guitar chords at the beginning of each measure. When I added a few grace notes into my solo jam that were not in the melody, I began to understand what Bee-Dee meant about getting into the heart of the musician. I wasn't thinking about the correct notes, or where the notes should be played; I was allowing the notes to be where they were.

We performed a few more numbers from my regular show, and the band breathed new life into each one of them. When we finished, the crowd stomped their feet, cheered and applauded. The display of appreciation was gratifying, and we went back to our table to find another round of drinks courtesy of Mr. Maddog.

I tried to express my admiration to each member of the band for his individual skills, but I was so overwhelmed by the experience I just kept repeating, "Wow! You guys are so cool! And hot!"

Sticks explained that any musician who had heard my songs as many times as they had since Billy's Lounge could play them in their sleep. His comment did not lessen my enthusiasm.

We walked out of The Devil's Den at six in the morning laughing and congratulating each other, not at all tired from being up all night. We followed Deke into the diner next door where an extremely friendly woman, named Mammy Bertha, served us a delicious breakfast of ham, eggs, pancakes, orange juice, and coffee. There was also something on my plate that I had never seen before, and Miss Bertha smiled from ear to ear when she informed me they were "grits." Even though I never ordered them anywhere again, their gummy texture and non-descript taste were improved when topped with butter and maple syrup.

We got on the bus, and headed back to Hamilton. I reached into my pocket to check on the safety of the quarter that Mr. Genoa had found and given to me. It was still there. I carefully took it out, and stared at the portrait of George Washington's left profile, then turned it over to view the majestic eagle.

As I curled up on the red vinyl-covered seat, I flashed on a thought of something my father always said when he referred to differing views of the same situation, "Every coin has two sides." I casually flipped the coin into the air, and caught it in the palm of my right hand. I opened my hand to reveal the engraved image of George Washington's head atop his pedestal neck looking away from me as if contemplating a secret. I flipped the coin a second time. "Heads" again. A third flip produced the same result, and I was suddenly struck by the notion that if I hadn't already looked at the eagle on the other side I wouldn't know it was there.

Weird thoughts out of nowhere were certainly no stranger to my brain, but this one was unique. There was no melody line, no orchestration; no sound whatsoever. Accompanied by my mental silence I flipped the quarter a dozen more times expecting the eventual appearance of "tails," but it always came up "heads." As I flipped the coin again, I heard Deke strumming his acoustic guitar. I smiled, recognizing he was playing a soft, slow version of "OUT OF MY MIND," and the coin landed in my palm. "Tails."

The ton of bricks that metaphorically hit my father whenever he had a revelation crashed down upon me. Something important had taken place at The Devil's Den. The coin had flipped. "Heads," I was a solo artist. "Tails," I was part of a group. Even though I was contractually bound to do so, it would be difficult to continue as a solo act. I loved the new way each of my songs had sounded, and I knew they would never sound as good with just me and a piano. I wanted a band, and I wanted Mr. Genoa's band to be my band.

I said a short prayer asking God to forgive me for coveting. I told Him I didn't feel comfortable with my desire, even though it was an honest one. As Deke continued to play, I put the quarter back into my pocket, trusting that God would handle my presence in the virgin territory of "tails" in His usual mysterious manner.

# opus thirteen

The Big Limo took us from Ashland, Kentucky, to Flint, Michigan, to Mansfield, Ohio, to Wilmette, Illinois, to Madison, Indiana, to Jefferson City, Missouri. We played in front of a sparse audience at The Kitty Kat Bar and Grill, for a packed dance floor at Roy's Roseland; we performed at places called Chuck's Cavern, Misty's, The Silver Star Lounge, Mule Head Harry's, Off The Road House, The Wayward Wind, and Aunt Mildred's Stage Door Dinner Theater (which doubled as a gun shop during the day). Four weeks had passed with no word from Mr. Genoa about his plans, but he continued placing the mysterious phone calls on a daily basis. No matter what town or club we were in, Mr. Genoa's only disclosure was that something was "gonna be great" somewhere on the horizon.

Our venues were as diverse as the people who attended; white collar, blue collar, and no collar. The men came dressed in everything from suits and ties to bib overalls and baseball caps. Most of the women who came to the "dinner and a show" settings wore clothes that looked to be their Sunday best. The women who came to the lounge and bar performances dressed more casually, though some of them wore jeans that were so tight I didn't know how they could sit comfortably for an entire show.

Fifty-two different audiences had passed before my eyes since my experience at The Devil's Den, and the dissonant sound of opposing melodies still played in my head. My performances were fine, but I was no longer satisfied with the low notes of the piano when Mr. Bop's bass would have sounded better. I knew there were chords from Deke's guitar that would compliment the ones I played with my right hand. I missed the hiss and snap from Sticks' hi-hat, and his crisp sizzling snare. I wanted to hear the warm tones of Pappy's saxophone dance around one of my melody lines. Envy had pitched a tent in my heart.

This green-eyed intruder, in concert with my knowledge of Mr. Genoa's secret plan, filled me with a sense of foreboding and made me eager for a resolution. Even though I had decided it was best to allow him to divulge his intentions on his own, I wasn't comfortable sitting silently on the powder keg of information.

I replayed my conversation with Miss Summer over and over in my head. Perhaps I had heard her incorrectly. Maybe she meant to say he planned to go to Broadway next year. Since I had never had a substantial conversation with Mr. Genoa, the idea of just asking him seemed out of the question. But I needed to know the truth. If he was leaving I could ask his band to be my band. If he was staying I still wanted his band to be my band. Whichever direction Mr. Genoa chose, the truth of what I wanted made me feel selfish and ashamed.

My self-absorbed attempt to alter the course of my life from the paved road of faith to the uncharted waters of worry came to an abrupt halt at

John's Bowl-O-Rama and Cocktail Lounge in Kensington, Iowa. Mr. Silverman's sudden appearance puzzled the band members, but considering the volume level of his private meeting with Mr. Genoa everyone agreed that something unpleasant was being discussed. Sticks asked if I could "dig the drift of the scene," but I saw no sense in divulging the information I had obtained from a third party.

It turned out that Miss Summer was correct, and for the second time I was the first to be informed.

"What are we gonna do, kid, huh? This is a big, big problem." Mr. Silverman had called me into the club manager's office to tell me that Mr. Genoa was leaving in the morning to begin rehearsals for a predominantly Caucasian version of PORGY AND BESS, which had been re-titled BILLY AND BETH. "We don't have another star of Vince's caliber waiting in the wings to take over for him," he said as he nervously ran his fingers through the sparse remains of what was once a head of hair. "You know what that means? Huh? Do you? It means we got a big problem! That's what it means! Are you listening to what I'm saying here?"

"Yes, sir. We have a big problem." I was happy he had such confidence in me that the predicament was our mutual concern, but I was also relieved that Mr. Genoa's plans were finally out in the open. Confessing prior knowledge of his Broadway debut would not improve the situation, so I tried to calm Mr. Silverman's frazzled nerves. "What can I do to help, sir?"

"Turn yourself into another Vince, kid. That's what you can do. Just magically become Vince Genoa for three weeks, 'cause other than that, kid, there's nothin' much anybody can do." His cheery yellow blazer, green paisley shirt and red slacks could not camouflage his distress. "I mean this is unexpected, right? He's just gonna break his contract, and run off to Broadway. What kinda guy does that, huh? I make him a star, and this is the thanks I get? God almighty, my name's gonna be mud. People are gonna point at me and say, 'You see that pile of mud over there? That used to be Sy Silverman.' Oh, this is bad, kid. Real bad."

Even though my father used to say, "Any problem can be made worse with a hasty solution," I quickly offered a possibility.

"I can't turn into Mr. Genoa, but I can do his show."

"You're kidding me, right? You can do his show? The whole thing, start to finish?" His mind whirled with the ramifications my suggestion presented. "Your show and his show; that's four shows a night, you know. Twenty-four shows a week is a lot of shows, so don't toy with me, kid. Don't make promises you can't keep. I got a weak heart." He made some swift mental calculations as the idea became more real to him. "Well, I might have to pay you more money, you know, for all those shows. Yeah, of course I would. You do twice as many shows I have to double your salary, right? No, make that more than double. How about we say two hundred a week, huh? How's that sound? No, wait, I got it! Two hundred and twenty-five! Triple salary for the remaining three weeks! Now, that's a generous offer, kid."

He was maintaining his usual conversational dynamic of not waiting for an answer, but his euphoria sank as quickly as it had risen. "Ah, who are we kidding here, huh? No one can replace Vince. He's an original, the bum. And what about his band? They might quit too for all we know. And you can't use his girls, 'cause he's takin' them with him. Promised them parts in the chorus. Oh, this isn't gonna work. I'm through. You hear what I'm sayin'? I'm gonna be a big pile of done, finished, kaput, over-with mud!"

He seemed a bit less defeated when I told him how well the band and I had performed together at The Devil's Den. When I mentioned I had information that led me to believe no one would quit as long as they were getting paid, he made his final decision.

"It's a deal! What other choice have I got, huh?"

When Mr. Silverman and I went to talk with the members of the band, he was surprised how quickly they agreed to the new scenario. Deke told him how much everyone enjoyed playing with me, and Sticks concurred, adding, "It's cool so long as the bread stays in the groove, you dig?" Pappy said the plan was definitely flight worthy.

Mr. Bop had a short, private discussion with Mr. Silverman after which I was informed my salary would be raised to six hundred dollars per week. Mr. Silverman was strangely subdued, and only nodded his head in agreement when Mr. Bop informed me of the revised financial arrangement. "It's more proper," was his explanation, adding that I was doing Mr. Silverman a tremendous favor and should be equitably rewarded.

It took a few moments for my eyes to return to their normal size after hearing the amount I would be paid, and I decided against mentioning that I enjoyed singing in front of people so much that I would do it for free. I was also pleased to learn that after Mr. Silverman deducted my monumental raise from the money he had been paying Mr. Genoa, Miss Goodard, and Miss Barner, he had enough left to double each band member's salary. I had no idea so much money could be made in this business, but Mr. Bop said we were still on the low end of the scale. Compared to the money I had been making less than an hour before, the low cnd looked like the top of a mountain.

Mr. Silverman, Mr. Bop and I sat down to discuss the plan for the last three weeks of the tour. Mr. Bop would handle the finances, and be in charge of the group. Mr. Silverman said he would contact the places we were to play, and tell them that Mr. Genoa had taken ill. I objected to telling a lie.

"Why not be honest with them?"

They both reacted to my question as if I believed babies came from cabbage patches.

"Tee-Bee. Sometimes you got to stretch the truth to smooth the road."

Mr. Bop's rationalization did not change my mind.

"Kid. The entertainment racquet is like politics. People expect you to lie. You want honesty? Go live with those monks who never talk."

Mr. Silverman was quite certain his opinion was correct, but I could not have disagreed more. I explained that I had been raised by two people who taught me that life was best lived under an umbrella of a few basic truths, and I related the ones that pertained to this situation.

"Everyone deserves respect. Lying is wrong, and following The Golden Rule is the easiest way to solve a problem."

Mr. Silverman broke the silence that had followed my personal philosophy. "Okay, kid. You wanna be Jesus Christ? Tell me what you think we should do?"

I suggested that he inform the remainder of the clubs on the schedule that Mr. Genoa would not be appearing due to another commitment. Any club that wished to cancel its contract with us could do so. Every club that didn't cancel would get a guaranteed show, meaning if their patrons didn't have a good time we would promptly refund their money with no questions asked.

"Are you crazy, kid? My idea agitated Mr. Silverman. "Bop, is the kid crazy? Tell me he's kidding. You're kidding, right?"

"I'm not kidding. My father used to say that the only people who can't get a refund are buried."

"You're not gonna be playin' cemeteries, kid."

"Mr. Silverman. You can deduct any money you have to refund from my salary." I thought this offer would do the trick, but it was Mr. Bop who put the icing on the cake.

"And if Tee-Bee's money don't cover it, you can take it from the band. And if that ain't enough for you Mr. Silverman, I suggest you get up and walk away from this table."

"All right, all right. You talked me into it. I'll guarantee the shows, but I'm tellin' you it sets a bad precedent. People are gonna say, 'Do business with Sy Silverman, and he'll give you your money back.' How's that sound, huh? Does that sound like good business? You know, a guy could go bankrupt doin' business like that. Straight to the poor house, no detour. You guys are gonna give me palpitations. That's what you're gonna do, you know. You're gonna send me to an early grave. But don't you go and put daffodils on my coffin. I hate those prissy yellow things."

There was one more issue to tackle. Tuxedo Bob could not open for Tuxedo Bob. The only way I could effectively succeed at following myself would be to perform Mr. Genoa's show using another name. Since there wasn't a lot of time to consider what to name me, I presented the idea for discussion.

"Use your real name." Mr. Silverman had momentarily forgotten I was already doing that.

Mr. Bop suggested I pick a name I liked the sound of, and he had a good laugh when I suggested Sylvia. "Would that be Tuxedo Sylvia, or Sylvia Bob?"

Even Mr. Silverman enjoyed a brief moment of lightheartedness. "Very funny, guys. Very funny, but it might be a hard sell. How about we pick something more normal like Frank or Tony?"

"How about Sam Ames?" My offering was greeted with looks of approval.

Mr. Silverman rolled the name through his lips. "Sam Ames. Hey, kid, that's not bad, you know? Sam Ames. Nice and short. Not a lot of letters. I'll call the clubs, and I'll tell them you got this alter-other personality thing that you do who sings real good like Vince."

"Tell them he's better than Vince." Mr. Bop was emphatic in his pronouncement, and it was the first time I ever heard him refer to Mr. Genoa in any form other than Mr. Vee.

"No need to push the envelope. The kid's got enough of a problem without setting his sights on being better than Vince Genoa, you know what I'm sayin'? Anyway, it's only three weeks. How bad could he be, huh?" Mr. Silverman had made his decision, but added, "Don't make me sorry, kid. I don't like bein' sorry. I don't like much of this whole idea, but you got me backed in a corner. You know what I'm saying when I say backed in a corner, kid? I'm talkin' against the wall with my hands tied behind my back, and a blindfold over my eyes. But hey, I'm kinda outta choices here, you know?"

"I'll do my best, sir."

Mr. Silverman smiled, and dropped his rapid-fire speech pattern as he put his hand on my shoulder. "You just go be the best damn Sam Ames I ever had the pleasure to represent without hearing first. Okay, kid?"

We shook hands, and he excused himself to get some sleep. In the morning he would place the phone calls to the clubs that remained on our itinerary, and inform them of their options. A message of the results of his efforts would be waiting for us at our next stop, The Roundabout Dinner Theater and Steakhouse in Sioux City, Iowa, which we hoped would still be among the remaining dates.

Because of the lateness of the hour, I did not bother Mr. Genoa, Miss Goodard and Miss Barner with verbal good-byes. Instead, I wrote short notes wishing each of them success on Broadway. I left the notes with the clerk at the front desk, and also left a brand new bag of Fig Newtons for Mr. Genoa.

We began loading The Big Limo, and as I carried Deke's guitar down the aisle, he asked how I had come up with the name Sam Ames.

"During my last discussion with Mr. Silverman and Mr. Bop my mind was busy composing a brief piano piece when all of the sudden this trumpet trio started playing a staccato figure that sounded like it was written for a king's entrance to his court."

Though Deke was listening intently to my explanation, his eyes expressed confusion. "Deke just ask about the new name, Tee-Bee."

"It's an acronym, Deke. The people playing those trumpets in my head were my Musketeer friends back in Kiamesha Lake. You remember them? Sylvia Aaron, Mr. Andrew Murphy, and Ernie Santos."

"Deke do believe Deke do." He nodded his head as he added, "They sure was nice people."

"Yes. Anyway, the first letter of each of their names spells Sam Ames."

His eyes brightened with comprehension. "That they do. They surely do." He paused for a moment, then whispered, "Deke know you got a gift, Tee-Bee. God never give nobody no gift without He got some plan to use it."

It was three in the morning by the time we were ready to leave. Bee-Dee was closing the luggage compartment of The Big Limo's underbelly when we heard Mr. Silverman calling from his motel room door.

"Chester! Come here a minute, would you?"

Bee-Dee complied, and returned with a small stack of letters wrapped with rubber bands. "You boys got some mail here from Mr. Silverman's office."

The general consensus was it could all wait until morning to be read. "Union jive and bills to pay more than likely," was Mr. Bop's decree.

Bee-Dee dropped the letters onto the front seat, and positioned himself behind the wheel. "Next stop, Paradise!" he called out as he always did when we left one city heading for the next.

God had answered my request for Mr. Genoa's band, and I gave thanks to Him for His gift. I added the superfluous request that He stick around for a few days to assist with the implementation of His plan, and quickly asked forgiveness for suggesting He would be anywhere else. As The Big Limo sped down the turnpike, I fell peacefully asleep unaware that God's gift of

Mr. Genoa's band was just one side of His Almighty coin. Heads: The Lord giveth. Tails: The Lord taketh away.

# fourteenth sonata

In the light of the bright August moon it is evident that the lush lawn, and ornamental shrubbery of Faraway Meadows are in the hands of an excellent caretaker. For those of us left behind it is a comfort to visit our departed relatives amid such finely manicured surroundings, and I can attest that the dense grass is a welcome change to my feet after miles of hard pavement.

From my vantage point I can see the large gray marble marker etched with the names Orville and Margaret Fledsper, and their expiration date of March 19, 1965. I take the quarter I have kept in my pocket for twenty-two years, and place it atop their current place of residence.

"I'm very proud that you're my parents." I speak the words aloud, though I know there are no words to fully express how grateful I am to have been raised by them.

I'm especially thankful to them for teaching me good manners, proper speech, and that being kind is more important than being right. I'm sorry I didn't say good-bye to them at the time of their internment, but a proper farewell was impossible. Twenty-two years ago they were buried under this ground, five weeks before I was aware they were dead. I remember exactly where I was when I found out. It is not a moment easily forgotten.

• • •

Bee-Dee had just parked The Big Limo in front of The Roundabout Dinner Theater and Steakhouse in Sioux City, Iowa, and was distributing the stack of mail given to him by Mr. Silverman the night before.

"This is cool, man. Dig it, ya'll! I got me a new nephew!" The postcard Sticks received announced the arrival of his sister's baby boy. "Named him Ethan. What kinda name is that, man?"

"Ethan Allen. Famous furniture guy." Everyone laughed at Mr. Bop's comment.

Deke and Pappy were given their union dues notices, and Mr. Bop read a copy of a letter sent from Mr. Napoli to Mr. Silverman expressing how pleased he had been with our performances at Pressman's.

Bee-Dee paused as he approached me with the last letter from the stack. I didn't know he had seen two black lines x-ing out my parents' names and address, and the word "deceased" written in the same casual manner one would write "please forward." Correctly assuming it would be a shock to learn via a piece of returned mail that my parents were dead, he handed the envelope to Mr. Bop and said, "This here needs to be specialty delivered."

Mr. Bop looked at it cautiously, and then asked me to accompany him to the gas station across the street.

"Tee-Bee, I'm afraid I've got some mighty bad news for you." He spoke slowly, and put his muscular left arm around my shoulders. "I'm so very sorry, son."

Time took a temporary vacation when he handed me that letter. A waterfall of tears quickly blurred my vision. I drew a few quick breaths in an attempt to compose myself, but only succeeded in making myself dizzy.

"Is there someone you can call? A relative?"

Mr. Bop's deep voice was gently consoling, and complemented the mournful sounds of the oboe and bassoon that had begun to play in my head.

"PETER AND THE WOLF." My comment was not an answer to his question. It was music he had no way of hearing. "PETER AND THE WOLF," I repeated. "It was my father's favorite. It's in my head."

Mr. Bop nervously shuffled from foot to foot, and kept his arm around me during the external silence that accompanied my internal instrumental. He couldn't hear the comfort that Sergei Prokofiev's most famous composition was providing for me, and he didn't know that "Please pass the potatoes" would be an appropriate comment. I nestled my head against his chest, and he patted me on my shoulder to show me he sympathized with my loss.

My father used to say, "Tomorrow is a good day for bad news." Tomorrow arrived in Sioux City, April 23, 1965, and dispatched its bad news under the red neon sign of a Gas 'N' Go. I wondered how many tomorrows would have come and gone had I not used Mr. Silverman's office as my return address. How many more letters would I have written to an empty house? Why had God taken them? I heard no answers mingling with Prokofiev's music, but any reply would have had no effect on the truth.

If tomorrow hadn't come today, my parents would still be dead. Death is part of the package God bestows upon the living.

I focused my attention on the nearby phone booth that could assist my desire for more information. I placed a collect call to Doctor Brigner, who had been my family's physician since before I was born. Nurse Perkins answered, and graciously accepted the charges. Before she put the doctor on the line she expressed how sorry she was for my loss, and asked how I was doing. I told her I was doing fine, and I thanked her for reminding me how neighborly everyone was in my hometown.

Doctor Brigner got on the phone, and told me about the accident on the highway between Minot and Schulberg that had extinguished the lives of Orville and Margaret Fledsper.

"They were on their way home from attending a national touring company's performance of THE MUSIC MAN when a manufacturing defect in one of the tires caused a blowout," he said in the same soothing voice I heard in my memory.

He calmly gave me all the details; their car flipped over several times before crashing into a tree, but it could have been worse had they not missed colliding with a Seattle-bound Greyhound bus by the narrowest of margins. Death greeted Margaret instantly, compassionately saving her from pain. Orville clung to life for several hours, but there was nothing that could be done to save him. He died in the middle of the night from massive internal injuries.

No one knew what town I was in, or how to contact me. Since my parents had no other relatives, Doctor Brigner accepted the responsibility for their burial in the plots at Faraway Meadows that Orville had purchased as

Margaret's nineteenth anniversary present. He said it had been a lovely service, and as he was familiar with my interest in such things, he told me they were interred in matching A-series bronze Utopia's Glory caskets lavishly lined with mounds of ivory satin and Danish lace. I thanked him for his efforts and his courtesy, and said I would repay all the expense he had incurred.

With an apology for adding to my distress he informed me that there were decisions I had to make regarding the disposition of property and personal effects. He gave me the name of my parents' attorney in Williston, and suggested I get in touch with her. I said I would, and thanked him again before hanging up the phone.

Mr. Bop asked if I was all right, and added, "You go home if you have the need, son."

His tender caring brought a smile to my face. I said I was fine, and after relaying what I had heard from Doctor Brigner, I told him there was nothing demanding my immediate attention in Schulberg that couldn't be handled from Sioux City. I checked into room number two-eleven at the Cochise Motor Inn, wondered why a motel in Sioux City bore the name of a famous Apache Indian Chief, and phoned Mrs. Amanda Winters.

"You're a very wealthy young man." Her initial statement regarding my parent's last will and testament sounded cold, as if their deaths were secondary to the benefits. But she was a lawyer, and I was certain she meant no disrespect.

She informed me that I owned my parent's house and the funeral home/tuxedo shop, everything inside both structures, and the five acres of land that surrounded them. She could administer the transfer and disposition of their bank accounts, plus my father's safety deposit box, and with my approval she would pay all their remaining debts, along with the Federal and State inheritance taxes. And she would handle the insurance policy settlements to make sure I got every penny that was coming to me. She was certainly thorough, and I was glad that she mentioned her hourly fee was quite reasonable and competitive. I would have never thought to ask.

I needed time to adjust to my new status as an orphaned heir. Since I was accustomed to keeping all of my belongings in a suitcase, this sudden acquisition of possessions was disconcerting. I hadn't fully assimilated that my parents were gone; how could I decide what to do with their things? Mrs. Winters said she understood how I felt, and agreed to meet me five days later at Scudder's Showtime Grill in Omaha, Nebraska, where we would complete the necessary paperwork.

I laid down on the bed, and closed my eyes to a soft chorus of flutes. I recalled the twinkle in my mother's blue eyes as she worked on a corpse, and the smell of my father's pipe when he sat on the porch watching a salmon-colored sunset. I heard their voices, and felt the loving touch of their hands. I imagined them walking through the pearly gates of Heaven, presenting their admission tickets to a satin-cloaked white-bearded usher, and waving good-bye to me before proceeding into the clouds.

Margaret is certainly out of a job in Heaven unless morticians are considered doctors. I figured she and Orville would still want to hang out together, and I pictured them overseeing the robe, wing, and halo industries.

Eternal life is not for the living to comprehend. It's hard to imagine anyone escaping the finality of death's darkness to walk the bright golden streets of God's kingdom, but I saw Orville and Margaret in a beautiful and peaceful place surrounded by cherubs and harps. The vision made me happy for them, but I was sad for me. I fell asleep wishing God would exchange what my parent's had left behind for what He had taken.

A knock on the motel room door woke me at six o'clock. Sticks entered with a tray of food, and was followed by the rest of the troupe. Bee-Dee hung up my freshly pressed tuxedos that he had so thoughtfully taken to a nearby dry cleaner. As I nibbled on the roast beef sandwich and french fries, each man expressed his condolences. I appreciated their sentiments of caring because any time of sadness is better spent in the company of good friends.

Mr. Bop told me he had spoken with Mr. Silverman, and not one venue had canceled a show. "You feel up to it, Tee-Bee?" he asked.

I wanted to say I didn't feel like singing, but regardless of my personal circumstances people were paying to see us perform. It would be unprofessional to allow my feelings to dictate a decision for the group. My silent thoughts allowed the band to offer their opinions.

"Deke say you don't got to do, if you don't want to do."

Sticks chimed in, "Deke ain't talkin' no jive, my man. You say the word and we're on board a hundred-thousand percent."

Pappy brought the point home. "What would your father say, Tee-Bee?"

"My father would say what he always said when faced with a difficult task, 'Only the dead stop what they're doing.'"

It was Orville's interpretation of the old cliché "the show must go on!" that resolved the situation. At eight o'clock that night in The Roundabout

Dinner Theater and Steakhouse in Sioux City, Iowa, our first show went on as scheduled.

The Tuxedo Bob portion of the first set was well received. I didn't mention the death of my parents to the audience, but I had internally dedicated my performance to them. Certain songs were affected by my personal tribute, particularly "I JUST LOVE TO COMPLAIN" and "MY LONG ISLAND COMA GIRL." Both sounded more contemplative and poignant, and failed to induce their usual amounts of laughter. As I was coming out of the third verse of my closing number, "CHOCOLATE TAPIOCA PUDDING," a new lyric entered my mind. I accepted its spontaneous arrival, and decided to decrease the song's tempo, and sing this alternate bridge and final verse as a soft lullaby.

> "Every time my mother made it
> I would stand right by the stove.
> I'd watch her stir my pudding
> on the tips of my toes.
> As soon as it was ready
> I would have my spoon in hand.
> Her chocolate tapioca was the best in the land.
> It's a great big world and I play my part.
> I'm happy to be livin' with a smile on my face.
> My mom and dad will always have a place in my heart
> along with chocolate tapioca pudding."

It was the only time I ever sang that improvisation. I acknowledged the applause with a bow, and I left the stage.

The band had watched from the wings, and everyone was overly generous with their comments about how much they had enjoyed my performance. Mr. Bop attached a red carnation to my left lapel.

"Now you Sam Ames."

"Thank you, sir." I smiled in an attempt to conceal my anxiety, but he wasn't fooled.

"Don't you worry about a thing, Tee-Bee," Mr. Bop said as he adjusted my boutonniere. "You'll do fine."

"I know." I took a deep breath to solidify my confidence. "Worry arrives upon the departure of faith."

"Your father?" Mr. Bop was highly perceptive.

"Yes, sir. Orville had a saying for every occasion."

"This gonna be hot. Get in the groove, my man, and dig it. Yeah!" Sticks had a high degree of nervous energy, and was more animated than usual. "You get jammed up Tee-Bee, you just stop, you dig? One of us'll nail a solo 'til you get back. Cool? Yeah, that's the situation. No jive. We alive. Come on. Let's dig it."

"Thanks, Sticks." Though I was fairly certain I knew Mr. Genoa's show forwards and backwards, I was grateful for his counsel.

The stout stage manager asked if we were ready, and we affirmed we were. "Okay, knock 'em dead!"

His statement bristled the band as if he had said, "I hope your parents have a car accident and die." Each one of them looked at me to see how I was reacting to what they perceived as an ill-timed use of show business jargon, but I had taken no offense.

I patted the stage manager on the back. "Dig it. We're gonna love 'em to death, my man."

The band walked onto the darkened stage, and adjusted the tuning of their instruments. I stood alone behind a green velvet curtain, waiting for the emcee's booming introduction.

"Ladies and gentlemen! The Roundabout Dinner Theater and Steakhouse is proud to present The Sam Ames Express!"

The name was Sticks' idea. He had quickly suggested it earlier in the evening when I hesitated to answer the question, "So what do you call yourselves?" asked by Mr. Cutleather, the owner of the dinner theater.

As The Express launched into "WHEN THE SAINTS GO MARCHING IN," Sam Ames ran onto the stage, smiling and finger-snapping his way to the microphone.

Upon finishing the song I shouted, "Is everybody having a good time?"

The crowd replied to my solicitation with hoots and hollers of emphatic agreement. In perfect imitation of Mr. Genoa's movements I patted my brow with a cocktail napkin borrowed from a nearby table, and looked at Mr. Bop.

"Let's do 'NOTHING CAN STOP ME NOW', all right? Hit it!" Though I knew I had said the entire phrase in the same 'I just thought of this' style of Mr. Genoa, everyone in the band started giggling. As they made attempts to compose themselves, I turned to the audience and said, "They love to hear me say 'Hit it!'"

After that moment of accidental spontaneity, The Express steamed ahead. Halfway through our third number, an up-tempo rendition of "TOWN WITHOUT PITY," I realized the crowd was not only eating me up, they were laughing hysterically.

I meant no disrespect toward Mr. Genoa as I mimicked his practiced sincerity, but the entire show was actually quite funny when viewed from a satirical perspective. When we were speeding through the closing sing-along, "BILL BAILEY," even I had trouble keeping a straight face. The number of patrons who asked for autographs after the show was astonishing, and I gladly signed "Love ya, Sam Ames" on an endless stream of cocktail napkins and souvenir menus.

The second set of shows was received in exactly the same fashion. There were laughter and tears during Tuxedo Bob, and a delightful party atmosphere during The Sam Ames Express. That first evening of my new endeavor had been a resounding success, and for those few hours I didn't focus on the waves of sorrow that rolled inside my heart.

• • •

Sioux City was so long ago, but I can't help thinking about it as I stand in front of my parent's grave. The day I found out they were dead had been my first appearance as Sam Ames, and those two events proved that my father was right as usual when he told me to remember that "Every ending is a beginning in disguise."

As the hungry wolf's French horns reach for the piccolo's escaping bird, I lay down on the soft cool grass in front of Orville and Margaret's gravestone. The mournful oboe of the duck welcomes the triumphant strings of Peter's victory as I cover myself with four tuxedo coats. I will sleep with my parents tonight — a final, though belated, good-bye.

# interlude

The damp chill of the early morning air caresses my face, nudging me awake. I open my eyes to find a light mist of fog rolling through the graveyard, surrounding me in a soft grayish-white blanket. Fog and cemetery are perfect mates; like a hot dog at a picnic, a hand in a well-tailored glove, me and a tuxedo, Orville and Margaret.

I sit up and stretch the memory of hard ground from my back and limbs. An unrestrained yawn completes the waking process, and I rise to my feet. As I pack away my four-jacket comforter, I take a last look around at the headstones that mark the homes of my parents and their neighbors.

Faraway Meadows has become the reunion site for a good many Fledsper Manor alumni of 1955's winter storm. Mr. and Mrs. Bartlett are next door to the right, Mr. and Mrs. Moore reside to the left, and the last person to scc my father alive, Dr. Brigner, rests four graves down the path. Mrs. Edwina Bailey, holding an oak leaf but otherwise inactive, preserves the silence a stones throw from the good doctor. Dear, sweet Mrs. Carver, of mashed canned potatoes fame, sleeps nonstop near the ivy-covered fence. Recalling the exquisite comfort that is synonymous with a Blessed Victory - Model 1000, I can't help but hope each of these fine people is eternally pleased to lie in whatever coffin was chosen for their remains.

I pat Orville and Margaret's headstone the same way they used to pat me on the head, and the cool marble absorbs the loving warmth of my hand. I take a deep breath amid a swell of violins, and walk the cobblestone path toward the cemetery gate. On the other side of the gate is the road, once formed of loose gravel and now smoothly paved with asphalt, which will lead me to my hometown.

As I make my way to the crest of the hill before me, I turn around for one more look at Faraway Meadows while it's still in sight. Its black, cast-iron fence surrounds the lush green lawn that covers a wide variety of my mother's handiwork and my father's formal wear. It would be fitting to call the cemetery Fledsper Memorial Park, but recognition was not important to my parents — to them an honest day's work was its own reward.

The steeple of The First Baptist Church is the first evidence of downtown Schulberg that comes into view. My heart beats with excitement to a chorus of trumpets, but when I reach the top of the hill and see what twenty-three years has changed, my internal brass is interrupted by a crash of cymbals.

The town of my youth has more than doubled its size. There are many more traffic lights and street signs. A mini-mall covers the baseball field where I once hit two singles in the same game. A housing development has sprouted over the area that was once Mr. Hogan's dairy farm. The drugstore lunch counter, where Mr. Brendan served root beer floats and penny pretzel rods with hot mustard, has been replaced by Taco Bell. Mr. Anderson's bar, where my father conversed with his friends, is a Pizza Hut.

Before heading into the city that bears little resemblance to the one I left, I direct my attention toward my old house on the hill at the north end of town. Years ago when the Conners family offered ninety thousand dollars for the property, both my lawyer and the real estate agent said it was worth twice that amount. I felt, as my mother believed in 1955, that Mr. Conners' demise in the living room warranted the consideration of a substantial discount. With that in mind (along with Mrs. Conners' statement that her family would continue both my parent's businesses) I accepted the offer. Her daughters, Becky, Karen, Mary Jo, Jane, and Wanda took over the tuxedo shop, and her son, Tom Jr., learned the undertaking trade. The deal also included a provision that I could trade-in my six-tuxedo inventory once a year, so it was a satisfactory transaction for all concerned parties with the possible exception of the property itself.

The oak tree that stood so proudly by the front window is gone. I trust the removal of my majestic friend was motivated by a natural cause rather than someone's decision that it just didn't go with the house. Either way I miss the graceful way its branches used to brush against the house's dignified pale ivory exterior that now shouts in bright hues of turquoise blue and banana yellow. The once white and now avocado green picket fence surrounds the property just as I remember. To the left of the main residence stands the black and white-striped (formerly red and brown) anniversary structure, which features a vibrant orange neon sign flashing the words, "Conners Funeral Home & Formal Attire Emporium."

I offer a prayer of condolence for the old homestead, and hope if a house has feelings that this house is happy. The Conners certainly had the right to do whatever they pleased with the property, and though I can't quite grasp their overall concept, it reminds me of what it must have been like to look inside Mr. Silverman's closet. I won't ask them what they were thinking when they chose the current color scheme because it's none of my business. As my father used to say, "You don't have to be concerned with another man's thoughts unless he's holding a loaded pistol."

I was eight when he said that, and had already developed the habit of responding to his axioms with either, "That's a good one, Father," or "I'll remember that one, sir." Whether or not I understood what each one meant at the time he said them, I do, in fact, remember every one. It was during the spring of 1965 when I understood that "loaded pistol" didn't necessarily mean "gun."

• • •

The end of my first professional road tour was two weeks away. Four days of high humidity and overcast skies had sedated the band's normal enthusiasm, and when The Big Limo pulled in front of Scudder's Showtime Grill in Omaha, the group decided it was best to continue napping. I had to cast a dissenting vote because of the scheduled appointment with my parents' attorney.

I walked across the parking lot to the bittersweet strains of a cello solo. The melody moved easily from A Minor to C Major, sad to happy, loss to encouragement. I was suddenly struck by the symmetry of the pattern, and the grief that had settled in my heart began to dissipate as I paused to add harmony. The structure was perfect, and the tune transformed my sorrow into a delicate peace. At that moment I knew the melody was a message from my parents sent through heavenly channels to let me know they were fine and I didn't have to be sad.

Having grown up around a mortuary, I knew that death was a part of life rather than just a fact of it. It was not up to me to question God's reasons for canceling Orville and Margaret's personal appearance tour on earth. It was His job to close the curtain on the final act. My job was to address the effects of His action.

I entered Scudder's Grill, and saw a slender gray-haired woman in a simple dark-blue pants suit sitting at a table by the stage. The soda bottle lenses of her black rimmed glasses magnified her eyes, and I thought this made her seem more like a smartly tailored bug than a representative of the legal profession. She extinguished her cigarette, and stood up.

"Mr. Fledsper, I'm Amanda Winters."

No one had ever called me Mr. Fledsper. It sounded peculiar, but this was my first legal discussion, and there were probably formalities involved that would be new to me. I shook her hand and sat down, eager to learn. She opened a large brown leather briefcase, and withdrew a small stack of papers.

"Let's get started, shall we? My plane leaves in three hours, and we've got a lot to accomplish."

She was all business. During our discussion she presented a dizzying number of elements regarding my parents' estate. Everything had been bequeathed to me, and everything included life insurance policies, real estate, equipment, inventory, bank accounts and more. I nodded my head a lot, and signed a dozen documents. I had no idea there was such a girdle of legalities encompassing the finality of someone's life. My understanding stopped with the preparation and burial of a body, but Mrs. Winters' expertise was in the dispensing, dispersing, and disposing of everything that accumulates over a person's lifetime.

"What are your plans?"

Her question caught me by surprise. I brushed aside the oboe recital that had been accompanying our discussion so I could think without interruption.

"I haven't given my plans much thought."

She responded before I could tell her I had given the same answer to Preacher Dave in 1956.

"Well, you've got quite a lot of money and property to consider, so let's make some decisions." She folded her hands on the table, and sat back in her chair.

"What if I wanted to sell everything?" I figured any plan was better than no plan, but she had no interest in a spontaneous remark. She wanted decisiveness.

"Then I would handle the selling of everything." She leaned forward. "Is that what you want me to do?"

"I don't know." I moved back slightly as I spoke because her magnified pupils were making me dizzy. "Do you think it's a good idea to sell everything?" My original question was back in her court seeking validation.

"Not if you're going back to Schulberg, and want to live in the house." She unfolded her hands, and leaned closer toward me as if she was a cat about to pounce on a dubious mouse. "Will you be returning to Schulberg?"

I couldn't answer. Even though it seemed reasonable to presume that I would return some day, my hometown seemed to be the place I was from rather than the place I was going. A clarinet and banjo sauntered across my thoughts playing a Dixieland melody that aroused images of popcorn and straw hats, and I instantly knew that whatever plan I had or didn't have, it would not immediately include living in a house on a hill in North Dakota.

Mrs. Winters drove out of the parking lot with signed documents giving her the authority to act as my representative in all matters involving the disposition of my parents' property. The house with its funeral home/tuxedo shop would be placed on the market, but could only be sold to someone who allotted a space in the attic to store my parent's photographs, souvenirs and memorabilia until such time that I could retrieve them. The rest of the contents of the house would be donated to The Salvation Army. After paying off debts, taxes and legal fees there would be about five thousand dollars left in the Fledsper bank account, which I decided could remain in Schulberg to accrue interest at a modest rate of three percent.

Orville and Margaret Fledsper were now both physically and legally gone. All that remained of them were my memories, and the cashier's check I held in my hands from Amalgamated Life in the amount of one hundred thousand dollars.

As I stood in the middle of the parking lot, a deep and familiar voice broke my train of thought. "That's a goodly display of zeros, Tee-Bee."

I was so engrossed with the events of the last few hours that I hadn't noticed Mr. Bop had gotten off the bus and was standing beside me. "Yes, it's a lot of zeros." I handed him the check. "What do you think I should do with all this money?"

What to do with the money became the main topic of discussion as the band set up the stage for the evening's performances. Sticks referred to it as "severe pocket change," and suggested it would be cool if I made a small donation to his favorite charity, "The Daddy Needs A New Set Of Skins Foundation." Both Pappy and Deke offered the opinion that I should invest it wisely, though neither could say how that would best be accomplished. Bee-Dee mentioned that The Big Limo might look "extra specially granditious on the highway back to New York if it was all dolled up by a splashin' of paint and some red velvety-like drapes."

Bee-Dee's comment about going back to New York had the same effect as an early morning plunge into an icy river. Everyone knew there would be an end to the tour, but no one had discussed what we were going to do, individually or collectively, when that moment came. Coming up with a plan instantly became more important than the cashier's check.

"Dig it, my fellow melody makers. We got a hot band, and a cool sound. There ain't no way we should slip from our groove." Sticks emphasized his remarks with a quick drum roll and cymbal crash.

"Deke say New Orleans the place. Got music in the air twenty-four hours a day. Ain't nothin' like our boy on Bourbon Street, so far as Deke know."

Deke described Bourbon Street as one long bar where the music never stopped, and suggested a few clubs where we might seek employment.

"Deke got a friend down there named Sweet Horn. Deke believe he help us."

My only knowledge of New Orleans had come from eighth grade American History, and while the band's excitement of Deke's idea mounted, I roamed my mental catalogue and found a number of references to France. I wondered if my findings might present a problem concerning a language barrier. Deke laughingly reassured me that everyone spoke English in The French Quarter, though it was sometimes hard to understand the local dialect.

"Cajun's what they call it," he explained. "It's a mushy sound. Like talkin' with a mouth full of food. But the city, Tee-Bee, Lord have mercy, the city is magic and music, music, music. Why Deke be happy just sittin' on Bourbon Street for the rest o' Deke's days."

New Orleans was quickly becoming the destination of choice, and I began to get excited by the possibilities such a place presented. I offered to use Orville and Margaret's insurance settlement for transportation and housing until we were once again being paid to perform. I was surprised when my philanthropic gesture was greeted with a high degree of resistance, so I explained my position with words from my father.

"A dollar spent in friendship is money wisely invested." When I pointed out that my father most certainly had the last word on the subject because he was dead, a hush enveloped the group. It was an uncomfortable moment for my friends, and I knew it was because they had avoided talking about my parents out of respect for my feelings.

"How about we all say 'Orville and Margaret have died and gone to Heaven' in unison."

My request stunned Sticks so much that he momentarily dropped his fidgety style of speech. "Sometimes you a bit too cool, my man, and we all don't know how to, you know, dig where you're comin' from. You dig?"

Mr. Bop set down his bass, and eased over toward me, "Everyone just trying to be sensitive, Tee-Bee."

"I know, and I'm lucky to have such considerate friends. But it isn't necessary to tiptoe around the subject. Even though my parents died unexpectedly, they went together, and I find that comforting. In fact, I'm sure they walked through St. Peter's pearly gate, strolled right up to God, and said, "Orville and Margaret reporting for duty, Sir."

Then I hummed a few bars of the tune I had heard prior to my meeting with Mrs. Winters, and told them how the melody had comforted me. The veil of uneasiness began to lift from their eyes.

"You sure you fine?" Mr. Bop asked in a way that told me the group would accept any answer I gave.

"Yes, I'm sure. When my father used to say, 'It's a waste of time to bury a clock with a body,' he was telling me that time is better spent on living. As far as I know he never lied to me."

"Deke do believe he never did." He walked over to me and gave me a warm hug. "You a good boy, Tee-Bee. Deke feelin' better now too."

My eyes misted a bit as Pappy, Sticks, and Mr. Bop also gave me hugs, and patted me on the back. It was a sweet moment of brotherhood.

"Now I can get to work on my new song about being an orphan."

The nervous giggles that followed my comment quickly became laughter when Pappy said, "Sounds like a plan."

"Yes it is," I said. "But none of you will have to learn it because it'll only be effective as a solo number."

Sticks thumped an emphatic beat on his kick drum. "You too much, Tee-Bee! Too much!"

When Mr. Bop suggested I finish the song as quickly as possible so he could go play it by himself, we were all laughing so hard that I could barely acknowledge the restaurant manager informing us that our dinner was ready. Fortunately, a nod when accompanied by the wave of a hand has universal meaning, and he understood.

We eventually calmed down, and went over to the table that had been prepared for us. The roast beef, mashed potatoes, buttered corn, rolls, and green salad looked and smelled divine. The friendly sharing of sentiments and laughter had a profound effect on our appetites, and we ate with ravenous delight.

Bee-Dee raised his glass of soda, and wished us much success on our adventure to Louisiana. The end of the current tour meant the end of his job as our driver, and he would be taking The Big Limo back to its garage at Celebrity Touring Service outside Kiamesha Lake. He would get another driving assignment, but as he explained, "No job's ever gonna capacitize my heart with soulful-lightness to the extra-remity this one did. No sir."

The band and I raised our glasses in response, and told him how much we appreciated his driving skills, sunny disposition, and personal feel for the English language. The clinking of the glasses sounded like lightly tapped triangles, and this complemented the violins I had been hearing since Bee-Dee had spoken the words, Kiamesha Lake.

I could almost smell the pine trees surrounding the still water that provided sanctuary for ducks, frogs, bass, and four small stones. The adventures with my first friends outside of Schulberg, Miss Sylvia Aaron, Mr. Andrew Murphy, and Ernie Santos, seemed so long ago, and I wanted to see them again. I started thinking of a way I could accomplish this. I certainly had enough money to fly them to New Orleans, but maybe they wouldn't be able to get off work at the same time. Maybe I should fly to see them instead. A hand on my shoulder ended my short daydream, and brought me back to the table. Everyone was staring at me.

"So, what do you think, Tee-Bee?" Pappy asked as he withdrew his hand. "Does it sound like a plan?"

"Sure," I said as I set aside my imaginary flight schedule. I thought I was confirming my agreement concerning the trip to New Orleans, but since violins had prompted a vision of Sylvia's gray-green eyes I had not heard the actual topic of their conversation.

Mr. Bop got up from the table and announced, "Okay, then it's settled. We finish the tour, and hitch a ride back to New York with Bee-Dee before heading down to Bayou country."

As everyone else got up and nodded in agreement to the plan as amended, I wanted to jump up and scream. But I felt it would be inappropriate. I had already inadvertently confirmed my approval of the idea, and a spontaneous display of excitement might lead everyone to think, correctly of course, that I had been ill mannered by not listening.

It was still two hours until showtime, and while the band and Bee-Dee went back to the bus to "snatch a zee" as Sticks put it, I sat down at the piano to tinker with the melody line my violins had been playing. The Scudder's employees, who were still finishing their meals, quieted their conversations as my fingers softly danced across the keys. My presence was not intended to be a performance, but when I completed the short sonata the quiet of the room was broken by appreciative applause. I smiled in gratitude for their indulgence unaware that the tune would resurface a few years later as an up-tempo Dixieland number called "THE ORPHAN STOMP."

I decided to take a relaxing walk around the neighborhood. It was a simple plan that only required exiting the restaurant, and turning either right or left. Compared to all the plans that had been made in the last few hours it was quite minor and insignificant, but as my father used to say, "God laughs whenever you tell Him your plans." I had forgotten to consider this during the day's decision-making processes, but God was about to reaffirm His divine right to keep Himself amused. As I reached for the handle of the door, it opened from the opposite side, and standing before me in the light of a Nebraska sunset were Messrs. Silverman and Napoli.

"Hey, kid! Surprised to see us? I bet you are, huh? You remember Mr. Napoli? Sure you do. Not a man to forget, right? Let's say we find a quiet corner where we can talk, okay? You're not gonna believe what we did for you, kid. It's the brass ring you want? Well, you're gonna get it, you hear what I'm sayin'? Are you listening? I said the brass ring. Hey, did I mention it's good to see you? Huh? Did I say that yet? Well, you look just great, kid. This tour's made a man of out you, and I'm not just sayin' that 'cause I have to, you know. Mr. Napoli thinks you look great too, kid. Right, Mr. Napoli? Ah, he loves ya, kid. Loves ya like a son. Oh, by the way, the guys on the bus let the cat outta the bag about your folks. Tough break, but hey, life goes on, right kid?"

Mr. Silverman took a breath allowing just enough time for Mr. Napoli to interject a mumbled hello before continuing his whirlwind commentary.

"Nice place, Omaha. Any nightlife? Of course there is. You're the nightlife in this town. At least for tonight, huh? Hey, this looks like a pretty good place. How's the food? Anything worth eating? I'm not hungry myself, but Mr. Napoli might want a bite to eat. Maybe a steak or somethin'. Is there some place we can sit down, or do you want us to just stand by the door here?"

"No sir, Mr. Silverman. I mean, yes, of course we can sit down. Right this way, gentlemen." I felt bad that he had to ask me twice for a table. Just because I was flustered was no excuse for bad manners.

We were quite a sight as we walked across the room to a secluded corner table. My tuxedo, and Mr. Napoli's shiny black Italian suit, black silk shirt and white tie were somber bookends for Mr. Silverman's bright green paisley sweater and pink slacks. I pulled out a chair for Mr. Napoli, and said a silent prayer as it creaked under the strain of his enormous weight. He put his big hands on the table, and spoke.

"Get me a glass of water, would ya, kid?"

I cleared my throat, which I remembered always having to do when I heard his voice, and said I'd be happy to. Their presence was puzzling, but I decided it was best to be patient and wait for the explanation that was surely somewhere on the verbal horizon. When I returned, Mr. Silverman had little beads of sweat dotting his brow.

"So, kid. What we have here is, well, something we refer to in the business as a situation, if you know what I'm sayin'." He gave me a wink as if I understood the meaning of his cryptic statement, then he nodded his head in Mr. Napoli's direction. "I'll let Mr. Napoli here fill you in on the particulars. But you're gonna love it." He squirmed around in his chair as if comfort had suddenly become elusive. "Really, kid. Trust me on this."

Mr. Napoli pulled some papers from his inside jacket pocket, and set them in front of me. I immediately recognized them as the contract I had signed with Mr. Silverman. He looked directly into my eyes, my preferred method for honest communication, but his stare made me feel naked and unprepared.

"Here's the deal, kid." He paused to take a sip of water, and then grinned with sly pleasure, as if each second that passed before revealing the deal was an inspired form of manipulation designed to make me more anxious, which it did. "Your friend Silverman got himself into a little jam, and I helped him out. That's what friends are for, right?" He paused again, but didn't reach for his glass of water. "Right?"

"Oh, I'm sorry." I had become so accustomed to the east coast method of speaking in question marks that a true inquiry was hard to spot. "Yes, friends should always help their friends."

He smiled. "You're a nice kid, so I won't bore you with the details. To make a long story short, I loaned your agent Silverman here a lot of money, and he didn't make timely payments."

He paused again, which gave me time to reflect on the lack of plot development in his description of this "situation," but even without details I knew it wasn't ethical to default on a loan.

"So, here's the deal," he continued from where he had started. "I bought your contract."

That statement, by itself, did not sound any alarms, but I took note of the bassoon droning across the back of my mind when Mr. Silverman, who was now sweating profusely, interjected, "Look, kid, it's a good thing. Mr. Napoli's got lots of connections." He wiped his forehead with a napkin, and his eyes darted back and forth between Mr. Napoli and me. "Can I tell him the news? Huh? Can I?"

Mr. Napoli casually shrugged his shoulders, which Mr. Silverman took as a sign of approval.

"You're goin' to Las Vegas!"

The words leapt from Mr. Silverman's mouth like a spontaneous "Praise God Almighty!" and he was filled with renewed energy.

"You heard me right. I said Las Vegas! Didn't I tell you it was the brass ring? Huh? Didn't I say that? You're gonna perform in Las Vegas! Oh, I envy you, kid. Look at me, will you? I'm turnin' green from so much envy. I can't even say Las Vegas without gettin' a chill. I just got another one. This is great, kid. You hear what I'm sayin'? It's great! Just great!"

Throughout Mr. Silverman's opinion on the grandeur of my career opportunity Mr. Napoli tapped his chubby fingers on page one of the contract. The prospect of performing in Las Vegas was certainly an interesting option, but for some reason the finger tapping caused me concern. I decided to sit quietly until I had all of the information.

"Mr. Napoli's got business partners at The Tropics. That's a big hotel and casino on the strip. First class all the way, and you're gonna get The Coconut Lounge! You heard me. The Coconut Lounge! Tuxedo Bob, Sam Ames, either one of you, kid. It doesn't matter, but, hey, The Coconut Lounge! I tell you, it's the chance of a lifetime. A dream come true."

Mr. Napoli informed me that this situation had actually begun months earlier when a deal was made for Vince Genoa to perform for a minimum of three years with The Coconut Lounge house band. Mr. Genoa reneged on the agreement, and this made him, "an ungrateful Guinea bastard who's got about as much chance being on Broadway now as that son of a bitch

Kennedy has coming back from the dead." Mr. Napoli's rasp sounded especially abrasive when uttering such harsh words.

"I hope he enjoys his tour of the East River. Anyway you look at the situation, the facts are still the facts. Vince is a fink. I need a replacement."

And I was the chosen one. From the day Sam Ames took over for Mr. Genoa on the tour, people representing Mr. Napoli's interests had been watching my performances, and sending back favorable reports. When my contract became the cure for Mr. Silverman's money problems, I became the satisfactory substitute to fulfill the terms of Mr. Napoli's deal with The Tropics.

I felt like a chess piece, but as Mr. Napoli politely, but firmly pointed out, I had signed a ten-year personal services contract that included a right of assignment clause. In short, I was collateral. When he directed my attention to the fine print in the middle of page three I knew it was too late to say I hadn't fully understood the ramifications of the clause because I hadn't actually read it. In the excitement of getting my first contract I had signed my name on a dotted line with a gun disguised as a fountain pen. Checkmate.

My present situation would not be improved by dwelling on what I should or should not have done, so I moved ahead, curious as to the extent these two gentlemen controlled my career. "How do we get to Las Vegas after the last show in Topeka?" I asked.

Mr. Napoli withdrew a plane ticket from his breast pocket, and handed it to me. "You fly. Jimmy Cossello will meet you at the airport in Vegas, and get you situated at The Tropics."

There was only one ticket so I inquired how the band would get there. Mr. Napoli looked at Mr. Silverman who nervously explained that the band was not part of the equation.

"You're gonna be using the house band, kid. Real professionals with a very today kinda sound. You're gonna love 'em. You'll do the same kind of shows you're doing now. First you sing some of your funny stuff, then you do the Sam Ames routine. Sam Ames and The Coconut Band. Is that a great name or what, huh? Three shows a night, six nights a week, three years with an option for another three, four grand a month, and free room and board. I'm tellin' you, kid, if I had any talent I'd be takin' the deal myself."

I measured my response to make certain it wouldn't contain an ounce of disrespect. These two gentlemen had obviously spent a great deal of time and energy planning the next few years of my life, and though I didn't want to seem ungrateful, I wanted to be clear about any situation that left Mr. Bop, Deke, Pappy, and Sticks behind.

"I'm sorry, but your plan is not acceptable, sir."

Mr. Silverman began muttering nervously to himself, "Oh boy, that's not good. Not good at all."

Mr. Napoli's chair squeaked in agony as he shifted his weight forward, and put his hand up to silence my former agent.

"What's not acceptable?" His tone was ominous, but no longer intimidating.

"It's not acceptable to perform in Las Vegas without my band." I stated my position with as much confidence as I could muster.

"Look kid. You don't have a choice." Mr. Napoli raised his left eyebrow, and addressed Mr. Silverman. "It would be a shame for this kid's career to end on such an unfriendly note."

Mr. Silverman turned to me with a pleading look that made me wonder about the consequences he would suffer if I didn't change my mind. "Ah, come on kid. This is Vegas we're talkin' about. What could it hurt, huh? It's just for a few years. I mean how bad could that be? How about if we let Mr. Napoli ask you again, huh? Only this time you say yes. How about that, huh? Can you do that for me kid?"

"No, sir." The more I thought about saying good-bye to the band, the more my confidence built.

Mr. Napoli tried again. "Kid, I'm not an unreasonable man. As a matter of fact I can be very fair sometimes. But I do have a business to run, and I can't have the people who work for me tellin' me what they will and won't do. You understand that, right? It makes me look ineffective. I don't like to look ineffective. It makes things unpleasant."

I appreciated his sentiment, but was not swayed by his beliefs. I told him I meant no disrespect to his abilities as a business manager, but my decision was final. "The bottom line of the contract may showcase my signature, but if the Las Vegas engagement doesn't include my current band I will not perform."

For almost nineteen years I had been pleasant and accommodating to everyone. I had been raised to believe that nice was better than nasty, and respect was more civil than indifference, but even so, I didn't care that Mr. Silverman was distressed by my refusal to perform in Las Vegas without my band. It also didn't bother me that Mr. Napoli had the legal right to ruin my career. My friends were more important than my professional reputation.

"You've got some balls, kid." Mr. Napoli was smiling. "The last time someone stood up to me like that? Well, you don't wanna know." He turned to Mr. Silverman as he slowly folded the contract and put it back in his pocket. "The kid's not a bad negotiator."

Mr. Silverman nodded rapidly, "You gotta respect that. I mean, what I meant to say is I gotta respect that. You don't have to respect it if you don't want to. I'm just sayin' that I respect it, and that's all I'm gonna say."

"Okay, kid. Your band goes too." Mr. Napoli's chair creaked with relief as he got up from the table. "I'll work out the details with Jimmy. Let's go, Silverman."

After they left for the airport where Mr. Napoli's private plane was waiting to take them back to New York, I broke the news to the band about the plane that would take us to Las Vegas. I was a bit apprehensive with my disclosure because I had made the decision without their counsel, but Pappy assuaged my fear with "Sounds like a plan."

Deke added, "Don't matter to Deke. Deke play wherever Tee-Bee play."

"Las Vegas it is," was Mr. Bop's comment, and then he gave me a glance that told me he knew there was something concerning my discussion with Mr. Napoli and Mr. Silverman that I had not divulged.

When Sticks whispered, "Gamblin' capital of the world. Dig it," everyone had agreed to the amended destination.

I was happy that I had succeeded in keeping the band together, but my victory had a price. The excitement everyone felt when Deke spoke about playing Dixieland music in New Orleans had been extinguished, and I would not be going to Kiamesha Lake to talk to my Musketeer friends about life on the road, and death in Schulberg.

# Las Vegas

"It's easy to be yourself when you have no hidden agenda."

Orville Fledsper

# do

On a Sunday morning in May at an airport on the outskirts of Topeka, Kansas, The Sam Ames Express flew off toward the desert, and Bee-Dee motored The Big Limo back to the land of the Musketeers. As the plane soared above the clouds I settled back in my seat, grateful to the four musicians who had agreed to follow me into the unknown in exchange for eight hundred dollars a month.

Other than questions about salary and accommodations, no one had asked for the particulars of my deal with Mr. Napoli. The contract's wordy and redundant legal terminology concerning twenty-five percent commission, song publishing and licensing, and the use of my image in advertisements or product endorsements was still pestering my mental orchestra, and I thought it best to keep the information to myself. There was no need to volunteer my concern that Tuxedo Bob was the wholly owned property of Mr. Napoli. For the moment it was enough to know that everyone's food and lodging would be provided, and that I could divide the "firm and final offer" of four thousand dollars a month by five.

I would have never thought of going to Las Vegas. The idea of performing in a town so famous for spectacular entertainment was intimidating, but it was the only option that would allow me to continue working with the band without legal entanglements. My mother had said it was a city more wicked than either Sodom or Gomorra, so I said a silent prayer asking God to spare it a similar fate during my minimum three-year stay.

As the fasten seat belt sign flashed, and we prepared for landing, I remembered something my father used to say. "The strength of a man's character is tested when he makes his bed with another man's sheets." I encouraged myself to rise to the challenge, realizing that Las Vegas was just another town called Paradise where people liked to hear music. Music was my job, not contracts, percentages, or negotiations; writing and singing songs was what I did, and I vowed to do my best shows ever. I touched the sacred quarter in my pocket, and also vowed to be much more careful the next time anyone said, "Sign here, please."

We were supposed to rendezvous with Mr. Jimmy Cossello, but no one greeted us as we deplaned. While we awaited his arrival we decided to greet a bank of slot machines situated outside a souvenir shop.

I put in a nickel, and watched as the spinning drums stopped on a colorful fruit salad of orange, plum and lemon. Sticks and Mr. Bop had the same luck as I, but Deke and Pappy each spun two cherries that paid a handsome reward of five nickels. They used the profit to purchase additional pulls of the handle, which resulted in nothing more than the nickels going back inside their respective machines. Recreation of this type may have been designed to create heart-pounding anticipation of a big pay-off, but all I could see was an invisible "Feed Me" sign.

A man who had been nervously scanning the throng of arriving tourists approached us. He was dressed in the felt hat, shiny silk suit-style that instantly classified him as an associate of Mr. Napoli, and I felt certain he was the person we were to meet.

"Hello," I said. "Are you Mr. Cossello?"

"Yeah, that's me. But let us not be so formal. I'm Jimmy The Nose, from Brooklyn. Welcome to the Gadden o' Eden." He pumped my hand vigorously and continued, "Four years I been here watchin' out for Mr. Napoli's interests, and I gotta say I am most definitely the luckiest guy in the world. I'm tellin' you this place's got everything. It's one big non-stop party with more good lookin' broads than you are ever gonna see in one place your whole life."

He looked at me, then at the guys in the band, then back at me again. I wasn't sure if his comment needed a response, but he seemed to be waiting for one. To coincide with his theme I offered, "The last party we went to was New Years Eve."

"Yeah?" He paused again.

"That's all. Just a New Years Eve party." I felt responsible for interrupting his train of thought. "So, Mr. Cossello, you were saying?"

"Hey, call me Jimmy The Nose. That's my name on the count o' I know everything there is to know about this town and everybody in it."

"That certainly suggests a high degree of awareness." I was intrigued by the notion that any one person could know everything about anything, and glad that the pace of our conversation was picking up.

"Without a doubt, I'm the go-to guy in this town." Mr. Jimmy The Nose turned his attention toward a well-endowed redhead who did not respond to his wolf-whistle as she passed. "Didn't I say the broads were unbelievable," he smirked as he jabbed me with an elbow to my ribs. "So, you gotta be Sam, right?"

"Yes, but you can call me Tuxedo Bob."

"On the count o' you wear a tuxedo, right? Mr. Napoli told me you got it on all the time, and not to make any big deal about it even if I think it's weird, which, by the way o' course, I don't." His voice had the sound of clogged nasal passages, and his demeanor reminded me of actors I had seen on the television show "The Untouchables."

"Mr. Napoli said you were his boy, and I gotta take good care with you. So that's what I'm gonna do. Anything you want, and I mean anything, you come to me 'cause like I said, I'm your go-to guy. Okay?"

He shrugged his shoulders as he talked, and I wondered if these were involuntary gestures or if he had an annoying itch in the middle of his back.

"Hey, Express guys, I did not mean to ignore you here. How's everybody doin', huh? Welcome to my town." He shook each band member's hand enthusiastically, and introduced himself. "So let's say we get outta here. You guy's got any bags, I'll have 'em picked up and delivered. Wait'll you see The Tropics. You're gonna love the place."

He led us through the airport at such a quick pace that I was glad he warned those in our path by repeating, "Watch your back," and "Comin' through." This eliminated any danger of accidentally striking a person with one of the instrument cases we carried. When we reached the exit door, Mr. Jimmy The Nose put on a pair of dark sunglasses before going outside, and as I followed him into the bright midday sun it was obvious that sunglasses were a necessary fashion accessory. I squinted my eyes at the object in front of me, which was reflecting a good deal of the sunlight, and saw what had to be the longest, shiniest limousine in the world.

Sticks exclaimed, "Dig the wheels, man! It's the big limo for real!"

We were soon cruising down a street called The Strip. It was lined with grand hotels and casinos, and its sidewalks were teeming with pedestrians rushing around in a manner that reminded me of Manhattan. Though it was the middle of the day, neon signs and multi-colored lights flashed from every direction. Mr. Jimmy The Nose said The Strip was even more dazzling at night. I was sure that it was, but I couldn't imagine paying for the electricity.

The hotels' gigantic marquees advertised the appearances of the greatest entertainers in the world, some of whom I'd seen on "The Ed Sullivan Show." Buddy Hackett, Sammy Davis, Steve and Edie, Liberace, their legendary names loomed large while smaller lettering announced the performances of newcomers like Lesley Gore or Paul Revere and The Raiders, and there were others who I assumed were just as talented, even though their names weren't familiar.

I wondered how "Tuxedo Bob" or "The Sam Ames Express" would look on the sign in front of The Tropics, or if there would even be a space allocated for either name. There was no signage clause in my contract, but I hoped that a minimum three-year engagement would present an opportunity to see one of my names in lights.

The Big Limo For Real pulled into a long curved driveway that was bordered by palm trees, and carried us to the front of our destination. Two bare-footed, sun-tanned women wearing grass skirts, brightly colored bathing suit tops, and flower necklaces opened our car doors, and welcomed us to The Tropics. Their welcome included kissing each one of us on the cheek, which I found to be quite friendly. Mr. Bop grinned, and informed me that I was blushing. Everyone laughed when I replied that I couldn't tell if he was having the same reaction.

We walked up the torch-lined pink seashell and white sand staircase toward two pineapples that opened automatically to reveal a massive lobby where the tropical paradise motif continued on an even grander scale. As I passed the large clamshell ashtray by the entrance I had to stop and catch my breath. This hotel was exhaustively impressive. I was amazed that someone had put so much thought and effort into the surroundings, and my feeling was best summed up by Sticks when he said, "Dig the fun house!"

Bellboys dressed as beachcombers waited for duty by a simple structure made of bamboo and thatch. On the wall to my left, a bank of elevators was disguised to look like the beach of a deserted island; hidden speakers played the sound of waves crashing on its imaginary shore, and strumming ukuleles were heard each time an elevator door opened. Large glass and wire cages hung from the rainbow painted ceiling, and each cage housed an assortment of multi-colored parrots, macaws, and cockatoos. Seven beautiful Hawaiian girls danced among hundreds of potted orchids to the percussive beat of congas and log drums in front of a three-story waterfall cascading down rocks on the wall to my right.

"Dig it. If Bee-Dee see this here joint, he'd say it's phantasmaglorious," Sticks remarked as he gazed around the room. "Got a groove all it's own."

Mr. Jimmy The Nose motioned us toward a volcano that served as the guest check-in area. As we approached the desk, Deke spoke the words we were all thinking. "Deke sure hopes the rooms is normal."

We lined up next to the glowing simulated lava flow that included intermittent puffs of real smoke and an ominous rumbling noise. As I waited for the key to my room, I wondered if my performances could ever be as impressive as these surroundings.

Before we could go to our rooms we had to register with a guard at the employees' entrance. He was a slightly built man dressed in an official looking uniform that set him apart from the other employee's tropical theme wear. With intense seriousness, he briefed us on the hotel's right to random searches, the importance of security, and how we must use this entryway exclusively whenever we desired passage into or off the premises. He took our photographs and fingerprints, and issued each of us a Tropics ID card. I thought to inform him that Mr. Napoli owned the rights to my face, but with respect to his position as a law-enforcement officer I kept the joke to myself.

We were finally shown to our rooms on the third floor which Mr. Jimmy The Nose said were "reserved for the exclusive use o' the hotel's finest entertainers." To everyone's relief they were furnished in traditional hotel room style with standard double bed, nightstand, and dresser. Had it not been for the wallpaper, which featured a colorful pattern of large chunks of tropical fruit, the rooms could have been in any town.

The window of my room was less than ten yards from The Tropic's huge neon sign, so I had an excellent view of its boldly blinking announcement that a "Gay-Paree Dance Extravaganza" was performed twice nightly in the main showroom. This information used every inch of available space on the majestic five-story sign, so I knew the show had to be quite spectacular.

Since the minimum three years of performances wouldn't begin until nine o'clock the next evening, there was ample time to scout around this fabulous resort. The band opted to relax in their rooms until free board was served, but I was too excited to rest, so I asked Mr. Jimmy The Nose to show me everything.

He took me straight to the casino where I was introduced to a number of security men. Some were obvious by their uniforms, but others were working undercover in various disguises, so as they were pointed out I pretended not to notice. I met men who were called pit bosses because, as Mr. Jimmy The Nose explained, "They handle all the action in the pit." Upon further inquiry I learned that the pit was the area where a pit boss worked.

Mr. Jimmy The Nose said hello to dozens of pretty cocktail waitresses walking around with trays of frothy drinks decorated with umbrellas. I admired their ability to nimbly perform their duties while wearing bright yellow polka-dotted bikinis, high heels, and attractive pineapple hats. They seemed friendly, but were understandably too involved with their occupation to engage in any form of conversation beyond a casual greeting.

At the tables in the center of the room I got to watch as people cheered or cursed each roll of the dice. They were playing a game that had the humorously inspired name of "Craps," and while I didn't watch long enough to grasp the rules, I did learn that a person could win a lot of money by placing a wager on snake eyes, and then rolling a two.

There were a few tables that featured a little white ball that bounced around a spinning wheel before coming to rest in a numbered slot. This game was called Roulette, and while there were numerous ways to win, the person who correctly guessed the ball's final resting place was the most cheerful.

The slot machine areas abounded with the music of jingling coins, ringing bells, buzzers, and shouts of joy or disappointment. According to Mr. Jimmy The Nose, the slots were the casino's biggest draw and moneymaker, and I could see why. Row after row, hundreds of people sat pulling handles in the hope that their financial worries would end upon the arrival of three lucky sevens. Most seemed content that their steady stream of nickels, dimes, or quarters produced payoffs in slow drips. Mr. Jimmy The Nose said the idea behind the slots' success was making people believe that their machine was just about to reward perseverance and investment with a jackpot. I noticed that most of the participants exhibited a casual disregard for the logic behind the slot machine's nickname, "One-Armed Bandit."

My favorite game to watch was Blackjack. The green felt tables were small, and since there were never more than eight players, it was easier to learn some of the rules. At first I thought the best card to get was a black jack, but I soon learned it had a value of ten, just like all the other face cards. The main goal was to get exactly twenty-one points, but a player could win with less if the dealer got twenty-two or more. "Splitting," "double down," and "insurance" were a bit more complicated, but as I started getting the hang of the intricacies of the game Mr. Jimmy The Nose escorted me from the table.

"It's against the rules to count cards," he said as he led me away.

I apologized for not knowing, but I had made eight people very happy by telling them not to take a hit because the dealer probably had fourteen points, and almost all of the cards remaining in the shoe were nines or higher.

When we had reached an area of slot machines, he relaxed his grip, and cracked a smile. "How'd you do that so quick?"

I explained that since there are thirteen cards in a suit and the same number of different musical notes, I had simply assigned a note to a card. An Ace was C, a Two was C sharp, and so on up to a B for a King. After a number of hands I had a bad melody line, but I heard very few notes above a G flat.

He said he had no idea what I was talking about, and asked that I not write any more songs at the blackjack tables. I agreed, and as he directed his attention to a pit boss who needed something I looked around at this peculiar place where knowing what cards remained in a deck was illegal, but the hope of lady luck smiling on one's fortunes was a way of life.

This was a carnival with all the commotion and excitement I had experienced as a child at North Dakota's State Fair in Bismarck only much more sophisticated. No one yelled, "Find the nickel!" but I heard machines being subtly urged to "Come on, come on!" or ordered to "Stop! Stop!" I recalled the look of intent on my father's face whenever he had attempted to topple some milk cans with a softball, and it was the same look the dice rollers had when they breathed on the dice and commanded them to "Roll daddy a seven!" Money was the prize instead of a kewpie doll, and I was not the only person wearing a tuxedo.

"Mr. Cossello?" He had finished his conversation, and I decided it was impossible to continue addressing him as Mr. Jimmy The Nose. "Can you show me The Coconut Lounge?"

"It's over this way, and what's with the mister? You don't like me or somethin'? Don't call me mister no more. I'm Jimmy The Nose. Mr. Cossello is what you call my father."

I offered a compromise. "How about if I just call you Jimmy?"

"Fair enough, seein' as how that is also my name," he said, and he led me toward a grove of fake palm trees at the edge of the casino.

Each palm treetop was adorned with a blinking letter that spelled out C-O-C-O-N-U-T L-O-U-N-G-E in sequence. Each letter was a different color, and just large enough to be appropriate in the hotel's decorating scheme of excessiveness. In case the blinking letters confused any of the non-English speaking patrons, there were signs attached to the trees on each side of the open entrance. Both signs featured a large painting of a coconut split in half by a machete. As I stepped into the club, I hoped that those symbolic pictures were not the handiwork of Destiny on a junket from New York.

The lounge was decorated to resemble a desert oasis. Cardboard silhouettes of camels and horses graced the wall behind a gurgling watering hole that surrounded the stage. In the middle of the stage a young woman sat at the piano performing "THAT OLD BLACK MAGIC" with such nonchalance that her boredom was transformed into an art form.

I felt sorry for her because her posture and vocal timbre indicated she fervently desired to be elsewhere, and after witnessing the response from the few men in attendance it was clear the feeling was mutual. Most of the men's attentions were directed toward the waitresses who were dressed in sequined belly dancer outfits that offered more than a subtle hint of what was underneath the sheer fabric.

"It's early." Jimmy said as he leaned against a fake palm tree between two empty tables. "Things don't start jumpin' here until after the dinner show in the main room, but after that? Whoa, look out! You'll see what I mean." He bent toward me, and spoke in a hushed tone so no one could eavesdrop. "We provide this place so our gambler's can relax. We want 'em to have a good time, and not go strolling too far from the casino. Mr. Napoli and his partners don't like it so much when somebody leaves the hotel, and goes someplace else."

"What happens if someone tries to leave?" I figured his last statement begged the question.

"We shoot 'em." He put his arm around me in a fatherly manner. "I'm just kidding, o' course. We got a good thing here, Tuxedo Bob. A guy can lose a couple grand at craps, and then come in here for a free drink and grab a little ass to forget about it. The waitresses don't mind 'cause they know it gets reflected in their monetary remuneration, if you know what I mean."

I nodded my head to indicate I knew most of what he meant, so he continued, "We give everybody a free drink, you give 'em a few laughs, 'cause I hear you're a funny guy, and then we get 'em back at the tables givin' us the rest o' their money." He paused to laugh at his sense of humor. "Jesus was right when he said, 'There's a sucker born every minute.'"

"I think that was P. T. Barnum."

"Yeah? Well, either way, we make money here as long as the lights are on." He gave me a friendly shove, and winked. "That's why we never turn off the lights."

Twenty-four hours a day the lights burned in the casino, the lobby, and on the marquee. The Tropics consumed more electricity in one day than Schulberg used in a month, but a large electric bill was insignificant compared to the amount of money I had witnessed being fed into the casino's coffers in the past hour. The well-lit gamblers were certainly at a disadvantage.

I thanked Jimmy for the tour and the information.

"Anything else you need, you just call me. Anything at all." His emphasis on the word anything seemed to imply that he had something in mind.

"I just want to go to my room, and relax."

"Say no more," he smiled. "I understand completely."

We said goodnight, and I returned to my room. I called Mr. Bop to tell him not to expect me for dinner, and to schedule a breakfast meeting with the band so I could discuss some ideas I had concerning our song sequence. He said to consider it a plan, and to enjoy my first night's sleep in my new home. I hung up the phone, content to have a mini-vacation before getting back to business tomorrow morning.

I hung up my tuxedo, and got into bed. My body sank into the mattress as if staking a claim, and the soft blanket covered me like a shield. I felt protected and serene in my new home. It was getting dark, but every inch of my living quarters was ablaze with the glow of flashing neon. Closing my eyes helped to partially block the twenty-four hour night-light that burned in the city that never went to sleep because there was money to be made.

A series of loud knocks on my door jolted me awake. I got out of bed, and after putting on the green terry cloth robe with a palm tree insignia of

The Tropics embroidered on both sleeves, I opened the door to find a young woman standing there.

"Hi. My name's Felicia. Jimmy sent me." Her hair was so blonde, her chiffon dress so yellow, and her voice so sweet she conjured thoughts of banana salt-water taffy.

Given the number of late night auditions conducted by Mr. Genoa I was not surprised by the presence of a young woman at my door at 1 A.M. Even though I had made no request for the services of a background singer, I assumed this was a part of the business I would eventually have to get used to. I wanted to appear professional, but being a late-night-audition-virgin I was unsure how one was conducted. Fortunately she started the ball rolling.

"May I come in, or did you want to do it in the hall?"

I knew that holding an audition in a hallway would be most unprofessional, so I apologized for being rude, and invited her into my home. She sat down on the edge of my bed, and I leaned against the dresser wondering how to best inform her that I didn't require her services.

"I'm afraid you might be under some misconception," I said. "There's really no room for an additional member in my small group at this moment."

With an understanding nod and smile she replied, "That's all right. I'm not looking to be one of your girlfriends. This can just be a one-time thing if you want. You don't ever have to see me again after tonight if you want it that way, but who knows? You might like me."

"I just might at that." She had such a good attitude about the lack of employment opportunity, I decided to tell her the truth. "I must confess, I've never done this before."

"You're a virgin?" She sounded surprised.

"Yes, I am. An acquaintance of mine used to hold these late night auditions, but I never watched."

"Well, there's a first time for everything." She sounded so positive I thought it best to follow her lead.

"Then you'll be my first. What would you like to do for me, Miss?"

"Felicia."

"Miss Felicia."

"You can pick another name if you don't like Felicia."

She was so compliant. I had no job for her, but she was letting me know right off the bat that she would accept any stage name she was given.

"Felicia's just fine. It's a very pretty name."

"It's short for one of my specialties."

"Do you want to perform that one?

"Sure. This is Jimmy's dime, and he said to do whatever it takes to make you happy." She shook her head, tossing the frizzy blonde curls from her shoulders. "So, how do you like it? Fast and hot, or slow and lingering?"

Since any song that could be performed in different ways aroused my interest, I told her either was fine, and gently inquired, "Which way are you the most comfortable?"

"I'm prepared for whatever you say." Though she stretched the limits of amicability, she was so nice it probably came to her naturally.

I continued the direct approach. "Okay. Do you want to sit or stand?"

"I can sit, stand, lay down, bend over, get down on my knees, whatever. Most guys seem to prefer a half and half."

I wasn't familiar with that number, and I didn't want to put her through any unnecessary physical gymnastics, so I suggested she perform something I recognized. "I think I'd be more comfortable if you do a standard."

"Sure. How standard do you want it to be?"

I wondered if Mr. Genoa had ever experienced this problem; a young girl who seemed eager to perform, but was reticent to begin.

"How about doing "OVER THE RAINBOW?" I congratulated myself for choosing a simple number that was surely in any singer's repertoire, but her response took me by surprise.

"Okay by me, but I've never done it before. It won't hurt, will it?"

"Well, Felicia, all I can say is the last time I did it, I made a lot of people cry."

She stood up, and in what I believed was a reference to Dorothy's ruby slippers, kicked off her high heels. I appreciated her desire to add a dramatic effect, but my assumptions were altered when she turned her back to me and asked, "Would you unzip my dress?"

Felicia, whose real name was Carol Jamison, left my room an hour later. In order to get her money from Jimmy she had to stay long enough to make him think she was performing her specialty number. She told me about her job instead. The details of what she did weren't important to me; I was interested in why.

She told me about her attempts selling shoes, ushering at a theater, and being a waitress, and how she had discovered that prostitution was the only industry that would provide her with enough money to follow her dream.

"Everywhere I worked my bosses were always hassling me into having sex, so I finally got smart and started charging them for it."

She said she didn't enjoy working as a call girl, and to illustrate her point she told me about an overweight client who had bad breath, and paid extra to hear her say how much she loved having sex with him. She was going to stop selling her body to strangers as soon as she could save five thousand dollars, and move to Hollywood. Once there, she planned to get into the movies, marry a big star, have babies, and move back to Dayton, Ohio. I respected her for having a goal, so I asked how much she had saved to date.

"Not very much," she replied. "I have to spend a lot on clothes."

A lighthearted guitar and piano duet interrupted my thought that her dream had no chance of coming true unless she became more frugal. The music was upbeat and gay; it was the opposite of what I would have expected given the circumstances. Then the words "He wants to think you do it for love, but you do it for money" attached themselves to the melody.

I chuckled out loud, and she asked me what was so funny. I confessed that her story about the obese client had provided some musical inspiration, and she laughed too.

"I always thought that people who heard music in their head needed to see a doctor."

I replied, "If that's true then I guess I need constant care."

She touched my cheek as she continued laughing. "It's refreshing to meet an honest man."

I thanked her for the compliment, and was struck by the thought that she was someone's daughter.

I opened the dresser drawer and withdrew my checkbook. "Miss Jamison, my father used to say that an honest man can afford to act on impulse."

Her first reaction upon receiving the check I wrote for five thousand dollars was handing it back. "This is too much money!" She took a deep breath, and quickly added, "I can't accept that. I didn't do anything."

"I haven't written a song in months, and you gave me inspiration. That's a wonderful present." I assured her I could afford to spend my money, and that I only wanted her to have a chance to put her dream in motion.

"You are just too nice," she said softly as she put the check in her purse and left my home.

I never saw her again in Las Vegas or in the movies.

At four in the morning I was still awake. I stared at the colored lights making patterns on the ceiling, and listened to the tranquil sound of flutes consorting with my thoughts of a young woman following her dream. Lyrics to the chorus of a new song lay on the nightstand, and even though "YOU DO IT FOR MONEY" was neither complete nor about Carol Jamison, I was grateful for the inspiration her story had provided.

Impulse struck again, and I jumped out of bed. If I could give a little help to a passing acquaintance I could certainly afford to offer the same consideration to my friends. I grabbed the phone, and dialed the hotel operator.

"I'd like to place a call to Pressman's Golf and Ski Resort in Kiamesha Lake, New York, please." It would be 6 A.M. there, so I planned to leave a message saying I would call back in three hours. This would allow Sylvia, Ernie and Mr. Murphy to receive my call together. I was so excited I didn't hear the operator asking for the number I wanted to reach until her third request. After a few minutes were spent getting the listing from long distance information, I was connected.

"Good morning. This is Pressman's Golf and Ski Resort located in beautiful Kiamesha Lake. How may I help you?"

"I'd like to leave a message for Miss Sylvia Aaron, please."

The receptionist asked me to hold while I was connected to that extension. I waited. One ring. Then another, and another. Finally a man answered. He sounded like I had woken him, and I silently chuckled at the image of one of Mr. Napoli's employees asleep at the message desk.

"Good morning, sir," I said. "I'd like to leave a message for Miss Sylvia Aaron."

"Who's calling?" The man was unnecessarily abrupt, but I attributed this to the early hour.

"This is Tuxedo Bob." I started to ask if he would let her know I'd be calling back at ten, and that she should gather The Musketeers, but I was interrupted with recognition.

"Hey, Tuxedo Bob, it's Charlie. Charlie Derbin. You remember? The bartender?"

Of course I remembered. “Hello, Mr. Derbin.”

“So, how’s the big tour? Wait. On second thought, you’d better tell Sylvia. I know she’s going to want to talk to you. Hold on.”

I was thinking how impressed I was by his willingness to work long hours behind the bar in Billy’s Lounge, and then man the message desk during the night. I even reprimanded myself for laughing at his having fallen asleep. He obviously was a hard worker, and could be forgiven a lapse in decorum. I figured he was getting a pencil or piece of paper to take my message, and I was only slightly confused by what I perceived to be the sound of rustling sheets and the word, “Honey.”

“Hi.” It was her voice, and that one word created a crescendo of brass and woodwinds. “How are you?” Three more words and a choir of angels joined the expanding orchestration.

A cymbal crashed in my ear, and the music stopped. She had accidentally dropped the phone, and as I heard the sound of two people giggling on the other end of the line I knew from the sinking feeling in my stomach that she was much farther away from me than the distance that separated the Nevada desert from a lake in the Catskills.

We talked for an hour. It was a friendly, warm conversation about everything that had happened since I left. Orville and Margaret’s death, The Devil’s Den, and the Vegas arrival of The Sam Ames Express were the highlights from my end. Falling in love with Charlie Derbin was the highlight from hers. She said he was gentle, kind, and considerate, which made me happy because it was the treatment she deserved, and she added that she hoped to be able to afford to go back to school soon. We wished each other well, and said good-bye after promising to stay in touch. I hung up the phone, and asked God's indulgence while I made a few plans.

Dawn was softening the neon glow in the room as I set my plans in motion. Letters and checks were written, and envelopes were stamped and addressed. My bank account in Omaha was down to sixty-five thousand dollars, but I was certain it was still more money than I needed. I felt good being able to use my resources to help my friends, and though I was sad there would be no Musketeer reunion, I knew there were four stones that would always be together at the bottom of Kiamesha Lake.

During the next few weeks, Sylvia Aaron received a letter from the Law Department of Boston University informing her of a full scholarship that had been given to her from an anonymous donor. The money covered all costs, including housing and other living expenses, so she could be a full-time student, and not have to wait tables. Though I never admitted I was her benefactor, she expressed strong suspicions in every letter she wrote. I continued to send her matchbooks, and advised her to repay whomever was responsible for her good fortune by graduating with honors, and becoming a top-notch lawyer.

Ernie Santos was drafted into the army, so he sent his check for five thousand dollars to his mother in Puerto Rico for safekeeping. He knew he wouldn't need it until he got back from defending his country's honor with the same energy he had defended Mr. Murphy's in Billy's Lounge. I prayed that he would be safe in Vietnam, and that he would be allowed to perform his military service away from the line of fire.

Mr. Murphy's immediate response upon receiving his check was to move back to Arkansas where the cornbread and ribs were the finest on earth. We kept in touch over the next few months. I filled my letters with stories about my Las Vegas musical career. His short notes were about fishing, and the colors of the sky at dawn. One night he closed his eyes, and fell peacefully asleep forever. It was a sad day when I received a letter from his neighbor informing me of his death, but I was certain Orville and Margaret had welcomed my good friend with open arms when he arrived at St. Peter's Gate.

# re

My first Las Vegas performance was less than twelve hours away when I met the band in the employee's cafeteria for our breakfast meeting. They helped ease my anxiety with a summary of what they had eaten at the ninety-nine cents "all-you-can-eat" dinner buffet that I had missed the previous evening, and then Sticks' recapped his adventures with a pair of dice.

"I was hot, you dig? Up a cool five bills, my man, when I let it ride for one more hard eight."

Everyone laughed when I asked if that meant he had lost.

"It's cool. It's cool. I bet your daddy used to say, 'you win some, you lose some.' I can slide when I lose 'cause it be so hip when I win, you dig?"

I dug him at his word, and felt no need to correct him with what my father had actually said on the subject, "You win when you learn a lesson from losing."

We moved on to discuss my idea that the forty-five minute sets required at nine, eleven, and one o'clock should be different from each other. Our current play list didn't contain enough material to fulfill my desire, but Deke offered a possible solution.

"Deke say we adds a little spice, and play like we in The Devil's Den."

His suggestion generated a flurry of enthusiastic agreement. Everyone spoke about how great we had sounded in Cincinnati, that lengthy solos would extend the songs, and that each musician would have a chance to shine in the spotlight. It seemed the logical direction we should take.

"Dig it, Tee-Bee. If the groove is cool, what we do about the Sam Ames jive?" Sticks' comment had the effect of an emergency brake.

"Sticks is right," I said. "Any suggestions on how Vince Genoa's show would be performed at The Devil's Den?"

Mr. Bop proposed, "We play cool behind Tee-Bee when you Tee-Bee, but we play Sam Ames with the Vee-Gee jive same as before."

"Won't fly," Pappy chimed in, and because it was a musical discussion he allowed himself to continue. "I say we dump the Sam Ames thing all together, but we keep the songs, and just play them with soul."

"Deke say Pappy done hit the nail on the head, and split the wood!"

Mr. Bop agreed. "Every song we play behind Sam Ames is a good song. Good songs should be played from the heart, and I don't know anybody got more heart than Tee-Bee. So let's not do The Express show no more. I say we Tuxedo Bob's band, pure and simple."

At ten hours to showtime, Sam Ames was dismissed from further service. Though his snapping fingers and speedy delivery were no longer needed, his songs would stay in the show. There was no danger of legal repercussions because he wasn't mentioned by name in my contract, and I knew I wouldn't sue myself for firing me without notice.

I thought some discussion was warranted to decide what our new name should be, and the band quickly voted as a bloc to veto any use of the words, "show," "band," "group," "ensemble," "parade," and "the." They wanted to perform in the middle of the simulated watering hole at the pretend oasis as "Tuxedo Bob."

"And what?" I asked.

The band responded by smiling in unison, vetoing "and" along with every other word in any language. We were "Tuxedo Bob" period.

Mr. Bop and I stayed in the cafeteria to map out the sets, while the rest of "Tuxedo Bob" went to The Coconut Lounge to check out the backstage area. Mr. Bop suggested I start with a solo, and then he would join me for the second song with the rest of the band being added during the third number. We wanted to showcase the band's versatility by featuring Pappy and Deke's abilities to play various instruments. At seven hours to showtime the band assembled in my room to discuss the completed play list.

"The sets are cool, my man," Sticks declared, "but dig it. When we hangin' backstage some group callin' itself Norman's Neon Light Revue was on the stage swingin' with our Saints and Bailey songs."

I didn't see the problem until Sticks pointed out that Norman's Revue preceded our nine o'clock show.

"I've got an idea that will solve the entire problem." All attention was focused on Pappy as he tore up the set list. "This is Vegas, my friends. To some people the entertainers in this city are on the top of the heap. This is our shot." He paused to consider his words. "What I'm trying to say is, Tee-Bee's got six songs that no one in this town's ever heard before."

"Unless there be some fanatics following us around the country," Mr. Bop interjected, causing a few laughs.

Pappy continued, "People want to hear new stuff. I say, as long as we're here, let's be unique."

"Deke say you clear-headed, Pappy. Deke only play Tee-Bee songs from here on."

Sticks looked around at everyone, his grin expressing a sly pleasure he was deriving from his thought. "Tee-Bee? Your papers say what groove you got to play, or can you just dig the scene?"

I told him there was no clause in my contract that required, or restricted any particular musical selection or genre. I was only obligated to perform to the best of my abilities.

"Cool. Then I say you perform what you want, my man. You dig?"

And with Sticks' vote the decision was final, and our plan was amended again. With less than six hours before our first Las Vegas performance, we had a six-song play list to fill three forty-five minute shows. I decided I had better finish "YOU DO IT FOR MONEY," and get busy writing some other new material. If I didn't, I'd be singing the same six songs, three times a day, six nights a week for at least three years.

The next five hours were filled with a flurry of activity. Deke got his guitar, and I taught everyone the chords and background vocals to the songs they were familiar with, but hadn't played before. I described a mandolin part that would fit beautifully in "COMPLETELY NUDE," I hummed a harmony line for "I JUST LOVE TO COMPLAIN" that would sound especially melancholy on an oboe, and I whistled a playful flute refrain that would round out the calypso flavor of "CHOCOLATE TAPIOCA PUDDING." In my excitement over the possibilities for these additions I wasn't very sensitive to the sighs of frustration coming from the band. Deke was the first to correct my behavior.

"Deke play a mean mandolin, but it ain't no good to be good at somethin' if Deke ain't got it to be good on."

"Deke's right," Pappy said. "I know how to play the flute, and the oboe, but I don't own either one. What good is that?"

It was a minor problem. My friends had additional talents to offer, and only lacked the means to present it. I got in touch with Jimmy, who the band addressed as "The Suit," and asked if there was a store that sold musical instruments close by. The man who knew everything said there was.

It was one hour to showtime when The Big Limo For Real brought us back to The Tropics from our trip to Instruments Unlimited. Deke had a new banjo, a twelve-string guitar, a mandolin, and a ukulele. Pappy had his oboe and flute, along with a soprano saxophone and a French horn. Mr. Bop had an electric bass and amplifier, and Sticks was the proud owner of a new set of skins. I was delighted to write a check for the purchases, because I knew that every penny spent would be repaid many times over in the form of their individual joyful noise.

We spent the final anxious minutes before our first Las Vegas performance crowded into the small room behind the stage. Sticks nervously drummed a rhythm on his leg as we sat in silence awaiting our cue. Mr. Bop's eyes were closed, and I could tell by the movement of his head that he was going over his bass parts.

"What chord the bridge in 'Nude' start on?"

"$B^b$," Pappy said in unison with Deke in answer to Mr. Bop's question.

"The key changes to F," I added, and we all went back to our own thoughts accompanied by the sound of Sticks' practice riffs.

Jimmy had informed me that he used various comedians between the musical acts, and they were also the emcees. After our introduction was made there would be ten minutes to set-up and tune the instruments to the piano, and then forty-five minutes of performance. It sounded simple, but ten minutes seemed a long time to ask an audience to wait for something to happen.

This would be the first time the band and I would perform my entire show together as a unit, and I had no idea how five of the songs would sound. "THAT'S WHAT I CALL LOVE" had already proven itself to be better as an ensemble number, but I had to trust that the inclusion of instruments would not detract from the dramatic effects of the slower songs.

Norman's Neon Light Revue had finished their set, and a young comedian was busy doing his best to induce laughter from the sparse audience. "Okay, now. How's everybody doin'?" The comedian was borrowing a page from Mr. Genoa, except he was yelling. "Hey! I'm talking up here! Is everybody having a good time?"

This produced murmurs among the hisses and boos from the free drinkers that sounded like, "Shut-up!" "You stink!" and "Get off the stage, you bum!"

"All right. All right. I can take a hint," the comedian laughed, "but I'm warning you, I'll be back after this next act." His declaration did nothing to lessen the audience's hostility.

I waited for my name to be announced, but the only additional words I heard from him were, "Sally, get me a drink." I peeked from behind the backstage door, and noticed he was no longer on the stage.

Mr. Bop put his hand on my shoulder, and whispered in my ear, "Go let the magic happen, Tee-Bee. We'll be right behind you."

I opened the door, climbed the short flight of stairs, and stepped onto the bridge that took me across the simulated watering hole to the piano. The band followed. While I played an A Major chord for their tuning purposes, I watched the two belly dancer waitresses attend to the needs of the four-man audience, and concluded that a small crowd was appropriate for a first rehearsal disguised as a performance.

Sticks installed his new snare and hi-hat into the house drum kit. Pappy made a minor adjustment to the mouthpiece of his alto saxophone, while Deke tuned the strings of his guitar. As Mr. Bop bowed some notes on his upright bass I realized I had not addressed our audience.

"Hello," I said into the microphone. "We're Tuxedo Bob."

A man who may have had too many free drinks yelled, "So what? I'm Harvey Davis!"

"It's nice to meet you Mr. Davis." I introduced myself and each band member, and I thanked Mr. Davis and the other three patrons for attending our first show.

Mr. Davis yelled, "So play something!"

I obliged his request, with a short improvisation of Bach's "BRANDENBURG CONCERTO #5." My intention was to kill time until the band was ready to go, so I was surprised when Mr. Bop began to play his bass in counterpoint to me. Then Sticks hit his hi-hat, and altered the classical 4/4 rhythm with a snare and cymbal figure that fused jazz with the beat of a Sousa march. Pappy started blowing his sax with a different melody line, and Deke's new mandolin gave Bach's composition its originally intended harpsichord sound.

We were cookin', and though we played the tune for less than a minute we couldn't have planned a better way to rid ourselves of the first night jitters. When we stopped, Mr. Harvey Davis yelled out that we weren't bad for a cheesy lounge act.

There was a second of uncomfortable silence as Mr. Bop stared at Mr. Davis. It was obvious that the rest of the band didn't appreciate the comment either, but I remembered Ernie had warned me about hecklers. I was pleased to be experiencing my first one, so I said, "Ladies and gentleman. I present for your listening enjoyment, the newly renamed Parmesan Players."

I turned to Mr. Bop, and gave him his cue to start the vamp to "THAT'S WHAT I CALL LOVE." Sixteen measures of thumping bass notes later Pappy and I played a single eighth note, and then rested for an additional sixteen measures while Sticks circled the skin of his snare with soothing strokes from metal-bristled brushes. Deke added his usual four inversions of each chord during what would have been the first verse had I begun singing, but I decided to delay my entrance and listen to Pappy play the melody on his sax.

The chorus began with Pappy, Sticks and Mr. Bop singing the three-part harmony background vocals, but I still had not sung any of the lyrics. I was content playing the piano chords, listening to the groove, and looking around the lounge. Our four-man audience was tapping their fingers on their tables, the waitresses were watching us, and the bartender had halted his conversation with the comedian. Having what appeared to be their undivided attention, I let the song continue as an instrumental.

When we got to the bridge section Pappy, Deke and I stopped playing, and Mr. Bop performed a repeat solo of the beginning vamp. The only lyric any of the eight people in attendance had heard was the title repeated in the background vocal harmonies. It didn't occur to me that they might be taken by surprise when I started singing.

> "You take my heart,
> and you throw it on the ground,
> and then you kick it all around,
> until it doesn't make a sound.
> Baby, that's what I call love."

There were giggles, then laughter. Mr. Davis laughed so hard he fell off his chair causing a waitress to drop her tray of empty glasses and ashtrays. Sticks acknowledged this auxiliary percussion with a few cymbal splashes and rim shots.

> "You'd turn your back if I was dyin'.
> Ignore the tears that I'd be cryin'.
> If I was standing on the edge of a bridge
> you'd probably give me a shove.
> You just can't hurt me enough.
> That's what I call love."

Hearty applause was our reward when we finished the song. As we started the second number, "I JUST LOVE TO COMPLAIN," more gamblers, ready for their free drinks and a few laughs, walked into the lounge. Some sat down while others stood, and the two waitresses raced around satisfying everyone's drink requests. With each passing minute more people wandered in, and by the time we closed our set with "COMPLETELY NUDE" the room was packed. Amid the hoots and hollers of "encore," I thanked everyone for their kind attention, informed them we would be back at eleven, handed the microphone to the comedian, and exited the stage.

One of the waitresses peeked backstage, and in a marvelous southern drawl excitedly informed us that she had made over one hundred dollars in tips during our show.

"That's a record for one set! You guys are great! Really. Thank you so much!"

She shook our hands, said her name was Sally, and informed us the other waitress was Beth. Her body jiggled and bounced as she giggled, "That parmesan thing you said was so funny. Made me about bust my gut."

"Well, I'm glad you didn't," I smiled. "Sounds dangerous."

"You are just too cute. Do you know how cute you are? Why I could just eat you right up." She tweaked my cheek, and left after gushing that if there was anything we needed to just ask.

"Deke know how cute you are, Tee-Bee."

That was the first of the "cutie-pie, sweetie-face" comments I had to endure from my friends over the course of the next several minutes.

"Dig it, Tee-Bee. Cool as cute is, that little fox be sniffin' around your den."

"Hey, listen up here. We got no time for this nonsense. We leave heckling Tee-Bee to the audience." Mr. Bop's words led me to believe he was rescuing me from further ribbing, until he added, "Though his face do possess more than its fair share of cute."

After the band was satisfied that they had made me blush as much as humanly possible, we discussed the few minor glitches that had occurred during our inaugural rehearsal/performance. Some chords had been missed, Pappy's microphone had stopped working, and I had neglected to prepare any beginning and ending cues for the songs. These problems were corrected before the second set.

"The Crazy Loco Coconuts" began filing into the backstage room, and after exchanging greetings we left in order to give them more space. We weren't due back for an hour, so Deke and Pappy went to their rooms, Sticks went off to throw some dice, and Mr. Bop and I sat down at a table in the now nearly empty club to listen to The Coconut Lounge's premier house band.

"Where'd everybody go?" I asked Sally.

"Back to gamble, I reckon. You want a drink or something?" The way she raised her eyebrows and softened her eyes when she said "something" caused a glimmer of Felicia/Carol to cross my mind.

Both Mr. Bop and I declined her offer since we still had two shows to perform. Before she moved on to another customer she smiled at Mr. Bop, and told him to ask me if I knew how cute I was. He attempted to repeat the question, but started laughing instead.

"That girl like a cat, and you the canary."

After promising not to let her clip my wings, I couldn't resist playfully adding, "So, how cute am I?"

The Crazy Loco Coconuts came on stage, and played songs that were currently popular hits by bands from England. "This next song is a big hit by The Beatles," the lead singer would say in a fake British accent, and the band would launch into another catchy tune. They played some songs by The Zombies, Herman's Hermits, and The Dave Clark Five, all of which revolved around one of two themes: "I love you and you love me" or "I love you even if you don't want to be with me anymore." The music was a little repetitious with no song containing more than four chords, but the group played them very professionally, and I thought they deserved a larger audience.

During their final number, a ten-minute medley of 50's rock and roll, Mr. Bop excused himself, saying he would meet me backstage. I stayed until the band had finished, and applauded their performance as they left the stage in the hands of the next emcee, a comedian named Max X. Mr. Ex proceeded to snarl a series of four-letter words disguised as jokes, and as I got up to leave he directed his humor at me.

"Hey, you in the tuxedo! Sit your lily-white dressed-up ass back down in that chair until I say you can go!"

I had seen Don Rickles perform a sanitized version of confrontational humor on television, so I played along by innocently pointing at myself. The audience responded with laughter.

"Yes, I mean you, penguin boy! Just where the fuck do you think you're going?"

I wanted to answer, but all I could think of was something my father used to say about the use of swear words to justify poor language skills. I sensed that Mr. Ex wouldn't be interested in this axiom, so I said nothing.

"Are you just going to stand there with your thumb up your ass, or what?" His persistence demanded an answer.

"I guess I'll take the 'or what' portion of your question, sir."

Mr. Ex accepted the chuckles from those in attendance as proof he was funny, and told me to "just get the fuck out."

I acknowledged his instruction with a nod of my head, and I left to join my band backstage. Mr. Bop, Pappy, and Deke were already there, and while we waited for the vitriolic comedian to finish, Sticks rushed in and told us he had seen "The Suit" in the casino. On the surface seeing Jimmy didn't seem to be exciting news to anyone but Sticks.

"Dig it. He got me a line of credit for a cool grand. I don't have to grease the joint in advance, you dig?"

I supposed that what he had received was cool, and did not allow the soft warning of trumpets playing in a far corner of my mind to deter me from quickly teaching everyone the new intro cues to the songs.

The second set went smoothly with the only exception being Sticks accidentally knocking over his appropriately named crash cymbal in the middle of "MY LONG ISLAND COMA GIRL." The third set was perfect, and we all felt comfortable with the new arrangements and our new surroundings. We had quickly settled in for the long haul.

Night after night we performed in the same professional fashion, and show after show The Coconut Lounge was crowded with patrons. As we entered our second month, an extra belly dancer and bartender were added to the staff from eight forty-five until two in the morning every day except Mondays. Jimmy, who hadn't been an audience regular, was now holding court at a front table during every show. He chomped on big cigars, drank champagne, and grabbed the waitresses in places that I had been raised to consider private.

Sally grew more flirtatious with each passing week. "Do you know how cute you are yet?" was her stock question. She would whisper it every time she brushed past me, and write it in notes she left on the piano. In what I imagined was an attempt to break my concentration, she would mouth it from across the lounge. Though I only answered her with a smile or an occasional nod, I knew how cute she thought I was.

I heard from her friend, Beth, that Sally wanted to have sex with me because she had a thing for singers. "It doesn't matter to her if the guy's a good singer or not."

Sally's "thing" was thinking singers were really cool. Considering the number of men who sang in Las Vegas, she had quite a list of targets, but as Beth pointed out, being in the same room made me more convenient.

"She don't even care if the guy's married, but she won't do comedians." I was glad to hear Beth say that Sally had some standards. "I don't want to see you gettin' yourself all hurt, so I'm just warnin' you, sex don't mean a thing to her. She's gonna get you in bed, then dump you the next day. Mark my words."

Her words were duly marked, but since I never had a physical desire toward Sally, the warning was unnecessary. I just wanted to maintain a good working relationship. Even though Sally never got the opportunity to dump me, I didn't mind that she continued to strive for the incentive to do so.

From my experiences with Felicia/Carol, Sally, and Beth I was able to complete "YOU DO IT FOR MONEY." It was not about them in particular, but they were the inspiration. The band thought it made a good addition to the show, and it's up-tempo, rock and roll arrangement made it a real crowd pleaser.

> "Take another diamond.
> Steal another dollar.
> You're never through.
> Roses and proposals are gathered by the dozen,
> so what's another heart or two?
> Hearts don't mean a thing to you.
> All of your friends are waiting in line
> with some change in their pockets
> to exchange for your time.
> You stand there, and smile
> while you say what you please
> to the ones that you'll trade-in
> for the ones that you'll leave.
> And I laugh, 'cause I think it's funny.
> You might fool them, but not me, honey.
> Everybody likes to think you do it for love.
> You do it for money."

One night, after two months of standing room only crowds, Jimmy came backstage, and unfolded a newspaper article that proclaimed, "*Go see Tuxedo Bob at The Tropics. You'll discover a unique blend of humor and musicianship rarely found within the city's limits.*"

"Pretty good, huh? You're the toast of the town, kid!" was Jimmy's take, and he started treating me as if I was his best friend.

Jimmy liked to have me come to his table after each set so he could pat me on the back, and introduce me to his cronies. The band didn't mind that I had been singled out for attention, and often kidded me by asking, "When you gonna get a suit like The Suit?" or "Does The Suit know how cute you are?" I took their jokes in stride, but I heard soft trumpets every time Sticks said, "I dig The Suit, man. He's super cool."

Jimmy's table was always the same. His male friends were dressed by the same Italian tailor, and had identical penchants for big cigars, bread and cheese, and woman fondling. Their female companions were always encased in tight dresses that overly accentuated their breasts, and made sitting down a difficult maneuver. The women's taste leaned toward iced bowls of caviar, and bottles of imported champagne, but these expensive perks rarely erased the looks of boredom on their faces.

"Hey! Get over here, ya bum!" was how Jimmy called someone to his table. A slap on the back always followed his question, "So, what's happening?" and the response he got in return was either a relaxed "Nothin' much" or an enigmatic "Forget about it."

"This here is Mr. Napoli's boy." That had become my moniker at Jimmy's table, and at times it preceded my name by as much as ten minutes.

Among Jimmy's friends and associates to whom I was introduced were Charlie The Horse, Jerry The Lip, Tony The Arm, Louie The Hammer and Sal The Enforcer. I didn't understand all their nicknames, but I was aware being Mr. Napoli's boy carried a great deal of importance. One night someone I recognized was invited to the table.

"Hey, Tuxedo Bob. You remember Frankie The Weasel? From New York?"

"Yes, we've met." I was cordial, and gave no hint of our previous altercation. "How are things at Pressman's, sir?"

He said, "Fine," but his abrupt tone indicated that he had not traveled across the country to converse with me. He pulled Jimmy aside for a private discussion, and left as quickly as he had arrived. Jimmy came back to the table with a worried look on his face. I was curious what had been said to make him so nervous, but I remembered that Frankie The Weasel had the same effect on me. When Jimmy asked me to accompany him to his private office, I figured some important message had been delivered concerning my performances.

Jimmy paced around the well-appointed room.

"Don't get me wrong. I'm happy you're a success. You're doin' better than anyone expected. Really, I mean that. No one ever listened to nothin' in the lounge before, and now you come along, and, well, what can I tell ya? You're real good. And Mr. Napoli? Well, he couldn't be more pleased. He thinks you're a very talented guy, and he'd tell you himself if he were here, but he's not so I'm relayin' his message." He shrugged his shoulders a few times, and adjusted his shirt cuffs. "The way it is, is this." He paused to put a finger over his lips, and collect his thought. "You gotta not be so good. You understand what I mean?" His hands made a pleading gesture for my response.

"No, sir."

He ran his fingers through his hair, and exhaled. "Look. You've become very popular in a very short time. That's a good thing. I mean, forget about it. I got lines of people standin' outside the lounge listenin' to you 'cause they can't get inside to see you. But you wanna know what else they're doin' while they're standin' outside the lounge? They're doin' nothin'. They ain't gamblin', and if they ain't gamblin', the casino ain't makin' any money. And if the casino ain't makin' money, that is not a good thing."

"Oh." I could see that Mr. Napoli had put Jimmy in a tight spot, and desired immediate action. "Why don't you just move some of the games over by the lounge entrance?"

It seemed the simplest of solutions, and would cease any further discussion that I should perform in a fraudulent manner.

"Hey, that's perfect!" Jimmy was smiling again. "It's downright beautiful! I gotta call Mr. Napoli right now, and inform him of my potential solution to the situation here." He picked up his phone and began dialing. "You're a smart guy, Tuxedo Bob."

I left and went back to the lounge to perform to the best of my abilities. The next day two blackjack tables, a craps table, ten slot machines, and a roulette wheel were positioned outside the entrance to The Coconut Lounge for any customers who wished to gamble and listen to my music at the same time.

# mi

Two more months went by so quickly that the minimum three-year obligation no longer felt like an eternity. Going to New Orleans was still a recurring daydream, but I was excited living in what was purported to be the recreation capital of the world. I knew there was a lot I could learn from Las Vegas, so any thought of a trip to Louisiana was assigned to a back burner for the duration of my contract.

The Coconut Lounge was packed every night "Tuxedo Bob" performed. Jimmy was happy that people would sit in the portable gaming area, and listen to me sing while they lost money. I imagined this also pleased Mr. Napoli because there were no more suggestions that I lower my performance standards. The combination of "Tuxedo Bob" and gambling was working, however, I wasn't satisfied that I was doing all I could to keep my performances fresh.

So while Mr. Bop, Pappy and Deke relaxed on their Monday nights off, and Sticks hung around his favorite craps table, I went around to the other hotels to look in on their entertainment offerings. Since I knew all the games were the same, I was curious to see what the competition was doing to entice a gambler's continued patronage.

Each hotel on the strip had several small clubs adjacent to their casinos where free drinks, hors d'oeuvres, and some form of diversion were provided in an attempt to prevent their gamblers from wandering off to another establishment. Each club had similarly good-looking women in revealing outfits serving cocktails with an umbrella or fruit garnish. Food temptations ranged from pretzels and salted peanuts to chef salads and sandwich platters. One hotel had a "High Roller's Club" where I met a man who had just lost seven thousand dollars playing Blackjack. He was being consoled with a free steak dinner, and he was quite jovial as he cut into his twelve-ounce sirloin gift, remarking, "Eight hundred more of these babies, and I'll be just about even."

The entertainment offerings varied from place to place. Vince Genoa-style singers performed show tunes, rock bands played the current hits, and instrumentalists presented old standards. Dozens of comedians told jokes, magicians performed amazing sleight-of-hand tricks, and jugglers tossed and caught bowling pins or sharp axes with equal dexterity. One entire hotel was designed as a circus, complete with trapeze acts, lions, elephants, and clowns. I was surprised anyone could focus on gambling amid such three-ring excitement.

The only main room show I had the pleasure to see was The Tropics "Gay Paree Dance Extravaganza," and it was an impressive display of beauty, style and grace. Forty tall women in gorgeous clothes walked sideways without looking while holding their arms straight out from their sides. Spiked high heels and enormous headdresses made this feat all the more difficult. The centerpiece of the show's glittery stage was an enormous staircase that was put to good use by the dancers who exhibited considerable proficiency at navigation. At the end of each dance routine all the women would take posture-perfect positions on the stairs, and pose for the audience. It was quite a spectacle, and since no cameras were allowed in the main showroom, the hotel gift shop sold censored picture postcards of these finales.

Every one of the dance numbers had unique and resplendent costuming. In one number the women wore fabulous dresses of gold that shimmered in the stage lights. In another they were adorned with huge feather fans strapped to their backs to give the appearance of proudly strutting peacocks. Delicate white lace and dense fog was the romantic motif in the only slow segment of the show. The rousing cancan encore was a kick-line of multi-layered ruffled skirts held up high to expose every inch of the dancers' long legs along with a colorful assortment of underwear.

The audience favorite was Cleopatra's Dream. It used the dense fog machine, and included five men wearing bright blue and red tuxedos which looked as if they had come straight off the hangers in Mr. Silverman's closet. The female dancer playing Cleopatra walked onto the stage wearing nothing but a gold crown and a large rubber snake that had been glued to the places most necessary to insure a modicum of propriety. The men pirouetted onto the stage, and took turns picking her up and spinning her around. It was fast paced, foggy, and featured a strobe light blinking rapidly to present an illusion of slow motion. The number ended with a flourish when the men surrounded her, and fell to their knees as if they were praising a goddess. I was amazed that no one ever bumped into the three large pyramids which were part of the set, but even more astonished that whenever the men passed Cleopatra among themselves, spinning her around and turning her upside down, her crown never fell off.

The Gay Paree Dance Extravaganza, or "Girl Walk," as it was named by Sticks, played to full showroom capacity every night except Tuesdays when it was closed, and it was easy to see why it was so successful. All the women in the cast were exceptionally beautiful, and they demonstrated the pride they had of their well-proportioned bodies by occasionally exposing their perfectly shaped breasts and derrieres – much to the delight of the crowd. The show was dazzling, and even though I couldn't think of a single formal gathering where the extraordinary attire, or lack of it, might be considered appropriate I knew this was truly Las Vegas style entertainment.

Antoinette, the show's spirited choreographer, explained the nudity to me one night in The Coconut Lounge.

"It is not naughty, mon ami," she said in her thick French accent, "it is art." Her tongue snapped the "t" in art like a lash from a whip. "Do you like art, Tuxedo Robert?"

I replied that I did indeed, and that I also enjoyed hearing her pronounce my name "Row-bare" with the slight gritty sound of fine sandpaper around the "row" part. She said she found me quite amusing.

The lavish production values of "Girl Walk" intrigued me. I wanted to create and perform something as grand and impressive, but I couldn't image how to make my dream a reality in the limited space I was given in the middle of a simulated watering hole. I decided that even with The Coconut Lounge's space limitations I would do all I could to improve my show.

It was obvious that costuming was an important Las Vegas element that I had never considered. Everyone in the band had always worn white shirts and thin ties accented with their own particular style; Mr. Bop's navy or brown suit, Sticks' black vest, Pappy's blue jeans and cream colored blazer, and Deke's weather-beaten pork pie hat. I decided to take the band outfit shopping to give our shows more of a visual impact.

"We off to find some pizzazz, my man," Sticks declared to the security guard as we left via our employer sanctioned egress.

We spent the next few hours in a clothing store called "The Glamour Palace" which I had picked from the yellow pages because its ad stated it catered to the special needs of the Las Vegas performer. Mr. Bop looked elegant in his choice of a three-piece navy blue suit with silver pinstripes. Sticks thought some brightly colored sequined vests would look especially hot under the stage lights. Pappy chose an all black silk ensemble, and he laughed when I suggested he add a white tie, and join Mr. Napoli's team. Deke spent an hour trying to find something that would go with his prized lucky hat. I was surprised when he eventually picked a beige trench coat, but he said he wanted one because it made him feel like his favorite character in the movie *CASABLANCA*. Since my only stipulation had been that the clothes be comfortable to perform in, I eagerly paid for three of each of their chosen costumes with the exception of Sticks who got six different vests.

Alterations would take several hours, but the accommodating sales woman assured us that all the clothes would be delivered to the hotel well ahead of showtime. As we thanked her and left, Sticks remarked that she should, "Come dig us tonight. We gonna look as cool as we groove."

Upon returning to my room I was startled by the presence of a man, dressed in the style of a Mr. Napoli associate, sitting on my bed. There was no sign of forced entry so I assumed there was a mix up with his lodging assignment.

"Hello. I'm Tuxedo Bob. I think there's been a mistake."

"I know who you are, and this ain't no mistake," he said. "I'm here to tell you that you got a slight problem."

It was clearer now. Jimmy had obviously sent this man to inform me of some issue involving the lounge that I needed to be aware of prior to the evening's performances. I invited him to continue.

"You got a guy name of Sticks workin' for you?"

"Yes. Is there something wrong in the area by the drum set?"

"I guess you could put it that way." His reply was stated with a slight smirk. "Your guy could end up with his thumbs broke if he ain't careful."

It was a potentially serious situation, and I was impressed that the hotel cared enough about the safety of its employees to personally deliver the information.

"I thank you for letting me know. I'll certainly tell Sticks to be careful, but may I ask what's being done to prevent him from breaking his thumbs?"

He looked puzzled by my question.

"What's being done?" he asked, repeating part of what I had said to make certain he had heard correctly.

"Is there any maintenance taking place which will solve the problem?" I wondered if I might be inquiring into an area that was none of my business, but it didn't hurt to ask.

"Jimmy only sent me to you as a courtesy. What happens now is up to this Sticks guy. Maybe you oughta talk to him."

I told him I certainly would, and thanked him again for passing along the information. He left before I realized I had no idea what the dangerous situation was, but I went to Sticks' room to relate what I had heard. Sticks was troubled by the news, and when I said I was sure the hotel would take care of the situation he responded that I didn't know what I was talking about. He was correct.

"I'm down eleven grand, my man." He stared at the floor, embarrassed to look at me. "I got on the losin' side of a streak, you dig? Credit line got heavy."

"And so you owe the hotel eleven thousand dollars?"

"No."

"You owe Jimmy eleven thousand dollars?" The sound of my voice indicated that I had a hard time believing that Jimmy had personally loaned him the money, but it was my only other choice.

"He just slid me the credit, but my scene ain't yours, you dig?"

"I'm your friend, Sticks. Whatever hole you've dug, we're digging it together."

I cashed a check for eleven thousand dollars, and gave the funds to Jimmy after obtaining his promise that Sticks' line of credit would forever be zero. Having paid Sticks' debt to avoid the breakage of any appendages, I felt compelled to ask Jimmy what kind of job mixed banking with bodily injury. He shrugged his shoulders, and said he didn't think there was any harm in telling me.

"I'm what's called a wise guy." As he explained this terminology further I learned he was not referring to his ample knowledge of Las Vegas.

He worked as part of a family under the watchful eye of a leader whose name was Don. Mr. Napoli worked directly for Don, and Jimmy reported to Mr. Napoli. The variety of oddly nicknamed gentlemen I had met, who reported to Jimmy, were also wise guys, but were called soldiers.

This made Jimmy the head wise guy, or as he put it, "If this was the army, which it is not, but if it was, I guess you could say I would be like a lieutenant." He laughed when he said some people called his group the mob. "You ever heard of the mob, Tuxedo Bob?"

"Only on television, but they're usually referred to as criminals."

He dismissed my response with an emphatic, "Hey, we ain't all crooks!" adding, "You should not believe hardly nothin' you see on TV. And that goes for the paper too. By the way, you should not take the event concerning your drum guy in any way personal. It's just business."

The nightly shenanigans at Jimmy's table began to make sense. It was a club where macho manners and bravado were important requirements for membership. Nicknames were given to identify a particular habit or physical characteristic. For example; "The Lip" was always talking, "The Squeeze" had a propensity for grabbing any woman's behind, "The Arm" and "The Tank" were very muscular gentleman, and "The Weasel" had thin, pointy facial features with beady eyes. Mr. Napoli's nickname was "The Boss," and in keeping with the format everyone called Don, "The Don."

Four hours after my monetary reminder that Manhattan wasn't the only expensive city in the country, I started the nine o'clock show by surprising the band with a new composition. I played the chords through a verse and the bridge to familiarize them with the structure, and when each man indicated he was able to follow along, I started singing.

> "If you're broke and you need money,
> I can loan you some of mine.
> You pay me in installments.
> Every Saturday is fine.
> Try not to miss a payment,
> or I'll have to break your thumbs.
> (It's just my job)
> I'm in the mob.
>
> My friends pretend they like me,
> though they think that I'm a jerk.
> I don't like them either, but I enjoy my work.
> I make a lot of money to hang around dem bums,
> but it's my job; I'm in the mob.
>
> This job requires no thinking,
> and the bonus I derive from not using my brain
> is I get to stay alive.
> I have to keep my mouth shut,
> or instead of shiny suits,
> I'll be fitted with a brand new pair
> of stylish cement boots.
>
> My clothing's silk Italian,
> and my Cuban cigar's big.
> I guzzle gin like water,
> and I eat just like a pig.
> I'm what you'd call a wise guy,
> but I like my women dumb.
> I love this job!
> I'm in the mob.

It was all in fun, and the crowd responded with more than the usual amount of laughter and cheers. The band also thought the song was humorous, and I had to wait a few moments to start the next number because they were having a difficult time maintaining a professional demeanor. The song list had grown to eight, and this newest entry allowed for more variance between each six-song set.

Jimmy, who the band now referred to amongst themselves as "Em-Gee" for Mob Guy, came up to me at the end of the show, and said he hadn't fully appreciated most of the words in my new song. I explained that it was meant to be funny, and that I hadn't intended it as a personal affront to either him or his soldiers.

"Putting how funny you are to one side for just a second, I would prefer you to not sing it anymore." Jimmy was most passionate in his request.

I apologized to him for any offense he had taken, and also made amends with everyone at his table. It was the proper thing to do, and my apologies were accepted. I was aware that everyone in the world was not going to think everything I wrote was funny, but I didn't intend for anyone to take my songs personally. However, "MOB SONG" had been my first composition with the unmistakable theme of "you in particular," and I figured it was best to try to stick with a "you in general" point of view in the future.

I was glad Jimmy had forgiven my impropriety, because I was soon working on a plan, inspired by Antoinette, which required his full cooperation. Whether or not I was Mr. Napoli's boy, I needed Jimmy as my ally, not my enemy, so "MOB SONG" was never performed in Las Vegas again.

## fa

Nicknames were as prevalent in the theater as they were among musicians and wise guys. I learned this in my new position as Antoinette's protégé; a status that enabled me to stand backstage, free of charge during Monday night performances of "Gay Paree Extravaganza." "Patty Taps," "Pretty Boy Roy," and "Princess" were nicknames for some of the dancers, "Change The Light Mike," "Big Red," and "Jelly Beard" were technicians.

It had become rare for anyone, other than strangers, to call me Tuxedo Bob. I was Tee-Bee to the band, and to most of the hotel employees. To Antoinette I was "Mon Cher" or "Mon Ami," and to the cast and crew I was "Le Pet." Due to my habit of addressing people as Mister or Miss, this moniker was altered slightly to Mr. Le Pet. When I mentioned that Sticks had nicknamed their extravaganza "Girl Walk" they retaliated by referring to my show as "Twisted Songs." It was an honor to be included in the fun.

A protégé should never impede the progress of the stagehands as they move props into position, change scenery, adjust lighting, or operate a fog machine. Viewing the inherent chaos of the backstage environment was a privilege I did not take lightly. The professional commotion was exciting, but there was always the potential that I could be trampled by the cast of forty women and five men as they rushed onto the stage, so I made sure I was never in anyone's way.

A twenty-two-piece orchestra played from the pit area in front of the stage. The pit boss position was occupied by a baton waving conductor, and he was as much fun to watch as the rest of the show. He was always smiling, slicing the air with the tip of his baton, and moving his arms and shoulders to the subtle nuances of the score. His shiny bald head bobbed from side to side in time with the music, and his lips moved as if each instrument was speaking through him. I sensed he was a hip cat with a cool feel for the groove.

"Girl Walk" was similar to Mr. Genoa's show because it was an exercise in precision timing with no room for improvisation. The dancer's steps, like finger snaps, had to be in synch with the music. The stagehands had to make certain that props were placed in their exact locations so the dancers didn't have to look for them, much like Mr. Genoa's microphone stand and water glass. The most difficult job in the main showroom was running the spotlight. Five people had been fired from Pressman's for being unable to keep a light on Mr. Genoa at all times, but I never saw the main showroom's light focused on anything but its intended target. Since I assumed that what I saw on Monday nights was the same every night, I concluded there were no slackers on the payroll.

Modesty had no place in the fast-paced world of the dancers. After the opening number there wasn't time for them to go back to their dressing rooms, so most of them made their quick costume changes in the backstage area where I stood. I had never seen so many naked women in one place, and since I had never fantasized about finding myself in such a situation it was shocking. At first I averted my eyes in an attempt to protect their privacy, but Antoinette pointed out that the women were proud of their bodies, and I could "look at them, but with respect." So I watched them work, and respected their dedication to the rigors of show business.

"Le Pet" blushed easily, and the dancers would inundate me with all sorts of references about sex and body parts. Miss Charlene, from Idaho, informed me that her perfectly round breasts were real, and I should touch them if I didn't believe her. Miss Angela, from Florida, asked me to come to her room so she could teach me how to delicately shave the bikini line she was always willing to display. Miss Sandy, from Tennessee, said I should take off my tuxedo because this would show her what kind of man I was. Her friend, Miss Bee-Jay, from Michigan, interjected that if I took off my tuxedo she would take the opportunity to show me what kind of woman she was. Politely declining all of their offers did not discourage their efforts. Even two of the male dancers, Messrs. Juan and Louis, joined in the fun by asking if I saw anything I liked when they were naked.

A betting pool was established among the cast concerning which of them would have sex with me first. My wager would have been "never," but I declined to participate because I didn't think it was appropriate to sanction the use of personal privacy as gossip cuisine. They were never able to declare a winner, and I never found out if there were prizes set aside for second and third place finishers.

After learning of my non-participation in the sweepstakes, Antoinette said, "It is hard to find someone with integrity in a business where ego is more important than backbone. You, mon ami, have that integrity."

I loved listening to her talk. "Is" sounded like ease, the letter combination "th" was pronounced "zee," and each part of every syllable was given a meticulous going-over as they flowed from her mouth. Her finely lined face divulged the intense beauty of her younger days. All the curves were still in place, but her body had the grace and poise of a mature woman. The no-bra look would not be in vogue for a few years, and she was a pioneer.

"I am sixty-one," she purred. "Men still send me flowers to tempt my favor. Sometimes, if the man is special enough, I am persuaded. It is not so bad, no?"

When she shared her views on life I was reminded of my father. Her definition of show business - "A fantasy factory that uses a performer's soul to feed the audience's desires." On what it takes to be a great director - "The ability to tell someone they have performed in a horrible fashion, and it is taken as a compliment." Love - "It is the best of all possible things, and makes all things possible."

She talked to me about how she had struggled for years to realize her childhood dream of becoming a prima ballerina.

"I gave everything I had in me to give. I performed in ballet companies all over Europe and the United States. I tried a very long time to be the one in the spotlight, but it was not to be. I was good, but I was not good enough. C'est la vie, such is life. I believe you Americans would say, 'screw it', but the meaning is the same. So I said, 'screw it', and became a successful choreographer instead of a big star."

She asked me if I wanted to be a big star, and I said, "I'm not sure. I think stardom has less to do with talent than it does with being in the right place at the right time."

"It is never the wrong time, mon ami, and the right place can be wherever you are. Unfortunately, you possess a gentle heart that beats in a world of diminished civility. You are a lamb among the lions, but if you decide to say screw it, and you want to be a big star, you must design a bigger show on a bigger stage." She giggled like a young schoolgirl, and performed a perfect pirouette. "And, of course, you will have me to direct and choreograph your creation into a work of art." She ended her sentence with a graceful bow.

I applauded her brief dance, and accepted her offer. If I chose a path to stardom, I wanted her as my guide. But stardom had never been a specific goal of mine. "Stars are larger than life," I reasoned. "I don't think my name belongs in the same galaxy as Mr. Sinatra or Miss Garland."

"And that thought, my pet, is the only thing that keeps you out of the sky."

Night after night I would lie awake while Antoinette's words danced in my brain among the woodwinds and violins, and the flashing neon sign with my name in lights. Antoinette believed I could do anything I set my mind to, and I had to admit that stardom was not outside the realm of possibility. Since an essential element of stardom was positive audience response I figured I was already a minor star, but that train of thought made me feel self-indulgent, so I dismissed it. Whether or not I was a star of any magnitude was not the issue. Finding happiness in what I was doing was all that mattered, and I was happy. If my path led to stardom I would follow, but being happy on that road had to remain at the heart of my ambitions.

The seed Antoinette had sown was germinating. If I wanted a bigger show on a bigger stage, how big did I want it to be, and how could I set any plans into motion? The show would have to be large enough to fill a stage equal in size to the one in the main showroom. Me, a piano, the band, and what else? I began to conceive an idea of a musical without a plot, which moved seamlessly from one song to the next before ending with dozens of dancers in the grandest of grand finales. I let my imagination run full throttle, sparing no expense on lavish costumes and flashy sets, and allowed the orchestra in my head to play with unrestrained inventiveness.

Turning my fantasy into reality would take a great deal of time and hard work, so I sought Antoinette's advice.

"I think you are very smart, mon ami," she said upon hearing my idea. "You have created brilliance in your head, yes? So now, I will help bring it to life, but prepare yourself for a failure."

"Why?" I asked. "I don't want to put on a show that will fail."

"Of course you don't. Neither do I, but failure is a part of this business." Her eyes looked at me intensely, then softened as she smiled. "I do not expect you to fail, mon cher, but try to remember that success is so much sweeter when it is not anticipated."

I thought about the day I met Mr. Silverman, and how excited I had been to receive my first professional assignment. I had no idea I would be successful, only that I would give my best effort. I enjoyed what I did, and that was sufficient. It was all I should continue to expect as I ventured onward.

With Antoinette's support and assistance in place I could move on to the next order of business, switching the band's night off from Monday to

Tuesday. This was an essential ingredient in the plan, and though I would miss hanging out backstage at "Girl Walk" on Mondays, changing my night off would coincide with Antoinette's schedule. I sought Jimmy's permission.

"Hey, whatever makes you happy," was his initial response to my request. "Monday, Tuesday? What's the difference?"

I was pleased that he was so amenable, but when I told him why it made a difference, his response fell short of whatever made me happy.

"Are you kidding? You want to rent the big room, and put on a show? That's crazy! You already got a show."

I assured him I was serious, and that I was hoping I could make some kind of agreement with the hotel to rent the main showroom since no one used it on Tuesdays.

"Do you know what kind of dough it takes to run the main room?" He pointed his index finger at me like a math teacher picking the most bewildered student to solve a difficult equation.

I answered in the simplest terminology, "No."

"Well, it takes a lot!" was his educated guess. "But that's not really the point on the count o' I don't think the hotel uses it as a rental property. I can't say for sure because it's not up to me. You're gonna have to go talk to Jerry about it, but I can tell you right now what he's gonna say. He's gonna say you been spendin' too much time in the sun."

I had met Mr. Jerry Owenthal, the Vice President in charge of hotel operations, one night in The Coconut Lounge. He had been very enthusiastic about my performance, and gracious with his compliments.

"You're joking, right?" Mr. Owenthal seemed pleasantly amused by my request, and though he expressed his wariness by saying my lounge show was too small for the expansive stage of the main room, he didn't say no.

I told him I was planning an evening of entertainment that would be appropriate to both the room's size and its reputation. As he nodded his head to indicate he was listening to what I had to say, it occurred to me that it was possible no one had ever asked to rent the room before. Maybe there were no guidelines to deal with such a request.

The door of negotiation cracked open as he leaned back in his chair, and folding his hands behind his head said, "Okay. Let's say, just for the sake of argument, that you've got the perfect show for the big room. Do you have any idea how much it costs just to staff it? I bet I pay more in one day for electricity, water, linen, flowers, and union fees for that room than you make in a month."

There was no refusal of permission included in his breakdown of the expenses, so I said I was prepared to pay all necessary costs. This may not have been a proper negotiating technique, but I thought it was a good place to start, and that he would accept it as a fair arrangement.

"Don't take this personally, but don't you think you can find a cheaper way to get your rocks off?"

I wasn't sure what he meant, but he still hadn't said no. I decided to mimic his earlier approach. "Just for the sake of argument, how much does it cost to operate the room for one night of the Gay Paree Extravaganza?"

Neither of us flinched when he said, "Fifteen thousand dollars for the dinner show, and another ten thousand for the late show."

I quickly multiplied two full houses times ten dollars per person, while he said something about "not including start-up costs." I proceeded with my calculations, and realized the hotel made a profit of about five thousand dollars per day.

"And we take in extra revenue from liquor and souvenir sales. I run a very profitable operation," he smiled proudly.

Indeed, I thought, and continued toward my objective. "Just for the sake of argument, if I gave you twenty-five thousand dollars, and offered the hotel fifty percent of any admission receipts over and above that figure, would you consider renting the room to me?"

Mr. Owenthal shook his head. I thought he was about to refuse permission, but instead he said, "Have you given any thought to what happens if no one shows up? You're out twenty-five grand, son. Minimum." His tone became paternal. "Why do you want to take a chance on throwing your money away? What do you want to prove? You're popular in your current situation. You've got a good following, you make a decent salary, and the casino's profits are up every night, except the night you're not performing. The Tropics considers you one of the family. Why mess with success?"

I knew I was on the brink. If I could supply the correct response to why I wanted to mess with success I would certainly gain his approval. But what was the right answer? 'It would be fun' was the truth, but it sounded foolish and unprofessional when I said it in my head. 'I wanted to do something more creative than my current show' was also the truth, but he might perceive it as ungrateful and arrogant. So I said, "I'm curious."

"That's all?" Mr. Owenthal laughed. "You're curious?" His expression indicated he had expected more than my two-word response.

I bounced the negotiation back to him with a modifier. "I'm very curious." Then I took out my checkbook, and wrote a check for twenty-five thousand dollars to show him I was also very serious. As I handed it to him I asked, "Aren't you?"

He looked at the advance payment, nodded his head, and smiled. "I suppose I am, but I also think you're a little crazy."

As we shook hands to solidify our agreement, I told him he wasn't the first person to express that opinion. He asked me to give him a thirty-day advance notice, and jokingly inquired about the check's validity.

"It's as good as my word," was my response.

I spoke with the band about my intentions, and what I had done to accomplish my goal. I said I would pay them five hundred dollars each to participate in the show, and their responses were pretty much what I expected. The exclamation "You must be crazy!" was repeated several times, but not as often as "We're with you a thousand percent."

Our night off now coincided with the night there was no "Girl Walk," and I had gained permission to use the showroom for my revue. I had paid Mr. Owenthal for the use of the room, the equipment, and the showroom service staff, but I hadn't paid for a cast.

I still had to pay for stage hands, set designers, musicians, an orchestra conductor, dancers, singers and any other persons who would be required to put on my show, but those expenses wouldn't become a necessity until a show date was selected. No date could be selected for my "one-night-only" special attraction because the show was yet to be written.

I had no idea how expensive it would be to produce my own Las Vegas extravaganza, but since I had prior experience with escalating costs from the restaurant bill at New York's Il Milano de Grazie I did not think I would be taken by surprise. My father used to say, "The greatest lessons can be the most expensive." I was prepared to pay for the lesson of a lifetime.

# sol

I spent every available minute working on what the band was now calling "The Recital." Every time they said it I was reminded of a Sunday afternoon in 1954 when I played a stirring rendition of Beethoven's "OPUS 27" in Mrs. Edwina Bailey's music room. I was one of seven pupils, and we each performed in front of a gathering of nervous parents. My digits played with confidence, so I was spared the sympathetic cringes and pained smiles some of the students received from their mothers and fathers. At the time I considered it to be my crowning achievement. But I was eight, and had no idea it marked the beginning of a journey that would lead to Las Vegas where I would perform eighteen recitals per week.

I was happy with my band, and made a point to let each of them know that The Recital was an addition to what we were doing, not a replacement. They understood I had music inside me that I wanted to express, and they didn't feel slighted that I desired the instrumentation to present it. They understood that an upright bass couldn't duplicate a chorus of bassoons, a drum set didn't possess the power of a percussion section, a guitar couldn't weep like a violin, and a single saxophone couldn't sound like a brass quintet. I needed an orchestra, and my newest recital would be the event that brought the instruments in my head to life.

Whenever I wasn't performing in the lounge, I was in my room sitting at the small electric piano I had purchased to translate my thoughts into action. I had also bought a Wollensak reel-to-reel tape machine that was quite valuable for working on instrumentation ideas. I could record a melody line from the piano, and play it back while I constructed harmonies or pondered various orchestral accompaniments until I heard the right combination of instruments. Antoinette (who was now the official director and choreographer) came by every day to check on my progress, and offer suggestions.

"That one is good for dance," she said about a new melody that was lyric-less for the moment. "It has the sound of dreams, and the structure is very classical, no? I do something very nice with it for you." She also advised me not to make the show entirely humorous. "People love to consider themselves, and their own lives. It's best to give them something to chew on."

Her comments always made me think, and it was this quality that made her a great collaborator and teacher. She pushed me to write in a more serious vein by giving me assignments designed to expand my orchestral imagination. "Pretend you are a tiger, and write something for a tap dancer." "Compose a waltz from the point of view of someone under the influence of too much to drink." "You are a hawk flying over the mountains, but do not tell me what you see. Let me feel it in the music."

It didn't matter if what I wrote actually ended up in the show. Antoinette believed it was advantageous to exercise creative fantasy, even one as pro-active as mine, and I exercised for over a year and a half. I wrote, edited, arranged, and orchestrated seven days a week, while performing six nights in the lounge. It was fantastic, and exhausting. As my father used to say, "The view from the mountain top is worth the climb."

Though I continued to write during the band's first vacation period, I took a few days off with them to visit some of Nevada's tourist attractions. I was passionate about the completion of my project, but I had never condoned a schedule of all work and no play.

Lake Mead was a nice place to visit, and I enjoyed watching the boats and water skiers. One of the lake's activities was parasailing which the band agreed looked like something fun to try. A rowboat took us two hundred yards offshore to a floating platform where we listened to an instructor talk about safety. His warning about the danger of unhooking the harness while in the air seemed quite unnecessary. While I was being strapped onto a kite and fitted with a crash helmet, Mr. Bop whispered, "Don't forget to write." It dawned on me that our group activity had become my solo performance.

"Deke watch you from here," was the last discernible thing I heard before the roar of the speedboat filled my ears, and I became an airborne screamer. I remembered Antoinette had told me to make believe I was a hawk, so I braced myself for the experience that would eliminate my need to pretend. I must admit that soaring high above the water did have a birdlike appeal, but closing my eyes and screaming in fear stopped me from fully assimilating the hawk's perspective. Being up in the air with nothing but a thin rope separating my life from certain tragedy made me think more about the reasons behind the name of my headgear.

The ride lasted for a very long two minutes before I was safely deposited back onto the platform. I was impressed by the precision, and while I couldn't deny it had been exciting, fear had put a lump in my throat that I didn't think would be good for singing. I decided this particular form of entertainment was best left to the creatures God had seen fit to supply with wings.

Driving to and from an immense dam named after President Hoover was a much calmer excursion. It pleased the band that Antoinette joined us on this trip because they had come to enjoy her company and accent as much as I did, and they considered her a friend. She had brought an instamatic camera along, and I asked her to take some pictures of the band.

She said it was a shameful thing that we had never had our picture taken as a group. "A picture is a memory one can cherish when friends are no longer together."

She took snapshots of us during our tour of the dam, and more when we returned to The Tropics where we found a surprise Jimmy had prepared for us.

Sticks was the first to see the black letters that had been added to the hotel's advertisement. "Dig it! We on the neon menu!"

The lower portion of the marquee read, "Tuxedo Bob Appearing Nightly in The Coconut Lounge." We quickly piled out of The Big Limo For Real, and gathered under the sign while Antoinette snapped away. I was thinking how much I would have liked to send one of these pictures to my parents, but that thought did not keep me from blurting out the obvious, "Wow! My name's in lights!"

Mr. Bop made a casual remark, wondering if the wording implied we no longer had a night off, and though the comment made everyone laugh, I asked Jimmy about it before our first show that evening.

"Relax. If I had put 'with the exception o' Tuesdays' up there I'd be cuttin' my nose off in spite o' my face, and I would not be "The Nose" no more," he laughed. "Anyway, you're good for business. Profits are higher every night you play, so if people think you're here all the time, what's the harm?"

I believed a little white lie was a lie nonetheless, and it made me uncomfortable. I expressed my concern that people might be upset upon discovering the chicanery, and Jimmy argued that the sign just slightly bent the truth.

"You perform nightly, just not every night." Then he ended the discussion by adding a clincher to his justification. "It ain't your sign. Forget about it."

Besides the sign, Jimmy provided another unique distraction during the time I spent writing my recital. On the morning of the second anniversary of President Kennedy's assassination he said, "I'm changin' your day off this week from tonight to tomorrow on the count o' you're goin' to the fight with me. You ever seen a fight?"

I had not seen one since the second grade when Andy Moore split Mickey Anderson's lip. The nasty cut required eight stitches, which Mickey proudly displayed to anyone interested in viewing swollen tissue, black thread, and dried blood. Andy had won the fight, but received a severe spanking from his father for resorting to violence after Mickey had called him a sissy. Mentioning this incident to Jimmy resulted in my being informed that I had not witnessed a real fight.

I accompanied him to a competitor's hotel to see a boxing match between former world heavyweight champion, Floyd Patterson, and the new champion, Cassius Clay. Both men were quite popular according to the cheers of support they received from the crowd when they were introduced, and after they had spent a few moments in the center of the ring conferring with the referee, the "real fight" commenced.

The contest lasted twelve rounds, each one starting with a pretty woman in a bathing suit walking around the ring carrying a sign displaying the round number. The crowd responded to her every move by whistling, and shouting that she should "take it off." Jimmy heartily pointed out that there were not many in attendance who were interested in her sign; they were interested in her "tits and ass." I suggested that those individuals might be happier attending the Gay Paree Extravaganza where the music was better, and their fun would not be interrupted by two men pummeling each other.

After the bathing beauty had finished her job a bell would ring, the fighters would fight for a few minutes, and then the bell would ring again to signal the end of the round. Both men sweated profusely, and confidently displayed a unique ability to pretend that there were no ill effects to being repeatedly hit in the face and stomach.

Mr. Clay bounced around a lot as if he had to go to the bathroom, but he never asked to be excused so he could relieve himself. I was surprised it didn't affect his concentration, but when I mentioned this to Jimmy, he said it was "Clay's style." After hearing his explanation, I rather enjoyed watching Mr. Clay dance around. Here was a warrior who added the threat of urination to his arsenal of weapons. This danger, along with several well-directed jabs to the jaw, was too much for Mr. Patterson to overcome, and Mr. Clay knocked him unconscious in the twelfth round. I was glad it was over, so my muscles could relax.

"Pretty great fight, huh? This kid Clay's gonna be great. You mark my words."

Jimmy was pleased with the outcome, as he had bet ten thousand dollars of Mr. Napoli's money on Mr. Clay being the victor. I failed to see the sport in a contest where a prize was awarded to someone who beat another person senseless, and I wondered if the fight had taken place because one fighter had called the other a sissy.

I returned to my room with a brass quintet playing a repetitive figure in my head. I liked its boldly defiant sound, so I sat down at the piano, and accompanied it with chords. The words "He's a bad man" emerged in conjunction with a melody line, and a new song was born. "BAD MAN" had nothing to do with the Patterson/Clay fight, nor was it musician jargon where "bad" meant "good." It was just a song about a man with less than honorable intentions, and it was a benchmark; the first composition I had written that wasn't intentionally or unintentionally humorous. I wasn't sure if it was any good, but Antoinette loved it when I played it for her the next day.

"You wrote about a character. That is perfect." Her blue eyes sparkled with youthful exuberance whenever she was excited. "I will choreograph a dance of modern jazz that you will like." She could tell I was pleased by her response, but she was not one to allow me to rest on my laurels. "Now you must write another new song, but this time think about the whole stage.

Place yourself in the audience instead of at the piano. Decide what emotion you want the people to experience before you start the composition."

Her direction propelled me into territory I had never considered. I started going to the main showroom early every morning to stare at the empty stage. This new perspective gave me the opportunity to create a larger mental image of what I wanted to accomplish. I pictured an on-stage orchestra as the backdrop for a multitude of dancers, tigers, magicians, elephants, ventriloquists, sailboats, and jugglers. I resisted the temptation to edit my thoughts, and gave myself permission to imagine. I was a painter, and the massive stage was my canvas.

One afternoon in late December I received a letter from Sylvia. She had become Mrs. Charlie Derbin, and was very happy with her life and studies, but she was sad to inform me that Ernie Santos had been killed by a sniper's bullet while on patrol near a demilitarized zone. My heart was heavy as I set her letter on the piano and cried. Earlier that day Jimmy had told me I didn't have to worry about the draft because Mr. Napoli had called in a favor owed to him by a Pentagon official. I was classified 4-F, and this spared me the experience of being sent overseas to be shot at by strangers. It was too late for my friend Ernie to benefit from my connections.

That night I dedicated the nine o'clock show to Ernie's memory, and to all the loved ones who had been lost in the Vietnam conflict. When I asked the audience for a moment of silence, the lounge became eerily still, then a strange and wonderful thing happened. The people closest to the palm tree entryway asked a few of the gamblers outside to be quiet, and to pass the request along. I had only intended for the lounge audience to be involved in my memorial, but a sudden wave of shushing noises skipped across the casino like a stone on a pond, and soon there was barely a sound. For thirty-seven seconds, no one lost money at The Tropics. It was a nice tribute.

On January 24, 1967, Antoinette and I picked the sixteen songs that would comprise The Recital. The eight songs that were in the lounge act would be performed with new arrangements, along with eight more numbers chosen from the twenty I had written during the last fourteen months. The new songs that made the final cut included a serious symphonic piece I had written after hearing of Ernie's death, a dreamy, classical melody written for ballet, and a large cast production number for the grand finale.

Antoinette made rough sketches of what the stage would look like during each song, placing emphasis on the lighting and dramatic effects. "Your soul will be on display, my pet," she said. "I will do it justice."

I had been paying Antoinette the token sum of one hundred dollars per month for her collaboration and guidance. Once we agreed on the entire concept, and Mr. Owenthal confirmed our request to reserve the main showroom for Tuesday, May 30, her fee as director/choreographer was due. While still maintaining her "Gay Paree" duties she would also be responsible for assembling crews to design and build the sets, auditioning and hiring dancers and performers, and overseeing all the staging and lighting elements. As it turned out, her expertise was worth many times the five thousand dollar salary.

My initial responsibility was to teach the band the new numbers and arrangements. Mr. Bop suggested we get away from the hotel to allow the band to work on the new songs without distraction. So the band's second vacation was spent in the modestly appointed confines of "Grand Vista Recording Studios."

Grand Vista was located three miles outside of town, and in keeping with its name, provided an excellent view of the city's water treatment center. The plant's machinery added a constant droning sound to the acoustics of our rehearsal room, which might have been annoying, but I discovered that the sustained tone, a D four octaves below middle C, was the perfect beginning for the second movement of my "SYMPHONY NO. 1 (THINK) in G Major" which would premiere at The Recital.

I started the first rehearsal by telling everyone that the extended solos they had become accustomed to playing in the lounge act had been cut from The Recital, but that there would be plenty of opportunity for each of them to show off their talents. I had prepared sheet music for each band member, and as I handed out the charts I said, "We'll learn the instrumentals first."

Deke's eyes were cast down at the floor as I approached him. "Deke don't read a note of music."

"I know, but you read chord symbols, so that's what I put on your sheets, and on Sticks'."

He smiled, "Deke thanks you for the consideration."

I sat down at the piano, and began playing the slowest of the three numbers; an orchestral piece called "MOONLIGHT." While they listened, and looked over their individual charts, I explained how Antoinette was planning to use a single ballerina dancing in a city street setting, unnoticed by the bustling crowd. When I got to the second verse Pappy began playing the saxophone melody, Mr. Bop thumbed his bass, and Sticks held down the smooth tempo. Deke smiled as he played guitar licks that complemented the chords. He said the song reminded him of a New Orleans sunrise.

The second instrumental was a Dixieland number called "BLESSED VICTORY," and there was a bit of laughter from the band when I said it had been named after a coffin. I told them it was part of a three-song "Bourbon Street" segment that would be in the middle of the show. Pappy and Deke were quite excited about the melody which had been written as a duet for clarinet and trumpet, and Mr. Bop said he could almost taste the gumbo. Sticks suggested that I add a trombone player to the band for this section of The Recital.

"Dig it. The trombone player from that jazz quintet that goes on before us Fridays and Sundays? Man, that cat is bad! He can howl with a growl, and glide on the slide, you dig?"

I dug that it was an excellent idea, and said I would ask The Fantasy Five's leader for permission to approach his trombonist upon our return to The Tropics.

"THAT'S WHAT I CALL LOVE" was next on the agenda. The band enjoyed playing in familiar territory, and they didn't mind that their solo performances had been shortened to make room for the orchestra's brass section.

"Sticks, when "THAT'S WHAT I CALL LOVE" ends I'll play a thirty-two bar waltz. On the downbeat of the last bar you start playing this drum figure." I finger tapped a rudimentary example on the top of the piano, and he understood what I was trying to communicate, filling in the blanks with perfectly accented rhythm.

"Is this the "BAD MAN" song?" Mr. Bop asked as he looked over his third sheet of music.

"No. It's a surprise I started writing for you guys in Omaha." My response was met with quizzical looks. "You'll understand in a second."

While Sticks kept playing and digging the groove, I played an intricate bass line on the piano. "This is your basic pattern, Mr. Bop." It was all I needed to say, as he picked it up immediately. I hummed a few bars of the simple trumpet figure for Deke, and when he started playing along with Sticks and Mr. Bop I added the piano chords. The four of us continued playing for a few minutes while Pappy waited for his instructions. His curiosity finally got the best of him.

"Hey, Tee-Bee. I'm feeling a little left out here."

"Like an orphan?" I said with a mischievous smile.

When I handed him the lead sheet for the saxophone melody of "THE ORPHAN STOMP," his eyes lit up like I had just given him a double-dip chocolate ice cream cone. "You son of a gun! You wrote it!"

"I did, and I trust no one's upset that it's not a solo number." No one was, and we jammed on the melody for almost a half hour.

By the end of the week, the band had memorized all the new songs, and the fresh arrangements of the old songs. I knew this would give them an important head start once they began working as part of a forty-piece orchestra. We headed back to The Tropics relaxed, and prepared.

The vacation was over, and we would go back to our job in the lounge, not only because we were under contract to do so, but because we derived a great deal of pleasure from entertaining hundreds of people six nights a week. The lounge was the meat and potatoes part of our career. The recital was the gravy, and the gravy was still three months away.

We returned for our first show in a week, and the lounge was so far over capacity that ropes had to be put up to control the crowd. I felt honored we had been missed, but I worried that it might be difficult for the band to perform our standard set now that the new arrangements were in their heads. I should have had more faith. Once we started, the guys played the old arrangements with fervor and pride. I looked at each one of them, and noticed a sparkle in their eyes, as if they were keeping a special secret. They played the old, but they were thinking about the new, and at that moment I knew I was a member of the coolest band on the planet.

# la

By the end of April there were seventy people on my payroll. I had already spent more than fifty thousand dollars, and Antoinette estimated I would incur an additional twenty thousand in costs before the curtain went up for The Recital. After recouping the initial rental payment, my share of ticket sales would amount to twenty-seven thousand five hundred dollars, if there were two sold-out performances. There was nothing to do but laugh at the prospect of losing forty-five thousand dollars. I reminded myself it was only money, and I would be richer from the learning experience. Some days I reminded myself several times, but no matter what happened, I was certain my plan for a bigger show on a bigger stage was not a big mistake.

The sets were taking shape thanks to the expert, but expensive, craftsmen Antoinette had hired for that purpose. Already completed was a city street with buildings, decorated store windows, revolving doors, and images of taxis and buses. A maze of dark, forbidding alleyways, crisscrossed with cast-iron fire escapes was under construction for "BAD

MAN." The interior of a strip club had been built for "COMPLETELY NUDE," and a Caribbean seaside resort was being readied for "CHOCOLATE TAPIOCA PUDDING." Deke said the nightclub in the Bourbon Street set, with its gaudy paintings of sultry, lingerie-clad women, was quite authentic.

Wardrobe and props are essential elements to any big show, and in mine they had their own departments. The people who worked in these areas spent a good deal of their time, and my money, combing Las Vegas shops to find "just the right touch" for each scene. According to Antoinette, everyone and everything would be ready by May 23rd for the first full-dress rehearsal.

Antoinette spent hours teaching routines to the dancers while I accompanied on the piano. She pushed, coaxed, and inspired each performer to perfection as she sculpted my music into three-dimensional form. It was magical watching her piece together the ballet solo that accompanied "MOONLIGHT." I was mesmerized by the musical noise the ten tap dancers created during "THE ORPHAN STOMP." I felt the tension generated by the chase sequences in "BAD MAN," and the precision kick line in the grand finale, "I JUST GOT THE BUSINESS FROM THE BUSINESS," amazed me. And though the dancers who performed the strip tease were never 'completely nude' as my song's title suggested, I was sure their proud presentations would satisfy any aficionado of the art.

On the morning of May 2nd, one hour before the first orchestra rehearsal was scheduled to begin, Antoinette and I had breakfast with "Girl Walk's" conductor, Cyril Pripton. He had agreed to act in the same capacity for The Recital, and he was very enthusiastic about my music.

"It's not bad. Not bad at all," he said of the score I had given him a week earlier. "I even took the liberty of having it copied, and distributed to the members of the orchestra. I assume that's what you wanted or you would have taken care of that minor little detail yourself."

Mr. Pripton's words were laced with criticism, and I quickly apologized for neglecting to include individual copies for each musician. Antoinette, with her usual grace, forgave my fumbled etiquette.

"Oh, you are so sweet Robert, but the 'liberty' to which Cyril refers is also Cyril's job. That is what you pay him to do, no?" She smiled, then turned to Mr. Pripton and said, "Do not think your 'liberty' includes a sharp tongue."

Mr. Pripton poked at his scrambled eggs. "I'm sorry if my remark was taken with offense. I'm actually looking forward to the rehearsal."

I was too, but upon hearing the word, my stomach did a flip-flop. Other than the one in my head I had never worked with an orchestra before, and I was nervous. While they calmly ate their eggs and sausage, discussing news, weather, and stage settings, all I could think about was the musicians assembling in the showroom.

As I sat with my thoughts, Mr. Pripton related a story to Antoinette about someone who had fallen out of his favor. I heard snippets of the conversation, and gathered that some fellow named Jamie, who Mr. Pripton had taken a liking to, had run off with a young waiter named Byron. Antoinette laughed when he referred to Jamie as a "heartless bitch," and she jokingly suggested that I write a song using the line.

Antoinette's direction had thus far proven flawless, so I took her request seriously. A series of bass notes, reminiscent of a training exercise Mrs.

Bailey had once given me to strengthen my left-hand technique, bounced around my mind.

"So, it is Jamie who has you so touchy this morning, Cyril," Antoinette smiled. "You forget that love is a game. Win or lose, it is only the desire to play that is important. There will always be another Jamie." She lightly patted my hand, and purred, "Robert, you have not touched your food. I think you should take your coffee, and relax with your orchestra for a few minutes. We'll be along shortly."

Antoinette's ability to sense the thoughts and emotions of those around her was, once again, right on target. I was too distracted to do anything other than go to the showroom, so I excused myself from the table. The restaurant exit took me directly into the casino where the house activity of "give a little, take a lot" was in full swing. I was as oblivious to the gamblers as they were to me. We all had our separate missions, and mine was a few yards down a bamboo-paneled hallway.

The walls of the gold-carpeted corridor leading to the showroom were lined with glitter-framed color photographs of the "Girl Walk" dancers. Red velvet ropes were draped from brass stanchions waiting to perform their function as crowd control devices. As I stepped closer to the showroom door, the sounds of spinning wheels and clattering dice were cleansed by the smooth tones of instruments being tuned, and musicians practicing the music on the charts Mr. Pripton had delivered. I heard Sticks thumping his kick drum, Deke strumming his guitar, and Pappy's unmistakable saxophone.

I reached for the handle, took a deep breath, and pushed the door open. At that moment I knew exactly how Dorothy felt when she opened the farmhouse door and gazed upon that garden in the land of Oz. The forty-five musicians assembled on the stage before me was a wondrous alternative to Munchkins and flowers. It was the first of many moments I would cherish during The Recital rehearsals, the most remarkable of which was hearing my mental orchestra come to life.

When I walked onto the stage, and took a seat at the piano I was greeted by Sticks who shouted, "This be the crowd you got inside your head, Tee-Bee?"

"All except for the chairs," I quipped, then remembering my manners I added, "Hello everyone. I'm Tuxedo Bob."

Some of the orchestra members nodded in my direction, others smiled and said hello, but the acknowledgment was momentary, and they quickly went back to their instruments and sheet music.

I decided it would be best to conceal my nervousness by taking a few minutes to fiddle with the new "heartless bitch" left-hand figure I had heard in my head. When I matched the bass notes with some right-hand chords, an idea about a man writing a letter to a woman who had left him began to form. I had just begun to compose the hook line for the song when I heard Mr. Bop's voice.

"What's that one, Tee-Bee?"

I looked up, and saw all the musicians looking at me. "I'm sorry." I knew my face was turning redder with each word I spoke. "Was I playing too loud?"

"Not at all," a cellist said. "I just can't find the song you're playing in my sheets."

"Neither can I," said a voice from the woodwind section.

"Which one is it?" said a man holding a cornet.

"It's not written yet," I answered sheepishly. "I was just noodling." I couldn't believe my rudeness. Everyone on the stage was unified for one purpose, to play my music, and I had made them uneasy thinking they had the wrong charts.

I got up from the piano, and walked among the musicians, introducing myself to each member with a firm handshake and direct eye contact. Mr. Caufield, the trombonist on loan from "The Fantasy Five" was the only person outside the band I had met before, so these individual greetings were the appropriate step to get back on the right side of good manners. By the time I had thanked everyone for coming, Antoinette and Mr. Pripton arrived.

Antoinette immediately went backstage to resolve a scenery construction problem, and Mr. Pripton wasted no time announcing we would begin with "MOONLIGHT." After everyone had the correct chart in position on their music stands, he silently waved his baton to indicate the tempo, and then pointed in the direction of the violins. My eyes filled with tears of joy as the opening strains filled my ears. The French horns, woodwinds, and cellos began playing at measure nine, and when the full orchestra entered at measure eighteen I knew that every penny I had invested had been well spent.

Nothing interfered with my euphoria. The false starts, abrupt stops, wrong notes, and repetition all added to my magical experience. Measure after measure, song after song — every note that had been conceived from within, breathed on its own.

Mr. Pripton was in full command of the orchestra, and all eyes were on him whenever he raised his baton. "No, no!" he chided the violin section.

"The glissando in measure ten is diminuendo! Not morendo!" His use of the Italian language caused me to dust off my knowledge of correct music terminology.

Thank you, Mrs. Bailey. Though it had been years since she had been my teacher, her lessons continued to pay dividends. I knew to say "molto sotto voce" if I wanted a passage to be played much softer, "larghetto" if the tempo was a bit too slow, and it certainly sounded more professional to say "pizzicato fortissimo" rather than "tell the violin players to pluck the strings louder."

My band had to get used to Mr. Pripton's style of direction, since they were accustomed to a less bulky language. But because they knew the songs so well they usually understood Mr. Pripton's hand gestures and body language. Palm down meant softer, a shaking fist meant more energy, and tapping the baton on the podium was the signal to be quiet and pay attention.

One afternoon Mr. Pripton took an unscheduled five-minute break so he and the orchestra could stop laughing. He had cautioned Sticks not to rush a certain passage, and Sticks had replied, "I dig it, my man. I be keepin' my groove below the allegro level."

Full cast rehearsals began on Saturday the 6th. Dancers and musicians made mistakes, and sometimes the ability of Antoinette or Mr. Pripton to speak pleasantly was overpowered by their urge to yell. Feelings were hurt, some dancers cried, a few musicians scowled, but Antoinette had told me that rehearsals were the place to "iron out the wrinkles." I understood this to be the first step toward producing a "a smooth show."

I was sure everyone wanted to do a good job, and I didn't mind when someone was out of position, or a measure was dropped; these were simply accidents, and accidents happen. During the second week of May, Jimmy had an accident that produced positive results.

The Recital's date and showtime were set, and if it hadn't been for the accident, I would have made a huge mistake on the admission price. I was sitting with Jimmy and his friends between lounge shows, talking about the Memorial Day recital. Jimmy was busy boosting my confidence by slapping his buddies on the back, and telling them it was a show they didn't want to miss.

"Mr. Napoli's flyin' in for the occasion, and he's gonna buy a whole table right up front on the count o' he wants to see his boy in action."

Jimmy's comment about Mr. Napoli's intended attendance created a chorus of responses.

"Mark me down for a couple!"

"I never miss a good show."

"I gotta get me one o' doze tickets."

Though everyone at the table may have agreed to attend in order to rub elbows with The Boss, at least ten tickets would be sold after they were printed and went on sale in five days. When his cronies began placing bets concerning who would get to sit at Mr. Napoli's table, Jimmy accidentally spilled his drink on his jacket.

"Forget about it," he said as The Hammer and The Thumb jumped to his assistance. "One of you guys just get me another drink. I was gonna send this suit to the cleaners anyhow." He reached into his pocket, and as he pulled out his handkerchief, two small pieces of printed cardboard fell on the table. "Hey, Tee-Bee, you remember this?" he asked as he handed me his discovery. "These are from when you and me went to the fight."

I looked at the stubs, and saw the names of the fighters, the date, and seating location. I also saw the price. “Wow! You paid two hundred dollars apiece for these?”

“No,” he said dabbing the wet spot on his jacket. “I got ‘em for free on the count o’ my position here, but it’s what a lotta other guys paid. The closer you are to the action, the more a seat is worth. Hey, in this town when you got somethin’ people want to see, you can charge ‘em up the ying-yang, and they’ll pay it.”

I quickly excused myself from the table, and went to my room where I had a diagram of the seating arrangement for the main showroom. Jimmy’s comment reverberated in my head along with cornets and kettledrums as I stared at the fifteen hundred-seat layout. I quickly circled the thirty tables positioned closest to the stage, and labeled them “prime.” “Almost prime” was the name I gave to the first and second tier of banquettes behind the prime tables. I considered the rest of the room the “choice” seats. I had been planning to sell every ticket for ten dollars, but a front row seat was much closer to the action than one in the back, so it had to be worth more. Since I viewed The Recital as something people would want to see, and at least as worthwhile as a prizefight, I would price it accordingly.

Tickets to “The Tuxedo Bob Memorial Day Recital” were printed with gold and silver tickets priced at one hundred fifty, and seventy-five dollars respectively. The white tickets were modestly priced at twenty dollars. Two full houses would bring in more than one hundred fifty thousand dollars, and on Sunday the 14th, seventeen days till showtime, the tickets went on sale.

Antoinette had recommended I purchase some newspaper advertising to coincide with the start of ticket sales, so a full-page announcement was scheduled to run for a week in the Las Vegas daily newspaper. A similar ad also appeared in the May 14, Entertainment section of the Los Angeles Times. The entertainment editor for The Times, Jonathan Christopher, authored a short, highly complimentary review of my lounge show, which was advantageously positioned on the page facing my advertisement. His article included a statement that my upcoming Memorial Day show was "certain to be the event of the year, and not to be missed." I was very pleased by this, but puzzled how anyone could say what something was going to be before it happened.

"Do not look in the mouth of your gift horse," was Antoinette's response when I asked her about the article. "Jonathan is a gentleman from whom I have accepted flowers on several lovely occasions." It was all she needed to say to let me know he was a very special gift horse.

A number of people must have had similar feelings for Mr. Christopher because by the afternoon of the 16th, both shows were sold out with most tickets being purchased by out of town phone orders. I was stunned, but pleased by the quick response. Mr. Owenthal said The Tropics had never seen anything like it, and asked Antoinette and me to consider adding a third show.

"You've just got to add another show. People are still calling, and they're saying they'll pay anything. Think about the money you can make! I'll give you sixty percent of the third house. What do you say to that?"

I was tempted, but Antoinette said I should refuse. "Two shows was the agreement and two shows are enough." She turned to Mr. Owenthal and continued, "To add another, people might think Robert is greedy, and, Jerry, we know that is not the case."

"Greed has nothing to do with it. It's sound business. I'll give you seventy-five percent. Come on, give me one more show." Mr. Owenthal was persistent, and though his final offer of a ninety-ten split was more than generous, I went along with Antoinette's recommendation.

Two years and nine months ago I had boarded a bus, and gazed at my parents for the last time. Today, on the morning of May 30, 1967, I stood at the window of my hotel room and stared at the words "The Tuxedo Bob Memorial Day Recital - Two Shows - Sold Out" ablaze in lights on the sign outside. For this one day Mr. Bop, Sticks, Pappy, Deke, and I were the only course offered on The Tropics' neon menu. It was twelve hours to showtime.

# ti

Four months of intense preparation had come down to one final day of last minute details. At nine hours to showtime, business as usual in the casino matched the bustle of activity in the showroom. While slot machines jingled and whirred, the stage crew was checking the showroom's sound and lighting systems. As dice bounced on green felt, the set pieces and props were put in their proper places. Blackjack continued to be dealt while costumes were cleaned and pressed, and roulette wheels were spinning as the piano was tuned. The hotel's kitchen staff was busy chopping vegetables and making sauces. The dining room tables were covered with black and white linens, and topped with white roses in black vases. Extra champagne was on ice.

Certain special guests found gifts in their hotel rooms compliments of Antoinette and me. Jimmy said Mr. Napoli and The Don appreciated their fruit baskets, and were looking forward to the show. Antoinette's knowledge of Mr. Christopher's preference for sharp cheeses and fine red wine was acknowledged with a plate of English Stilton and Vermont cheddar along with a bottle of Bordeaux from my favorite chateau. Sylvia and Charlie Derbin could not attend due to her final exams, so I sent them a souvenir ticket along with two Tropics T-shirts.

It was seven hours to showtime, and I had just finished a light lunch in my room when the phone rang.

"Hey, kid! It's me, Sy!" and just in case I might confuse his rapid-fire cadence with another Sy in my life he added, "Sy Silverman! So, how ya doin', kid? By the way, thanks for the invite. You know, I've been thinking about you. I'm being sincere here. You've been on my mind, and I mean even before you sent me the ticket. How's Napoli treatin' you? You need anything? Oh, thanks for the fruit. I had one of the pears already 'cause I was hungry. A person could starve eating airline food, you know. It's the worst! And I'm not just sayin' that to hear myself talk. Who's Antoinette? Her name was on the card with the fruit. You got yourself a girl? Can she sing? She got an agent?"

After answering his questions, I told him I was glad he had come. "It means a lot to me, Mr. Silverman. Everything that's happening in my career is because of you. Thank you."

"Kid, one of these days it's gonna be you and me again. I promise you that. I got my money problems all straightened out, and I signed a mentalist. The guy can bend spoons without touching them, and he communicates with spirits. Speaking of spirits, did you hear they found Vince floatin' in the East River?"

I said I hadn't heard, and that I was sorry to hear he had died during the tour Mr. Napoli had hoped he would enjoy.

"Yeah, it's too bad, kid. Hey, do you remember what I told you about Vince bein' the best? Huh? Do you? Well, I gotta say you're better than Vince. Yeah, you heard me. I said better. May God strike me dead right here in the desert if I'm lyin'..

I assumed God was satisfied with his statement because he continued to talk for several more minutes. I invited him to come backstage after the first show, and watch the second one from the wings if he desired. He accepted, and we hung up after he advised me to "break a leg." Since I knew this was show business jargon for "good luck," I said I would do my best to break both of them.

At six o'clock I had showered and shaved for the second time, donned my tuxedo, and was walking down the bamboo hallway to the main showroom. Black and white satin streamers hung from the ceiling, and a dozen tuxedo clad mannequins stood in front of the glittery "Girl Walk" photographs. The gold carpet had been covered with a black and white rug, and the showroom doors had been painted to resemble the upper half of a tuxedo ensemble.

I walked into the showroom, and looked at the stage. In a few short hours it would be filled with my band, an orchestra, dancers, singers, scenery, and me. The dress rehearsals had gone so well that Antoinette told the cast to consider tonight's shows as "a chance for two audiences to practice the fine art of applause." All the cast and crew had worked so hard during the past few months, and I trusted the three thousand in attendance this evening would appreciate everyone's efforts.

As I went into my dressing room, I reflected on some of the things all the preparation for a bigger show had taught me. I could tell the difference between a floodlight and a pin spot, and I had found out the little plastic things that changed the color of the lights were called gels. A gofer was the person to ask for a cup of coffee, and I had learned how to apply make-up; a skill Antoinette assured me was not considered feminine in the theatrical community.

I sat down at the small vanity, and began the procedures that would make my face worthy of all the attention the lighting crew was preparing to bestow. A medium-tone pancake was applied first as the make-up base, then blue eye shadow, black eye-liner and mascara, a touch of rouge, pinkish-plum lip gloss, and a light dusting of powder. The women who do this as a daily ritual should be considered candidates for sainthood.

On the ceiling in my dressing room was a small speaker that piped in sounds from the showroom. At one hour to showtime I heard the doors open, and the quiet tinkling sounds of last minute touches were replaced with a great murmur as the audience arrived for the dinner show.

The first part of The Recital began as soon as the doors opened. Two performers, one dressed in a white jumpsuit, the other in black, stood at opposite ends of the stage, each juggling a trio of black and white balls. Jugglers in Las Vegas are a common sight, and this wasn't meant to be the most exciting of opening acts, just a non-intrusive form of entertainment for those who wanted something to look at while dining. Later, Jimmy told me he made two hundred dollars when he bet Mr. Napoli that neither juggler would drop a ball.

The hotel chef had prepared a menu which offered a choice of either poached salmon on a bed of saffron rice, hickory-smoked chicken with corncakes, or prime rib and baked potato. All dinners would be served prior to showtime, but the majority of the audience would still be eating by the time I went on stage. Since the aroma of such fine fare would certainly make every performer's mouth water, a dinner buffet of cold cuts and salads had been set up in a backstage room. This was provided free of charge by Mr. Owenthal, and I appreciated his thoughtfulness.

When the house lights dimmed at eight o'clock, the jugglers disappeared into the darkness, and a mahogany grand piano was rolled out to center stage by two stagehands dressed in long white coats. A white spotlight, using an effect of moonlight shining through a barred window, illuminated the piano. There was no deep-voiced emcee's reverberating introduction as I walked onto the stage. I was greeted with polite applause, and I nodded my head in appreciation of the audience's pre-approval as I sat down at the piano. I adjusted the height of the microphone, and thanked everyone for coming. A pin dropping to the floor at this moment would have made quite a racket. As I began to play the opening bars of "THE SANITARIUM SONG," I overheard Mr. Napoli whisper, "Hey! I know this one," from his front row table.

A curtain of sheer black and white panels served as my backdrop, and was positioned in front of the orchestra. They were unseen by the audience until the violins began to play in the second verse. At that point a gentle radiance of light, beaming from the floor behind the orchestra, cast elongated silhouettes of the musicians onto the curtain. Pappy's mournful oboe solo was the highlight of the number, and the audience responded to his talent with a warm round of applause.

"OUT OF MY MIND" began with a swirl of strings and pounding percussion. The sheer curtain behind me was raised, and the audience could now view all forty-five members of the orchestra and the back of Mr. Pripton. The background vocals were handled by four very capable young singers who stood on a platform to the right of the stage. Antoinette had suggested hiring this group, "Lulu and the Loo-Loos," after she heard them perform at a competing hotel.

Upon the completion of the second number the backdrop for the city street set was lowered to prepare the stage for "MOONLIGHT." Two stagehands dressed as policemen rolled the piano and me to the left side of the stage, while other crew members, dressed as construction workers, put the various set pieces into place. Cardboard taxis and buses were moved across the stage, and expressionless pedestrians, dressed in beige, walked from shop to shop as the violin section played the somber opening measures. When the ballerina made her entrance, dressed in pink and white, a spotlight followed her every movement. Even though this lighting was intended to keep the audience's focus on her as she danced around the stage, I noticed a number of patrons glancing in my direction throughout the song. I think they were waiting for me to start singing, and it wasn't until the song ended that they realized "MOONLIGHT" was an instrumental.

The next backdrop and three fire poles quickly descended from the ceiling. The scenery depicted the interior of a strip club, and as Sticks kicked off the song with a flurry of sharp rim shots, six exotic dancers slid down the poles and began gyrating to the beat.

> "I don't buy big diamond rings.
> I don't drive big fancy cars.
> I have no use possessing things.
> Impressing only goes so far.
> All I want is you.
> I want you completely nude."

I could tell "COMPLETELY NUDE" was a success by the number of wolf whistles from the men in the audience, and I found it humorous that any man would yell "take it off" to someone who was already doing so.

"YOU DO IT FOR MONEY" started immediately at the end of "COMPLETELY NUDE." The piano and I were pushed back to center stage by two crew members dressed in tie-dyed T-shirts and bell bottom pants, and I was quickly surrounded by two dozen dancers dressed in similar fashion. Strobe lights flickered like flash bulbs, and the strip club set was quickly removed to once again reveal the orchestra. This song was a favorite among the bassoon players because their services were rarely requested for rock and roll.

The intensity of the show was building, and I could tell from the expressions of the patrons at the prime tables that they were eating everything up. As "YOU DO IT FOR MONEY" ended with a shower of paper money confetti raining down on the audience, it dawned on me that some guests might not like having bits of paper drop into their food. But it was too late to change what may have already happened, and there was no time to worry about it.

The main curtain of the stage was brought down so the crew could put together the intricate pieces of the next set in private. While this was taking place, a group of four young men, who performed as "The Four Barbers" six afternoons a week in The Coconut Lounge, made their entrance. They were dressed in white pants, red and white-striped shirts, and blue straw hats. With their squeaky-clean good looks, the costumes gave them a wholesome all-American appearance. They stood in front of the curtain, and sang "MY LONG ISLAND COMA GIRL" a cappella. Their perfect four-part harmony marked the first occasion anyone other than myself had publicly performed one of my songs. This barbershop quartet segment went over so well with the audience that two of the barbers asked for more money shortly before the start of the second show. This angered Antoinette, but my offer of an additional four hundred dollars guaranteed that the second audience would not be deprived of their marvelous voices.

"BAD MAN" started with a brass ensemble. The curtain raised as the opening thirteen-note figure blared from the metal horns. The stage was dressed to resemble a dark alleyway with a maze of twisting fire escapes, broken window frames, and swirling fog. Twelve women dressed in bright red skin-tight outfits entered, followed by a male dancer who wore a black cape over a black leotard. The set and costumes combined for a sinister effect to match the lyrics.

"He's a bad man keepin' out of sight.
He's sneakin' up your stairs
in the middle of the night.
He's a madman lookin' for sin.
If he knocks on your door don't let him in."

The female dancers darted up and down the fire escapes, and in and out of the windows while the 'bad man' chased them. Most got away, but the ones who were caught joined him in erotic dances of passion and surrender. Louis was very believable in his role as the menacing bad man, and as the audience roared its approval when the number ended, Louis' boyfriend Juan blew kisses from the wings.

The main curtain was lowered again, leaving me alone at the piano on the left of the stage. I performed a new ballad, "I DON'T WANT TO BE IN ANYBODY'S DREAMS," with its majestic orchestral accompaniment, followed by my lounge act standard, "I JUST LOVE TO COMPLAIN." When I finished, the applause gave me enough time to go behind the curtain and join my band and the trombone player from the Fantasy Five for the Bourbon Street segment. When the curtain raised, the stage looked like one of the clubs on New Orleans' most famous walkway. We played "BLESSED VICTORY" while Mardi Gras beads were distributed by the waitresses and busboys to everyone in the audience. "THAT'S WHAT I CALL LOVE" followed in true Dixieland-jazz style, and the thundering tap dance that accompanied "THE ORPHAN STOMP" received a standing ovation.

Antoinette predicted the New Orleans sequence would be popular, and had advised me that instant gratification to an audience's requests for "more" was good show business. The band and I remained on the Bourbon Street club bandstand, but curtains were partially drawn to allow the stagehands to assemble the scenery for the song that would follow our planned encore.

I was isolated in a blue spotlight as I started singing:

> "Our song was just on the radio;
> I listened very close.
> The words were very haunting;
> I shared them with your ghost.
> This is my third martini;
> I'd like to propose a toast.
> No, instead of that
> I think I'll just compose a little note.
> If I can find the perfect words,
> some sense will come of this.
> Dear hardheaded, cold-blooded, evil,
> heartless bitch."

The audience laughed, and I was grateful for having heard Mr. Pripton's sentiment concerning his lost love. I would have never thought of it myself. When the song ended I knew I had another number that would fit nicely into my lounge show.

One of the great things about Las Vegas is its abundance of musicians. I had always wanted steel drums and marimbas for "CHOCOLATE TAPIOCA PUDDING," and when the curtains parted to reveal a Caribbean island setting, the audience saw the results of my wish. "Jamaica Jam" was a lounge act at The Sands, and I had rented three of their members for the evening. Their spirited playing was so delightful that the audience began clapping in tempo with the beat. The claps turned into applause when the waitresses started serving free samples of chocolate tapioca, and by the time the song was over everyone understood why it was my favorite dessert.

The stage lights dimmed as four large screens descended slowly from the ceiling. Two were staggered on my left, the others to my right. Photographs of wild flowers, snow-capped mountains, and waterfalls were projected onto the screens; each picture more beautiful than its predecessor. Antoinette and I, with the assistance of Mr. Christopher and The Los Angeles Times, had assembled over two hundred slides to use during the performance of my most ambitious composition, "SYMPHONY NO. 1 (THINK) in G Major." The color pictures of nature's beauty matched the sound of the violins as they began playing the song's main theme. Interspersed with the natural wonders were black and white shots of people. Some showed proud men in front of grand mansions, others were of proud men who lived in less fortunate circumstances. There were happy children, hungry children, mothers holding babies, mothers crying, people of all colors together, people alone, and for Ernie, who had been the song's inspiration, there were pictures of brave young men fighting in Vietnam.

"We talk about life,<br>
and talk for hours on end<br>
of things we think we know that we don't know.<br>
We speak the same of love;

using tender words
to smoke screen any feeling we won't show.
But that's our way to hide what's in the heart.
We choose a side to stand on, so we stand apart.
Think about it."

There was no clattering of dishes, or tinkling of silverware. No sound came from the room of fifteen hundred as the ten-minute symphony progressed from the verse into the chorus.

"Think about the days and nights,
and wrongs and rights,
and all that should have been.
Think about our hopes and dreams,
and our sideways schemes,
and all that could have been.
Think about the goods and bads,
and the haves and hads,
and all that would have been.
And while the clock is ticking,
we still have time to think there's
time to figure out the things we think about."

The second movement began with the droning sound inspired by the water treatment plant. Sweeping violins and graceful flutes accompanied the heart-melting duet of Pappy's oboe and Deke's mandolin. The delicate beauty of the second movement's theme was a respite from the serious nature of the first and fourth movements, and I took the stillness of the audience to mean that they were as mesmerized as I was the first time I heard this grand orchestra play my work.

At the start of the third movement pictures of amazing sunsets and starry skies filled the screens. This section was a ballet that featured all the dancers. Their bodies moved like fluid silk, gliding around the stage as the orchestra played with an ever-increasing crescendo of passion and power. The ballet ended precisely on the last beat of the movement, and the dancers scattered off in all directions as the pulsating percussion and staccato bass figure began the fourth and final segment of the symphony.

The screens were withdrawn, and the children's choir from Las Vegas Elementary took their positions on stage. They looked angelic in the new robes I had donated to their school, and I was certain they would also enjoy the new piano that was part of the performance agreement Antoinette had made with their choirmaster.

The children sang the final chorus beautifully, and when the symphony's final chord resounded through the showroom many in the audience stood up and responded with shouts of "bravo" and "encore." The outpouring of acknowledgment was deafening, but as we took our bows and the curtain lowered, I could hear the faint splash of my tears hitting the stage.

The standing ovation continued, and the curtain was raised so the entire cast could acknowledge the praise with more bowing before the curtain was lowered again. The curtain rose a second time in recognition of the sustaining applause, and Antoinette joined us to take her bow. She presented me with a dozen red roses, and I pulled one out to present to her as the curtain lowered for the third time.

Antoinette had mapped out this curtain call as "Plan A." In the absence of sufficient praise "Plan B" called for an immediate start of the closing number, but since "Plan A" was flying, the last song became the encore. Whatever happened, and whatever we called it, everyone quickly took their places for the grand finale.

The curtain rose while the orchestra played a four bar introduction. I was sitting at the center stage piano, next to a stack of black silk top hats. As the applause died down and the audience retook their seats, I began to sing the song I had written for Antoinette.

"I remember when I started out,
I thought I'd hit the top.
I'd reach the highest of the heights.
I'd see my name ablaze in lights.
There'd be "standing room only" every night.
But all I did was flop."

All the female dancers came onto the stage dressed in tuxedos. They twirled silver canes while performing a soft shoe, so named because their feet were very quiet.

"I packed my bags, and I hit the road.
I worked hard, but remained unknown.
I sang my songs; no one clapped.
I told some jokes; no one laughed.
And after that, though I was busted flat,
I kept on dreamin', and I kept on schemin';
one day I would make it to the top.
But I just got the business from the business.
I gave my all,
and all I've got to show is nothing.
I just got the business from the business.
Fame and fortune I will never know."

When the children's choir came out to join in the singing of the final chorus, the dancers grabbed top hats, kicked off the pads that covered their taps, and performed a spectacular leg kick routine that stirred the audience to a frenzy. The balloons, confetti, and streamers dropping from the ceiling added to the grand display.

"I just got the business from the business.
I gave everything I had to give,
and all I got back
was a great-big-giant-fat nothing.
I just got the business from the business.
Fame and fortune I will never know.
But c'est la vie, mon ami, on with the show!"

I thought everyone in the audience would have tired of slapping their palms together by the time we finished the song, but that was not the case. The stomping and cheering, yelling and whistling, and cries for more didn't stop even after the house lights were turned on. An announcement was made over the loudspeakers informing everyone that the room had to be cleared for the second show, and gambling was available in the casino. This broadcast, along with a dozen members of hotel security, finally cleared the room.

Backstage, Antoinette and I congratulated everyone on a fine performance, and asked for one more. The jubilant cast ran off to their dressing rooms while the stage hands adjusted the lighting, and put everything back in order for the late show. There was less than an hour until the jugglers would take their positions.

Antoinette had told me it was a show business custom for people from the audience to make their way backstage to acknowledge a performance, so the band and I spent the hour in my dressing room talking about the show with those who followed this tradition. Mr. Napoli came back and reported that The Don was very impressed, and asked that I accept an invitation to join them for breakfast in the Aloha Suite. I had heard this was the best room at The Tropics, and I was excited to see the decorations. Mr. Christopher stopped by to offer congratulations, as did a number of other people, and I thanked them all for attending The Recital. Without them it would have been just another rehearsal.

Sticks defined the entire experience with one concise sentence, "Cool!" Pappy and Deke agreed, and so did Mr. Bop, but he was more reserved.

"You think it's gonna be easy bein' back in the lounge after a night like this, Tee-Bee?"

"If anything," I answered, "it'll be easier."

"How's that?" he said with a skeptical look. "Songs won't sound the same without the orchestra, and they won't look the same without all the razzmatazz."

"That's true, but we've got it all in here," I said pointing at my head. Then I pointed at my heart. "And in here. We'll never forget how the songs looked and sounded, or how they felt, and that's how we'll play them."

The second show was as successful as the first. Mr. Silverman, handsomely dressed up in a light blue tuxedo, watched from the wings. I jokingly introduced him to the stagehands as my protégé to sanction his backstage access, and he told anyone who would listen that I was his discovery. When anyone asked, I said it was true.

The next morning I arrived at the door of the Aloha Suite at precisely eight o'clock as scheduled. When Jimmy opened the door I noticed the lush tropical decor of the hotel had been abandoned, and in its place were rich tones of walnut and teak. Exotic silk fabrics covered the walls, and fine leather furniture with sculptures of brass and glass filled the room.

Jimmy mumbled something about not being nervous as he escorted me toward the dining room where Mr. Napoli and The Don were waiting.

"Come in, my boy," The Don said. "Sit here, next to me." He patted the top of the empty chair to his left, and I complied.

The Don started the conversation with the customary small talk. "How are things?" "Do you like Las Vegas?" "How's everyone treating you?"

During this initial question and answer period, Jimmy seemed to be uncomfortable, but he relaxed after my response to The Don's third question, "Everyone's very kind to me, sir, especially Mr. Cossello."

Breakfast of steak and eggs with hash-brown potatoes, bagels and cream cheese, orange juice and coffee was served, and this provided a break in the conversation. It was quite a feast, and I was sure I wouldn't be hungry for the rest of the day. After we ate, The Don snapped his fingers and Mr. Napoli pulled a set of papers from his jacket pocket. Although their actions reminded me of something from The Great Zarbino Brothers magic act, they were not performing a sleight of hand trick. Mr. Napoli was simply handing my contract to The Don.

The Don set the papers on the table. "So, Tuxedo Bob, we're in business together."

"I believe that's a correct statement, sir." I didn't know what to expect, but I knew I should be on my best behavior.

"I'm gonna ask you something," he said staring straight into my eyes while rubbing his lower lip with the tip of his index finger. "You would honor this contract?"

It seemed an odd question since my signature was my word, but he didn't know me and probably wanted reassurance. My answer was a clear and forthright, "Yes, I would, sir."

"So, if I say you're playin' the lounge for the next seven years, that's okay with you?"

"Yes, sir."

"No ifs, ands, or buts?"

I wasn't sure what he was driving at, but I replied, "Yes, sir."

He leaned closer to me. "You're a talented young man, but more than that, I hear you're an honest one."

He paused and I said, "Thank you."

"No need to thank me yet." He leaned even closer, and I could smell the coffee and steak on his breath. "You impressed me last night. Not just with the show, which was very entertaining, but the way you pulled it off. Renting the room and putting the whole thing together, that takes a certain amount of brains. Isn't that right Jimmy?"

Jimmy jumped in his seat at the mention of his name. "Yes, sir. He's as smart as they come."

"Shut-up, Jimmy." The Don's brusque order was obeyed immediately, but there appeared to be no hard feelings. I figured it was the nature of their relationship. The Don continued, "I hear things, Tuxedo Bob. You want to know one of the things I heard?" He was speaking to me, but he was looking at Jimmy. "I heard it was your idea to put those gaming tables outside the lounge. Did I hear right?"

"Actually, sir, the idea developed during a discussion between Jimmy and me, so if I was given all the credit, then you heard wrong."

"Then I am corrected." His eyes again focused on me. "Let me tell you what I have in mind. I want you to agree to play the lounge for six more months. After that you can follow your career wherever it takes you, but you pay me ten percent of your action for the next ten years. If you promise me that, I'll tear up this contract right now."

I couldn't believe my ears. "I promise, sir. And you have my word as a gentleman."

He smiled, and tore up the contract. "That's what I thought you'd say."

My second gift horse of the month went on to explain that "action" meant every dime I made, and included any dimes that were paid on my behalf. The money was not an issue with me, and I reiterated my understanding of the new agreement. He gave me a New York City post office box number where I was to send a money order on the first of every month for the next ten years, and I left the Aloha Suite walking on air. I was accompanied by a Dixieland melody dancing with my thought of being able to go to New Orleans sooner than I had expected.

Mr. Silverman was booked on an early morning flight back to New York, so I met him in the lobby after my breakfast with The Don.

"Big things are gonna happen for you, kid. I can feel it! You got charm, you know that? I said charm, and I know a lot of people who would love to have one ounce of the charm you got. And, as I'm sure you know, I'm not just sayin' that to hear myself talk." He winked at me, and smiled. "We could have been a great team, kid."

"We are a great team, Sy." When I called him by his first name I thought I saw a mist in his eyes.

"I better get out of here, kid."

Sy Silverman picked up his bag, and walked toward the pineapple doors. He didn't turn around, but I heard him say, "You take care of yourself," as he left the hotel. It was the morning after showtime, and it was the last time I ever saw him.

# resolution

After recouping the twenty-five thousand dollars I had paid for the rental of the showroom, my share of the admission receipts not only covered all the money I had spent to put on The Recital, but netted a profit of twenty-seven dollars as well. My bigger show on the bigger stage also provided a handful of benefits for the people most responsible for its success. Mr. Owenthal signed Antoinette to a five year contract that gave her a free hand to produce extravaganzas of her own choosing, Mr. Pripton was allowed to add ten more musicians to his orchestra, and Jimmy got a raise.

It was easy to get back into the daily routine of three performances, and I was pleased that the lounge continued to be packed to capacity. Mr. Owenthal instituted a new policy of charging a five-dollar admission fee for each Tuxedo Bob performance, and even though the gamblers could see any other lounge act in town for free, the cover charge did not become a deterrent. People lined up an hour before each show, and the gaming tables outside the entrance became some of the casino's biggest moneymakers.

I rearranged some of the songs from The Recital, so they could become part of our lounge repertoire. The diversity enabled the band to play three different sets each night, and this pleased our repeat customers. However, the shows were no longer comprised solely of humorous songs. My reputation for writing offbeat songs caused some of the audience members to think that everything they heard was supposed to be funny, but I didn't see this as a problem. I was happy that people felt comfortable enough to laugh whenever they felt the urge.

Mr. Napoli tripled my monthly salary for the remainder of my Coconut Lounge performance contract, and I divided this largess equally among the band. Sticks called it "good money in the extreme." Jimmy told me that the entire salary would be paid under the table, and though he never actually handed it to me in that fashion, it was all paid in cash.

"Don't go tellin' nobody about our new arrangement," Jimmy cautioned upon handing me the first twelve thousand dollars.

Since it would never occur to me to discuss my personal finances with anyone, I took his statement to be a combination of friendly advice and parental admonition. I didn't know that "under the table" was the opposite of "above board," but during the next year I learned there were legal ramifications attached to accepting cash without a receipt.

Along with the new salary and lounge admission, The Tropics acknowledged the band's popularity by selling coconuts that had been painted to look like chubby men dressed in tuxedos. The gift shop charged five dollars for each overweight Tuxedo Bob, but I considered this a bargain because it couldn't have been very easy to paint the surface of a coconut. "The Tropics - Tuxedo Bob - Las Vegas," monogrammed in rich gold lettering, added to the value. Though they looked nothing like me, they did bear a slight resemblance to Bee-Dee, so I sent him one. I was certain he would be amused by the prestige associated with becoming a souvenir item. I imagined him opening the package, and with a wide grin exclaiming to his wife, "Lookie here! Tee-Bee done sent a curi-oddity!"

My agreement with The Don called for just six more months before I was allowed to make my own schedule, so the band began planning our trip to New Orleans.

"Deke call a few friends, and maybe have us a gig by Thanksgiving."

"Sounds like a plan," Pappy said per his usual style of agreement. "But," he added, "we should have a back-up in case something unexpected happens."

"Pappy's right." Mr. Bop's remark was accompanied by a thoughtful glance in my direction. "Won't be too good if Deke finds us a gig, and we still here."

It was certainly something to think about. We were all aware that God enjoyed interceding in our plans, so it seemed prudent to consider additional options. Agreeing to deliver our services based on the premise that we could predict our future put us on shaky ground at best.

"Dig it. We makin' some hip coin. I say we stash the cash, and groove here for a while. We can scope the scene in Dixie once we actually there."

Sticks' solution was the simplest one, and it placed no demands on anyone to make a firm commitment. We agreed to allow providence to decide when we should make our move.

Jimmy had a girlfriend, Miss Edwards, who worked as a teller at The Las Vegas National Bank and Trust. At his suggestion I opened an account there, and Miss Edwards expertly handled the transfer of my funds from Omaha. Since I was receiving so much cash I thought this was a good idea, and I was able to save the added expense of out-of-town banking.

The band was paid once a month, but Jimmy's salary was paid every Friday. When I started banking locally, he asked me to deposit his money into my account as a favor to him. "The Don does not allow me to have a personal account," was his explanation, and since I wasn't privy to the machinations of high finance, or his personal business, I agreed to help.

The transactions were simple. Jimmy would come to my room with a paper bag full of cash, I would take it to Miss Edwards for deposit, and a few days later I would withdraw the money and give it back to Jimmy. Each bag was filled with well-worn ten, twenty, and fifty dollar bills, and I was certain Jimmy appreciated the crisp hundred dollar bills he received in exchange. I was quite impressed by the size of his salary, and did not heed the dissonant chorus of muted trumpets that always accompanied the transactions. I figured they were playing because it was important to exercise caution when carrying such a large amount of the city's most valuable commodity. In spite of Jimmy's constant reminders that our dealings were just between the two of us, and Miss Edwards' penchant for nervous glances, I gave no thought to impropriety.

I hadn't been able to see as much of Antoinette as I did when we worked on The Recital, but I knew she was busy working on a new show. She had asked permission to use some of my songs in her next extravaganza, and I agreed without hesitation.

"MOONLIGHT" and "THE ORPHAN STOMP" were two songs she wanted to use, and at her request I rewrote the lyrics to "I JUST GOT THE BUSINESS FROM THE BUSINESS" as a four-person ensemble number. Antoinette was supportive of my plan to go to New Orleans, but sad that I would miss the show's debut which was scheduled for December.

"It is going to be very spectacular with much more dancing than walking," she said with a twinkle in her eye. "I am going to call it "Antoinette Gilbeau's Night in Paris." What do you think, mon ami. It is good, no?"

"It's very good. You deserve to have your name in lights." I wanted to add that she should have her name written in the stars, but when I realized I had just heard her last name for the first time, all I could say was, "My last name is Fledsper."

"Fledsper," she repeated with extra emphasis on the "d." "It sounds like a rock. Is there something in the middle?"

"Bob," I replied.

"No, my pet," she giggled. "A middle name. Something between the Bob and the Fledsper. Mine is Simone."

"That's a very pretty middle name. I don't have one. Should I get one?"

"It is not so bad to have no middle name, but if you like, you can use part of mine. Monsieur Robert Simon Fledsper." She arched her eyebrows as the name rolled from her tongue. "No," she said wrinkling her nose. "On second thought, you must always be Tuxedo Bob. There is no name better than that for you."

The Fourth of July, Labor Day, Halloween, and Thanksgiving passed in the blink of an eye, and the band had made no decision concerning our exodus. I knew it was because we were making more money than ever before. My savings had grown to over one hundred forty thousand dollars, and since making money can be as intoxicating as the lack of it is sobering, I didn't find fault with our procrastination. Each man had opened his own savings account to put money aside for our eventual departure, so I was confident that whenever we got to New Orleans our financial picture would be as rosy as my view of life.

As it turned out I was still in town when Antoinette's show opened on December 6th, and I sent each person in the cast and crew a congratulatory bouquet of flowers. I had seen the final dress rehearsal the night before, and hearing my songs performed while I casually observed was a treat. The show earned Antoinette rave reviews, and she had every reason to be proud of her success. The words "Antoinette Gilbeau's Night in Paris" flickered in neon on the marquee in front of The Tropics directly above "Tuxedo Bob Appearing Nightly in The Coconut Lounge" until the middle of June 1968.

I had written a Christmas song that the band performed from Thanksgiving through Christmas Day. Antoinette liked it so much she asked me to sing it during her dinner show on Christmas Eve, and I was happy to accept her invitation. On December 24th, after my nine o'clock Coconut Lounge performance, I went to the main showroom. Being backstage again, among the dancers and the busy stage crew, was like returning to Oz. In all my euphoria I would have definitely missed my introduction if Miss Charlene had not nudged me and said, "Hey, Mister Le Pet! You're on!"

I was still awed by the size of the theater when I walked on stage, but I calmed down by the time I sat down at the piano and thanked the audience for their generous applause. I smiled at Mr. Pripton as he readied his baton over the charts I had prepared and delivered to him the week before. A chorus of trumpets followed by a downward spiraling glissando from the woodwinds sounded the beginning. When the orchestra paused, my digits took over while I sang the simple prologue.

"Eleven months of every year
Santa and his eight reindeer
take vacations away from the north pole,
because that place gets much too cold.
This leaves all the toy maker elves
to make the toys all by themselves.
Mrs. Claus stays to oversee,
but if she needs Santa,
she knows right where he'll be."

Mr. Pripton signaled with his baton and the orchestra entered as I got up from the piano, snapping my fingers to the bouncy beat.

"Santa Claus loves Las Vegas.
It's his favorite town.
He unwinds from his one-day grind,
and you can find him sitting down
at the blackjack tables, or shooting dice,
sipping scotch with a splash on ice.
Santa loves Vegas that's why he's here
eleven months out of the year.
Comet lives in Phoenix; Cupid's in L.A.
All the other reindeer
have not told me where they stay.
They say they're incognito;
I think that's overseas.

But they all head north
December twenty-fourth
for their one day odyssey.
Santa gives toys to all the boys,
and all the girls around the world.
Accomplishing this is no easy task,
so I don't think you have to ask
why Santa Claus loves Las Vegas,
or why you'll find him here.
Santa Claus loves Las Vegas
eleven months out of the year."

The audience responded so well that Antoinette came out on stage, and asked the crowd if they would like to hear me sing another number. The cheers and applause indicated their endorsement of her proposal. Mr. Pripton held up a sheet of music to "SILENT NIGHT," and I smiled as I nodded my agreement. I had told Antoinette a few stories about the road that led me to Las Vegas, and one of them had been about my "SILENT NIGHT" performance at Pressman's. I wasn't suspicious that Antoinette had planned this encore in advance, I was certain.

I never imagined I would get to sing that beautiful melody with any orchestra other than the one in my head. It was truly inspirational, and I felt blessed to play a part in Antoinette's show. I bowed when I finished, and waved to the audience as I made my exit. When I got to the wings I embraced Antoinette, kissed her on the cheek, and told her I loved her.

"Of course you do, mon ami," she said with a knowing look in her eyes. "You do not know any other way to feel."

Another New Years Eve celebration, an extra day in February, and the Ides of March came and went. Jimmy was happy that the band was sticking around longer than promised, and that I had continued making his deposits and withdrawals on a weekly basis. His job performance must have pleased Mr. Napoli because he was always getting fantastic raises. I congratulated him on his most recent salary increase, although I did wonder what service he provided that was worth forty-five thousand dollars per week. If Jimmy's arrangements had been any of my business, I would have inquired why bags of cash had replaced our paychecks.

On an April evening Martin Luther King was killed outside his motel room in Memphis, Tennessee. He was not the same man who had shouted "find the red lady!" on a Manhattan street. This Mr. King was a doctor who had dedicated his life to a non-violent fight for the equality of all people.

"Deke know it's a cryin' shame losin' Dr. King that way."

"Damn," was all Pappy could muster, and Sticks just shook his head and wept.

Mr. Bop suggested that we perform the first movement of "SYMPHONY NO. 1 (THINK)" during our shows that night to honor this great man. The five of us had not played this number since the rehearsals at "Grand Vista Studios," but we played it together that evening with a passion that rivaled the finest orchestra.

Over the next few days I was confused when some people paid tribute to Dr. King by rioting and looting, but then I remembered something my father said after President Kennedy's assassination. "Son, there are three kinds of people on this earth: those who dream the world can be a better place, those who dedicate their lives to make the world a better place, and those who are unable to imagine either possibility."

The senseless murder of Dr. King was followed by two more. The one that received the most media attention was the killing of Mr. Robert

Kennedy. He was campaigning to become the Democratic Party's candidate for President when someone decided that the Kennedy family had not suffered enough from the tragedy of five years earlier. For the second time in two months a nation mourned, and the band performed the first movement from the symphony in remembrance of another fallen loved one.

The lesser of the reported assassinations took place outside of the Murray Hill Station Post Office in New York City. Mr. Napoli and The Don had picked up some mail from their post office box, and were getting into their limousine when a hail of bullets from an assortment of high-powered weapons ended their lives. Jimmy informed me of their deaths late one night when he came to my hotel room. I had never seen him so agitated, and before he related the details of the killings he shut my window blinds and turned on the faucets in the bathroom.

"Tell me somethin', kid. Have you seen any suspicious lookin' characters hangin' around?" Before I could answer that I had not, he pulled me closer and whispered, "I'm gettin' outta this town in the morning, kid, on the count o' somebody's sending a message, and it would not be to my better interests to stick around for the call."

There was fear in his voice, but I couldn't figure out why a man who knew everything and everyone was afraid of anything. When I asked if he knew an address where I could continue to send ten-percent of my salary to The Don's family he gave me an odd answer.

"Are you kiddin'? The family killed him!"

He said he would see me around sometime, and left my room. I never saw him anywhere after I watched him carry two large suitcases out the pineapple doors at nine the next morning.

Within the next three days the entire hotel was in a state of upheaval. Room Service deliveries ceased, pit bosses weren't reporting to their pits, the volcano belched more smoke than was probably healthy, and there were no dancers in front of the lobby waterfall. No one seemed to know who was in charge, and amid the chaos the band voted to leave Las Vegas for the next journey to Paradise. When we went to the bank to withdraw our funds, we found that providence had a stinging retort to our proposed departure.

"Excuse me," the tall man in the dark blue suit said as he displayed an extremely official looking ID. "I'm Special Agent Carstairs from The Internal Revenue Service. Would you gentlemen follow me, please?"

His request seemed more like a command, so we followed him into the bank manager's office where another man, dressed in the same dark-suit style, was sitting behind a desk. From my experience with Mr. Napoli and his associates I was sure that these two men worked together.

Sticks' forehead was covered with beads of sweat, and he kept whispering, "It's the Feds, man."

I saw no reason for any of us to be worried, and since Mr. Carstairs had been kind enough to introduce himself I returned the gesture.

"I'm Tuxedo Bob, Mr. Carstairs." That was as far as I got before he interrupted me with a correction.

"Special Agent Carstairs. If you'd all take a seat we'll be with you in a moment." With that, he turned his back on us and began a discussion with the gentleman behind the desk. Proper introductions would have to wait, and the band and I sat down on the folding chairs that were lined against a wall.

As they scrutinized some documents on the bank manager's desk, I overheard a few comments of their whispered conversation. "This one's twenty grand." "Here's a couple for forty." I surmised that the bank's records were somehow involved, and since the band and I were bank customers, I thought it was a good thing that these special agents were so concerned with the safety of our money.

A third man in a dark blue suit escorted Miss Edwards into the office. She was wringing her hands, and her eyes were red and swollen from crying.

"Hello, Miss Edwards," I said. "Can I get you a glass of water or something?"

She sat down on the couch by the window, and sobbed, "Jimmy's gone. Jimmy's gone."

I felt badly that Jimmy's absence was making her so upset. I wanted to comfort her because she had always been so nice to me, but the newcomer who had escorted her into the office quickly seized my attention.

"Yer in a heap o' trouble, boy." His southern accent reminded me of Sally from the lounge, but the grin on his face seemed out of place.

"I'm Tuxedo Bob, sir. You are?"

"I'm the guy who knows the trouble yer in, boy." He positioned himself near the window, and alternated his glances between looking across the room at me, and downward in the direction of Miss Edwards' cleavage. He continued grinning, so I assumed he was quite pleased with both the view and the information he possessed.

Ten minutes passed, and I had never known the band to be so quiet, especially Sticks. When I started humming along to a new melody in my head Mr. Bop touched my arm, and said very softly, "This ain't the time for composition, Tee-Bee."

Special Agent Carstairs finally turned toward us, and announced that the band could leave, however, the pleasure of my company was still required.

"If Mr. Tuxedo Bob stays, then we stay." Mr. Bop's deep baritone spoke for Pappy, Deke and Sticks, who nodded their heads in agreement.

The man behind the desk finally spoke, "I can have you gentlemen removed if that is your preference." The ring of authority in his voice made it clear to me that he was the person in charge.

"It's okay, guys" I interjected. Just close out your accounts, and I'll be with you in a few minutes."

"More like ten to twenty years if you ask me." The grinning southerner was beginning to display a personality that might actually become irritating over a period of time. Special Agent Carstairs must have been aware of this characteristic because he asked his cohort to keep quiet.

"Shut-up, Arthur," were his exact words.

The band and Miss Edwards left the room, leaving me alone with the three men.

The man in charge began tapping his pencil on the desk. "You've been running some large amounts of cash through your account. That sort of activity raises a few red flags."

"You'll forgive me, but I find it difficult to have a conversation without being properly introduced," I said extending my hand. "I'm Tuxedo Bob."

He set down his pencil. "I'm Special Agent John Mickelson. You've met Special Agent Carstairs, and that's Arthur Rumpling, one of our field agents."

We shook hands, and they all presented their leather-bound IRS ID's for my inspection. If I had not been required to relinquish my Tropics ID to hotel security I would have shown it to them, but they took my word that I was who I said I was.

"Our records show you've deposited and withdrawn over one and a half million dollars in a little less than a year. Can you tell me where all that money came from, and where it went?" Special Agent Mickelson's manner was abrupt, but his direct question deserved an answer.

"No, I can't," was my honest reply, but it was clearly not what he wanted to hear.

Special Agent Carstairs leaned over, and with his face inches from mine said in a threatening tone, "You can't, or you won't?"

"I can't say because it wasn't my money." I explained the situation about Jimmy's inability to have his own account, and how I had agreed to help him out.

The three men listened politely to my story, and when I had finished each of them had a rather blank expression on his face. Mr. Rumpling slapped his forehead exclaiming, "Is this guy stupid, or what?" Since he was speaking to no one in particular, I didn't feel compelled to respond.

Special Agent Mickelson explained that since the money had been in my account it created a Federal tax problem. Even though Mrs. Winters had been diligently filing my taxes from her office in Williston, this money was looked upon as unreported income. Since I couldn't prove the money wasn't mine, I owed the government the back taxes, penalty and interest. Now I understood Mr. Rumpling's prediction about my "heap o' trouble."

"How much?" The breath I took after asking my short question was quickly released upon hearing Special Agent Mickelson's answer.

"Somewhere in the neighborhood of four hundred thousand dollars."

I had one hundred forty-nine thousand, seven hundred sixty-two dollars and thirty-nine cents in my account, and a quarter in my pocket. Special Agent Mickelson agreed to let me keep the quarter, and we signed some papers to transfer everything else to the IRS in full settlement of the debt. After shaking everyone's hand, and inviting them to look me up if they were ever in New Orleans, I left the office.

Mr. Bop was furious that Jimmy had put me in such a perilous position, but I reminded him that my father used to say, "Ignorance is neither an excuse nor a defense." I had agreed to the situation, so I had to accept the responsibility for my actions.

"Sometimes you too nice, Tee-Bee," he said with a disapproving shake of his head.

"A person can never be too nice, Mr. Bop. Or too forgiving. Or too polite."

Sticks put his arm around me, and smiled, "Dig what he say, Bop. Tee-Bee got a hip message, but he left out a person can be too broke."

I laughed at his joke, but Deke interrupted with an unusually sharp tone in his voice, "Listen up here. Long as Deke got a dime, Tee-Bee got a dime," and with that he handed me all the cash he had taken from his account.

"Sounds like a plan," Pappy said as he also handed me his money.

"Ain't no jam you in without me, you dig?" Sticks gave me his cash, and both of his drumsticks.

Mr. Bop put his money on the top of the pile. "A person can't have too many friends."

We went back to the hotel to gather our things, and as I packed my suitcase thoughts of friendship and casino profit skimming waltzed through my head. I found the whole idea of gamblers hoping to win jackpots, and finding myself in a jackpot relatively amusing. It was, after all, only money, and while it made life more comfortable it had nothing to do with life itself.

I closed the door to my home at The Tropics for the last time, and rushed down to the main showroom to meet Antoinette for a final good-bye. She was sitting at one of the prime tables, facing the door so she could see me when I entered.

"Do not come any closer, mon cher!" she shouted as the door closed behind me. "I want to look at you like I would gaze upon the moon and the stars."

"But I have something I want to give you."

"What more is there, my pet, that you have not already given to me?" Her voice softly trembled as she spoke. "Say your good-bye, Robert, and follow your heart."

"Thank you for everything." I meant it, but the words sounded so flat compared to the depth of my feelings. "I love you, Antoinette."

"And I love you, Monsieur Tuxedo Robert Fledsper. Now walk out the door, and leave me to my memories."

"I'll miss you," I said through an onslaught of tears.

"Your journey is far from over, and it no longer requires my presence. Adieu, dear, sweet Robert. I think if you are not an angel, then angels do not exist."

I closed the door behind me, and wiped my eyes. In my hand was the bow tie that I had wanted to give to her, but I couldn't go back in. I knew my tears were matched by her own, and she did not want me to see her cry. I walked down the gold-carpeted bamboo hallway, and stopped at her picture adorning the wall beside the entryway. I kissed the glass over her cheek, pinned the bow tie to the bottom of the frame, and walked through the casino crying like a baby.

I found the band waiting for me in the lobby. The volcano, and the waterfall had been turned off, and no birds flew above us. Word had spread that The Tropics was under new ownership, and a massive redecorating plan was in the works. It was eventually torn down to make room for a huge hotel built by an entertainment conglomerate, but by then Antoinette had retired, and my path had taken me from the Gulf of Mexico to the Pacific Ocean.

I carried my suitcase out the pineapple doors, and into the bright Nevada sunlight. After a four-year stopover in the city my mother had believed was high on God's list of endangered locations, I was going to New Orleans — blessed by the presence of four good friends and the quarter in my pocket.

# New Orleans

"Memories are what keeps those who have died alive."

Orville Fledsper

# twenty-fourth nocturne

## *sempre nesto*

Mr. Deacon "Deke" Brown passed away on August 23, 1973. His death certificate listed a faulty valve in the left ventricle as the cause of his heart attack. The Coroner said it was a congenital defect, but regardless of his medical diagnosis, Deke's heart was one of the finest I had ever known.

Walker's Funeral Home on Conti Street took care of the arrangements, and on the stiflingly hot afternoon of August 27th, Deke was buried. The ceremony was long — four and a half hours — but it was done in the manner befitting a cherished New Orleans' musician. Tears of sorrow and joy, expressions of love and respect, and music all mixed together in a celebration to grieve his passing, and rejoice that he had gone home.

I entered the viewing room an hour early to spend a few quiet moments with my friend. The room was peaceful, but in my head I could hear the sound of his guitar, his trumpet, and his mandolin. It hardly seemed possible that five years had gone by since the hazy June morning he excitedly informed the band, "We here!" and we all jumped off a freight train outside the city limits.

• • •

By the afternoon of that first day in New Orleans we were sprawled on the floor of a sparsely furnished apartment on Burgundy Street. It belonged to Monroe "Sweet Horn" Jefferson, a friend of Deke's "from way back," who said we could stay there "so long's ya'll needs a place to crash." He charged us twenty-five dollars a week, plus half the utilities, but since he did not have a stove or hot water, the electric bill for the refrigerator didn't amount to much.

I remember being happy to be in a room that wasn't moving. We had spent the greater part of three days either on a bus or inside a railroad boxcar. Since Deke was the only member of our group who had ever been to New Orleans, we had allowed him to make the travel arrangements from Las Vegas.

"Deke say we gets a bus to Phoenix, and whilst our instruments goes on to New Orleans, we takes a train or two."

His suggestion seemed simple enough, and since no one asked for his definition of train travel, he didn't offer one. I had never been on a train, but I had a Lionel set when I was six, and enjoyed watching it go around in circles. I figured our route would be less round, and that there would be comfortable accommodations available. I discovered that comfort was only given to those passengers who had purchased a ticket.

On the bus ride to Phoenix, Deke explained that hopping a freight train was "akin to thumbin' down a road." The train was going where we wanted to go, and there was always room to be found in an empty boxcar. This tradition had gained popularity during The Depression when people had little or no money, but had to travel to find work. Since the IRS had depleted my funds, and the band wanted to work in New Orleans, we agreed to Deke's plan. Actually, I hesitated at first because the idea sounded like a theft of service, but I accepted Mr. Bop's opinion that I had already paid for the privilege.

"Trains are subsidized by the government, and you did your share of subsidizing the government this morning. Seems only right they let your behind occupy a little government space."

We jumped on a slow moving freight train just outside of Phoenix; three days and two trains later we were in our new home two blocks from Bourbon Street. Train hopping was far more dangerous than parasailing, but it had certainly beat walking. I didn't know it at the time, but I would help myself to some free train travel again when my financial picture dictated I make similar traveling arrangements.

• • •

"Dig it, my man. Seem like this whole town know Deke."

Sticks' comment jolted me from my thoughts. The room had filled with so many mourners that a second room was opened to accommodate the crowd. Mr. Walker, the soft-spoken owner, didn't mind the overflow. I overheard him tell Sweet Horn that it was his honor and privilege to have his establishment become Deke's Place for a few hours.

The band was standing beside Deke's coffin — a brass and mahogany Heaven's Harmony — and I joined them to accept condolences from those who had come to pay respects. Sweet Horn came over, and with a generous laugh related the story about how he had given Deke his first trumpet back in the thirties.

"We was playin' in "The Firehouse Gang," and Deke here was the band's guitarist." He pointed toward Deke's body to make sure that any curious stranger who had wandered in off the street would know who was being honored. "Deke had an ear for music. Everybody know he did, and I tell you what, he pick up any instrument he like and make it sing. Gospel truth!" He moved closer to one of the large fans that was helping to disperse the heat more evenly throughout the room. "Deke had special affection for the trumpet, you know, and he like to blow on mine if'n I ever set it down. Got to be where it made no sense him not havin' his own, so I give him an old one I found in a pawn shop." His belly bounced when he chuckled in recollection, "Tarnation, it was a hunk o' junk! Valves was always jammin', but Deke sure loved playin' on that ol' horn."

Hearing Sweet Horn talk about deficient valves reminded me that God is sometimes subtle where His prophecies are concerned, but I kept the realization to myself.

The funeral service began with Mr. Bop's reading of Deke's favorite Psalm. He changed the pronouns just like Deke had always done each night before going to bed. "The Lord is Deke's Shepherd. Deke shall not want."

Pappy followed the scripture reading with his story about how he met Deke in New York City. "I was standing on a subway platform at Lexington and Third, when all of the sudden I heard a guitar. Now, a person can find all kinds of musicians playing in the subway system. Some are good, some are," he paused before completing his thought, and then he laughed. "I was about to say 'some are bad', but Tee-Bee's sitting there looking at me, and I know Deke's up in Heaven listening; I learned a lot from those two about being nice, so what I mean to say is some subway musicians are good, and some are better." He smiled at me, and then down at Deke. "How was that?"

I had heard Pappy's story before. Deke was hired on the spot, and Pappy discovered he had actually employed three musicians in one because of Deke's equal dexterity on the guitar, trumpet and banjo. Their weekly gigs at Eddie Condon's and Jimmy Ray's became part of the history of New York's famous Fifty-second Street music scene. My favorite section of Pappy's tale was about the night Deke broke two strings on his guitar during a performance of "TAKE THE A TRAIN," and he improvised a solo that earned him a standing ovation. I didn't have to imagine Deke playing through this kind of calamity because the same thing had happened our first night in New Orleans.

• • •

The sun had gone down, and the band and I had gotten up from the floor of Sweet Horn's apartment to go listen to him perform. We walked down to Bourbon Street, where the sultry night air danced with the sound of Dixieland Jazz, and we entered "The Swamp Club." Once through its moss covered doorway we were in a room thick with cigar smoke and the sweet smell of rum. I thought that the odors, along with the fishing nets and stuffed alligators decorating the walls gave the place a real Louisiana Bayou quality.

We sat down at a corner table, and ordered a bucket of boiled crawfish that Deke said were "sorta kin to a shrimp." When they arrived I remarked that thcy looked like little lobsters.

The waiter explained that the proper "N'Awlins" technique for eating a crawfish was a two-step process. "Ya suck da haid! Den peelaf dat shell, and eat dat tail-meat, f'sur!"

Deke translated by showing us how it was done. He selected a crawfish from the bucket, and without hesitation ripped off the head and sucked the juice from its interior. Then he removed the shell from the decapitated remains, and ate the meat. His smile of delight informed the rest of us that it was quite tasty.

"Dig in. Deke know you gonna love eatin' the mudbug."

The local delicacy with the cute nickname of "mudbug" was very good, but quite spicy, and I guzzled three pitchers of ice water in an attempt to cool my mouth. Mr. Bop suggested I try beer instead, but I declined. Three pitchers of beer would have certainly put me face down on the floor, and I would have missed most of our first night out. All the ripping, sucking, and tearing was messy, but it was fun to play with my food without wondering if sloppy table manners would cause a loss of dessert privileges. A melancholy clarinet quickly accompanied the joy of the moment. It echoed softly in my head, and I was reminded how much I would have given to hear a parental reprimand.

Sweet Horn's five-piece band started to play at nine-thirty, and continued until three in the morning. Even though they were allowed a ten minute break each hour, the performance demands on a New Orleans' entertainer seemed much more grueling than three shows a night in Las Vegas. When I heard the band only made fifty dollars a day, I calculated a per-hour rate of one dollar and eighty cents per musician. The modest living arrangements made much more sense after this discovery.

Deke, Mr. Bop, Sticks and Pappy each sat in at various times during the evening, and during the final set Sweet Horn asked me to play a song. The style of music being performed dictated I do something suitable, so the band joined me in playing "THE ORPHAN STOMP." Deke broke a string at the beginning of the song, and another during his solo, but he played around the malfunction with such expertise that Sticks commented "You was hot, my man. I know them disobedient strings is sorry they missed bein' part of your groove."

The audience gave Deke a standing ovation; even in their fairly inebriated state they recognized superb musicianship. One person in the crowd, who was especially impressed by Deke's ability, owned a bar a few doors down the street. Mr. Peter Taylor approached us at the end of the evening, and asked if we would be interested in performing at his club on Wednesdays and Saturdays for twenty-five dollars a night. We agreed.

After eight performances Mr. Taylor hired "Tuxedo Bob" as his house band, and raised our salary to two hundred fifty dollars a week. For the next five years we played six nights a week at Mr. Taylor's club on Bourbon Street. The club was named Paradise.

After a month of sleeping on the floor at Sweet Horn's, Pappy found a two-bedroom apartment on St. Peter Street just around the corner from Paradise. The rent was forty dollars a week, but the added luxury of hot running water made the price seem reasonable. The band moved in, and with our pooled finances we bought a small refrigerator, stove, table and chairs, couch, and five mattresses from a nearby thrift shop. The apartment on St. Peter Street was the first place that felt like home since I had left Schulberg.

• • •

Deke seemed comfortable laying in the clouds of vanilla silk that lined Heaven's Harmony - Model MB73. His hands were folded over his heart, his eyes were closed, his lips frozen in a contented smile, and he looked quite dapper in the first tuxedo he had ever worn. He used to say that he wanted to wear one only once. "Deke put on a tuxedo at Deke's funeral." A phone call to Tom Conners resulted in the speedy delivery of Deke's size forty-four "After Six" ensemble, and from that day forward Deke and I were not just brothers in music; we were brothers in style.

Sweet Horn followed Pappy, making a short speech about how much he had admired Deke's musicianship, and repeating his "first trumpet" story. He was followed by a few other players from around town who also extolled Deke's abilities. Admiration for Deke was in abundance.

Mr. Charlie "Shoes" Watson, a tap dancer who had ridden the rails with Deke "long before you was even in the plannin' stage" as he liked to tell me, hobbled to the front of the room. He suffered from an arthritic condition that had taken the spring from his step, but did not affect the joy in his heart. Mr. Watson didn't say a word when he got to the coffin. He just stood there looking down upon his friend. After a few minutes of silence he started dancing. It was a simple shuffle-step that only lasted a moment, and when he finished he patted Deke on the head. "Deacon," his voice crackled like crisp cereal, "I know you always did enjoy the sound of my shoes. I'll dance for you again one of these days."

Sticks was next on the program. He walked up to the front of the room carrying a drumstick in one hand, and a white carnation in the other. He placed the flower on top of Deke's folded hands, and laid the drumstick in a fold of silk next to the new set of guitar strings Deke had bought the day before he died. "You remember Joe Dunbar, my man. He remember you," he whispered as he stepped up to the podium.

"Everyone here hip to our friend always sayin' 'Deke' when he be talkin' 'bout hisself. I could dig it, you know, so I never ask why he had his particular habit 'til I hang around him a couple years. I didn't think it be cool checkin' his personal business, you dig? Anyways, Pappy never said nothin' about it, and he be runnin' with Deke a whole lot longer than me, so I kept my nose on my face where it belong."

Sticks paused to wipe the nervous sweat from his brow. Even though he would have preferred to be sitting behind the protection of a drum set, it was important to him to participate in his friend's memorial service.

"Anyways," he continued, "when I finally do think it be cool askin' why he always say Deke, he laughed and say 'Deke just enjoy the sound of it.' That was it. No jive; no detective needed. Man just like the way his name sound. He say it make him think o' hittin' a guitar string every time he hear it, so he say "Deke" instead o' "I" or "me." Got to be Deke's special thing that Deke do to make Deke happy." His voice faltered, and he struggled to regain his composure with a deep breath. Bowing his head to let his tears drop to the floor, he continued softly, "Good ol' Deke. Man, you sure could play that guitar." He touched the edge of the coffin, and looked at Deke's peaceful face. "Dig it now, my brother. You go on up to God, and you tell him proud, 'Deke ready to play in the band.'"

• • •

Deke was always ready to play, and some of his best performances were during the annual Mardi Gras. After performing at Paradise he would take his guitar or trumpet and join the throng of musicians who added music to the parades. For five years I saw him as an integral part of the celebration, and though Mardi Gras would continue, it wouldn't be the same without him.

The biggest night of Mardi Gras was the Fat Tuesday before Ash Wednesday when every street in the French Quarter was packed with people who wanted to be as decadent as possible prior to the start of the more solemn Lent event. This had something to do with wanting to be a good Catholic, and the idea that God would be satisfied watching His flock tow the line during the four weeks prior to the anniversary of the resurrection of His Son.

Mardi Gras featured beautiful floats, good-natured yelling and screaming, numerous parades, gregarious laughter, flamboyant costumes, colorful masks, nudity, sex, and drinking. Those last three items were the ones that the majority of good Catholics would swear to avoid after a smear of ash was placed on their foreheads the following day. The Catholics with less fortitude would only vow to avoid sweets or television.

The parades were the most fun to watch. People on stilts, jugglers, and magicians walked among the floats that were decorated with enough glitter to rival any Las Vegas hotel. The streets became a Las Vegas floorshow without the tables. Getting drunk and catching shiny beads were the primary activities of the crowds. There were women, men, and men dressed like women, who enjoyed displaying sections of their bodies that are most often covered. Bare breasts were the most common display, and for those who enjoyed watching inebriated women pull up their shirts, Mardi Gras was the best show on earth. Those who loved good music could be found in the vicinity of Deke.

• • •

The service ended with everyone standing to recite "The Lord's Prayer." It was time to begin the long walk to the cemetery. There were two sections to the procession: the first line and the second line. The first line was comprised of The Grand Marshall, the band, and the coffin; the second line was everyone else. The job of Grand Marshall was always performed by someone who was a close friend of the deceased, and it was mandatory he or she wear a tuxedo. Since all I needed was a top hat to fulfill the necessary requirements, I was the logical choice for this position.

When the participants in the procession were taking their positions behind me I was reminded of the flurry of activity that takes place backstage prior the beginning of a show. Our curtain rose when the front door of Walker's Funeral Home opened, and we were greeted by a large crowd that had gathered on the corner of Burgundy and Conti Streets. The crowd was expected because a New Orleans' funeral procession was considered a tourist attraction.

I acknowledged the throng with a tip of my hat as I walked down the steps to the street. The band followed behind me playing "NEARER MY GOD TO THEE." It was a dirge standard, known by every Bourbon Street musician, and its mournful melody reflected the sadness of Deke's passing. Sticks, strapped onto a large bass drum, struck the downbeat of each bar. Pappy played his saxophone, Sweet Horn was on trumpet, and Mr. Bop jingled a tambourine because the upright bass was not designed to be a parade instrument. The band was followed by the pallbearers, then came the rest of Deke's friends followed by the swarm of tourists and onlookers.

Our pace was slow and respectful as we made our way down four blocks then turned left on Chartres Street toward the first of four scheduled stops. When we marched past the bronze statue of Andrew Jackson, we had arrived at the steps of St. Louis Cathedral. In accordance with ceremony, I removed my hat, and placed it over my heart. This gesture was to show respect for the places that were important to the deceased.

Deke used to love walking through the cathedral looking at the stained glass, artwork, and beautifully painted ceiling. He said his heart soared whenever he heard the pipe organ, reputed to be one of the best in the country. A few months before his death, he had gained permission from the cathedral's bishop for me to play that organ during the coming Christmas holidays. I was excited at the prospect of playing such a massive instrument, and I had attended several classes given by the church's musical director in order to learn its functions. Deke's untimely death had prompted me to ask the bishop if I could move my performance to an earlier date, and given the circumstances, he agreed.

The procession tiptoed into God's house as Mr. Bop and I took our positions in the organ loft. His bass was already there, and he would accompany me because I had not learned to play with my feet. Mrs. Bailey had done a wonderful job with my digits, but after a few organ lessons I discovered that my toes were not qualified to participate in my musical career. So Mr. Bop thumbed the staccato "feet" parts on his bass, and we played "MARCH OF THE MAGI" by Mr. F. Flaxington Harker. The song was from the cantata <u>THE STAR OF BETHLEHEM</u>, and it was Deke's favorite piece of music that didn't fall into the jazz category.

The religious aspects of this instrumental concerned The Three Wise Men (Balthazar, Caspar and Melchior) and their journey to honor the baby Jesus. Mr. Harker had most certainly written it in praise of The Lord, but knowing The Lord's generous heart and compassionate spirit I was sure He wouldn't mind sharing some of His praise with Deke for a few minutes.

The growing procession's next stop was the club called Paradise. Our last performance there — the night before Deke died — was as festive and playful as the four thousand eight hundred and twenty-nine that preceded it. There had been no soft trumpets playing in my head to make me believe a catastrophe was waiting in the wings. It was just Deke's time to go home, and join those who had made the journey before him. I was not prepared for the end of the road.

The band was playing "SWING LOW, SWEET CHARIOT" when we arrived at Paradise's black-ribbon-draped doorway. Mr. Taylor had closed the bar in memoriam to Deke, and as I placed the top hat over my heart I saw the small sign in the window indicating that Paradise would reopen on Tuesday, August 28, and that all drinks would be half price. The band and I were scheduled to participate in Mr. Taylor's reopening, but performing as four-fifths of our former selves seemed foreign to me – as foreign as carrying one-fifth of us to a final resting place.

I led the two lines slowly up Dumaine Street to a spot on North Rampart Street that Deke held in the highest regard. Back in the 1910's, a bullet from a gun (discharged on a dare) sent a young teenager to the "Waifs' Home for Boys" for eighteen months. While there, he played the drums as a member of the "Coloured Waifs' Band," and exhibited such musical prowess that the band director promoted him to bugle. When he graduated to trumpet he created a style of playing off the beat that became known as "swing," and he helped alter the course of musical history. The young man was Louis Armstrong, and the top hat over my heart at the site of the gunshot was Deke's salute to him.

Six blocks east to Esplanade Avenue, and the procession turned left to walk the remaining blocks to Deke's fourth and final stop. St. Louis

Cemeteries were divided into three separate graveyards, and they were numbered sequentially: One, Two, and Three. Number Three was where we headed as the band played "YOU WONDER," the only song I had written in New Orleans. It was primarily a saxophone piece for Pappy, but contained two eight-bar breaks that Deke had filled with sweet notes from his guitar. The band decided that only Mr. Bop's tambourine would play during Deke's sixteen measures, however, as we walked to the grave site I knew we all heard Deke's guitar in our heads. Years later I renamed the song "DEKE'S THEME," and when I had the opportunity to record it I included those sixteen bars of silence in homage to him. My producer thought the gesture was "a pointless waste of valuable studio time." I found it ironic that the recording industry referred to my tribute as "dead air."

Dead air was an apt description for the oppressive heat that beat down on those who still remained in the procession. The first line was still intact, but the ranks of the second line had thinned during our journey to the cemeteries known to the locals as "Cities of the Dead." The stone mausoleums and vaults, tightly packed on both sides of the pathway, intensified the heat making them more suitable for baking than housing.

The pallbearers were doing an excellent job carrying Deke (never faltering, never out of step) as they followed the band and me along the twisting path that led to the final resting place. Mr. Walker had arranged the purchase of a gray-marble crypt where the body of my friend would be interred. I was grateful that Mr. Walker had handled all the burial details as professionally as my mother used to.

St. Louis Cemeteries One, Two, and Three were located in the oldest section of The French Quarter (a run-down neighborhood that both tourists and residents were warned to avoid — especially after dark). Some people, lured by fables of flesh-eating zombies, disregarded the five o' clock news reports of murders and robberies that occurred in this area. My lack of "zombie" curiosity was complemented by my lack of desire to wind up as a featured story on those five o'clock news programs, so I was glad Deke's funeral was a daytime affair.

Though I heeded the warnings of the dangers that lurked in The French Quarter, Cafe Du Monde was an excellent place to sit in the daytime and drink chicory coffee while watching the world pass by. I spent many quiet afternoons there writing letters to Antoinette, and to Mr. and Mrs. Charles Derbin. I always enclosed a few matchbooks for Sylvia, and drink recipes for Charlie. Antoinette liked little trinkets so I sent her voodoo charms, or any small souvenir that had a "French Quarter" imprint. I loved the name French Quarter; Antoinette was from France, and I always had a quarter in my pocket.

The procession arrived at Deke's crypt, and as his coffin was placed inside I said, "God rest his soul," and the band immediately broke into a rousing rendition of "THE ORPHAN STOMP." The solemn occasion became a party atmosphere, and in the commotion no one heard me whisper, "May I have another napkin, please?"

When I was first told about the New Orleans tradition of closing a funeral with a ruckus I thought it sounded highly inappropriate. Sweet Horn explained the custom, telling me it was a symbolic gesture to express happiness for a loved one who had finally escaped the misery and hardships of life. His description of life certainly made it sound like there was a reason to rejoice, even though I had never known Deke to be miserable about anything.

The crowd yelled "Hallelujah!" and "Praise The Lord!" while they danced and clapped their hands to the music. The somber group that had walked for hours now ran with the fever of a Baptist revival. It was fun to jump up and down, and bang on Sticks' bass drum as I escaped the cemeteries, but I was still sad that Deke was gone. It was a familiar sadness, and I was comforted by the thought that my personal welcoming committee had already embraced Deke when he walked through the pearly gates.

That night the band and I began to talk about what we had been avoiding for five days — finding someone to take Deke's place. Replacing him might require hiring several musicians because there were not many so blessed with his proficiency. Musical ability aside, we would be looking for someone whose personality and temperament matched those already in place. Finding the right fit would be important. The task was formidable, tantamount to making the group decision to leave Las Vegas, and after a number of hours and countless suggestions we opted to think about it in the morning.

Sleep did not come easy. My mental orchestra worked overtime playing a mixture of soft sonatas and resounding overtures, all featuring a guitar or trumpet. Nostalgic visions spanning eight years floated among the notes: The band's first impromptu performance at The Devil's Den in Cincinnati, our first engagement at The Roundabout Dinner Theater and Steakhouse in Sioux City, Iowa, a bowling alley, the big limo, Kansas, a billiard club, hamburgers and fries, Nebraska, Las Vegas, St. Peter Street; all roads led to Paradise.

A few days after the funeral the band was still trying to decide what to do. Mr. Taylor wasn't happy that we hadn't returned to Paradise, and though he said he understood our line-up problem, he installed another group as his house band, and wished us well.

"Not a very nice kiss-off, if you ask me." Mr. Bop had not taken Mr. Taylor's firing lightly.

"Wasn't no kiss-off! What the man did was a kick-out." Even if it sounded like disagreement, Sticks concurred with Mr. Bop's assessment.

"Won't fly, treatin' us that way. Taylor should show more respect," Pappy said.

"You can't blame Mr. Taylor for doing his job." My words calmed the band's upset. "He wants a band, and right now we're not a band."

It was the truth, and the band knew it, but as my father used to say, "Knowing the truth isn't the same as accepting it." I repeated his wisdom, and proposed the only solution I could think of to solve the problem of replacing Deke. "We continue as a foursome."

A decision had to be made, and Mr. Bop was its instigator.

"Tee-Bee," Mr. Bop spoke my name gently, as though he was afraid it would break. "It don't make sense to me why you want to go on doin' the same thing you been doin'."

"I like to sing," I replied with a rush of violins in my head, "but you have a point. We've been here for five years, and maybe it is time to leave. We could go back out on the road for a while." I thought my suggestion had merit. "I could call Mr. Silverman. Maybe he can book another tour." I wanted to let Mr. Bop know that time had not dampened my enthusiasm.

"That's not what I mean, Tee-Bee." Mr. Bop's voice dropped even lower and softer, "I think you should be makin' some plans for yourself."

I was momentarily stunned by his recommendation, but I collected my thoughts and replied, "Mr. Bop, my father used to say, 'The difference between what a man thinks, and what a man says can usually be found between the words he speaks.'" I looked into his soft brown eyes, and saw my friend was hurting. "What's going on?"

Sticks answered, "Dig it, my man. You be livin' here five years now. How many new songs you write?"

"One," I answered, "but what does that have to do with what we're talking about?"

"Everything, and everything!" Sticks was adamant. "You got skills, Tee-Bee! But you ain't usin' 'em, and you ain't gonna use 'em long as your butt stay here in Bayouville, you dig?"

"Tee-Bee," Pappy interrupted, "What we're trying to tell you is something we've all been talking about for a long time, Deke included." Pappy had never been the demonstrative type, but he put his arms around me and gave me a hug. "You know we all love you."

"You've told us a lot of things your father said, and I want to tell you somethin' my daddy said to me," a tear was traveling down Mr. Bop's cheek as he spoke. "I was seven years old when my daddy left, and I remember askin' him why he was leavin', and he said, 'Son, sometimes the best thing a man can do for his family is to go.' That's what he said." Another tear followed the path of the first, and I knew it was for me when he said, "Tee-Bee, son, it's time you go."

A swirl of discordant instruments circled my head as I tried to speak, but there were no words to say. I felt something brush against my wrist, and I looked down at the envelope Pappy was trying to put into my hand.

"There's eight thousand dollars in there that Sticks, Bop, Deke, and I were keeping in the bank. We saved it for you so you'd have some extra money when you left us. You've got a great gift, Tee-Bee. We all want you to use it."

I opened my hand, and accepted the envelope. These men were my friends, and I knew that whatever plans they had, they had my best interests at heart.

Mr. Bop explained the rationale behind the band's decision. "Your road has to go on, Tee-Bee, and we think we been holdin' you back. Not at first, mind you. At first you needed us to make yourself better than you were. We, and I know I'm speaking for Deke too, we all loved playin' behind you, and you made us better than we were. It was an equal partnership, but now, well, now you don't need to be playin' here no more."

"My man," Sticks said shaking his head, "you got to be hip to the whole picture. Bop, Pappy, and me can jam the same groove, and be happy we doin' it; your groove got to move or it go stale. You got to know that be true, my brother. I sure know it, and you much smarter than me."

"We think you should call the man that give you his card back in Vegas," Mr. Bop said. "Remember? He told you to check him out if you ever in Hollywood."

I remembered the man, and I still had his card. He had given it to me the day after The Recital, telling me to come see him at his record company in California, but in all the excitement of my agreement with The Don I had put it aside. New Orleans was the next city on the band's agenda, and California was in the opposite direction.

“So here’s the bottom line,” Pappy said. “We’ve been kicking around in different groups all our lives, but we want something better for you. I think Bop and Sticks will agree that we’ve been a little selfish keeping you here as long as we did, but we did know this day would come. We want you to take every opportunity that comes your way. That’s the plan, Tee-Bee.”

“And it flies,” added Mr. Bop. “You know it’s not Deke’s dyin’ that brought us to this; it’s Deke’s life, and the life of everyone in this room.”

“It’s no kiss-off, my man. It’s a love tap.” Sticks smiled. “Dig it. I’m gonna get me one of those outfits o’ yours, and call myself Tuxedo Sticks.”

The decision was made; Tuxedo Bob was once again a solo act. I was as certain the correct decision had been made as I was that the hole in my heart would never heal. Antoinette’s photos from Hoover Dam, and the one of the band in front of my name-in-lights-marquee were more precious to me than ever.

I looked out the window of the Greyhound bus, and waved good-bye to Delroy “Bee-Bop” Washington, Joe “Sticks” Dunbar, and Charlie “Pappy” Donovan. They seemed to be moving backward as they waved their farewells, but it was just an illusion. The platform was stationary; I was pulling away. I sat back in my seat, and closed my eyes; headed toward a state called “golden,” and a city of angels.

# Hollywood & Home

"There is no doing it all over again."

Orville Fledsper

# twenty-fifth concerto

The Big Rig Motel, just north of Schulberg on U.S. Route 85, isn't the most glamorous place I've stayed, but it's the first home I've had in my hometown in twenty-three years. Across the highway Trucker's Haven is still serving "Good Food - 24 Hours a Day," and Doris Simmons is still smiling behind the counter. Until I decide what to do with the rest of my life there are hot meals available within walking distance.

On the bed of motel room #17 is a suitcase much older than mine; its age endorsed by fraying corners and a handle that hangs from its remaining strap. It belonged to my mother when she was Margaret Thrombull. Thrombull was her maiden name, and according to the ID tag she was a resident of Bruskin Hall at St. Mary's College for Girls. Also in my possession are six brand new "After Six" tuxedos per my long-standing yearly exchange agreement with Tom Conners Jr.

There was lump in my throat when I walked up the front steps and knocked on the door of the Conners, nee Fledsper, house this morning. I used to run up those same steps when I came home from school; I bounced balls off them; they used to be mine. Tom Jr. certainly made me feel welcome when he invited me inside, and immediately offered the use of a bathroom so I could shower and shave. He told me that after I had gotten "the train washed off" I would find six new tuxedos on the bed in the guest room in exchange for my old ones. In years past we had handled this transaction via the U.S. Postal Service.

After I was refreshed and dressed in my '87 model "After Six," Tom Jr. escorted me to the kitchen where I was introduced to his wife Betsy.

"How about some breakfast before Tom takes you on the grand tour?" Betsy said with a smile.

I gratefully accepted, and over bacon and eggs they told me all the news about Schulberg: the new high school where their twin daughters were members of the honor roll, Betsy's election to the town council, and Tom Jr.'s induction into the Elk's Club. I told them a little about the towns and cities where Tom Jr. had been sending my replacement tuxedos. Good manners prevented me from laughing out loud when Betsy asked, "So, what are your plans?"

They took me on "the grand tour," and as I followed from room to room the sad feeling I had when I first walked up the front steps gradually disappeared. The house looked smaller than I remembered, and Margaret's flair for decorating was missing. The corner in the living room where she used to sit on the overstuffed couch was now occupied by a floor lamp behind a director's chair; the area of the den where Orville had rocked in his favorite recliner had been taken over by a computer; the antique silver and crystal chandelier in the dining room had been replaced with track lights. Tom Jr. and Betsy had made it their home, and I was a guest who had come to pick up the vestiges of the Fledsper family belongings that were stored there.

The suitcase on my motel room bed had been tucked away in the dusty darkness of the Conners' attic where it had served a spider's need for housing support. I thanked the spider for standing guard over my mother's things, and apologized for relocating the edge of her delicate handiwork to a corner of a box of Christmas ornaments. She did a little eight-legged jig while I carefully reattached her home, and cautioned her that this new location would only last until December. She crawled over to the ornament box, and tapped it twice with one of her legs as if to say, "Gone. Christmas."

Opening the suitcase took several minutes as the locks had oxidized, but when the latches finally popped I lifted the lid and peered inside. The first thing I saw was the plaster handprint I had made in kindergarten. The indented hand looked so small, but the digits were long and thin; perfect for playing the piano.

• • •

I arrived in Los Angeles thinking that it was going to be just another city where I would perform my music. "Smooth sailing," "an even keel," and "steady as you go" were nautical terms I had heard in a pirate movie on late night television, and I applied them to my journey. My path had been paved with good fortune, and I had no reason to believe that I would encounter anything more than a small bump or two. I thought Los Angeles was just another city called Paradise.

At the end of my first Greyhound bus ride to Chicago, the driver had proudly said, "Here we are folks, the Windy City." When I arrived in New

York the driver barked, "Port Authority! Everybody out!" In Los Angeles the bus driver casually announced, "Last stop, Los Angeles." When I walked out of the Los Angeles bus depot I was on the corner of 6th and Los Angeles Street. My immediate thought was I would be living in a city that was either devoted to repetition or had a high regard for self-promotion.

I didn't remember New York City having a "New York Drive" or "Manhattan Avenue." New Orleans had an "Orleans Street," that was close, but it was in the oldest part of town, so it was probably "Old Orleans Street." I quickly learned a second difference between Los Angeles and Anytown, USA. Pedestrians had the right of way in Anytown; in Los Angeles they had the right to remain silent.

"Didn't you see the "Don't Walk" sign?" the officer asked. He adjusted his hat, then pulled out his ticket booklet to begin recording my offense.

"Yes, sir, officer, I did," I replied, "but the light was still green." I should have known better than to present my take on the legality of the situation.

"The light's for cars, the sign's for people," he said without looking up. "What's your name?"

"Tuxedo Bob, sir." I extended my hand momentarily, but quickly withdrew it as I could see his hands were busy.

He shook his head as he wrote my name in the space provided for the perpetrator of a crime. "You must be a comedian."

"No, sir."

"Well, you've sure got the name for it."

I thought he was making a joke, but he wasn't smiling, so I didn't either.

"What's your address, Bob?"

I informed the officer that I had just stepped off the bus, and had not had the opportunity to find lodging. He was kind enough to give me directions to the YMCA in Hollywood that had offered daily accommodations to single men since the late 1920's. After he remarked that I was a very well dressed transient, he gave me my ticket and went on his way. I thought the twenty-five dollar fine was a reasonable price to pay for the valuable information I had received.

A number 83 bus took me up Wilshire Boulevard, and after transferring to a number 85, I disembarked within a few blocks of the YMCA. During the ride the bus driver had informed me that there were streets to identify every area of the city; Santa Monica, Westwood, Venice, Century, and Hollywood all had their own Boulevards. As I walked toward the YMCA I saw huge letters on the top of a hillside that spelled out H-O-L-L-Y-W-O-O-D. I wondered if all the cities the bus driver mentioned used similar advertising campaigns.

I remember laughing out loud when I flopped down on the lumpy mattress in my room. Here I was again — big city, room rented by the day, a wallet filled with traveler's checks, a business card in my pocket, and a suitcase of tuxedos at my feet. It was as though my mental orchestra conductor had tapped his baton, and issued the instruction "Da capo!" - from the beginning.

I wanted to find an apartment as quickly as possible because the YMCA did not allow its residents to play musical instruments. I learned of this rule as my electric piano was being delivered from the bus depot.

"Is that what I think it is?" was the warning issued by the desk clerk. "We run a quiet place here, no noise allowed. You can keep that thing in your room, but don't be playin' on it."

For three days I walked into any building within a forty-block radius of the YMCA that displayed a "For Rent" sign. I was embarrassed each time I wrote "jay-walking" in the "Have you ever been convicted of a crime" section of the applications, but most of the landlords I met told me they didn't consider my offense to be significant.

My "currently unemployed" entry on the applications, along with "The Tropics — Las Vegas" under work history, caused the most raised eyebrows and questions. I was astonished by the number of times I was asked, "Are you currently engaged in any criminal activity?" I always answered with an emphatic "No, sir!" or "No, ma'am!" but since the root of criminal activity is deceit, I wasn't sure anyone believed me. Even though there were many nice comments about New Orleans, I found that most Hollywood apartment owners frowned upon the idea of renting to an out-of-work jaywalker who had done time in Las Vegas.

After filling out sixty-seven forms at various buildings, I finally succeeded in renting a furnished studio apartment just off the corner of Franklin and Vine, overlooking The Hollywood Freeway. Even though I had given the seventy-year-old blind manager, Mrs. Mabel Robertson, the same information I had given everyone else, she simply put her hand on my face and proclaimed that I looked like "a nice young man." I signed a lease, and gave her three-month's rent in advance. It was my home for fourteen years, and its close proximity to a freeway full of speeding cars and trucks negated the need for any rules concerning unnecessary noise.

Five days after my arrival I went to the offices of Eclipse Records, and asked to see the man whose name was on the card in my pocket. The receptionist informed me that Mr. Kelvin Ballard had left town after the earthquake in 1971 leveled his apartment.

"That was, like what, two years ago?" She blew an enormous pink bubble of chewing gum, and it popped to accentuate her point.

I had heard that earthquakes were one of the natural disasters that occurred in the area, and that people often decided to move away after a really big one. But since shaky ground had not ceased the activities of Eclipse Records, it was logical to assume that Mr. Ballard's position as Director of Artists and Repertoire had been filled. "Is there someone else I can see?" I asked.

"Just a sec, hon." She put down her nail file to answer the ringing phone. "Eclipse Records. Oh, hi there Mr. Chambers. Yeah, I would say he's expectin' your call." Her gum popped when she chewed; her mouth moved in the slow circular motion most predominant in the cow family. "Yeah, 'pissed' is a good word. I don't think he was too happy pickin' up the morning paper and seein' a picture of your client fightin' with a cop." She giggled at something Mr. Chambers said. "Oh, you are bad! Look hon, I got somebody here, but the answer is yes, okay?" She pushed a button to forward the call, and looked up at me. "So, where were we?"

"May I see the person who acquired Mr. Ballard's position?"

"Walter doesn't see anyone without an appointment."

"May I make an appointment to see Mr. Walter?"

"It's Mr. Honikey, and no, you can't. He doesn't make appointments unless he likes your tape. Do you want to leave your tape?"

God had been kind enough to instruct me on my need for a tape nine years earlier in New York City. As I left the offices of Eclipse Records I silently apologized for making Him repeat Himself.

Strolling up Hollywood Boulevard reminded me of Bourbon Street the morning after Fat Tuesday. The sidewalks were littered with newspapers and plastic cups, young people slept in doorways, and the smell of urine permeated the air, but to my knowledge there had been no parade (and the air in Los Angeles was called "smog.")

I had been so involved with getting my apartment and visiting Eclipse Records that I really had not taken the time to notice anyone around me. That was not like me at all, and I quickly remedied the situation by leaning against a street sign to inhale the endless stream of people who walked past me on their way to somewhere.

Men were letting their hair grow past their shoulders, and had taken to adorning themselves with beaded necklaces and earrings, and carrying purses. Women had discarded modesty enhancing undergarments in favor of less restrictive clothing, and it must have been the close proximity of Pacific beaches that made sandals the common choice of footwear for both sexes.

I was familiar with the fashion trends that included Nehru jackets and medallions, the topless swimsuit, bellbottoms and tie-dyed caftans; I had heard about smoking banana peelings, acid rock, sit-ins, marijuana, bra burning, and free-love. All of these current cultural preferences seemed to me to be as significant as powdered wigs, whalebone corsets, bathtub gin, marathon dances, sugar rationing, bomb shelters, and ducktail haircuts had been to previous generations. Fads come and go, but I didn't recall the trends I was viewing on Hollywood Boulevard having the same profound impact in any of the cities I had previously visited.

While I watched the parade my mind kept itself busy composing piano and flute counterpoints to the compositions of Jefferson Airplane, The Doors, and Buffalo Springfield that blared from competing neighboring storefronts. I was so preoccupied that I didn't notice the tall man with tightly woven braids of shiny, fuzzy black hair as he approached me.

"Hey, man. You want some hash?" he whispered in my ear.

Though I was startled, I did not forget my manners. "No thank you, sir. It's kind of you to offer, but I'm not hungry."

"Everybody's hungry, man. Come on. Ten bucks. Primo Lebanese Blonde. Fine hash, man. You won't be sorry."

He was a persistent salesman, and under normal circumstances I might have made a purchase, but his unkempt attire and dirty fingernails caused me to be concerned about his sanitation procedures. "No thank you, sir. I had some in a diner once — corned beef, pink with little diced potatoes; I didn't care for it."

"No problem, man. Peace," he said raising two fingers in the shape of a vee.

He turned away to approach someone else with his sales pitch, so he didn't hear me respond, "And peace to you too."

• • •

U-2, a rock-and-roll group from Ireland, is the most popular band in America as I sift through my late mother's keepsakes. Some of my memories are included among her treasures: my high school yearbooks and old report cards, a plain white envelope containing a few folded sheets of Margaret's favorite daffodil-yellow stationary, an object wrapped in newspaper, and my parent's wedding photograph that used to be displayed on the mantle in the living room. The picture of Orville and Margaret brought a tear to my eye, even though I didn't know the happy couple at the time it was taken. They looked so young in their pre-me days.

I thumb through the report cards, and smile at the recurring notations from my elementary school teachers: "excellent manners," "gets along well with others," "has a tendency to daydream." I remember my teachers telling me to pay attention. They didn't understand I wasn't daydreaming; I was orchestrating their lessons. I thought any subject matter could be improved by adding a string section.

I looked through the yearbooks recalling the innocence of my youth. The scribbled notes from classmates were amusing: "Stay as sweet as you are," "2 good 2 B 4 got 10," "Q: What do you get when you cross a chicken with a tuxedo? A: A well-dressed bird." I was voted "best-dressed" four years in a row, and the caption under my senior picture read "always wears a smile, but most likely to become testy if "After Six" ever goes out of business."

When I reach for the white envelope, the sheets of Margaret's stationary fall out and drop to the floor. I retrieve them, but I set them next to her suitcase because their inexplicable fall from my grasp alerts me that I should save them for last. I am well aware that there are no accidents.

• • •

One typically sunny Los Angeles morning I was taking a walk, and turning the corner at Franklin and Highland I bumped into a young man as a policeman was handcuffing him. Ever mindful of God's mysterious ways, I knew that bumping into a stranger was not an accident, but a sign. I apologized, and paused to study the young man for a moment. His attire was not well maintained, and he had what looked to be an unfinished tattoo of a red cross on his right forearm. My mother would have said he needed some serious soap and water. As the officer recited a city code concerning vagrancy laws, the young man kept repeating something about not having "a pad." I decided to leave well enough alone because I couldn't be sure that God's plan didn't include the young man's incarceration. I continued on my way, unaware that I would again encounter this young man fourteen years later.

The days passed in a flurry as I attempted to comply with the request of the Eclipse Records receptionist. I couldn't find a pinball arcade that had a recording machine, and after several phone inquiries to various amusement establishments I discovered that my idea of recording was not the one commonly shared within the music community.

A recording studio was what I needed, and I found a small one that touted itself as the most affordable in town. Three hours and two hundred dollars later I emerged from Omega Sound Studios with a tape. I had chosen four songs to record, but when I listened to the playback they sounded nothing like the way I heard them in my head. Eddie, the person who operated the recording equipment at my session, had said, "It sounds kinda lame with just your voice and a piano. You need a band, bro."

I remembered that Sticks had made the same statement on the big limo outside Warsaw, Missouri, and decided to call the band I needed. After discovering the phone in the apartment on St. Peter Street had been disconnected, I called Sweet Horn. He informed me that they had left town to gig as a trio in New York City at The Blue Note and The Village Gate.

"They goin' by the name of TRINITY now," Sweet Horn said. "That means three." He laughed when he told me they had adopted my preference for performing in a tuxedo. "They lookin' right fancy, sur'nuf."

Sweet Horn suggested I give them a call, but I felt it was best to leave well enough alone. I sent a congratulatory note to one of the clubs Sweet Horn had mentioned, and for several years I corresponded with Pappy because he had been elected the group's biographer. Sticks married a woman he called "Super Fox" who occasionally sang with the band. Mr. Bop developed arthritis in his digits, and in the winter of 1979 when his condition prevented him from playing, TRINITY went their separate ways. Sticks supported his wife and her three children by working as a studio musician, Mr. Bop moved to Holland and opened a jazz record store, and Pappy bought a piece of Jimmy Ray's Club playing his saxophone there until he died in the summer of 1981 and reunited with Deke.

But those future events were not drifting among the notes of the flute concerto I composed as I perused the Yellow Pages in February of 1974. My old band was not available, and I needed musicians. Under that heading I found "The American Federation of Musicians," and I went to their offices to inquire about the use of their services. After I had completed and submitted all the necessary paperwork I became a signatory, which meant I was authorized to hire union musicians and pay them "union scale," which meant expensive.

Eleven thousand dollars was all the money I had left after bus fare, housing, and one inferior-quality tape, but it seemed like more than enough to achieve the sound quality I was looking for in my second recording venture. This time I booked three days at a sixteen-track studio called The Album Factory because one of the employees at the musician's union informed me "anybody who's anybody records there."

The studio was loaded with all sorts of electronic equipment that my recording engineer/producer, Jason Ravans, said was needed to make a professional recording. His exact words on the subject were, "Yeah, bro, this stuff comes in handy."

Mr. Ravans' services were included in the package price of the studio, and he came with a well-groomed ponytail hanging down to his waist, a studio-logo T-shirt, blue jeans, and boots that were previously lizards. I was impressed when I saw his name under the "Presented To" imprint on three of the gold records hanging on the studio walls. Since my career had started in the gold-record-lined halls of Pavilion Music, I took this as a good sign.

"We're laid-back here, bro, so let's call me Jason," he said in his nonchalant manner of speaking.

The booth where Jason sat surrounded by electronics was separated from the recording room by a thick wall of glass. When I first sat down at the piano and put on my headphones I had difficulty getting his attention, and I thought that what he called "laid-back" was actually a lack of interest. I soon learned that he couldn't hear me until he turned my microphone on, and I couldn't hear him unless he pushed the talkback button. Sometimes when he pushed the talkback button I would receive a jolt of feedback in my headphones. The occurrence of this sharp earsplitting noise was always blamed on my proximity to a live microphone, and I apologized each time it happened.

I recorded five songs with three union-scale musicians that Jason knew "from way back." The cost was thirty-five hundred dollars, well within my budget boundaries, but Jason said the tape was not complete.

"They're decent rhythm tracks, bro, but you should add some more sounds, you know, to increase the vibe." He inhaled some granulated white powder from a small mirror into his nose. "I know this guy, bro," he continued while pinching his nostrils, "who books overdub dates. Hey, you wanna toot, bro?"

"No, thank you," I replied, "but yes, please, to your idea about your friend's help with the sounds."

Seven thousand dollars, eighteen overdub musicians, and countless expressions of "bro" later, I had a tape that sounded like a record. I delivered "COMPLETELY NUDE," "YOU DO IT FOR MONEY," "BAD MAN," "CHOCOLATE TAPIOCA PUDDING," and "OUT OF MY MIND" to the Eclipse Record offices, and hurried back to my apartment to wait for Mr. Honikey's phone call.

I was sure his call would come, but after a few weeks, and less than five hundred dollars in my local bank account, I thought my time waiting might be better served seeking employment. Fortunately, devising a plan for additional income was easy in a city where there were a number of restaurants that hired the services of piano players. I was confident that my prior performing experience would impress any prospective employer, but when I applied at Maisonette de la Casa, it was my tuxedo that proved to be my most valuable asset.

The restaurant/piano bar was located on Santa Monica Boulevard between Sanchez and Robertson. When I saw the Robertson Boulevard sign

I couldn't wait to get back to my apartment, and tell my landlord she had a street named after her. When I walked into the restaurant, I was dazzled by the walls that had been painted to give the impression that a dining room had been constructed in the middle of a dense forest. Dark greens and browns were the main colors with just a hint of blue sky peeking out from behind the leaves and branches. The tables were dressed with crisp white linens, green tapers in tall silver candlestick holders, and single stems of red roses rising from crystal vases; the brown velvet chairs looked plush and comfortable. In the front of the room was an ebony Steinway baby grand that had a luster as prominent as the shine on my patent leather shoes.

"So, my friend, I see you are already dressed for my fine establishment." That was the first thing Mr. Carlos Cruvette said to me as he escorted me to the bar. After a few minutes of questioning he said, "You have excellent manners, Tuxedo Bob, and I like the way you listen. Here's what I want to do for you. I already have a piano player on the weekends, but I want you to fill the empty slots on Tuesday, Wednesday, and Thursdays. I'll let you do that, but you have to also maître d' for me on Fridays, Saturdays, and Sundays. So, what do you think of my offer? I'll even pay you," he chuckled, "since you probably came here looking for a paying job. Five dollars an hour, one meal, one drink, you keep all your tips. Is that an acceptable arrangement?"

That arrangement was sealed with a handshake, and I started that evening. Mr. Cruvette had one addendum to his offer that altered my performance technique. "Did I mention no singing?" It was a major minor detail, but it gave my digits an opportunity to practice their instrumental skills. I had been relying on words to communicate a song's intent; my music would have to speak for itself.

I had never performed as a maître d', but since it was a Wednesday, I got to watch Mr. Cruvette's seating procedures during my breaks. I quickly learned the table numbers, and discovered there were three types of customers: those who ate dinner, those who came to be seen eating dinner, and those who wanted to sit where deceased famous people had eaten dinner.

Maisonette de la Casa featured a mixture of French and Spanish cuisines. Sizzling grilled meats with rich sauces were served with rice and beans. The house specialty was Tacos Provencal, one of the most popular appetizers was Caviar Guacamole, and Plantain Flambé was considered the perfect finish to any meal. My most requested number was "The Orphan Stomp."

After a few years passed with no word from Eclipse Records, I figured Mr. Honikey was not interested in my musical style. Disco was the type of music most often heard from the radios of the cars cruising the boulevards, and I didn't have a song that sounded good with a booming bass drum pounding every beat. I was happy playing at Mr. Cruvette's restaurant, and he treated me like one of the family. He had even granted me permission to sing during my last set because it was, "almost closing time, and no one will be bothered."

On my musical nights off I enjoyed greeting the customers and informing them how long they had to wait for a table. Tips to the maître d' were paid by the secret handshake method. I usually received ten dollars from those patrons who felt I was putting them ahead of someone else on my reservation list, and twenty dollars was the industry-standard accompaniment to a customer's statement "see what you can do" after I said the wait would be at least an hour.

Tips to a piano player are a much more open transaction. At first I borrowed the glass water pitcher that the weekend performer, Mr. Harvey "Magic Fingers" O'Malley, used. It sat on the piano, and had no outstanding characteristics other than a simple hand-painted sign taped around its middle that said "kitty." Customers felt obligated to "feed the kitty" whenever their song requests were honored, and some did it as a manner of habit. (Or as my father used to say, "The habit of manners.")

One night I decided to replace the "kitty" sign with a sign of my own. My sign said "pitcher." I thought it was more accurate since a pitcher looks nothing like a cat. The correct labeling did not hinder my nightly tip total, so I figured this literary adjustment did no harm. However, Mr. O'Malley wasn't pleased when he discovered that I had tampered with his property.

"What is this?" he questioned upon seeing my sign. "Is this some kind of joke?" He looked down his nose around the room at the restaurant employees. "I want my kitty sign back, and I want it back this instant!"

"I've got your sign, Mr. O'Malley. I forgot to change it last night. I'm sorry." I regretted causing him anxiety, but he wasn't interested in my apology.

"How dare you touch my property, young man! I consider your offense an outrage." He grabbed his sign from my hand with such fury that it ripped in half. "Now look what you've done!" he screamed, and he stomped off to the kitchen for his free board.

I spent the next twenty minutes constructing a new "kitty" sign with the hope that this would ease the tension between us. However, when he came out of the kitchen it was he who apologized to me.

"My behavior was completely unacceptable. I extend my hand to you in friendship with deepest sincerity." He clicked his heels together, and bowed his head slightly to magnify his surrender.

I shook his hand, and presented him with his new sign. I figured it must have been hunger that had made him so volatile, but a waitress named Carmela informed me he was always nicer after taking his valium. Whatever his reason, I decided it would be better to get my own tip container.

I wanted something nice, so I went to a Thrifty drug store, and bought a glass jar of dusting powder. It was faux cut crystal, and I thought it would dress up the Steinway. The added look of luxury, along with the scent of lilacs that remained after I had given the powder to Carmela, pushed my tips to a fifty-dollar per-night average. This prompted Mr. O'Malley to politely inquire if he could use it instead of his pitcher. I agreed, of course. He was really a very pleasant gentleman when he took his pills. I had not heard about the discovery that there was a link between bad temperament and deficient levels of valium, but if it worked for others like it did for him then it was certainly a miracle drug. Every weekend while he happily counted the extra dollar bills he was receiving in the fancy kitty, I counted my blessings that my body was naturally producing a sufficient amount of valium.

• • •

The object that had been carefully wrapped in a page of old news from the Williston Daily Herald is the lead-crystal jar I gave my mother for her birthday. It still has the faint scent of roses, and I remember what she said to me the day she used the last of its dusting powder. "This is going to be my treasure jar." I can see it holds a few items that she considered worthy enough to be included in her treasury.

I open the jar and discover the four letters I had written to my parents. The first one, from New York City, has the Chinese fortune cookie slogan "You Are Forever Happy!" enclosed, and though twenty-three years have passed, its forecast is still correct. The second one is the Christmas card I had sent from Pressman's, and I smile at the photograph of Mr. Murphy standing next to the sign in front of Billy's Night Life Lounge. I had forgotten about the photo, and I'm glad my mother had the foresight to keep it. A few dried yellow rose petals are also in the card's envelope; Margaret also saw fit to keep a memory of the flowers I had sent. The short "I love you" letter from Pressman's is here, along with the letter I had sent from Lake Geneva that contains the Vince Genoa Express itinerary. The fifth letter to my parents had long ago found its way back to me; I take it from its home in the elastic side-pocket of my suitcase, and add it to the pile.

One more paper item lies at the bottom of the jar, and the folded sheets of daffodil-yellow stationary still sit next to my mother's suitcase. I pause before continuing to stimulate sadness with happy memories.

• • •

I had taken a long break from song writing while in New Orleans. That, along with Deke's death, had been the main reason for the decision to travel to Los Angeles, and I finally started writing again during the spring of 1974. The first new song I wrote was called "ANYTHING TO WIN," and it came to me one afternoon while I was sitting in my apartment pondering the lack of response from Eclipse Records. The lyric "I don't understand this business" came into my head. Immediately following that was the memory of Mr. Napoli mumbling, "What's a decent kid like you doing in a business like this?" I smiled at the symmetry between the thoughts, and began to compose a melody to accompany them.

> "I don't understand this business.
> It doesn't seem to make any sense.
> There's not a lot of small-town, down-home feeling
> in a business like this.
> It's just my opinion, but I think it's kind of strange
> that the only thing I see from the bottom
> is something I want to obtain.
> I could decide to push aside all my morals,
> and claw my way on up to the stars.
> But if I play the game will I find fortune and fame,
> or my heart in a jar?
> And the answer so far?
> Do anything to win.
> Throw away your pride.
> Bargain with your soul.
> If you have to, lie.
> Once you're on the top never give an inch,
> because someone's right behind you
> with a new idea doing anything to win."

The lyrics to "ANYTHING TO WIN" seemed to indicate I had become quite cynical about pursuing a career in show business, but they were written to be a humorous response to the late Mr. Napoli. I was still having fun on my road to success.

Although Mr. Cruvette had sanctioned the addition of vocal selections to my last set, he requested they be the type of songs that "no one in the restaurant would have to pay attention to." I didn't think my most recent composition fit into that category, so taking his advice to heart, I wrote some songs with repetitive choruses. I still wrote songs that told a story, but by singing the same words over and over I didn't annoy any customers with anything they might have to think about.

To my benefit, people enjoyed listening without thinking. Mr. Cruvette told me that I had begun to acquire what is known in show business as a "following," and due to my popularity he lifted his restriction concerning vocals in my early evening performances.

"I think your voice goes very nicely with food," he said.

He mentioned that he and his business partners were quite pleased to own a restaurant that no one could get into without a reservation. Holidays and special events were booked months in advance, and by the end of 1979 I was relieved of my maître d' duties.

"Magic Fingers quit, and I want you to take over his nights. Will you do that for me?" Being a successful restaurateur required excellent manners, and Mr. Cruvette always spoke with a tone of respect. He was a short man – no more than five and a half feet tall — with a small mustache that was perfectly trimmed, and he kept his graying hair significantly shorter than the current trend. He liked the wide-lapel open-collared shirt style of the era, and he invested heavily in gold chains, which he proudly displayed around his neck. When I agreed to his request he said, "Excellent. Here's a favor I'll do for you in return."

I thought he would say he was taking over as maître d', or he would let me train the new maître d'. I never expected the favor he had in mind.

"I have some friends joining me at the restaurant New Year's Eve. Actually, they're more than friends; they're my investment partners." Whenever Mr. Cruvette was pleased with something, he pushed out his upper lip in a way that made his mustache bunch up in the middle and appear smaller than usual. That was how he looked when he said, "They want to meet the entertainer who has given them such a good profit margin. If they like your music as much as I, then we will look for ways to capitalize on your popularity."

I wasn't sure what he meant, and he must have sensed that from the look on my face. Without mentioning specifics he explained that he and his friends owned a number of companies, and perhaps an agreement could be reached for me to record some of my songs. A short tribute from my internal trumpets made it difficult to pay close attention as he continued presenting his idea, but I heard the words "percentage of any deal" and "anything you record" before he finished with "but those are standard things any artist would expect."

New Year's Eve arrived, and so did Mr. Cruvette's friendly investment partners. After I was introduced to them and their wives, they introduced me to the guests they had brought to the celebration. Mr. Cruvette had already told me they were bringing the new president of one of the companies they owned, but I was not prepared for the mental crash of cymbals that announced God's latest edition of "His Mysterious Ways."

"Tuxedo Bob, I'd like you to meet Janet and Walter Honikey. Walter's our new president over at Eclipse Records."

Smiling prevented my mouth from remaining agape for more than a millisecond. "It's nice to meet you. I hope you enjoy your dinners, and may I say Happy New Year to all of you." Decorum prevented me from skipping to the piano.

• • •

I retrieve the last crumpled piece of paper from the bottom of my mother's treasure jar. So little of my parents' lives remain. The money from their insurance, the oak tree, their businesses, and the way they laughed at a funny joke; everything's gone except these few scrapbook items on my motel room bed and the bank account that was transferred to my name. As I unfold the paper in the light from the window, I see a glint of gold from my mother's wedding band. I remember when she told me she had put it away because of her allergy. I was four, and had asked why she didn't wear a ring like father.

"It makes my finger swell up like a balloon," was her response. "I keep it upstairs in my drawer, tucked away in the piece of paper your father gave me to honor our first anniversary."

I can still hear the soothing sound of her voice — it fits perfectly among clarinets and flutes. Her ring fits my little finger, and since I've never worn jewelry I decide to keep it on for a while to see if my digit will react in a similar balloon-like fashion.

The piece of paper that had been housing the ring features the familiar, but now faded, red Coca-Cola symbol imprinted on the top. It's a stock certificate that my father must have purchased when he sold America's favorite beverage because it's dated February 19, 1931. Seven years later he presented it to Margaret to commemorate their paper anniversary. I have no idea if two hundred shares from so many years ago are worth anything, but the question merits a phone call to Williston.

"Hello, stranger. I haven't heard from you in years." Mrs. Amanda Winters had retired from her law practice in 1977, and though she no longer filed my taxes, I still considered her an expert in the matters of money. "What have you been up to?"

I gave her a brief rundown of all that had transpired over the course of my final years in Los Angeles. She was particularly interested in the part about Eclipse Records.

• • •

In the spring and summer of 1980 I recorded eighteen vocal compositions, four instrumentals, and two symphonies by virtue of the financial backing provided by Mr. Cruvette and his partners and the free studio time at Eclipse Records. Including the five songs already in Eclipse's possession, I had recorded almost every song I had written since leaving Schulberg in 1964. I excluded "MOB SONG" per my non-performance agreement with Jimmy, and "SANTA CLAUS LOVES LAS VEGAS" because I wanted to save it for a future album of Christmas songs. Everyone who had been at the table that previous New Year's Eve loved the finished tape; everyone except Mr. Walter Honikey.

"I don't hear it. But it's a good tape; the songs are well written; the production's top-notch, except for the dead air you put in that instrumental; I have to pass. I just don't hear it."

I was sitting in his office when Mr. Honikey played the entire tape but didn't hear it. I watched him nod while he didn't hear the plea to rekindle a love affair in "SAY YOU LOVE ME." I saw him smile when he recognized himself in the second verse that he didn't hear from "DON'T FORGET ME." I felt his foot tapping the floor to the beat while he didn't hear "SHE'S GONE." And I noticed a look of contemplation on his face during the entire ten minutes when he didn't hear "SYMPHONY NO. 2 (WHISPER) in $E^b$ Minor."

"Mr. Honikey's opinion is not a problem," Mr. Cruvette said as he drove me back to the restaurant. "He will put out your record if my partners and I tell him to put it out."

There wasn't time to contemplate the difference between "if we tell him" and "when we tell him" because Mr. Cruvette began to frantically point toward a thick cloud of black smoke. Traffic was at a standstill, so he hastily pulled the car over, and we ran the remaining two blocks to find Maisonette de la Casa had become Maisonette de la Flambé. A fireman told us that a fuel truck had been unable to effectively negotiate a left turn, and the failed maneuver resulted in the formation of a blazing river of gasoline flowing through the dining room.

I patted Mr. Cruvette on the shoulder. "I'm sorry you lost your restaurant, sir."

"It's insured," he said. Then he told me to go home, and he would call me when he had some news about my record. His final words to me were, "Don't you worry about a thing."

After four weeks of visiting the ashes which used to be my place of employment, and no word from Mr. Cruvette, I found two things I could worry about: did I have a record deal, and could I get a copy of my tape? I made several inquiries at Eclipse to see if any of my recordings had been scheduled for release. My last telephone call to them was transferred to the company's legal department where an attorney informed me, "Certain recordings are made for tax write-off purposes, and never scheduled for release." He added that I had not heard that from him.

I had heard what the attorney said, and having experienced the deaf environment at Eclipse Records, I knew he had provided the answer to both of my worries. An emphatic, "No!"

• • •

Mrs. Winters said it was a shame I had been treated so callously. "You should have called me. I might have been able to help, but maybe I can still light a fire under them. What's their phone number?" Mrs. Winters' frail voice expressed her good intentions, and I thanked her for having been so attentive to my story, but there was no hill to charge, no windmill to joust, no company to call. Eclipse Records had gone out of business in 1983.

It would serve no purpose to inform her that I had placed a call to her the same afternoon I had spoken with the legal department at Eclipse. It was the same day she had been admitted to the hospital to have a number of varicose veins removed. Instead of handing her my problem in the fall of 1980, I had sent a dozen roses and a get-well card.

• • •

With Mrs. Winters in the hospital, I tried to reach Antoinette. She had been in show business for many years, and I was certain she would have some suggestions about what I should do. But The Tropics had been demolished, and the management of The Grand Hotel and Casino that had been built in its place had no idea who I was talking about. Information found no listing for any Gilbeau in Las Vegas, so I called the Los Angeles Times, and asked to speak with Mr. Jonathan Christopher. I was connected to the Entertainment department where a man named Fred informed me that Mr. Christopher had taken early retirement and moved to France with a choreographer from Nevada.

Though I silently wished Antoinette and Mr. Christopher all the happiness they deserved, I was disheartened. I had been in Los Angeles for almost eight years, and though I still had a place to live, I had no job, no money, no connections, and no tape. Starting over one more time from the beginning again was getting redundant.

Logic prompted me to look in the classified section of The Times under the heading Employment Opportunities, and respond to the ad: PART TIME HELP WANTED - GIFT SHOP - WOODLAND GREEN MEMORIAL CEMETERY. If I had to go back to the beginning, I was going to go way back.

Since my mother had been a mortician and I was wearing a tuxedo, I would certainly be among the most desired applicants. I spoke quietly during my interview to show that I had as much respect for the dead as I did for the living; I was hired immediately.

The Gift Shop sold a variety of items: postcards with pictures of some of the elaborate vaults on the grounds, plastic replicas of statues and grave markers, and glow-in-the-dark key chains stamped with the name of a movie star buried in the cemetery. I mentioned to my supervisor that it might be a good idea to sell small replicas of expensive coffins.

"People collect model cars and airplanes, so well-detailed miniature caskets could become big sellers." I should have been more aware of the blank look on Mr. Saperstone's face, but I continued, "And to make them even more collectible, you could have them made into music boxes. A customer lifts the 'Souvenir of Woodland Green' imprinted lid, and hears a sweet tinkling of "THE WAY WE WERE." My enthusiasm for the job was noted, and I was fired before my first allotted break.

Based on Mr. Saperstone's success with the plastic grave markers and key chains I thought my proposal had merit, but he thought my suggestion was the closest thing to blasphemy he had heard in the fifty-seven years he had operated the Gift Shop. I was asked to leave the premises, and this allowed me to go back to the beginning again for the second time in eight hours.

I was angry with myself during the entire bus ride back to my apartment. I walked up the three flights of stairs, and for the first time in my life I slammed a door. I was aghast at my behavior, and would have sent myself to my room without any dinner, but it was a one-room apartment and there was no food in the refrigerator. To compensate for the lack of punishment, I went down to Mrs. Robertson's apartment to apologize for the noise. A flustered young woman I had never seen before answered the door, and without looking at me yelled, "What took you so long?"

Since I had only slammed my door a few moments earlier, I was sure that I was not whom she had expected.

"Oh, I'm sorry. I thought you were the paramedics. My aunt's in the back room. I think she's dead."

The young woman grabbed my arm, and pulled me down the hallway to her aunt's bedroom. Mrs. Mabel Robertson lay dead on the floor.

My landlord was buried at Woodland Green three days later, but I did not venture near the Gift Shop after the service. I did, however, begin a friendship with the deceased's late-husband's brother's daughter, Angela Robertson.

Angela was an actress who had appeared on television, and was about to make her first movie. I was impressed that she worked in the profession she claimed to have. One of the mysterious things about Los Angeles was that most everyone said they were something other than what they were. Waiters and waitresses didn't wait on tables; they were actors waiting for the right part. Mailmen, cabdrivers, and cable installers were screenwriters. I told Angela I was an unreleased recording artist with a rap sheet who couldn't hold down a job. While she thought my comment was funny, she suggested I develop a more positive attitude. I said I would try.

Angela introduced me to the two men from Saudi Arabia who were producing her movie. They made a lot of money in the oil business, and when she told them I wrote music they gave me a job as a go-for. Running around for coffee, cigarettes and whatnots wasn't difficult, and it was an honest day's work that paid more than minimum wage. It also turned out to be a job with potential for advancement.

The movies they made were action-oriented with a high percentage of roles for attractive women. Angela was always cast in the attractive woman role with the most screaming, and I worked as an assistant go-for on two more pictures before being promoted to head go-for when filming commenced on a third. By the fourth picture they decided to give me another promotion.

At Angela's insistence, and I think because one of the producers had more than a few sweet thoughts about her, I was asked to write the theme song for their new picture. I asked what they wanted the song to be about, and one of them said he didn't care as long as it contained the words "LOVE SLAVES ON THE PLANET VENUS." This, I was told, was the picture's title.

I began working on my first movie theme song, but the lyric parameters were difficult; very few words rhyme with Venus.

"Hey there, you men of Earth!
We are the love slaves on the Planet Venus.
You're on that big blue ball we see in the sky,
and there's an awful lot of space between us.
So, get on your rocket ship, and come see us.
Land on Venus, and free us.
There's no greater love in the galaxy.
If you think there is, it's a fallacy.
Bring your species and bring your genus
to the love slaves on the Planet Venus."

"CAW, CAW, CROW" was a masterpiece by comparison. Listening to myself sing it at the recording session might have been my life's most embarrassing moment, but the two Saudi Arabian gentlemen loved it, and I was not embarrassed enough by my endeavor to refuse their check for five thousand dollars. I thanked God that the picture was never released on the unsuspecting public. I also thanked Him for including Angela and her producers in His plan.

• • •

I pick up the daffodil-yellow pages of my mother's stationary again. They do not fall from my grasp this time, and I unfold them to find what I had expected. Margaret's crisp handwriting style is as familiar to me as the creamy texture of her chocolate tapioca pudding. In the salutation I see her extra curl at the top of the capital "D," and the perfectly round "o" she nestled on the elongated final stroke of the capital "R." As I read the words, the sound of her voice in my head is as warm as woodwinds.

Dear Robert,

Forgive me for addressing you by your original name, but Tuxedo Bob is your creation. Robert was, and is, your father's and mine. I don't know where you are today, but I imagine you are well and safe. I suppose I could look at that itinerary you sent, but the names and places you visit sound so foreign. You know me; I'm pretty much of an old homebody.

Your father and I are going to see a musical in Minot tonight, and this might sound silly, but I was struck with a sudden urge to write to you and tell you I love you. I know you are aware of that, but it's your mother's prerogative to say it as often as she likes. Loving goes with the territory of being your parent, but I would love you even if you were not my son because you are such a fine young man. Everybody says so. Just the other day Mrs. Hogan was remarking what a fine young man you are, and asked how you were doing. When anyone asks about you, I tell them you're out in the world climbing your ladder to success.

Your father would want me to remind you about that ladder. He says to watch your step, and be nice to everyone on the way up because you'll need them on the way down. Now I usually don't have any idea what your father is talking about, but in this case I'm sure he just wants you to be careful. He took a spill from a ladder once while trimming the oak tree. You should have heard him holler. He broke his big toe, but that was a few years before you were born. Gave him a lot of pain for months, and he's been a bit skittish around ladders ever since.

Well, this letter could just ramble on and on if I had the time, but I have to put my good dress on and get ready for my evening out. It's snowing here, and the ground looks so beautiful. I can almost see you in the front yard building your snowman. I thought it was so cute, but I don't think your father would want you to use his only size 54 as the decoration again. He wasn't too pleased that he had to undress your snowman and bury Mr. Overton in a wet tuxedo, but between you and me, I don't think Mr. Overton minded one bit.

Your father's calling from downstairs now, so I have to stop writing. I love you, Robert. I know I already said that, but I'm your mother, and a mother never gets to say it enough. I'll finish this letter when I get back tonight, and mail it tomorrow to one of the addresses you'll be at next week. That way it will be waiting for you, as I wait for you. (I promised myself I wouldn't write something like that, but I wrote it anyway).

I can't ask you to come home because I miss you; that would be a most unfair thing for me to do. Missing a child is natural for a parent, and I have to miss you without being selfish. But while you're doing what makes you happy, please remember that success, fame, and fortune are not what are important. You just be the kind, generous, thoughtful, loving person you've always been, and let God decide what you will attain. That's my two cents worth of advice, but you can never fail using that recipe.

Oh, there's Orville again. Says he'll wait for me in the car, which you remember is his way of letting me know I'm taking too long. I hope when you read this letter you understand that I'm just trying to say how proud I am that you're my son. Your father is too, and even though he doesn't say it, I know he misses you.

Love,

Your Mother

Her plan to mail the letter didn't coincide with the plan God had made for her life and the life of my father. She and Orville had left the house for the last time. I tuck her message in the inside pocket of my jacket, over my heart, where my parents reside.

They died after seeing THE MUSIC MAN. By coincidence or design a musical was part of the reason I decided to leave Los Angeles, and travel back home to Schulberg.

• • •

The two Saudi Arabian movie producers were Prince Ali and his business partner, Mr. Menoham Mohammed. Based on their enjoyment of the song I had written for their space adventure, they decided I should write an entire musical. Even though I explained I had never written a musical before, hiring me for the job made perfect sense to them.

"Mister Tuxedo Bob, sir. You had never written a movie theme song before, but both Prince Ali and myself were very much pleased by the composition you presented to us. Since you fulfilled our request so well, and you did not know what you were doing, the fact that you have never written a musical is too hard for us to resist."

Their logic seemed foreign to me, but their proposal included an offer of twenty-five thousand dollars to begin writing the musical, and an additional twenty-five thousand upon my presentation of the script and music. They did not have to ask twice.

There had been no parameters set for a specific lyric to be included in the musical, so I had no framework from which to build. My free hand quickly became the idle hand attached to the arm of someone who had a chorus of voices in his head singing, "What, who, where, why, when, how?"

Mr. Mohammed was kind enough to instruct me on the industry standards for correct script formatting. Among the rules were proper margins, tab spacing, indentations, the use of fades, cuts and dissolves, abbreviations, and the admonition, "Don't put a brad in the middle hole of the three-hole-punched paper or everyone will know that you have never before written a script." There were many more, and I was sure these rules were made to make it easier for anyone who knew the rules to read a script. Still, I had the freedom to write whatever I wanted to write as long as it fit the format; I was a professional screenwriter.

I sat in my apartment for a week, pen in hand, staring at a clean tablet of writing paper and my notes of Mr. Mohammed's rules. I didn't sleep very well as I wondered when I would start earning the money I had been paid. If I felt like eating, which was not often, my meals alternated between peanut butter and tuna fish.

On the eighth morning of no ideas I went into the bathroom to splash some cold water on my face, and I began to giggle uncontrollably when it crossed my mind that I could write a musical based on the story of a tired, malnourished man splashing water in his face. My parents would have said I had experienced "a fit of the snickers" because I was laughing at something that wasn't funny.

I calmed down and looked up into the bathroom mirror. For a split second the face I saw reflected wasn't mine. I was so startled by the brief hallucination that I jumped backward and banged my head against the towel rack. Applying ice to my minor injury would have been my next move, but I was too distracted by my mental orchestra as it began playing a series of melodic themes. One theme was brave, another was sweet, and one that started out charming turned dark and sinister. Cymbals crashed, horns blared, strings soared; this was it!

I rushed over to my tablet of blank paper, and began to write a story about a young man whose rose-colored vision of the world is shattered by a well-mannered-but-evil villain trapped inside a mirror.

> "There's a chill in the air tonight;
> a sinister stillness that cuts like a knife.
> It moves with the wind,
> and hides in the darkness.
> It puts locks on your houses,
> and fear in your soul.
> It's out of your hands, so it's out of control.
> You try to ignore it, then it knocks on your door;
> Danger!"

Those were the first lines I wrote; the song became "TONIGHT IS THE NIGHT; DANGER." Eight hundred forty-seven days later I wrote the word "BLACKOUT," and my first musical screenplay was completed.

Mr. Mohammed said my compositions for the musical were even better than "LOVE SLAVES ON THE PLANET VENUS." Prince Ali was elated, and authorized the purchase of a small recording studio so I could make demonstration tapes of the musical's songs at my convenience. It was during one of these sessions that I happened to see a painfully thin young woman sing a song on a music-video television program. She was the stimulus behind the last pop song I ever wrote.

> "There's a skinny girl who cannot sing
> on MTV in her underthings.
> I could change the channel; look at something else,
> but I think I'm in love; I can't help myself.
> I got bad taste."

It was kind of Prince Ali to allow me to record "I GOT BAD TASTE" during the "Mister Moore" sessions. Mr. Mohammed wanted to know the identity of the "skinny girl who cannot sing," but I politely refused to divulge the name of my song's inspiration. Since she became quite famous in the field of celebrity gossip, I'm glad I kept her name a secret.

Citing the producer's prerogative clause detailed in our yet to be written formal agreement, Prince Ali and Mr. Mohammed added their names to the writer credits of <u>THE MIRROR OF MISTER MOORE</u>.[2] Then Prince Ali informed me the musical was too costly for him to allow his company to finance on its own.

"The risks are too great," he declared. "I spend less than three million dollars on my pictures. This one will cost at least fifty million dollars if it can even be done at all."

The "if it can even be done at all" part of his declaration alluded to the number of special effects included in the script that would require specialists (which meant expensive) in the field of computer programming. Special technology would have to be created in order to make the effects appear real enough to satisfy a movie audience. It was pointed out that having my

---

[2] **<u>THE MIRROR OF MISTER MOORE</u>** is included in its entirety beginning on page 443.

villain appear and disappear in a mirror was easy, but creating the appearance of him dissolving into broken glass fragments, and then adding a swirling tornado effect as the fragments come together to re-form an unbroken mirror, and then having the mirror bend and put itself back into its frame on the wall was going to cost three hundred thousand dollars if the special effects people could get it right the first time. In short, fake realism was expensive.

Even though Prince Ali had a great deal of money, I learned that the movie business followed a basic rule of thumb: "It is far better to spend someone else's money." My father had a competing axiom, "A wise man builds his own house."

Prince Ali and Mr. Mohammed put together a consortium of individuals who agreed to assist with the movie's financing. All of the people in the consortium called themselves "producers," and Mr. Mohammed gave himself the title of Executive Producer. Prince Ali was happy just being a prince. One of the producers in the deal was the head of a large movie studio. Mr. Collin Lancer agreed to foot fifty percent of the production costs on the condition that I perform at his daughter's wedding. I thought this was an odd way to do business, but Mr. Mohammed explained that Mr. Lancer had taken his daughter, Debbi, to The Recital in Las Vegas. Twenty years later Debbi still had her autographed gold ticket stub displayed on her bedroom wall. He explained further that Hollywood was a city where the scratching of another person's back was all part of the negotiation process.

Debbi's wedding was going to be a huge affair. I had a meeting with the orchestra conductor where I gave him the music charts I had made for the forty-two musicians hired to perform at the reception. There would be no tap dancers, no sets, and no special lighting, but in the words of Vince

Genoa it was "gonna be great!" All I had to do was sing for an hour, and my first screenplay would be made into a movie.

Mr. and Mrs. Lancer graciously invited me to attend a luncheon at a restaurant so exclusive there was no name or address on the door. My directions were to walk sixteen paces east from the mailboxes on the corner of Melrose and Orlando and wait. I performed my sixteen steps perfectly, and after waiting several minutes, a door opened and a muscular gentleman escorted me into a posh dining establishment.

Even if a person knew about this restaurant, he would have to "know someone" to get inside. That is what Mr. Lancer told me before introducing me to his daughter and her fiancé, Derek Dreardon. In Hollywood "knowing someone" was quite different from having a friend. If you knew someone, it had to be the right someone, but the right someone was not always the same from day to day. If the right someone suddenly became the wrong someone, then no matter what, you never knew him. That's what I gleaned from the rest of Mr. Lancer's answer to my casual remark about a business being able to survive without advertising.

Debbi was so excited to meet me she spilled her glass of cabernet all over Derek's white leather jacket. He excused himself from the table, and gave his soon-to-be partner in marriage a look that reminded me of the way Mr. Brian Ackerman used to glare at his wife. As the waiters rushed over to change the tablecloth, Debbi looked at me as if the entire episode was a lark.

"So I'll buy him another precious coat," she said rolling her eyes. "White leather is so queer, anyway."

Debbi Lancer had the most perfectly formed features I had ever seen outside a Barbi doll, and I complimented her parents on their daughter's beauty.

"It's not from heredity, trust me," Debbi interjected. "I bet you don't remember me, but I came backstage after I saw your show in Las Vegas. I was seven years old with buckteeth, a big nose, and no chin. You gave me your autograph after you asked, 'Who's pretty little girl are you?' Daddy didn't say anything." She scrunched her flawlessly arched eyebrows together, and passed her father the same glare she had received from her fiancé.

Mrs. Lancer stepped in and admonished her daughter's moment of disrespect. "Mind your manners, missy."

"Your father probably didn't want to intrude on our private conversation," I said in an attempt to ease the tension that apparently coincided with wedding preparations.

"Yeah, probably," Debbi responded, blowing her bangs from her perfect forehead. "You told me if no one claimed me I could be your pretty little girl."

"Well, it was my loss for not keeping that pretty little girl because she's become a very pretty young woman." I remembered a gawky child who had asked for an autograph, but Debbi's face bore no resemblance to the one I saw in my mind.

"I have my plastic surgeon to thank. He also gave me great boobs, see?" She puffed out her chest, and the cleavage at the bodice of her pink dress confirmed her statement.

"Debbi, you're embarrassing Mr. Bob," the more embarrassed mother of the bride-to-be said.

"It's all right, Mrs. Lancer. I spent a few years in Las Vegas, and a lot of women there purchased the same two items."

Miss Debbi Lancer became Mrs. Derek Dreardon on a beautiful Saturday afternoon in May of 1987. I was supposed to be waiting for them in the ballroom of The Beverly Hills Hotel, but I was not there. I was sitting in the hallway outside my apartment door holding the hand of a frightened and very sick young man who still had no pad.

I was on my way to my first wedding reception performance, and as I stepped from my apartment door I had every intention of singing for Mr. and Mrs. Dreardon. Instead I tripped over the leg of a person who had decided the wall next to my front door was as good a place as any to enjoy a dose of whatever had been in the syringe lying next to his arm. He didn't respond to my attempts to apologize because he was barely conscious. His skin had a ghostly pallor, and he smelled like he hadn't bathed for quite some time. My first thought was pity; it was a shame that this stranger was wasting his life in such a manner of self-loathing. I was about to continue on my way when I heard him whisper three words between two coughs: "wow," "pad," and "bro."

The stranger's expressionless face was vaguely familiar, and when I saw the half-finished red cross on his right forearm I knew he was the same person I witnessed getting handcuffed on the corner of Franklin and Highland fourteen years earlier. As I looked down on his crumpled body, I was saddened by the thought that he had been traveling a road of personal destruction ever since I had first bumped into him by accident. The words "by accident" slammed the brakes on my thoughts.

A rush of adrenaline jolted my body as I pondered a course of action. I couldn't just leave him there, but I had a performance to give in one hour. "A plane to catch," "a car to wash," "a dog to feed." Those phrases of excuse whirled around in my head smashing the violins, trashing the woodwinds, and crashing through the horns before colliding into "a performance to give." I looked up at the ceiling, and though it was solid mass, it did not stop my gaze toward Heaven.

"I gave my word!" I yelled to God. "What should I do?" I appealed to Orville and Margaret. "There are people waiting!" I shouted to Mr. Murphy, Ernie, and Deke, but I only got a moan from the young man in response.

I knelt down next to him, and asked him his name. If he regained enough consciousness I might still keep my appointment. "What's your name?" I asked again, this time shaking him a little.

"Paul," he said in a wheeze.

"Okay, Paul, do you want to try to stand up?"

He coughed, then whispered, "Paul," again.

"Hello Paul, I'm Tuxedo Bob. I'm going to help you up now."

I tried to lift him, but lifting unassisted dead weight was a difficult assignment, and his jelly knees collapsed under him.

"Paul Matthews, bro." He pronounced each syllable quietly as he slowly slumped back against the wall.

Hearing his full name gave me the strength to pick him up, and carry him into my apartment. I dialed 911, then called the Beverly Hills Hotel. When the paramedics arrived I was still on hold waiting to be connected to

Mr. Fawnlin, the orchestra conductor. The operator came back on the line, and informed me that the extension was still busy. I left a message of apology stating I was detained because I had to take care of a sick friend.

When I was young, Pastor Paul Peters of Schulberg's First Baptist Church read Matthew 25: Verse 40 to the congregation, then gave a sermon on its topic: "Whatever you do to the least of these, you do also to Me." When Paul Matthews had said his name, I heard Pastor Peters reciting his sermon from that faraway Sunday. The answer to my plea concerning what I should do was as crystal clear as the sound of Pastor Peter's voice; my scheduled performance seemed trivial. So, instead of playing for Debbi and Derek and all the "right people" they knew, I accompanied Paul Matthews to the hospital.

When he was admitted it was discovered that he had no insurance, no family or friends, and no money, so I signed forms declaring myself as his guardian. During his first night the doctors found that he had an addiction to heroin and a number of complications in his immune system from a disease called AIDS. The negative baggage he carried around with him was discarded when he died on the evening of his fifth day in Room 4628. For those five days I held his hand, and sang to him. I sang every song I had ever written, humming the instrumentals and solo passages, and I told him every story I knew about life, friendship, love, death and taxes.

The Hollywood film community (like musicians, thespians, and studio personnel) has its own brand of jargon, and I found out that the phrase "taking care of a sick friend" meant "I have a drug problem." While it was true I had a drug problem, it had belonged to my sick friend. No amount of explaining could appease Prince Ali or Mr. Mohammed. No apology was accepted by the Lancers or the Dreardons. The five days I had spent sitting with Paul Matthews in his hospital room got me blacklisted by the film industry. To put my predicament in the words of Sy Silverman: the pile of mud occupying the studio apartment on Franklin Avenue overlooking the Hollywood Freeway used to be Tuxedo Bob.

Even though there was money in my Schulberg bank account, I sold my electric piano to pay rent. I had made a promise to myself that I wouldn't touch my hometown savings until I had a permanent home. My father used to say "A dishonest man breaks the promise made to others; a soulless man breaks the promise made to himself." My hometown savings and soul were intact, and I believed the only blemish on my record of being "good on my word" had come from "doing the right thing." I don't think Orville disapproved when I added, "but any promise can be broken when motivated by common decency" to his axiom.

It was August, and the air was hot and thick as so many August days are in Southern California. It didn't matter that my air conditioner was broken because my phone and electricity had been shut off. The lack of these necessities was an additional perk for the blacklisted. After paying Paul Matthews hospital bill and burial expenses, I was broke again. Broke except for the quarter that was on the dresser next to my suitcase.

I picked up the quarter with President Washington and the eagle positioned on opposing sides of the same situation. I kissed George on his nose, and the eagle on its beak, and flipped the quarter into the air. "Heads" I would stay; "tails" I would leave. The song "I JUST GOT THE BUSINESS FROM THE BUSINESS" began to play in my head as I watched the majestic eagle land in the palm of my hand. If George had shown his face I would have gone for two out of three.

I tucked the quarter into a pocket of my last clean tuxedo, and packed my suitcase with the five tuxedos in need of dry cleaning service. I looked out the window, and said good-bye to Hollywood. I had a train to catch.

# coda

I had just stepped out of the shower when Mrs. Winters called with the news. I answered the phone dripping wet and naked in my room at the Big Rig Motel that August morning in 1987. There was excitement in her voice, but I was toweling water from my ear, and missed what she said except for "money" and "how about those apples!"

"I'm sorry, could you repeat that please, ma'am?" Then I remember having to sit down on the bed.

I had already discovered that twenty-two years of interest compounded daily had doubled the value of my five thousand dollar savings account. I believed this was an adequate safety net, and would certainly be sufficient while I considered my future. Mrs. Winters repeated the reason for her call, and my knees buckled when I learned that during the last fifty-six years the world's passion for "The Real Thing" had created a sizable increase in the value of the piece of paper my mother had used as a ring repository.

"One million dollars," Mrs. Winters said.

My adequate safety net became an ostrich-sized nest egg — Amen.

Tony Garrman, who had been held back two grades for failing math when he was my classmate in high school, was now the vice-president and investment counselor at Schulberg Savings and Loan. He graciously advised me about the ins-and-outs of tax-free bonds and high-yield mutual funds.

"You have to divide your money between solid and liquid assets," was just one of the things he said that went in one of my ears and out the other. But a lack of understanding did not prevent me from taking his advice and purchasing several municipal bonds, T-bills, and certificates of deposit. Tony also suggested I buy a house, sit back, and watch my money grow. I purchased a house, and found that watching grass grow was far more interesting than the vocation he mentioned.

Buying a house marked my decision to stay in Schulberg. I had spent years following the invisible map of the plan God drafted for my life, so discovering a million dollars in my hometown made me believe I should stick around to see what else He had in mind. As my father used to say, "Every good plan has its purpose."

The house I bought was a two-bedroom split-level located on a half acre of land that used to be part of the Hogan family farm. A contractor had purchased and developed the land into what was now called "Nearby Meadows - A Quiet Community." All of the houses were similar in design, and painted in an array of pastel colors. Mine was pale yellow with a big yard, a two-car garage with an electric door, and some small trees that the real estate agent pointed out "would get bigger." I liked its hardwood floors, big windows, and porch swing, so the "For Sale" sign went into the garage, and my name went on the mailbox.

Days passed like a lazy stream meanders through a pastoral countryside. My mental melodies became accustomed to the accompaniment of crickets, chirping birds, and wind-blown leaves instead of car horns, police sirens, and garbage trucks. Friendly neighbors stopping by to chat over a slice of pie and a hot cup of coffee replaced musicians, business executives, and musketeers. And my front porch swing and backyard garden received more attention than the Steinway baby grand in my living room.

I named the flowers and vegetables in my garden after my friends. The practice began when my first daffodil bloomed, and I recalled Sy Silverman had referred to them as "prissy-yellow things." So I started addressing all the daffodils as "Mr. Silverman." My Mr. Murphy tomatoes blushed by the dozens during the summer, a bounty of Sylvia Derbin chrysanthemums flourished in the fall, and in winter blankets of snow safely covered everyone until the first Antoinette crocus pushed her head above ground in early April. The pleasure I received from watching the Margaret yellow roses bloom was as satisfying as any standing ovation, and certainly as mysterious as any event that had happened along the winding road that led me back to Schulberg.

Since mystery and serendipity are God's specialties, it seemed silly for me to think that anything in my life happened by chance. But, by chance, in the fall of 1990 my next-door neighbor, Mary Anderson, peered over our mutual backyard fence and asked if I would like to see her daughter perform in the Schulberg High School senior class musical production of BRIGADOON.

"Joe's boss canceled at the last minute, so I have an extra ticket," she explained.

Mary's maiden name was Eberly, and she had met her husband-to-be Joe when they were toddlers in my attic during the winter storm of 1955. It was gaga at first sight, and they got married the day after they graduated from high school. Joe had become an expert in the field of heating and air conditioning, and worked for a company that promised to "keep it warm in the winter, and cool in the summer," according to the logo on his truck.

I had never seen a production of BRIGADOON before, but I couldn't imagine any cast executing this delightful musical fable as professionally as Schulberg's high school seniors. Ashlee Anderson was very believable as a Scottish maiden living in an imaginary town, and her parents beamed with pride when she said her line, "It's Harry Beaton!" The show was truly a family event for Tom and Betsy Conners Jr. Their twin daughters, Heather and Meadow, played flute and tuba respectively in the small orchestra, and Tom's sister, Wanda, was listed in the program as the costume designer — she certainly had a way with plaid.

Afterwards I followed the show-business custom of going backstage to congratulate the cast and crew on a job well done. I particularly wanted to acknowledge the show-must-go-on spirit of the young actor who inadvertently knocked over one of Brigadoon's cardboard houses during the exciting chase sequence. I had such a wonderful time attending this "by chance" evening of outstanding entertainment that I hardly noticed the sign on the wall as I exited the school: "Third Annual Magazine Subscription Drive."

The next day I answered a knock at my door, and was greeted by a boy no taller than my knee. He was very well dressed in a light brown suit and bow-tie, and his head was tilted back as far as it would go so he could look at me with his big blue eyes.

"Good morning mister sir. My name is Danny Hopper, and I'm selling magazine prescriptions."

He looked uncomfortable holding his head in a position to retain eye contact, so I knelt down.

"It's nice to meet you, Danny Hopper. My name's Tuxedo Bob."

"I know. My mom says you're a nice man with a different time zone."

"That's kind of her to say." I couldn't recall meeting a Mrs. Hopper, but receiving a complimentary review is always pleasant whether from a friend or a stranger. "Selling magazines is a very important job, Danny Hopper. May I ask why you're doing it?"

"Yes, sir. It's to help buy insta-ments for the school band. Would you care for a magazine, sir?"

I had dealt with a few door-to-door salesmen, but Danny was certainly the most direct.

"I might care for one or two, but first why don't you tell me what instrument you play in the band."

"Oh, I'm not in the band, sir. I'm only in the first grade, but when I get to the sixth grade I want to play the guitar if my mom gets me one. Guitars are cool." His eyes sparkled with delight as he savored his thought. "My brother's in the band. He's in the eighth grade. He plays trumpet."

"So, you're helping your brother. That's a very good thing."

"David, that's my brother, he had to hang out with his friends," Danny said handing me an order form with a list of magazines. "He said if I didn't sell any he'd beat me up."

It was certainly an effective sales pitch, but I hoped it wasn't true. "He said that, did he? Well, we can't let that happen, so I'd better pick out a few." I went over to my desk, and asked him what kind of magazines he liked.

"I like the ones that have pictures of stuff I haven't seen," he replied. "Like outer space and lions; stuff like that."

"That's some pretty cool stuff, Danny." I looked over the list, and circled some names of publications that suited his age and preferences. I asked him where he lived, and printed his name and address in the provided space. Then I wrote a check payable to the Schulberg High School Band Instrument Fund.

"Is that your piano?" he asked pointing to my Steinway.

"Yes, would you like to play it?"

"No thank you, sir, but my mom might want to. Can my mom come over and play it?"

"Certainly," I said.

"My mom used to have a piano, but yours is bigger."

"Well, you tell your mother that your friend Tuxedo Bob says she can play his piano whenever she likes." I walked back to the door, and handed him the check along with the order form. I knelt back down again so we could see eye to eye. "Danny, I want you to go with your brother when he gives that check to whoever's in charge of the magazine drive. Will you do that?"

He nodded his head in agreement, but asked, "Why?"

"Because the person in charge might have a question or two, and you'll be there to say that Tuxedo Bob is a friend of yours who wanted to help purchase some instruments."

"Okay," he said extending his little hand for a shake. "It was nice meeting you, sir."

"It was nice meeting you too, Danny," I said accepting his gentlemanly gesture. "You come back anytime."

"I can bring my mom?"

"Certainly, and your dad and brother also."

He let go of my hand when he said, "My dad doesn't live with us, but it's not David or my fault, and my mom and my dad still love us very much. That's what my mom says. Dad lives in Ohio with Amy. That's who my mom says is the fault."

Danny said good-bye, and I watched him as he took little hops down the front steps and ran to his bike. I closed the door, and sat down at the piano to accompany the guitar melody that had begun in my head when Danny said he knew he was loved regardless of his parent's matrimonial situation. I was interrupted in the middle of composing the duet by the ringing of my telephone.

"Hello, Tuxedo Bob residence."

"I'd like to speak with Mr. Tuxedo Bob, please. Tell him Danny Hopper's mother is calling."

"This is Tuxedo Bob, Mrs. Hopper, and may I say that Danny is a remarkable young man. I'm sure you're very proud of him."

"Yes, I am. I'm calling to tell you that I don't think the joke you played on him was very nice at all."

"I'm sorry, Mrs. Hopper, but I don't recall playing a joke on your son."

"Well, let me remind you, sir." she said tersely. "You filled out a magazine order, put my son's name on it, and then wrote a phony check to pay for it. Does any of this ring a bell? Tell me, what kind of man would do such a thing?"

"Mrs. Hopper," I said calmly, "the kind of man you mention would not be welcome in my home. I assure you that my intentions and the check are good."

"We'll see about that!" She slammed her phone down, and we were disconnected.

I was disappointed in myself for not accompanying Danny, consequently putting him in a situation where my donation was misconstrued as a prank. After obtaining Mrs. Hopper's phone number from information I tried to call her back to tell her I was ashamed of my behavior, but there was no answer. I figured she was off to verify the validity of my check, and though I was satisfied she would discover the truth, it would still be necessary to apologize for upsetting her.

I answered a knock at my door to find a very neatly dressed woman with jet-black hair, bright blue eyes, and a slightly embarrassed look on her face.

"I am so sorry, sir. Please forgive my rude behavior," she amplified her conciliation by casting her eyes toward the ground and wringing her hands.

"You must be Danny's mother, and it is I who should apologize to you," I said with a friendly smile. "Would you like to come in for a slice of peach pie and some coffee?"

She returned my smile, albeit weakly, and stepped into my living room. "I would understand if you never wanted to speak to me again after the way I sounded on the phone."

"You were only acting in the best interests of your son. I'm sorry I caused you aggravation. Please sit down." I walked toward the kitchen and asked, "How do you take your coffee?"

"With cream and two lumps of humility," she responded.

I laughed at her remark, and called from the kitchen, "So Danny tells me you play the piano."

"Yes, but I haven't played for a few years," she responded.

"Why is that?" I asked returning with our refreshments.

"The short version is I'm in the middle of a divorce, and I sold it to make a car payment."

"I understand. If you delete 'divorce', and insert 'rent' for 'car', I once had to do exactly the same thing."

We had a pleasant conversation, some excellent peach pie, courtesy of Miss Annie's baking talents at Trucker's Haven, and coffee that was good to the last drop, courtesy of Maxwell House. I learned that Mrs. Cynthia Hopper was thirty-seven; she worked as the high school librarian, read romancc novcls, listened to country music, and preferred her bicycle over her car as a means of local transportation. Her favorite flower was the tulip, which currently bloomed in assorted colors in her garden, her favorite perfume was "Joy," but it was too expensive, and she hoped to buy her sons a dog for Christmas.

The next day I received a personal visit from the high school principal, the high school band director, and the twenty-seven member high school marching band, which began to play "Under The Double Eagle" as soon as I opened the door. I was embarrassed by the display, but when Principal Phipps shook my hand, I took the opportunity to extract his promise that he would purchase a ukulele for Danny Hopper's small hands after deducting the cost of four magazine subscriptions from the one-hundred thousand dollar check I had written.

"Where is our little mascot?" Principal Phipps said as photographs were taken. "Bring him up here for a picture!"

Danny Hopper had been elected the band's mascot until he was old enough to be a member, but he was not tall enough to be seen behind a tuba and bass drum. The players stepped aside, and Danny walked proudly toward me carrying a sign that read, "Schulberg Band Loves Tuxedo Bob" (the "Loves" was in the shape of a red heart, but I knew how to interpret the symbol.) Danny looked like a pint-sized version of me dressed in his size four "After Six" tuxedo.

A few days later I sat on my porch swing smiling at the thought of Mrs. Hopper's surprised expression when "Williston Keyboards" arrived at her doorstep to deliver the new piano I had sent as a gift. I anticipated the phone would ring any second, but when I saw her pedaling her shiny green bike up my street I was glad I was getting a personal visit instead. I stood up to greet her, prepared with my response in case she asked, "What kind of man sends a woman a piano?" (A man who wants a woman to have a piano.)

"Tuxedo Bob, I cannot accept such lavish presents," she said skidding her bike to a halt. "I really can't," she said during her dismount. "Really, I just can't," she continued as she walked toward me.

I had not prepared a response for rejection, and was momentarily caught off guard. "Why not?" I asked.

"Because!" she stammered, "I mean, a piano, and my favorite perfume?" She had listed the items I sent, but had not answered my question. "What's next?" she continued. "A few romantic novels? Some country records? A dog for my sons?" The pitch of her voice rose with each question. "Did you think I told you those things so you'd go buy them for me?"

"No," I said calmly, "but that's the nice thing about unexpected presents. Take your sudden appearance here for example. I thought you would telephone, but you took the time to ride over and see me personally. I call that an unexpected present, so we're even."

"We're not even!" Her voice ascended into high soprano range. "You must have spent at least two-thousand dollars! Are you crazy?"

"No, but the question has been raised on several occasions, Mrs. Hopper," I said with a smile.

"Cynthia, please," she requested. She returned my smile, and her voice recovered its natural alto range.

"And you call me Tee-Bee," I responded. "Cynthia, I've been listening to you, but I still haven't heard why you can't accept my gifts."

She exhaled a huffing sound that was part exasperation, and part concession. "Because I don't want you to get the wrong idea. Tee-Bee, I don't want to get involved." Her tone was softly soothing. "I've got two kids, and even though my girlfriends tell me I'm stupid, I still love my soon-to-be ex-husband. I just can't get involved. Okay?"

"Involved with what?" I asked.

She looked at me quizzically as if she couldn't believe she had to say, "With you!"

"Me? Mrs. Hopper, Cynthia, please forgive me for causing you anxiety." Now I was the one who was stammering. "I wasn't aware that the giving of gifts included an involvement requirement."

"Pardon me for being blunt," she tilted her head slightly, "but I thought you sent me those things because you wanted me to sleep with you."

"I just wanted to give you a piano and a bottle of perfume. My father used to say, 'It's a foolish man who gives a woman a gift, and expects anything other than a simple thank-you in return.'" I paused when I saw tears beginning to form in her eyes.

She expelled another breath. "I'm sorry for thinking that, but that's been my experience with guys who give presents and compliments." I handed her my handkerchief, and she continued, "When I was a teenager my father told me, 'Cynthia, guys only want one thing from you!'" She mimicked her father's stern voice between sniffles. "'Guys just want to get in your pants!' I'm thirty-seven years old, and I still hear him saying that."

I put my arm around her, and patted her gently on the back. "I'm sure he just said that so you'd be careful."

"No, he said it because he was right."

It was hard to hear what she said next because she was face-first against my shoulder, and her words were muffled against my jacket. I leaned back a few inches, and said, “You’re a beautiful woman, Cynthia, but any guy who gives you something just because he ‘wants to get into your pants’, to use your father’s words, isn’t worth thinking about.

“Thank you,” she said blowing her nose.

“So, you’ll accept my gifts with no strings attached?”

“Yes, thank you, and I’m sorry for crying.” She handed back my mascara-stained handkerchief.

“There’s no need to apologize. I think it would be sadder if you couldn’t cry.”

Cynthia Hopper, and her sons Danny and David, became my good friends. We got together every Tuesday evening, and she and I took turns playing the piano. Danny could not be separated from his ukulele (Cynthia said he even slept with it), and I taught him the “G,” “A,” and “D” chords I had learned from Deke. He strummed those three chords in every song his mother or I played regardless of the key. David, the recipient of a new trumpet from the high school band department, reluctantly practiced his scales with us after several pleas from his mother.

Now a freshman in high school, David had a world of things to think about that were much more important than spending time at home. These thoughts were usually expressed in the generalizations: “There’s nothing to do,” “We never do anything fun,” and “Everything is so stupid.”

One Tuesday night, David groused more specifically, “There isn’t any cool place in town to hang out. You know, a place where me and my friends can go to have fun without the fossils breathing down our necks. No one saying ‘do your homework, clean your room, get a haircut’ — stuff like that.”

His mother interjected with the parental corrections, "That's 'my friends and I', David, and I'm not a fossil."

He glanced at his mother, and then looked back at me. Rolling his eyes to the heavens he responded with his favorite word, "Whatever," before sulking off to his room.

"Whatever" was his way of saying he had more to say, but preferred to keep it to himself. I understood that his lack of desire for earnest communication with anyone he considered a member of the museum generation was linked to his teenage growth hormones, but he was a musician, so I followed him to his room. Standing in the doorway of his bedroom I told him I had not come to bother him with any "When I was your age" stories, so he invited me in.

I knew that an adult receiving an invitation to enter a teenager's room was a high honor, so I entered with humility. "It's a drag there's no place to hang out," I offered.

"Yeah," was his initial response, but as I was about to ask for his ideas on the subject he continued. "There's no club or place or anything except 4-H and nerdy stuff like chess and Elks. My dad was an Elk." He huffed like his mother, and flopped down on his bed. "Mom keeps telling me I should join the junior Elks!" He huffed again, "No way I'm doing that jerky stuff. I want someplace way cool."

Cool was important to musicians of all ages, and employing his teen-age inflection I told him I would "way" look into the town's lack of a cool place for kids to hang out.

"And I hate the trumpet!" he added as if he needed to get it off his chest.

"Hate is a very strong word," I replied. "Do you mean you don't like to play the trumpet?"

"No," he mumbled staring at his feet.

"'No', you don't like playing it, or 'no' it's something else."

He sat up and said, "I want to be in a cool band someday, and cool bands don't have trumpets, okay?" He slumped back on the mattress, and sighed to the ceiling, "This town is so nowhere."

I looked around the walls of his room, and saw the posters of popular rock groups that occupied his dreams the way pictures of buildings and pedestrians had captured mine. I left him to his thoughts after reaffirming my promise to look into the cool hangout situation. I would have to give some thought about a future "coolness of trumpets" discussion.

I phoned my friend, and town-council member, Betsy Conners Jr. the next morning, and asked if there were any municipal codes that would prevent opening an establishment for teenagers. There were none, so I called David and asked him to get a group of his friends together, and meet me in front of Old Man Farmer's warehouse on the corner of Wheat and Winter Streets.

Old Man Farmer owned "Old Man Farmer's Nut Company of North Dakota," a very successful mail order enterprise, and everyone in town knew he preferred being called Old Man rather than Horace. A couple of months ago he moved his operation to larger quarters, and asked me to purchase his empty warehouse. Old Man Farmer was just one of many in Schulberg who had approached me with a business proposition, or asked for a donation, or simply asked for money. I listened politely to everyone, but I kept an eye out for the woodwork from where Cynthia said the solicitors had crawled prior to arriving at my door.

When a group of high school alumni asked me to purchase additional computers for the science department, I readily agreed. But when that same group asked me to build luxury boxes at the football stadium, I politely declined. I appreciated their offer to rename the stadium "Tuxedo Bob Arena," but I didn't think the addition of luxury boxes would improve any student's athletic ability.

I had bought some books for the public library, but I did not buy a set of encyclopedias for Mr. Janson's son. "Eddie, he don't like goin' to the library alone, and I sure ain't got time to take him," Mr. Janson had explained. "The Mrs. has got me runnin' from sun-up to sun-down."

I sympathized with his hectic schedule, but reasoned that the library already had the books his son needed. I told Eddie I would be happy to be his escort anytime he wanted to go to the library, and we went almost every Monday and Thursday afternoon.

I donated money to a number of charities, but I declined Mrs. Ferguson's request to help pay for the expensive designer prom dress her daughter, Virginia, had found in a fashion magazine. I agreed that her daughter would look smashing in the Oleg Cassini original, but suggested she take the picture to Wanda Conners who had a reputation for exchanging her expert sewing skills for household chores.

When David and his friends met me on the corner of Wheat and Winter, they deemed my idea for a youth center "way cool," and wanted to occupy the building immediately. I appreciated their enthusiasm, but told them they would have to wait until it was legally habitable. I called Old Man Farmer, and told him I had changed my mind about purchasing his property. The price, previously quoted as "a measly thirty thousand measly dollars" and "a steal," had jumped to thirty-five thousand dollars. He said the higher price was due to inflation, and I didn't quibble. Even though Cynthia said he raised the price because I told him how much I wanted it, he didn't know I would have paid much more.

There were a number of comments offered by the adults in the community concerning a place that was going to be just for kids. "They'll get tired of it," "They'll trash it," and "They won't appreciate it" were some of the negatives. "At least my kids will be out of my hair," and "I hope you like heavy metal music" were some of the more optimistic. But before any of their children could use the building, all the electrical wiring, plumbing, and what David and his friends labeled "all that other stuff," had to be safe and in proper working order. Since I didn't understand the workings of any of the "stuff," I required the services of a professional contractor.

"That's what my dad does," Danny said while swinging on my porch swing. David and I were playing catch in my front yard, and Danny had overheard us discussing our way-cool plans for the warehouse.

"It's what he used to do, dummy," David retorted.

"I am not a dummy. I'm a Danny," Danny refuted correctly.

"Dummy Danny, Danny dummy — what's the difference?" David knew how to acquire his brother's goat.

"Shut-up, dummy David! Tell him to stop, Tee-Bee!" (Danny and his brother were my friends, and I had gained their mother's permission to allow them to address me in the manner I preferred.)

"Danny, if I fight your battles you will never know victory, and if you go to war over name-calling you will only learn defeat."

"Yeah, Danny, It's like that sticks-and-stones stuff dad says. You know, like water off a duck's back. Don't let it bug you. Dad doesn't do that contractor stuff anymore."

David usually offered Danny big-brother advice after I had offered mine, and his comment brought me back to where the confrontation had begun. His dad is, or was a contractor. I called Cynthia who confirmed the "he is" statement, and she also told me that Donald would be in town the next week to visit his children.

It occurred to me that since Cynthia was such a wonderful woman, Donald had to be a decent man. Maybe he had just responded to an urge to get into Amy's pants, and once there, he had trouble extracting himself from the web of his ill-considered action.

Another tangled web had been created when big-city developers came into Schulberg during the North Dakota oil boom of 1980. These big companies had built the Taco Bell and Pizza Hut, they renovated the library and the bank, and they had turned the outlying farm areas into housing developments. They had moved in for a quick buck, and pushed the local contractors to the brink of bankruptcy by placing ridiculously low bids on available contracting jobs. The practice was called "low-balling," so both of Donald's problems were similar in theme.

When Donald's business as the town's biggest smaller contractor was threatened, he had turned to cheating on his wife as a way to reaffirm his manhood. Cynthia was too hurt and embarrassed to consider the connection, so Donald took his excuses and left town. As Cynthia expected, her husband Donald came back to town the following week to see his kids. She did not expect that he would stay, but my mind was open on the subject.

"So, do you think you can fix the place up?" I asked Donald as we stood in the middle of my dilapidated building.

"Well, the beams are in good shape," he said looking up at the high ceiling. "The structure's sound, but it'll take a lot of work. Maybe about three months, once the plans are approved."

"What plans?" I asked.

"Building and Safety in Williston will have to approve your architectural drawings before any construction can begin. Have you hired an architect?"

"No. Isn't that something you would normally handle?"

"Yes, but like I said, I'll be leaving town in a few days. I'm only looking at your building because David asked me to."

"Yes, David said you have to get back to Ohio."

"Maybe I can put you in touch with someone."

"I don't want someone, Donald. I've heard you're the best person for the job, and I want you to do it." There was no reason to be anything but direct. "I think your sons want you to do it also."

"Look, I know you and my boys get along well, but don't tell me what they want," he snapped. "They're my boys, you remember that."

"I never forget it," I responded.

"Are you implying I do?" His tone increased in sharpness.

"I said I never forget they're your children."

His eyes softened, allowing me to peer deeper into his soul. "Don't get me wrong, Tee-Bee, I know I threw away something special. But don't think that I don't love my kids." He gave me an atta-boy pat on the back, and continued, "No hard feelings, buddy. You're a good guy, and Cindy's a great lady. I know the two of you have gotten close, and hell, it's what I deserve. Congratulations." He stepped away from me, began fiddling with some wiring, and commented, "This'll have to be replaced."

I walked over to him, and put my hand on his shoulder. "Donald, your wife and I are friends, and neither of us has ever behaved in a manner that would cause anyone to believe otherwise. Cynthia is devoted to your sons and to you." I could tell by the look on his face that he realized I was telling him his wife would welcome the chance to be a family again.

"You mean you and she aren't, you know," he finished the sentence by diverting his eyes to the wire in his hand. "God, forgive me for being such an idiot."

"God already has," I said. "Maybe you should ask Cynthia."

Donald and Cynthia finally sat down and discussed the correlation between his behavior and his fear of being a failure. I wasn't involved in their private conversations, but Cynthia forgave him, and Donald never went back to Ohio. David was happy having his father back on a full-time basis. Donald spent time teaching him how to throw a curveball, and David helped his father build the youth center. Danny could usually be found somewhere near his father's feet, playing his ukulele and singing the songs he made up about banging hammers, drills, his brother, and anything else that came to his mind. Cynthia gave me some tulip bulbs as a thank-you gift, and pink, yellow, and red Hopper tulips bloom in my garden every spring as a colorful reminder of our year-round friendship.

Donald re-started his construction company, and he and his crew did an expert job on the renovation project. The one-story building on the corner of Wheat and Winter Streets, previously described by most of Schulberg's adult population as "a dilapidated eye-sore," was now "way-cooler than cool" according to David.

The City Council decreed that the town's youths could make all the rules governing the club's operations with two exceptions. The council's referendum required that there had to be two adult chaperones on the premises at all times, and the club could not be open during school hours nor on Sundays. The rest of the decisions were made by the town's residents who met the club's under-eighteen voting requirement. The first vote taken was to name the youth center "The Club-Club," and a second vote was taken to elect members to "The Club-Club's Council-Council." David Hopper was sworn in as the council's first president, and I was named "Founding Father" and "First Chaperone."

After several months of spirited planning sessions, ballots were cast to decide on the colors of the walls, the brands of sodas and snacks dispensed from the machines, and which rock group and movie star posters would be displayed. David handled all the voting in a very democratic manner, and even studied "Robert's Rules of Order" at the library so he could "run the place like Congress," as he put it. His friends started calling him "Senator Dave," and he got a kick out of that. A number of perceptive adults remarked, "Congress should run so well."

One of the Council-Council's unique decisions proclaimed that all the town's youngsters could take turns hosting theme nights. In order to select a theme your name had to be drawn from a hat. Once your name was drawn it went into a second hat, which would be used once the first hat was empty.

This was a fair system, and every kid in town knew his or her turn would eventually come. Tom Conners Jr. donated a top hat, and his sisters donated a frilly bonnet for the name-drawing purposes.

The first four months of themes were set before the club opened its doors. Poetry night, disco night, scary movie night, sing-a-song night, finger-painting night, fashion show night (not a boy favorite), sport night (not as unpopular with the girls as the boys had imagined), and hobby night were some of the more recurring themes. During the school year the theme from Monday through Thursday was decreed "group study night," and it was mandated that any student with less than a B average had to attend or risk losing club privileges. The hours of operation were painted on the door: "After school until dinner" — "After dinner until bedtime" — "Closed on Sunday."

One of the Council-Council's resolutions concerned the club's opening night, and it was voted that I, as founding father, would perform on the club's stage. I considered this a great honor, and duteously accepted their commission to present a thirty-minute set.

The Hoppers and I had kept up with our Tuesday evening musical get togethers, and since David and Danny had learned a few of my old songs, I asked them if they would join me on stage to assist my performance of "BLESSED VICTORY."

"On the stage?" David said with a pained expression. "In front of all my friends?"

"Yes, that is if your friends show up," I responded.

Danny accepted my proposal immediately. "Live! On Stage! Me!" he squealed. Since I had transposed "BLESSED VICTORY" to the key of G,

Danny understood how good it sounded to play the correct chord at the right time, and he was eager to display his musicianship.

David continued to contemplate the disaster of appearing uncool in front of his friends. "Oh, man," he whined shuffling his feet, but since he was a "Senator" he knew it would be inappropriate to decline. "Okay, but just that one song. You have to cross your heart, and say, 'I swear that David only has to play that one song.'"

I crossed my heart with an "ex" and said, "I swear," but I didn't inform him of the plan I had set in motion to alter his perception of just how "cool" cool can be.

• • •

"Dig it, my man. Sticks has arrived in the sticks. This town be toppin' my middle-of-nowhere list."

I welcomed Sticks with a big bear hug, and invited him inside my middle-of-nowhere house. When he accepted my invitation to come to Schulberg, I had arranged his flight into Minot, and reserved a "big limo for real" to bring him to my door. His hair was a little grayer, and he wore glasses now, but it was so good to see him I wondered why I had never thought of doing this before.

"Man got to be born in this town to find it," he said. "Super Fox digs you getting me out of the house for a few days, you dig? Says I be sittin' around with too much procrastination on my mind. She's hip to long words like you, my man. Studio gigs be dry this summer, but it's cool. Got booked to play the skins for a Broadway musical, so the bread be back in place come September. Dig it, Tee-Bee, Sticks be on Broadway kickin' out the jam."

While Sticks and I chatted over cherry pie and coffee, Schulberg's adults were inspecting "The Club-Club." The safety features, which included smoke alarms, sprinklers, fire extinguishers, emergency lighting, and first aid kit, were admired. The interior was designed to be harmless. No sharp corners, skid-proof flooring, temperature controls on the water faucets in the bathrooms, unbreakable furniture, and shatter-proof glass were some of the measures taken to ease the worries of any parent whose child was accident prone. Contractor Donald and Senator David hosted the daytime affair, and every parent in attendance was asked to sign a statement giving permission for their children to use the facility. The adults were very impressed with "The Club-Club," and all signed without reservation.

At six that evening, Sticks and I kicked out the jam, and the opening night party began. We started with "THE ORPHAN STOMP," and even though it was not the style of music most teenagers listened to, they were impressed by Sticks' amazing drumming skills. I sang "CHOCOLATE TAPIOCA PUDDING" next, and then followed with a song I had not sung since I was in the fifth grade. The smaller children enjoyed "CAW, CAW, CROW" so much that I turned it into a sing-along. One little girl giggled the name "Barney" a few times, so I took her cue and inserted "Caw, Caw, Barney" into the third chorus.

I introduced David and Danny as "two fine local musicians who will assist Sticks and me for one song." Danny ran on stage followed by his coolly nonchalant brother. Our quartet performed "BLESSED VICTORY" as scheduled with Danny strumming his chords as instructed, and David doing an admirable job playing the melody on his trumpet. When we finished, Danny bowed several times in response to the applause, and ran off the stage. His brother David stood still, smiling and staring at the faces of his friends who were responding to his "uncool" trumpet in the coolest of fashion. His smile may have had something to do with Connie Adams, a pretty, red-headed school-mate who was standing in front of the stage looking at him like her heart was about to leap from her chest. I knew somewhere in his mind the words "This is way cool" were being spoken because he turned to me, and asked if we could play another song.

"MOONLIGHT," I asked?

"Cool," he replied.

"Give me the count, my man," Sticks said. "Dig it, you be playin' your first encore."

David grinned with satisfaction as he snapped his fingers, and in true musician style said, "One, two, three, four."

What David lacked in nuance he made up with precision, and he played "MOONLIGHT" perfectly while keeping his eyes focused on the face of Connie Adams. For a few seconds I heard Deke playing in New Orleans.

At the end of the festivities, Sticks and I went to the Hopper house for drinks and conversation. Danny put up a mild fuss before finally agreeing to go to bed. It was not so much the excitement of the evening as it was the sound and rhythm of Sticks' voice that caused his unwillingness to retire.

"Would you please talk some more, sir?" Danny asked a number of times.

Sticks complied with, "Dig it, my hip small-fry. You cool on the uke. Give me five, and no jive."

Danny slapped Sticks hand and proclaimed, "I'm so hot, I'm so bad!" while he ran around in little circles and giggled.

Because he was older, David was allowed to stay up longer, and it was then that Sticks and I told him stories about our good friend Deke, and the coolness of trumpets. A few years later "Senator Dave" entered college in pursuit of a career in political science, and he helped his parents with the expenses by earning money playing his trumpet (which he would always consider the coolest of instruments) in a jazz band.

Sticks and I spent a few days relaxing; we talked about old times and old friends, and walked together in my garden. I pointed out the "hip shade of green drumsticks" that I called "Sticks asparagus," and he thought it was hot having a vegetable named after him. When I showed him the paper-thin petals of the deep-orange Pappy poppy he said, "Pappy be smilin' down on us right now."

As Sticks stepped into the "big limo for real" that would begin his journey from my house in the middle-of-nowhere to New York and his preparations for a Broadway debut, he said, "Dig it, Tee-Bee. When the band split in New Orleans I forgot to thank you."

"Thank me for what?" I asked.

"Everything, and everything. That be a lotta years comin', but I say it now. Thank you, my brother. When my heart beats, you there."

"And you're in mine," I said as a crescendo of strings soared in my head, and the limo drove away.

Danny was almost eight by the time his name was drawn from the top hat allowing him to choose a personal theme night. He changed his mind countless times; "Ukulele Night," "Baseball Trading Card Night," and "Gummi Bear Night" were in the running, but all were ultimately discarded in favor of "Everybody Has To Wear A Tuxedo Night."

On a snowy Wednesday evening in February of 1996, every boy and girl under the age of eighteen showed up at "The Club-Club" wearing the black and white symbol of civility and manners that I had worn and loved for so many years. On that Valentines Day, I was not alone. Danny christened me his guest of honor, and he and I performed a rousing duet of "CAW, CAW, CROW" for piano and ukulele. The children in attendance spent the entire evening bowing and pretending they were Schulberg's most cultured citizens. They addressed each other as "ma'am" or "sir," and used "please" and "thank you" in every sentence. They spoke to each other with respect and kindness, and I overheard a number of conversations that included the phrases, "I see your point, sir," and "That's an excellent idea, ma'am." One of the adults serving the grown-up style canapés of peanut butter and spun chocolate was so impressed by his son's demeanor that he remarked, "I wish he'd wear one of those penguin suits all the time."

When I got home that night, I went into my garage, and retrieved the old "For Sale" sign that had been in the front yard when I bought the house. As I painted it white, I thought about every stage where I had performed in front of countless strangers, and all the places I had been that now seemed like blinks of the eye — towns as big as Los Angeles and as small as my own. The words "my own" repeated in my head to the lilting sound of flutes and piccolos.

I opened the small bottle of gold leaf paint I had bought when The Hoppers and I made Christmas ornaments the previous December, and began to inscribe the quick-drying white paint with a name I had almost forgotten. With sign and hammer in hand I walked across the millions of snowflakes that covered my front yard, and pounded my homemade handiwork into the frozen ground. It seemed like such a small gesture, but it marked my arrival home. I looked up into the falling snow and cast my gaze far beyond the clouds.

"Thank You for everything, and everything," I shouted to the heavens. "You let me know what's next. I'll be right here." I took a deep breath, patted the top of my sign, and walked into my house. The sign said "Paradise."

# d. c. al fine

## *author's note*

Tuxedo Bob originally agreed to be interviewed for a "whatever happened to so-and-so" article that Susan and I were writing for a Las Vegas newspaper. After speaking with him on the phone we realized we wanted to write more than a two-column story about the Memorial Day shows he had performed in 1967.

We traveled to Schulberg and spent three weeks in his living room listening to him talk about his life, and watching him give free piano lessons to anyone in town who wanted them. On the occasion of our last interview we asked if there was anything we could do for him in return for all the time he had given to us. After all, we had gotten more than we bargained for; we started with an assignment for a small article and ended up with enough stories for a book. Surely there was something we could do for him.

He looked at us curiously, "My father used to say, 'The best gift for a talker is a pair of ears.' I think he meant that people who do a lot of talking should also do a little listening, but I bring it up because it's the gift you've given me. I talked; you listened. You gave me two pairs of ears, and for that I thank you."

There was a momentary silence, which was broken by Susan. "Well, I think a lot of people are going to thank you for talking to us when they read the book."

Tuxedo Bob folded his hands in his lap, smiled, and replied, "It's humbling that you think a lot of people who I've never met are going to want to read a book about me."

"Well," I interjected, "we certainly hope a lot of people will read it."

He got up from the piano stool, and walked over to his desk. "I would like you to include a note from me in your book. Will you do that for me?"

Of course, Susan and I said yes.

*Dear Reader,*

*I want to thank you for spending some time reading about my life. It would be my pleasure to hear about yours, so please stop by my house if you are ever in Schulberg.*

*Sincerest regards,*
*Tuxedo Bob*

# Reprise

"Popularity is rarely based on merit."

Orville Fledsper

## THE SANITARIUM SONG

Four walls around me painted green.
Bars on the windows instead of screens.
Life's very safe in the sanitarium.
I think I'll stay here awhile.

Nurses bring me coffee.
Doctors give me tests.
My family put me in here,
and I can use the rest.
Life's very safe in the sanitarium.
I think I'll stay here awhile.

When I need a vacation
I walk down the hall to recreation.
There I can string some beads,
or basket weave,
or play with papier-mâché.

I have peace and quiet;
when that gets boring I can start a riot.
The nurses know it's all in jest,
and I get blessed with love from the medicine chest.

And then I do not feel worried.
I don't feel pain.
(I don't want to feel too much 'cause I might go insane).

Life's very safe in the sanitarium.
I think I'll stay here awhile.

## OUT OF MY MIND

If I had known you for a day before I met you,
I would have shot you on sight.
If I could leave you now I know I could forget you,
but I stay here for spite.

You hold your breath waiting for something to excite you;
you wouldn't know if it came.
If dogs could talk maybe they'd tell you why they bite you,
but they'd bite just the same.

You don't know how to be tender.
You don't know how to be kind.
You must be crazy, and I must be OUT OF MY MIND.

You call our friends, and tell them all how you adore me.
I wish they'd spray you with mace.
You never tell our friends how much you just ignore me.
When you fall from their grace, I hope you land on your face.

You don't know how to be tender.
You don't know how to be kind.
You must be crazy, and I must be OUT OF MY MIND.

We go around in circles.
I don't know why we stay with each other.
You serve no useful purpose for a stable state of mind.
And I don't think you're a very good lover.

If I could live with you by telephone
I know that I would never dial your number again.
Just give me some idea of where our story's going,
and we'll go to the end.

You don't know how to be tender.
You don't know how to be kind.
You must be crazy, and I must be OUT OF MY MIND.

## COMPLETELY NUDE

I don't buy big diamond rings.
I don't drive big fancy cars.
I have no use possessing things.
Impressing only goes so far.

All I want is you.
I want you COMPLETELY NUDE.

Don't need no mansion on a hill.
I don't need to dock a yacht.
Owning things gives me no thrill.
I don't need the stuff I got.

All I need is you.
I need you COMPLETELY NUDE.

Take off your shoes, drop your dress, and slowly turn around.
Throw your bra and panties on the floor.
A smile is all you need to wear.
I just need to sit and stare.
With you COMPLETELY NUDE, I wonder who could ask for more?

So strip my rainbows from my sky,
and stop my sun from shining.
Make my mighty rivers dry.
You won't find me crying.

All I want is you.
I want you COMPLETELY NUDE.

I just want to see you nude.
Nothing on, COMPLETELY NUDE.
All I want is you COMPLETELY NUDE.

## YOU DO IT FOR MONEY

Everybody was mighty impressed
when you came back to town with the best of the west.
But most of your friends are so easily swayed,
and your too-cool manners never give you away.

I laugh, 'cause I think it's funny.
You might fool them, but not me, honey.
Everybody likes to think you do it for love,
but YOU DO IT FOR MONEY.

All of your friends are waiting in line
with some change in their pockets to exchange for your time.
You stand there and smile, while you say what you please
to the ones that you'll trade-in for the ones that you'll leave.

I laugh, 'cause I think it's funny.
You might fool them, but not me, honey.
Everybody likes to think you do it for love,
but YOU DO IT FOR MONEY.

Take another diamond, steal another dollar;
you're never through.
Roses and proposals are gathered by the dozen,
so what's another heart or two.
Hearts don't mean a thing to you.

Everybody is down on their knees.
You've got 'em all thinkin' that you know what they need.
What you know is your friends wouldn't stay so impressed
if they found out that you couldn't care less.

I laugh, 'cause I think it's funny.
You might fool them, but not me, honey.
Everybody likes to think you do it for love,
but YOU DO IT FOR MONEY.
YOU DO IT FOR MONEY.

## MY LONG ISLAND COMA GIRL

MY LONG ISLAND COMA GIRL,
are you happy to see me today?
Is there anything you'd like to say?
Would you like to go outside, and play in the sun?
I wait for your answer, but I do not get one.

MY LONG ISLAND COMA GIRL,
there's something that's puzzling to me.
When I open your eyes do you see?

I don't know your secrets.
You don't know my touch.
I don't hear your laughter.
You don't talk so much.
You've been plugged to the wall since the day you arrived,
but isn't it joyous just being alive?

The doctors say you are confined to your bed.
They're recording a brainwave from inside your head.
They will keep you alive; they must use any means.
If you fail to respond, they will get more machines.
The drugs that they give you can stop any pain,
but wouldn't it be nice to feel something again.

And your mother and father, who by your side linger,
would get so excited if you just moved one finger.

Your family and your friends don't want your life to end.
Everybody seems to care about you,
but I know you do not want to live without you.
So I'll give you a hug as I pull out your plug.
Good-bye, MY LONG ISLAND COMA GIRL.

## BAD MAN

He's a BAD MAN; keepin' out of sight,
and sneakin' up your stairs in the middle of the night.
He's a madman; lookin' for sin.
If he knocks on your door don't let him in.

I have warned you.
I've tried to inform you; don't go messin' 'round with that man.
If you want trouble, you'll get it double.
Listen to me, understand.

He's got a heart that's a little rock.
He's got a stare like ice.
He's got a touch that burns too much.
He's not very nice.

Oh, no, he's a BAD MAN.
Hear what I say.
If you give him your love he'll just throw it away.
He's a madman; he'll spend all your money.
You'll be a fool if you mess with him, honey.

He will promise diamonds.
He will promise gold.
He'll hold you with empty arms, and you'll be out in the cold.
Don't get too close.
He won't let you close.
You can't get too close to the BAD MAN.

He's keepin' out of sight,
and sneakin' up your stairs in the middle of the night.
He's a madman; lookin' for sin.
When he knocks on your door don't you let him in.
He's a BAD MAN; steppin' out of line.
If you give him attention you'll be wasting your time.
He's a madman who's up to no good.
Stay away from him, honey; you know you should.

## I DON'T WANNA BE IN ANYBODY'S DREAMS

You see me on the street.
You ask me for the time.
You talk a little nervous,
but you're lookin' pretty clean.
You act a little coy,
but I know what's on your mind.
I DON'T WANNA BE IN ANYBODY'S DREAMS.

Take another look.
You can see it in my eyes.
Everything I say is exactly what I mean.
You can play a part,
but it's only for the night.
I DON'T WANNA BE IN ANYBODY'S DREAMS.

You tell me that you're looking for a live-in lover.
Well, everybody's looking for 'the love so right.'
I am only looking for the undiscovered.
I don't wanna be in your dreams tonight.

You can have a choice,
but only you can make it.
Most can't move, and others just lean.
If I had a heart,
you would only break it.
I DON'T WANNA BE IN ANYBODY'S DREAMS.

## I JUST LOVE TO COMPLAIN

Sixty-four and lonely.
My life is fading fast.
There's no one here except for you,
and you remind me of the past.
There's nothing much to do today except stare at the grass,
but I feel no pain.
I JUST LOVE TO COMPLAIN.

The TV set is broken.
I just ran out of beer.
The neighbor's cat just killed our dog,
and you didn't shed a tear.
I don't blame the children for not wanting to be here,
but I feel no pain.
I JUST LOVE TO COMPLAIN.

My social life is spent with all the friends I used to know.
Sometimes I think I'd like to run away.
But then again, I don't know of any place where I can go.
So I'll just sit and stare from my uneasy chair
with nothing much to say.

I pull up closer to the fire.
I'm feeling bitter cold.
The dreams I used to have for us have all been bought or sold.
I wanted to have everything, and all I got was old,
but I feel no pain.
I JUST LOVE TO COMPLAIN.

## THAT'S WHAT I CALL LOVE

You take my heart, and you throw it on the ground,
and then you kick it all around, until it doesn't make a sound.
Baby, THAT'S WHAT I CALL LOVE.

You take my life, and you toss it in the air,
and then you shoot it with a gun and say you just don't care.
Well, baby, THAT'S WHAT I CALL LOVE.

You'd turn your back if I was dyin'.
Ignore the tears that I'd be cryin'.
If I was standin' on the edge of a bridge
you'd probably give me a shove.
You just can't hurt me enough;
THAT'S WHAT I CALL LOVE

Sometimes, honey, it don't feel so good.
But I believe when you say,
"It feels the way that it should."
Baby, THAT'S WHAT I CALL LOVE.

You'd turn your back if I was dyin'.
Ignore the tears that I'd be cryin'.
If I was standin' on the edge of a bridge
you'd probably give me a shove.
You just can't hurt me enough;
THAT'S WHAT I CALL LOVE

You put a pain in my head, and an ache in my heart,
but I think things'll change, 'cause I'm not very smart.
You've got me down on my knees, just where you want me,
beggin', please! Please! Please!

Please take my heart; throw it on the ground;
kick it all around until it doesn't make a sound.
Baby, THAT'S WHAT I CALL LOVE.

## HARDHEADED, COLD-BLOODED, EVIL, HEARTLESS BITCH

Our song was just on the radio; I listened very close.
The words were very haunting; I shared them with your ghost.
This is my third martini; I'd like to propose a toast.
Instead of that I think I'll just compose a little note.
If I can find the perfect words, some sense will come of this.
Dear HARDHEADED, COLD-BLOODED, EVIL, HEARTLESS BITCH.

Now that's a good beginning; the thought is very clear.
No chance for misunderstanding, because you're not here.
But if you were I'm certain you'd know exactly how I feel.
And once again I'd see your love as something that was real.
Or would I see a fantasy?
My mind still questions this.
You HARDHEADED, COLD-BLOODED, EVIL, HEARTLESS BITCH.

I'm getting repetitious.
I really must move on.
I want to finish up this letter before dawn.
Anger sticks inside my throat; I want to scream it out.
When I put my thoughts on paper, the words leave little doubt.

But I still don't know the reason.
I can't explain the why.
As I sit and think of you my eyes begin to cry.
You're searching somewhere else
for all the things you think you lack.
You'll find out you don't need me;
you won't be coming back.
I wish that I could give you everything you think you want.
You're just a hardheaded, cold-blooded, evil, heartless...
Sincerely yours forever, and sealed with a kiss.
You hardheaded, cold-blooded, evil, wicked, heartless bitch!

## CHOCOLATE TAPIOCA PUDDING

It's a great big world, and I play my part;
happy to be livin' with a smile on my face.
Everyone has always got a place in my heart,
and chocolate tapioca's got a space on my plate.

I love it with a passion; I could eat it all day,
but my parents wouldn't like it very much if I did.
So I wrote to the President, and asked him to say,
"Chocolate tapioca pudding's very good for your kid."

I love the way it squishes.
I love the way it feels.
It's hard to wait sometimes for the end of the meal.
Don't offer me vanilla, banana, orange, or mocha.
All I want is chocolate tapioca.

I'm a member of the Clean Plate Club,
and I pay my dues eating broccoli, asparagus,
and other green things.
Because I know what's coming when I finish my food:
CHOCOLATE TAPIOCA PUDDING.

I love the way it squishes.
I love the way it tastes.
I lick the corners of my mouth when it gets on my face.
It's good in any season.
Any reason is fine.
I don't know where it comes from, but I'd eat it anytime.

Yes, it's a great big world, and I play my part;
happy to be livin' with a smile on my face.
Anyone can always have a piece of my heart
as long as chocolate tapioca's got a place on my plate.

## SYMPHONY NO. 1 (THINK) IN G MAJOR

*First Movement*

We talk about life,
and talk for hours on end of things we think we know that we don't know.
We speak the same of love;
using tender words to smoke screen any feeling we won't show.
But that's our way to hide what's in the heart.
We choose a side to stand on, so we stand apart.
THINK about it.

THINK about the days and nights, and wrongs and rights,
and all that should have been.
THINK about our hopes and dreams, and our sideways schemes,
and all that could have been.
THINK about the goods and bads, and the haves and hads,
and all that would have been.
And while the clock is ticking,
we still have time to THINK there's time to figure out
all the things we THINK about.

We talk of the times.
We talk of moments we pretended that our conscience was our guide.
Now only the years that pass too quickly
will judge us for the things we did,
and the things we never tried.
But isn't that our way?
Never to be wise.
We wash our hands, and calmly close our eyes.
THINK about it.

THINK about the days and nights, and wrongs and rights,
and all that should have been.
THINK about our hopes and dreams, and our sideways schemes,
and all that could have been.
THINK about the goods and bads, and the haves and hads,
and all that would have been.
And while the clock is ticking,
we still have time to THINK there's time to figure out
all the things we THINK about.

## MOB SONG

If you're broke and you need money,
I can loan you some of mine.
You pay me in installments.
Every Saturday is fine.
Try not to miss a payment,
or I'll have to break your thumbs.
(It's just my job)
I'm in the mob.

My friends pretend they like me,
though they think that I'm a jerk.
I don't like them either,
but I enjoy my work.
I make a lot of money to hang around dem bums,
but it's my job;
I'm in the mob.

This job requires no thinking,
and the bonus I derive from not using my brain is I get to stay alive.
I have to keep my mouth shut, or instead of shiny suits,
I'll be fitted with a brand new pair of stylish cement boots.

My clothing's silk Italian, and my Cuban cigar's big.
I guzzle gin like water, and I eat just like a pig.
I'm what you'd call a wise guy, but I like my women dumb.
I love this job!
I'm in the mob.

## I JUST GOT THE BUSINESS FROM THE BUSINESS

I remember when I started out, I thought I'd hit the top.
I'd reach the highest of the heights.
I'd see my name ablaze in lights.
There'd be "Standing Room Only" every night,
but all I did was flop.

I was a trooper who believed the show must go on,
and I'd go on, from dusk 'til dawn.
Sometimes when I'd be singing to an audience of four,
I would end my closing number, and start heading for the door.
Then some drunken so-and-so would scream he wanted an encore.
I found that harassing,
and quite embarrassing.

*My father used to say, "Embarrassment is like a broken heart.*
*You eventually get over it, but you never forget how it made you feel."*

I JUST GOT THE BUSINESS FROM THE BUSINESS.
I gave my all, and all I've got to show is nothing.
I JUST GOT THE BUSINESS FROM THE BUSINESS.
Fame and fortune I will never know.

I packed my bags, and I hit the road.
I worked hard, but remained unknown.
I sang my songs, no one clapped;
I told some jokes, no one laughed.
And after that, though I was busted flat,
I kept on dreaming,
and I kept on scheming;
one day I would make it to the top.

I JUST GOT THE BUSINESS FROM THE BUSINESS (continued)

But I JUST GOT THE BUSINESS FROM THE BUSINESS.
I gave my all, and all I've got to show is nothing.
I JUST GOT THE BUSINESS FROM THE BUSINESS.
Fame and fortune I will never know.

I tried my damnedest to succeed.
I dared to dream the dreams I dreamed.
I tried new jokes, but there was not a smirk.
I was out of patience, cash, and work.
Then my agent turned out to be a jerk,
and I finally realized the career that I was striving for
might not ever happen.

I JUST GOT THE BUSINESS FROM THE BUSINESS.
I gave my all, and all I've got to show is a big fat zero.
I JUST GOT THE BUSINESS FROM THE BUSINESS.
Fame and fortune I will never know.

I JUST GOT THE BUSINESS FROM THE BUSINESS.
I gave everything I had to give,
and all I got back was a great-big-giant-fat nothing.
I JUST GOT THE BUSINESS FROM THE BUSINESS.
All I wanted was a little respect,
and all I got was a lot of rejection.
I was looking for wealth and glory,
and dozens of gossipy tabloid stories.
I wanted to prove that I could do it,
but I never did, so screw it!
Fame and fortune I may never know,
but c'est la vie, mon ami, on with the show!

(Original lyrics coauthored with Amanda George)

## SANTA CLAUS LOVES LAS VEGAS

Eleven months of every year,
Santa and his eight reindeer
take vacations away from the North Pole,
because that place gets much too cold.
This leaves all the toy-maker elves to make the toys all by themselves.
Mrs. Claus is there to oversee,
but if she needs Santa
she knows right where he'll be.

SANTA CLAUS LOVES LAS VEGAS.
It's his favorite town.
He unwinds from his one-day grind,
and you can find him sitting down at the blackjack tables,
or shooting dice; sipping scotch with a splash on ice.
Santa loves Vegas that's why he's here eleven months out of the year.

Comet lives in Phoenix; Cupid's in L.A.,
but all the other reindeer have not told me where they stay.
They say they're incognito; I think that's overseas,
but they all head north December twenty-fourth for their one day odyssey.

Santa gives toys to all the boys,
and to all the girls around the world.
Accomplishing this is no easy task,
so I don't think you have to ask why
SANTA CLAUS LOVES LAS VEGAS,
or why you'll find him here.
SANTA CLAUS LOVES LAS VEGAS eleven months out of the year.
Santa loves Vegas that's why he's here eleven months out of the year.

## ANYTHING TO WIN

I don't understand this business.
It doesn't seem to make any sense.
There's not a lot of small-town, down-home feeling in a business like this.
It's just my opinion, but I think it's kind of strange
that the only thing I see from the bottom is something I want to obtain.

I could decide to push aside all my morals,
and claw my way on up to the stars.
But if I play that game will I find fortune and fame,
or my heart in a jar?
And the answer so far?
Do ANYTHING TO WIN.
Throw away your pride.
Bargain with your soul, if you have to, lie.
Once you're on the top never give an inch.
There's someone right behind you
with a new idea doing ANYTHING TO WIN.

Always try to take advantage; it's just a version of the golden rule.
You've got to do unto everyone else
before they get the chance to do unto you.
But don't believe it's quite that easy,
(though they make it easy at the start).
The more you succeed the greater the greed, and the smarter they are.

Be prepared to change your positions when people try to hold you back.
Be a little deceiving, it's better, believe me, if you put on an act,
but underneath that do ANYTHING TO WIN.
Throw away your pride.
Bargain with your soul, if you have to, lie.
Once you're on the top never give an inch
There's someone right behind you
with a new idea doing ANYTHING TO WIN.

When I decide to push aside all my morals and claw my way on up to the
stars, I'll have to use my heart for a sidewalk if I want to get very far.
ANYTHING TO WIN.
Throw away my pride. Bargain with my soul; if I have to, lie.
Once I'm on the top I'll never give an inch to anyone behind me
with a new idea doing ANYTHING TO WIN.

## RUMORS
(You said, he said, I said)

Did you hear what he said about her?
Did you hear what she said he said about me?
It's a sad old game, and the rules don't change.
It just takes a word overheard in some small conversation.

Someone we know didn't show up for school today.
We hear she's pregnant, but nobody knows for sure.
You should turn your back on your friend down the hall.
If you heard what I heard I don't think you'd like him at all.

Light a match, and you've started a fire.
RUMORS are matches of truth to a liar.
But no one takes credit for starting the RUMORS
when someone is hurt, and crying.
So, all their hurt just smolders in anger,
and all their anger builds while it looks for a way to explode.
And nobody notices.
He said, I said, you said.
I said, you said, he said.
You said, he said, I said.

They're a knife in the back; they're so hard to ignore.
They crawl down the alley, and creep under the door.
They're like dirt on your hands that won't come clean.
If RUMORS are spreading about you, you know what I mean.

Light a match, and you've started a fire.
RUMORS are matches of truth to a liar.
But no one takes credit for spreading the RUMORS
when someone is hurt, and crying.
So, all their hurt just smolders in anger.
And all their anger burns while it looks for a way to explode.
And nobody notices.
He said, I said, you said.
I said, you said, he said.
You said, he said, I said.

## DISPLAYS

I was looking for a dreamer.
You were looking for a dream.
I had never cared who or when or where.
You were more demanding it seemed,
so I began to spend my days watching your DISPLAYS.

You were never very certain.
I could never make you sure.
I was not aware what was really there.
I was only hearing the words you used to hide what you wouldn't say.
You always seemed to find a way to hide behind your DISPLAYS.

Placing you above another might have been my big mistake.
Thinking you could see every part of me
might have pushed me further than fate would have permitted me to go.
I may never know.

I was not aware what was never there.
I was only hearing the words you used to hide what you wouldn't say.
You always seemed to find a way to hide behind your DISPLAYS.

I will always be a dreamer, and we will always be apart.
Maybe I will find the passing time
can patch every hole in this heart that thinks about you every day.
I miss your DISPLAYS.

## SAY YOU LOVE ME

You made me think you were the only one for me.
I played your fool for much too long.
I gave you everything and now you set me free.
I took a chance and I was wrong.

I know I must forget you,
and I'm sure I will as soon as I know how.
But for now, SAY YOU LOVE ME, and hold me tight.
Stay and love me all through the night.
Say you'll keep me safe and warm.
Wrap me in your arms until the morning light, then I'll be all right.
Say you're thinking of me;
stay and SAY YOU LOVE ME, tonight.

I'm not pretending when I say you broke my heart,
and you shattered all my dreams.
If I were stronger then I wouldn't fall apart.
This is not the way I want to be.

It's hard to live without the one
who seemed to make the sun come up each day,
but I'll find a way; I'll be okay.

SAY YOU LOVE ME, and hold me tight.
Stay and love me all through the night.
Say you'll keep me safe and warm.
Wrap me in your arms until the morning light, then I'll be all right.
Say you're thinking of me.
Stay and SAY YOU LOVE ME.
Make believe that everything's all right, tonight.
SAY YOU LOVE ME.

# A LITTLE BIT OF LOVE

You look so sad and lonely.
I bet you count the tears you cry.
Well, take off that long face there's a knock at your door.
It's time you let someone inside.

A LITTLE BIT OF LOVE will awaken your heart.
A LITTLE BIT OF LOVE makes your day worthwhile.
So give a little love.
It can start with a smile.
You just might get it back, and you can't do better than that.

Get that chip off your shoulder.
Open up, let down your guard.
You might see someone who's been waiting for you.
Just look around you.
Is that so hard?

A LITTLE BIT OF LOVE will awaken your heart.
A LITTLE BIT OF LOVE makes your day worthwhile.
So give a little love.
It can start with a smile.
You just might get it back, and you can't do better than that.

You can care for me.
I can care for you.
That's the best thing we can do.

A LITTLE BIT OF LOVE will awaken your heart.
A LITTLE BIT OF LOVE makes your day worthwhile.
So give a little love.
It can start with a smile.
You just might get it back, and you can't do better than that.

## DON'T FORGET ME

Don't ever settle for less than you can afford to settle for.
Make sure you cover your bets.
Watch for your backside on a closing door.
One thing more:
DON'T FORGET ME.

DON'T FORGET ME.
Like the river remembers the sea,
DON'T FORGET ME.

Don't try to save what you spend.
You can replace what you discard.
Be sure of your lovers and friends.
Always remember: anywhere you are, I'm not far.
DON'T FORGET ME.

DON'T FORGET ME.
Like the river remembers the sea,
DON'T FORGET ME.

Don't ever take what you can't accept.
Try not to say things you might regret.
Always forgive what you cannot forget.

Don't ever settle for less than you can afford to settle for.
Make sure you cover your debts.
And don't let your heart become a closing door.
One thing more:
DON'T FORGET ME.

DON'T FORGET ME.
Like the river remembers the sea,
DON'T FORGET ME.

SHE'S GONE

What happened?
What did I sleep through?
I feel so sad.
I've lost her.
It would have been something.
Now I hurt so bad.
I must have just been crazy.
I let the best thing that I ever had slip through my fingers,
at such a cost;
I never figured I'd be so lonely and lost.

SHE'S GONE.
She had enough, and SHE'S GONE.
She didn't try to hold on.
I turned my back for too long, and my girl is gone.

Where am I, and how did I get here?
I feel so strange.
I miss her, and I wish she were here with me,
but everything's changed.
Now I don't know what I'm doin',
but I have to do something to change her mind.
I'll tell her I'm sorry.
Oh, no, that's no good.
I don't think she'll forgive me.
If I were her, I would.

SHE'S GONE.
She had enough, and SHE'S GONE.
She didn't try to hold on.
I turned my back for too long, and my girl is gone.

I let the best thing that I ever had slip through my fingers,
and now I'm feelin' so bad 'cause SHE'S GONE.
She had enough, and SHE'S GONE.
She didn't try to hold on.
I turned my back for too long, and my girl is gone.

## SYMPHONY NO. 2 (WHISPER) IN $E^b$ MINOR

*First Movement*

*The Whisper In The Wind*

All around you go, spinning in circles.
You can't close your eyes to make everything fine for a while.
Some thing that seemed so important is not anymore.

It's a sensation so strong.
You can't stop it.
The rule is now the exception.
Life has disarmed you, but who needs a shield or a weapon?

Can you hear it?
THE WHISPER IN THE WIND.
Can you feel it?
It's something that gets under the skin.
You never see it.
THE WHISPER IN THE WIND.

Run the same old race.
It doesn't matter.
Get up, and fall down all you like;
over and over again until something inside you runs into a wall,
then you can't ignore it at all.
You're in for the race of your life.
You're running the race of your life, but there's nothing to run to
and nothing you need to be running from.

Can you hear it?
THE WHISPER IN THE WIND.
Can you feel it?
It's something that gets under the skin.
You never see it.
THE WHISPER IN THE WIND.

## SYMPHONY NO. 2 (WHISPER) IN E$^b$ MINOR

*Third Movement*

*We Give The Best We've Got*

How do we stand the test of time?
What do we have inside that's everlasting?
How do we keep our hearts aligned,
and put all of our faith and trust in each horizon?
We can only do the best that we can do.
Ask no more of me, I ask no more of you.

There isn't a thing we have to prove.
Nothing that happens here is so important.
We can only try as hard as we can try,
and as we watch the days go by
we'll give the best we've got.
Try the best we can, and we can give the best we've got.
It's not so hard.
Everything is easier when we're feeling our hearts rise,
and fly on the wings of a dove.
Only our best is enough, and WE GIVE THE BEST WE'VE GOT.

Only the best we have will do.
Less than our best won't see us through bad moments.
You are in me, and I'm in you.
In everything that's all that really matters.
When the two of us are strong and we believe,
then moving mountains is easy to achieve.

WE GIVE THE BEST WE'VE GOT.
Try the best we can, and we can give the best we've got.
It's not so hard.
Everything is easier when we're feeling our hearts rise,
and fly on the wings of a dove.
Only our best is enough, and WE GIVE THE BEST WE'VE GOT.

## I JUST WANT YOU TO BE HERE

I wait for you,
but you're not here,
and I'm by myself; alone.
But I still wait for you;
forever.

I long for you.
I make a wish for you on every falling star.
What if I beg for you,
and stand out on the streets and plead?
Will you come home to me?

I JUST WANT YOU TO BE HERE.
I want you here so badly;
I want to hold you in my arms.
I JUST WANT YOU TO BE HERE.
I'm lost inside this aching heart,
and I want you to be here.

I live for you.
You're the breathe inside me;
I'd die here on my own.
What can I give to you to make you change your mind and stay?
Oh, I can't go on this way.

I JUST WANT YOU TO BE HERE.
I want you here so badly;
I want to hold you in my arms.
I JUST WANT YOU TO BE HERE.
I'm lost inside this aching heart,
and I want you to be here.
I'm lost inside this aching heart.
I JUST WANT YOU TO BE HERE.

## DO YOU EVER THINK OF ME AT ALL?

I never knew; you never told me what was wrong.
You closed your heart, and said good-bye; I never knew why.
And now that you're gone,
I think of a reason everyday to pick up the phone to say, "Hello,"
but I don't.
The hard thing about all this?
What I've lost is what I miss.
I wonder if I saw you today, how would I act; what would I say?

I'd say, "Hey, what's new? You're looking fine.
I haven't seen you for sometime.
What have you been up to lately?
Yeah, I've been busy too, but I'm doing well; got no complaints.
The girl I see now, she's a saint.
I hope there's someone special in your life who's loving you."
And I'd make believe I'm happy.
I'd pretend I don't recall how many nights I sat alone
with the sound a teardrop makes when teardrops fall.
DO YOU EVER THINK OF ME AT ALL?

Sometimes I tell myself it's a waste of time.
It's a waste of my time to want you this way,
to need you this way, to love you this way,
but there's nothing I can do about it.

The sad thing about all this?
What I've lost is what I miss.
I wonder if I saw you today, how would I act; what would I say?

"Hey, what's new? You're looking fine.
I haven't seen you for sometime.
What have you been up to lately?
Yeah, I've been busy too, but I'm doing well; got no complaints.
The girl I see now, she's a saint.
I hope there's someone special in your life who's loving you."
And I'd make believe I'm happy.
I'd pretend I don't recall how many nights I sat alone
with the sound a teardrop makes when teardrops fall.
DO YOU EVER THINK OF ME AT ALL?

## I GOT BAD TASTE

There's a skinny girl,
who cannot sing,
on MTV in her underthings.
I could change the channel;
look at something else,
but I think I'm in love;
I can't help myself.

I GOT BAD TASTE;
I don't deny it.
If it's bad I'll buy it.
No use lyin', I'm not gonna try to change.
Give me anything that dulls my brain,
I GOT BAD TASTE.

I want special effects,
and girls that scream.
Give me blood and violence on my TV screen.
It'll keep me involved as long as it's got
one-dimensional characters, and no plot.

I GOT BAD TASTE; I don't deny it.

I crank up the volume because I found
life's much better in Dolby sound.
I'd even watch the news if all the talking heads
were grabbed by monsters that ripped them to shreds.

Keep the crap coming;
I'm one of the sheep.
Give me more car crashes;
keep my brain asleep.
Keep the dialogue simple,
and the visuals intense.
It's the best entertainment that makes no sense.

I GOT BAD TASTE; I don't deny it.

Tuxedo Bob's Instrumental Works

MOONLIGHT

BLESSED VICTORY

THE ORPHAN STOMP

SYMPHONY No. 1 (THINK) in G Major
*2nd movement: "Musique de la Femme Antoinette"*
*3rd movement: "Heartless"*

DEKE'S THEME

SYMPHONY No. 2 (WHISPER) in E$^b$ Minor
*2nd movement: "Musketeer's Theme"*

# Finale

"An honorable man lives his life as if there is no reward."

Orville Fledsper

# The Mirror of Mister Moore

written by

Tuxedo Bob, Prince Ali, and Menoham Mohammed

Music and Lyrics by Tuxedo Bob

THE MIRROR OF MISTER MOORE

**SONG: <u>THE OVERTURE OF THE MIRROR</u>**

FADE IN:

EXT. NEW ENGLAND COUNTRYSIDE - DAY

WE SEE a car driving through the quiet, peaceful New England countryside at the height of the fall foliage season. The car passes a large sign at the border of a small town. The sign reads:

**WELCOME TO FAIRMOUNT, MAINE**
**- established 1699 -**

**PLEASE DRIVE RESPECTFULLY**

WE SEE the serenity and picturesque charm of the town as the car makes its way to Fairmount University - A group of ivy-covered buildings nestled among majestic oak and maple trees blushing with autumn's hues. The car passes a sign at the university entrance.

**FAIRMOUNT UNIVERSITY**
**HIGHER LEARNING FROM HIGHER IDEALS**

WE SEE many STUDENTS, caught up in the excitement of the fall semester, scurrying about as the car passes various campus buildings; GOODMAN HALL, THE STUDENT UNION, and the DORMITORIES. The car slows down as it passes SIX NEW ENGLAND-STYLE HOUSES, and pulls up behind the Mayflower moving van that is parked in front of the SEVENTH HOUSE. Just as the car stops, the moving van pulls away from the curb and drives away.

**SONG: <u>THE OVERTURE OF THE MIRROR</u>** ends

CUT TO:

EXT. HENRY JACOBS' HOUSE - DAY

SARA WAGNER, a bright young graduate student, wades through the numerous boxes piled on the lawn as HENRY JACOBS, a young history professor wearing a tweed jacket, white shirt and jeans, gets out of the car. Henry is followed by his big, fluffy sheepdog, HAWTHORN. Sara stands next to an antique grandfather clock, and WE SEE her annoyed expression reflected by the large mirror that leans against one of the taller boxes.

HENRY
Why did they leave?

SARA
Because I paid them.

HENRY
But they're not done. They didn't take anything into the house.

SARA
They couldn't get into the house, Henry. And don't you think you should apologize to me for being two and a half hours late?

HENRY
I ran out of gas.

(CONTINUED)

SARA
An excuse is not an apology.

HENRY
I'm sorry I'm late, Sara.

SARA
I don't forgive you.

HENRY
That's okay. I'm still sorry
I'm late. So, why couldn't
you get into the house?

SARA
The door's locked.

HENRY
Didn't your uncle tell you he
put the keys in the mailbox?

Sara gives him a chastising look.

HENRY
I probably should have told
you.

SARA
It would have helped.

HENRY
Again I'm sorry.

SARA
Again I don't forgive you.

Henry and Sara make their way toward the
mailbox on the front porch.

(CONTINUED)

Hawthorn is over by a basement window sniffing about. He makes a hollow growling noise, and slowly backs away from the window.

HENRY
Hey, what's the matter Hawthorn? Did you see the Boogie Man?

Hawthorn barks.

SARA
It was probably his own shadow.

Hawthorn barks again, and runs over to them as they climb the three steps to the front door. Henry takes a key from the mailbox, and opens the door. Sara opens her purse, and pulls out a small brass plaque. She removes a piece of protective paper from the adhesive back, and affixes the plaque onto the mailbox. It is engraved: PROFESSOR JACOBS.

CUT TO:

INT. HENRY'S HOUSE - DAY

The turn-of-the-century house is partially furnished; dust and cobwebs indicate that it has been vacant for quite some time. Henry swats a cobweb from his path as he walks down the hallway past an ornate wooden staircase. Sara sets her purse down on a small side table by the stairs, and follows Henry into the living room.

(CONTINUED)

In the center of the room WE SEE a couch, a coffee table, a desk and desk chair, and a small round dining table with two chairs. Mahogany bookshelves cover three walls. The fourth wall has two doors; one leads to the kitchen and back door, the other leads to the basement. Henry blows some dust from the top of a small desk.

HENRY
How could anything be better
than this?

**SONG: <u>LUCKIEST GUY IN THE WORLD</u>**

HENRY
I'VE GOT A NEW HOUSE,
A NEW JOB,
A NEW CAR, AND AN OLD DOG.
EVERYTHING THAT'S WONDERFUL
IS HAPPENING TO ME.
IT'S A QUAINT HOUSE.
IT'S A GOOD JOB.
IT'S A NICE CAR.
HAWTHORN'S A GREAT DOG.
AND I'M IN LOVE WITH A
BEAUTIFUL GIRL.

SARA
And I still don't forgive you.

HENRY
I'M THE LUCKIEST GUY
IN THE WORLD.

SARA
Let's get to work, Lucky.

(CONTINUED)

During the song Henry and Sara clean the house, and move the boxes and possessions from the lawn into the house.

HENRY

HOW COULD ANYONE'S LIFE
BE BETTER THAN MINE?
WHO COULD BE MORE HAPPY?
WHO IS MORE CONTENT?
ANYONE WHO SAYS HE IS
HASN'T SPENT A MINUTE
IN MY SHOES,
AND LOOKED AT YOU.
I do believe that your face
is the sole reason God gave
me eyes.

SARA

And all this dust is the sole reason God gave you hands.

HENRY

Oh, not the only reason.

He reaches for Sara, but she avoids his grasp.

SARA

Dust is all you're getting your hands on for the time being.

HENRY

Killjoy.

She puts a fingerprint of dust on his nose.

SARA

Now I forgive you.

(CONTINUED)

*(song "LUCKIEST GUY IN THE WORLD" continues)*

DISSOLVE TO:

EXT. HENRY JACOBS' HOUSE - NIGHT

Sara carries the last box into the house.

*(song "LUCKIEST GUY IN THE WORLD" continues)*

CUT TO:

INT. HENRY'S HOUSE - NIGHT

Henry straightens some clothes in his dresser drawers that sit on the stairs, and sees Sara enter with the last box.

HENRY

HOW COULD ANY ONE NIGHT
BE BETTER THAN THIS?
WHAT COULD BE MORE PERFECT
THAN BEING HERE WITH YOU?
I CAN'T THINK OF ANYTHING THAT
I WOULD RATHER DO
THAN BE WITH YOU.
CAN YOU?

He tries to put his arms around her as she passes, but she playfully maneuvers away from him.

SARA

KEEP YOUR MIND ON CLEANING,
HENRY, WE'VE GOT TO GET THIS
DONE. AND KEEP YOUR HANDS
JUST PUTTING THINGS AWAY
WHERE THEY BELONG.

<MORE> (CONTINUED)

SARA (CONT'D)
TOMORROW WHEN THE MORNING
COMES YOUR CLASSES START,
PROFESSOR.
SO NOW'S THE TIME
TO DO THE CHORES.
DUST THE STAIRCASE,
SWEEP THE FLOORS.
THESE WALLS AND HALLS
AND DOORS ARE YOURS,
PROFESSOR.

HENRY
I'm just renting.

He feigns exhaustion, and collapses on the staircase.

HENRY (continuing)
Moving into a new place and expecting to get everything cleaned and put away in one evening is a lot to ask of the youngest professor ever to be hired in the long and hallowed history of Fairmount University.

SARA
Don't be pompous, Henry.

HENRY
It's the truth.

SARA
Then it's the pompous truth.

(CONTINUED)

HENRY
You want a beer?

SARA
No, I want you to put away all those books piled on your desk. Besides, you don't have any beer.

HENRY
You want to give me a back-rub? I've got a back.

SARA
How about you and your back getting back to work!

Henry reluctantly complies.

*(song "LUCKIEST GUY IN THE WORLD" continues)*

DISSOLVE TO:

INT. HENRY'S HOUSE - NIGHT

WE SEE the grandfather clock; it is almost midnight. There are a few empty boxes on the floor, and some papers strewn on the desk, but the place looks clean. Henry and Sara are exhausted.

HENRY
HOW COULD ANYONE'S HEART
BE FULLER THAN MINE?
HOW COULD ANYONE'S LIFE BE
RICHER? I'VE GOT NO COMPLAINTS,
BUT IF I LIFT ONE MORE FINGER, I
REALLY THINK I'LL FAINT.

<MORE> (CONTINUED)

Henry puts his arm around Hawthorn, and poses pathetically.

HENRY (CONT'D)
WE'VE HAD ENOUGH OF THIS.
GIVE US A KISS?

Sara smiles at Henry's absurd pose.

SARA
YOU'VE GOT A NEW HOUSE.

She wipes the dust fingerprint from his nose.

SARA
A NEW JOB.

She kisses him on the cheek.

SARA
A NEW CAR.

She kisses him on his other cheek.

SARA
And good old Hawthorn.

She pats Hawthorn on the head.

SARA
EVERYTHING THAT'S WONDERFUL
IS HAPPENING TO YOU.

HENRY
IT'S A QUAINT HOUSE.

SARA
IT'S A GOOD JOB.

(CONTINUED)

HENRY
I've got a nice little car.

SARA
And a silly old dog.

HENRY
Plus, I have the added benefit
of being IN LOVE WITH A
BEAUTIFUL GIRL.

SARA
You keep mentioning that.

HENRY
I'M THE LUCKIEST GUY IN THE WORLD.

SARA
Are you trying to convince me?

HENRY
I'M THE LUCKIEST GUY.

SARA
You are the luckiest guy.

BOTH
THE LUCKIEST GUY IN THE WORLD.

**SONG: LUCKIEST GUY IN THE WORLD** ends

They kiss, unaware that Hawthorn has walked behind them. Henry takes a step backward, and stumbles to avoid stepping on his dog. He slips on Hawthorn's toy ball, and bumps against the large mirror propped against the wall. The mirror begins to fall.

(CONTINUED)

HENRY
Uh oh.

Neither Henry nor Sara can stop its inevitable crash to the floor. They can only watch it shatter to pieces.

HENRY
I'm glad I'm not superstitious.

DISSOLVE TO:

INT. HENRY'S HOUSE - NIGHT

Henry is dumping the last of the shattered mirror into a box. Sara stands by the open basement door balancing some boxes in her arms while flipping a light switch.

SARA
You might want to reconsider being superstitious. Your seven years of bad luck is starting with no light in your basement.

CUT TO:

INT. HENRY'S BASEMENT - NIGHT

Henry and Sara carefully walk down the stairs into the basement. She carries a candle while he carries the boxes. When they get to the bottom of the stairs he sets the boxes down, and looks for another light switch.

(CONTINUED)

Henry pulls a cord that dangles from a light fixture on the ceiling. The cord breaks, and falls to the floor.

SARA

This is a creepy basement.

HENRY

It's just a basement.

SARA

It's creepy.

The candle goes out.

SARA

Creepy and dark.

Henry lights a match, and relights her candle. Sara and he look around and see two laundry tubs and an old wringer washing machine to their right, and to their left a furnace behind which Henry thinks he sees a glint of reflected light.

HENRY

What's that over there?

SARA

What's what over where?

HENRY

Behind the furnace.

He walks over to investigate. Sara's candle goes out again.

(CONTINUED)

SARA
Okay, Henry, I'm going back upstairs. Henry?

He doesn't answer.

SARA
You are so not funny.

Henry lights another match.

HENRY
Honey, there's something back here.

SARA
Oh, wow! Really? I'm still going upstairs.

Henry sees a light switch on the wall next to him, and flips it on. A dim light shines from the ceiling. He blows out the match.

HENRY
Voila! See? My luck is improving already. Now come over here, and help me with this. Please?

Sara disapproves, but goes over to him. They drag a large wooden-crated object from behind the furnace. It is caked with dust, and looks like no one has disturbed it for decades. Henry pulls off a rotting piece of one of the boards, and sees a reflection of his face.

HENRY
It's a mirror!

(CONTINUED)

SARA

Oh, yippee. Can we go back upstairs now?

HENRY

Doesn't finding a mirror after breaking a mirror erase the seven years of bad luck?

SARA

I thought you weren't superstitious.

HENRY

I'm not superstitious. I'm curious.

Sara leads as they carry the crate toward the stairs. She has her back to Henry who continues to gaze at his reflection, which appears to be changing. His eyes aren't quite his own. His skin looks blotchy and yellow. Suddenly his reflection turns hideous and monstrous, and seems to leap out at him. This startling occurrence causes him to shift the majority of the weight of the crate onto an unsuspecting Sara.

SARA

Hey! This thing's heavy.

HENRY

Sorry.

SARA

Sorry doesn't make it not heavy.

Henry feels a cold draft on the back of his neck as they start up the stairs.

CUT TO:

INT. HENRY'S HOUSE - NIGHT

Henry and Sara pull the crate from the basement doorway.

SARA
I don't see why this couldn't have waited until morning.

HENRY
Never put off until tomorrow what you can...

He stops in mid-sentence when he notices Sara's disapproving glare.

HENRY
I have class in the morning.

They prop the crate against a wall, and Henry quickly pulls off the remaining boards to uncover the mirror. The mirror's frame of reddish-brown leather is covered with swirling designs, and there are two unusual markings carved into the upper left corner. The reflective surface of the mirror shimmers with an almost hypnotic iridescence.

HENRY
This is cool.

Hawthorn growls softly, and leaves the room.

HENRY
What's wrong with him?

(CONTINUED)

SARA
He thinks you're making a mess.

HENRY
Yeah, well, he doesn't have to clean it up.

The grandfather clock "bongs," and they see the time is one-thirty.

SARA
And neither do I.

Henry follows her as she exits to the hallway.

HENRY
You're leaving?

SARA
I have to.  I've got a few things of my own to take care of before dawn, Professor Jacobs.

She grabs her purse from the small side table. Henry helps her with her coat.

HENRY
I can't believe you're leaving. I haven't seen you for two weeks.

SARA
Don't whine, Henry.  It's so unattractive.

(CONTINUED)

HENRY
I was trying to elicit a little sympathy by sounding pathetic.

SARA
The perfect path to any girl's heart.

HENRY
I'm just nervous about tomorrow.

She puts her hand on his cheek.

SARA
Oh, Henry. Your students are going to love you almost as much as I do.

HENRY
You think so?

SARA
You do have a certain charm.

HENRY
You really think so?

SARA
Why else would I put up with you?

She gives him a peck on the lips as he opens the front door. She shivers, and pulls her coat collar tight around her neck.

(CONTINUED)

SARA
There's a chill in the air
tonight.

CUT TO:

EXT. HENRY'S HOUSE - NIGHT

It is a beautiful starlit night. STUDENTS are walking in various directions on the main campus path that fronts the house. Sara starts down the steps as Henry watches from the doorway.

HENRY
Do you want me to walk with
you?

SARA
No, I'm all right.

HENRY
But I'm not done saying
goodnight.

She comes back, and gives him another kiss.

SARA
Then say goodnight, Henry.

HENRY
Goodnight, Henry.

SARA
That's so original.

She walks down the steps.

(CONTINUED)

HENRY
Don't forget we have dinner
tomorrow night with your uncle.

SARA
I won't.

Henry jumps down the steps to her.

HENRY
What do you want to make for
dinner?

SARA
Henry, I'm going home now,
and nothing you can do or
say is going to stop me.

HENRY
Are you sure?

SARA
I'm sure. Now goodnight!

She gives him a passionate kiss that causes his knees to wobble.

**SONG: <u>I'VE FOUND SOMEONE</u>**

HENRY
That was cruel.

He staggers backwards up the stairs to his front door.

HENRY
It was very nice, but it was
cruel. Goodnight, my princess.

(CONTINUED)

Henry bows to Sara as a knight bows to a lady, and then he goes into his house, and closes the door. Sara looks up at the starry sky, smiles, and lets out a sigh. She turns away from the house, and begins walking down the main pathway (which winds through the campus) toward her rooming house.

SARA

THE SKY IS FULL
OF TWINKLING LIGHTS.
IT MUST KNOW HOW I FEEL TONIGHT.
I WISH I MAY,
I WISH I MIGHT
FEEL THIS WAY FOREVER.
THE MOON THAT SHINES
ABOVE THE TREES
SENDS MOONBEAMS DOWN
TO DANCE WITH ME.
YOU ASK WHY I FEEL LIKE THIS?
I'LL TELL YOU WHAT THE REASON IS.
I'VE FOUND SOMEONE.
SOMEONE WHO MAKES ME LAUGH,
AND MAKES ME HAPPY.
I'VE FOUND SOMEBODY WHO LOVES ME
THROUGH AND THROUGH.
I'VE FOUND SOMEONE WHO
MAKES MY DREAMS COME TRUE.

She walks past some STUDENTS who toss a football to her. She catches it, smiles, and throws it back. She sees TWO STUDENTS kissing as they lean against a tree.

SARA (continuing)

IT'S NOT SO VERY HARD TO SEE
HOW EASY LOVE IS MEANT TO BE.

<MORE> (CONTINUED)

SARA (CONT'D)

IF YOU'RE IN LOVE,
THEN YOU AGREE
TO BE IN LOVE ETERNALLY.
BUT IF YOU DOUBT
I FEEL THIS WAY,
WELL, THE ONLY THING
THAT I CAN SAY IS,
IF YOU HEARD MY HEART
YOU'D KNOW WHY I'LL NEVER
LET THIS FEELING GO.
I'VE FOUND SOMEONE.
SOMEONE WHO MAKES ME LAUGH,
AND MAKES ME HAPPY.
I'VE FOUND SOMEBODY
WHO LOVES ME
THROUGH AND THROUGH.
I'VE FOUND SOMEONE WHO
MAKES MY DREAMS COME TRUE.

She continues to walk down the path past Goodman Hall and the Student Union.

SARA (continuing)

I'M IN LOVE WITH A WONDERFUL GUY.
HE'S FAITHFUL, HONEST AND TRUE.
HE'S KIND, HE'S SMART,
AND HE'S IN MY HEART.
HE MAKES ME FEEL BRAND NEW.
I'VE FOUND SOMEONE.
SOMEONE WHO MAKES ME LAUGH,
AND MAKES ME HAPPY.
I'VE FOUND SOMEBODY WHO LOVES ME
THROUGH AND THROUGH.
I'VE FOUND SOMEONE WHO
MAKES MY DREAMS COME TRUE.

*(song "I'VE FOUND SOMEONE" continues)*

CUT TO:

EXT. SARA'S ROOMING HOUSE - NIGHT

Sara arrives at her door, and takes a set of keys from her purse. She wistfully looks back in the direction of Henry's house.

SARA (continuing)
HE MAKES ME LAUGH,
AND HE MAKES ME HAPPY.
I'VE FOUND SOMEBODY WHO LOVES ME
THROUGH AND THROUGH.
I'VE FOUND SOMEONE WHO
MAKES MY DREAMS COME TRUE.

She leans against the door, and looks up at the stars.

SARA (continuing)
THE SKY IS FULL
OF TWINKLING LIGHTS.
I KNOW JUST HOW
THEY FEEL TONIGHT.
I WISH I MAY,
I WISH I MIGHT
FEEL THIS WAY
FOR ALL MY LIFE.

**SONG: I FOUND SOMEONE** ends

A sharp gust of wind blows through the bushes and trees, and a person's shadow dashes across the side of the house. Sara is too dreamy-eyed to notice the shadow as she puts her key in the door, but she is startled by the sound of something hitting the side of the house.

(CONTINUED)

SARA
Hello? Is there someone there?

She hears the sound of someone moving in the bushes.

SARA
Hello?

DAVID CARTER, a stylish Ivy-League type with extreme good looks, steps from the bushes carrying a football.

DAVID
Just when you think you've lost a football, you find a former fiancée. Go figure.

SARA
David Carter? What on earth are you doing here?

DAVID
I was tossing this football with some of my new friends...

SARA
What are you doing here in Maine?

DAVID
Well, my terse darling...

SARA
Don't call me darling.

(CONTINUED)

DAVID
You're not happy to see me, Ms. Wagner?

SARA
Can't you tell that I'm perfectly thrilled? David, why are you here?

DAVID
As you may or may not recall, with the grades I earned at Harvard I'm able to pursue what is commonly referred to as higher education anywhere I choose. I chose tranquil, quaint, pastoral Fairmount University. Imagine my shock finding you here too.

SARA
Yes, what a shocking coincidence.

DAVID
Maybe it's destiny. Is this where you and Professor Jackal live?

SARA
His name is Jacobs, I live here, and it's none of your business.

DAVID
Ooh, you're not this testy when you're sleeping with someone, so I must surmise that you and he are...

(CONTINUED)

SARA
Also none of your business.

She opens the door.

DAVID
Aren't you going to invite me in?

SARA
Gee, let me think...No!

DAVID
Suit yourself. I'll see you around campus.

SARA
Thanks for the warning.

She goes inside, and closes the door with authority.

DISSOLVE TO:

INT. HENRY'S LIVING ROOM/STUDY AREA - NIGHT

Hawthorn is soundly asleep on the floor. Henry sits at his desk, jots down a few notes, and puts the last of his papers into neat little piles. He looks at the grandfather clock, and sees it is ten minutes to three.

HENRY
I'm going to bed my alert and fearless protector.

He rises from his desk.

(CONTINUED)

He walks past Hawthorn toward the staircase and his newly hung mirror. He yawns, and then laughs as he sees the mirror's reflection of the clock.

HENRY

Ten after nine. Oh, it's so much earlier in there.

Hawthorn barks. Henry turns to tell his dog to be quiet, but Hawthorn is no longer in sight. He turns back toward the mirror, and to his astonishment the reflection of the clock is no longer a reversed image. It looks normal, and the hands read ten minutes to three. He quickly turns his attention to the clock in the living room, and it is also ten minutes to three. He turns back again to the mirror, and the reflection of the clock is once again a mirror image (a backwards reflection of the clock's hands as if the time was ten minutes after nine).

HENRY

The ability to hallucinate must increase with lack of sleep.

He moves closer to the mirror to examine his reflection. The flesh on his face begins to change; his features begin to distort. His eyes take on a sinister gaze; his smile displays rotted teeth; tentacles of worm-like hair sprout from his head, and oozing abscesses grow on his face. As he jumps back with revulsion, the mirror begins to fill with swirling clouds.

**SONG: <u>THE MIRROR OF MISTER MOORE</u>**

(CONTINUED)

A low rumble of thunder comes from the mirror, and another face fades into view. It is the face of MISTER MOORE; a countenance not quite handsome, but possessing a certain compelling charm. There is something sinister lurking behind his hypnotic brown eyes. Henry feels dizzy, and places his hands on the wall to steady himself.

MISTER MOORE

HELLO, HENRY JACOBS.
I AM MISTER MOORE.
PERMIT ME TO ENLIGHTEN YOU
WITH WHAT I HAVE IN STORE
FOR YOUR AMUSEMENT, HENRY JACOBS.
LOOK DEEP INTO MY EYES,
AND TELL ME IF YOU SEE HOW SOON
YOU'LL LEAD TO YOUR DEMISE.

Henry pinches himself on the cheek, Mister Moore vanishes, and the mirror's reflection returns to normal.

HENRY

MY NAME IS HENRY JACOBS.
I'M THE ONLY ONE WHO'S HERE.
THE VOICE
I THINK I THOUGHT I HEARD
DID NOT COME FROM THIS MIRROR.
I KNOW I MUST BE RATIONAL.
AN HALLUCINATION'S REASONABLE.
I'M TIRED AND OVERWROUGHT,
I'M OVERWORKED,
AND NEED A REST.
A GOOD NIGHTS SLEEP
WOULD SURELY BE THE BEST.

He turns off the lights.

(CONTINUED)

*(song "THE MIRROR OF MISTER MOORE" continues)*

DISSOLVE TO:

INT. HENRY'S BEDROOM - NIGHT

Henry tosses and turns in bed.

*(song "THE MIRROR OF MISTER MOORE" continues)*

DISSOLVE TO:

Henry dreams that he is falling through an endless darkness.

*(song "THE MIRROR OF MISTER MOORE" continues)*

CUT TO:

INT. HENRY'S BEDROOM - NIGHT

The dream continues: Henry plummets through darkness, and then crashes through the ceiling and lands on his bed. Mister Moore sits atop Henry's dresser. He is dressed entirely in black from his shoes to the long cape that drapes from his shoulders.

MISTER MOORE

WAKE UP, HENRY JACOBS.
DON'T THINK THAT YOU CAN HIDE.
YOU CAN'T ESCAPE ME
IN YOUR SLEEP.
I CAN'T BELIEVE YOU'D TRY
TO GET AWAY FROM ME, YOU RASCAL.
I'M REALLY QUITE UPSET.
IF YOU PERSIST IGNORING ME,
THE MORE UPSET I'LL GET.

He leaps from the dresser.

*(song "THE MIRROR OF MISTER MOORE" continues)*

CUT TO:

EXT. THE CAMPUS LIBRARY - DAY

The dream continues: Henry's bed is on the lawn in front of THE LIBRARY. Mister Moore's leap from the previous scene concludes with him landing at the foot of the bed.

SARA (O.S.)
Hello, Professor.

Sara, dressed in ultra-sexy lingerie, giggles and waves at Henry as she and a gathering crowd of MALE ADMIRERS walk past. Henry reaches out, but his hands go through her as she, her admirers, and Mister Moore evaporate into thin air. Henry looks left and right, then quickly turns around to discover Mister Moore behind him, hanging upside down in mid-air. Mister Moore grabs him by the lapels of his pajamas, lifts him off the ground, and pulls him close to his face. ZOOM-IN to a CLOSE-UP of their faces.

MISTER MOORE
FACE ME, HENRY JACOBS.
YOU CAN'T AVOID THE TRUTH.
LOOK INTO THE MIRROR,
AND SEE IF WHAT YOU SEE IS YOU.

*(song "THE MIRROR OF MISTER MOORE" continues)*

CUT TO:

EXT. A CLIFF OVERLOOKING A DEEP RAVINE - DAY

The dream continues: ZOOM-OUT from the CLOSE-UP from the previous scene. WE SEE Mister Moore now hangs upside down from the limb of a tree holding Henry by the lapels of his pajamas over a deep ravine.

MISTER MOORE (continuing)
WHAT'S YOUR DEEPEST
DARKEST FANTASY?
ARE YOU ALL THE MAN
THAT YOU CAN BE?
WE COULD NEVER BE DISHONEST
WITH EACH OTHER, WHAT'S THE FUN?
COME ON, HENRY JACOBS,
LET'S BE CHUMS!

He lets go of Henry's pajama lapels, and gleefully watches him plunge to the bottom of the ravine.

*(song "THE MIRROR OF MISTER MOORE" continues)*

CUT TO:

INT. HENRY'S BEDROOM - NIGHT

The dream continues: Henry's fall ends with him crashing through the ceiling, and landing on his bed again. Mister Moore is perched atop Henry's dresser; the mirror hovers over Henry's head. Mister Moore jumps off the dresser, leaps upward into and is absorbed by the mirror. His arm reaches out from the mirror toward Henry.

MISTER MOORE
TAKE MY HAND,
PROFESSOR JACOBS.
<MORE> (CONTINUED)

MISTER MOORE (CONT'D)
PLEASE DON'T BE AFRAID.
I MIGHT BE THE MOST IMPORTANT
FRIEND YOU'VE EVER MADE.

The mirror disappears, leaving Mister Moore floating above Henry.

MISTER MOORE (continuing)
YOU CAN TRUST ME, HENRY JACOBS.
THE CHOICE IS YOURS TO CHOOSE.
IF I'M MERELY YOUR IMAGINING,
WHAT HAVE YOU GOT TO LOSE?

He throws his cape over Henry.

*(song "THE MIRROR OF MISTER MOORE" continues)*

CUT TO:

INT. A CLASSROOM - DAY

The dream continues: Henry throws the cape off himself, and finds that he is standing at the front of a classroom. There are dozens of STUDENTS crawling on the floor, and reaching out to him. Mister Moore rises from underneath the discarded cape, and taking Henry by the arm he walks over the Students to get to the mirror that is the classroom door. Henry tries his best not to step on anyone.

MISTER MOORE (continuing)
I'M GETTING ANXIOUS
AND FRUSTRATED;
AND YOU'RE BEING SUCH A BORE.
WHY SHOULD WE BE LIKE THE
MASSES CRAWLING ON THE FLOOR?

<MORE> (CONTINUED)

MISTER MOORE (CONT'D)
TOGETHER WE ARE DIFFERENT.
WE'RE VIBRANT,
COOL, AND CONFIDENT.
THERE'S NOTHING TO ACCOMPLISH
BY BEING DISTANT OR REMOVED.
BUT THERE IS EVERYTHING TO
GAIN BY JUST ALLOWING ME TO
PROVE THAT YOU AND I ARE ALL
YOU NEED; TOGETHER WE ARE YOU,
PROFESSOR JACOBS!

He turns suddenly to face Henry.

MISTER MOORE (continuing)
Touch me, Henry.

He telescopes backward into the mirror as if pulled by an unseen force. Blackness surrounds the mirror and envelopes the scene.

*(song "THE MIRROR OF MISTER MOORE" continues)*

CUT TO:

EXT. A BLACK HOLE IN SPACE - SPECIAL EFFECT

Henry and the mirror twist and tumble through the darkness as they are sucked toward the hole. Hurricane gusts blast from the mirror toward Henry, but the force of the wind doesn't push him further away; it draws him closer. Mister Moore's hand extends slowly from the mirror, and beckons Henry to grab hold. As Henry reaches for the hand the dizzying speed of the tornado-like maelstrom surrounding the mirror increases.

(CONTINUED)

Previous scenes from Henry's dream appear, and fly past him. They are misshapen - like images in fun-house mirrors. He tumbles closer toward the mirror and Mister Moore's outstretched hand. Exploding fireworks and carnival sounds add to the cacophonous confusion. Suddenly Mister Moore's hand disappears, and Henry crashes headlong through the mirror.

*(song "THE MIRROR OF MISTER MOORE" continues)*

CUT TO:

INT. HENRY'S BEDROOM - NIGHT

Henry wakes up with a jolt. His pajamas and bed linens are soaked with sweat, and he is out of breath.

HENRY

I AM HENRY JACOBS.
MY SENSES MUST BE RAW.
THE FACE I THINK I'VE SEEN
IS NOT A FACE I REALLY SAW.
I'M JUST EXHAUSTED,
I'VE IMAGINED THINGS.
THERE'S NO POINT
IN ALARMING ME.
I'LL WAKE UP IN THE MORNING,
EVERYTHING WILL BE ALL RIGHT.
A GOOD NIGHTS SLEEP
IS ALL I NEED,
GOODNIGHT;
GOODNIGHT.

**SONG: <u>THE MIRROR OF MISTER MOORE</u>** ends

DISSOLVE TO:

INT. HENRY'S HOUSE - DAY

Henry is dressed for his first day of class, and he walks down the staircase whistling a happy tune. His jaw drops when he catches a glimpse of his living room as reflected in the mirror. All of the papers that were on his desk are scattered across the floor.

HENRY
Hawthorn, what the...!

Henry looks at the grandfather clock, and sees the time is seven-twenty.

HENRY
You are so lucky I have a little time before class to clean up after you.

He walks around picking up the papers, and hears a noise in the hallway.

HENRY
You're a bad dog, Hawthorn!

He steps into the hallway to investigate, but Hawthorn isn't there. He glances at the mirror, and is astonished to see the reflection of the grandfather clock's hands spinning around the dial. He turns toward the clock in the living room, sees the hands aren't spinning, but the time reads eight twenty-five.

(CONTINUED)

HENRY
Maybe I'm still dreaming.

He looks at this watch. It also reads eight twenty-five.

HENRY
I'm late!

He rushes into the living room, quickly gathers the papers from the floor and stuffs them into his briefcase. Hawthorn walks in from the kitchen with his ball in his mouth.

HENRY
I'm late, and it's your fault!

Hawthorn wags his tail, drops the ball, and barks as it bounces across the floor.

HENRY
The cute and innocent routine won't work.

Hawthorn barks again as Henry hurries toward the front door.

HENRY
I don't want to hear your excuses. You're a very bad dog!

Henry dashes out. Hawthorn stands up on his back legs with his front paws on the wall next to the mirror. He growls, then whimpers and runs off toward the kitchen.

MISTER MOORE (O.S.)
Bad dog indeed!

CUT TO:

EXT. THE MAIN PATHWAY THROUGH CAMPUS - DAY

Henry races down the path. He drops a folder he was trying to stuff into his briefcase. As he stoops to pick it up, he drops his keys. He reaches for the keys, and drops his briefcase. Henry hurriedly picks everything up, and runs directly into Sara's uncle, DR. FRANKLIN ARMISTICE. Dr. Armistice is a kind-faced, gray-haired man in his seventies who walks with the aid of a cane, and whose rumpled appearance belies a keen intelligence.

DR. ARMISTICE
Whoa, Henry! Where's the fire?

HENRY
Dr. Armistice! Hello! It's really nice to see you, but I'm in a hurry. We'll catch up at dinner later, okay? Great. I've got to run. You know, first day and all. I didn't want to be late.

DR. ARMISTICE
You didn't want to, and you're not.

He points his cane to direct Henry's attention toward the large clock atop Goodman Hall. The time is seven thirty-five. Henry looks at his watch, and sees the time is seven thirty-five.

(CONTINUED)

DR. ARMISTICE
Seems to me you've got enough time to run around campus a few times, and still make your first class, Professor.

HENRY
I thought it was after eight.

DR. ARMISTICE
And now you see that it isn't.

HENRY
But I was so sure.

DR. ARMISTICE
And now you are surer. Anyway, the ability to read a clock is highly overrated. Maybe you're just a little nervous, first day and all?

HENRY
Maybe I am.

DR. ARMISTICE
Well, you needn't be. Henry, when I told the dean that you'd make an extraordinary addition to the faculty, your ability to tell time never entered the conversation.

HENRY
I hope I can live up to your expectations.

(CONTINUED)

DR. ARMISTICE
Poppycock! You have nothing to prove to me or to anyone. Just be yourself, Henry.

DISSOLVE TO:

EXT. GOODMAN HALL - DAY

**SONG: ANOTHER YEAR OF COLLEGE**

STUDENTS walk up the gray granite steps, and go into the building.

*(song "ANOTHER YEAR OF COLLEGE" continues)*

CUT TO:

INT. CLASSROOM - GOODMAN HALL - DAY

STUDENTS walk into the room. Some greet old friends, some talk in small groups, some try out various desks to see which one they like. JASON, KELLY, and KATE enter, and acknowledge their friend STEPHEN, who is busily copying a list from the bulletin board.

JASON
HAS ANYBODY SEEN HIM?

KELLY
HAS ANYONE FOUND OUT
WHO THIS HENRY JACOBS IS,
AND WHAT HE'S ALL ABOUT?

KATE
I HEAR HE'S FAIRLY HANDSOME.

(CONTINUED)

STUDENT ONE
WORD IS HE'S RATHER SMART.

Henry enters, and stands at the rear of the classroom. With his young age and demeanor he is easily mistaken as another student.

HENRY
I'VE HEARD HE'S QUITE
A PLEASANT GUY.

STEPHEN
He's probably some old fart.

KELLY
That would be consistent with last year's faculty choice. I mean, who could forget good old 'I-feel-so-alive-when-I'm-boring-you-to-death' Woodson.

KATE
Hey, have some respect. Woodson died last month.

KELLY
No kidding? How could anyone tell?

JASON
If I had to listen to one more of his lectures on nothing whatsoever to do with anything, I think I'd attempt to kill myself by reading an entire Faulkner sentence without taking a breath.

(CONTINUED)

KATE
I think that's what killed
Woodson.

STEPHEN
Well, this reading list will
be the death of all of us!

FEMALE STUDENTS
HAS ANYBODY SEEN HIM?
HAS ANYONE FOUND OUT?

MALE STUDENTS
JUST WHO PROFESSOR JACOBS IS,
AND WHAT HE'S ALL ABOUT.

STUDENT TWO
I'VE HEARD HE'S STIFF,
AND STOIC.

STUDENT THREE
OLD FASHIONED, DULL,
AND STAID.

STUDENT FOUR
AND NOT TOO SHARP A DRESSER.

STEPHEN
I wonder how he grades?

KELLY
Maybe he doesn't grade at all.

KATE
Maybe he's the progressive type
to whom a grade is merely an
insult to the intellect.

(CONTINUED)

JASON
Archaic symbols of competition that have no place in a true academic environment.

KELLY
Here, here!

STUDENT TWO
Well said!

JASON
Thank you.

STUDENT THREE
Maybe he uses the honor system.

STUDENT ONE
On my honor, Professor! Aliens stole my term paper!

STUDENT FOUR
Hey, maybe he'll let us grade ourselves.

KELLY
If I grade myself I'll probably pass!

KATE
Not necessarily.

Stephen pulls the list he has been copying from the bulletin board, and holds it aloft.

STEPHEN
Not one of these books is available at Blockbuster!

(CONTINUED)

FEMALE STUDENTS
IT'S ANOTHER YEAR OF COLLEGE.
WE LOVE THE STRESS AND STRAIN.
WE HOPE SOME BITS OF KNOWLEDGE
WILL SEEP INTO OUR BRAINS.

MALE STUDENTS
IT'S ANOTHER YEAR AT FAIRMOUNT.
ANOTHER YEAR TO LEARN.
AND IF WE DON'T
THE DEAN WILL NOT
ALLOW US TO RETURN.

JASON
ONE MORE YEAR
OF READING, WRITING.

KATE
TAKING TESTS,
AND PRAYING THAT WE PASS ONE.

KELLY
WISHING EACH EXAM
WILL BE THE LAST ONE.

STEPHEN
LET'S HOPE THIS YEAR
IS A FAST ONE.

STUDENT ENSEMBLE
ONE MORE YEAR
OF READING, WRITING.
LET'S MAKE THIS YEAR
MORE EXCITING.

ALL
IT'S ANOTHER YEAR OF COLLEGE.
WE LOVE THE STRESS AND STRAIN.
<MORE> (CONTINUED)

ALL (CONT'D)
AND EVERY NOW AND THEN
SOME KNOWLEDGE SNEAKS
INTO OUR BRAINS.
COLLEGE CAN BE FRIGHTENING.

FEMALE STUDENTS
FAILING'S WHAT WE FEAR.

MALE STUDENTS
THE FRIGHTENING THING
WOULD BE THE BARS IN TOWN
RUN OUT OF BEER!

KELLY
College without beer?

JASON
I don't even want to entertain
the possibility of such an
occurrence.

STEPHEN
It has to be illegal.

KATE
And downright un-American.

KELLY
It would certainly make headlines.
"Beer Drought In Fairmount Maine!"

KATE
"Students Take To The Streets!"

STEPHEN
"Budweiser Airlifts Supplies!"

(CONTINUED)

JASON
It'll never happen. I've been
here three years. Nothing ever
happens in this town!

FEMALE STUDENTS
IT'S ANOTHER YEAR OF COLLEGE.
WE LOVE THE STRESS AND STRAIN.

MALE STUDENTS
WE HOPE SOME SPECK OF KNOWLEDGE
FINDS ITS WAY INTO OUR BRAINS.

Henry strolls down the aisle to the front of the classroom.

ALL STUDENTS
IT'S ANOTHER YEAR AT FAIRMOUNT.
ANOTHER YEAR TO LEARN
THE THINGS THAT PASS FOR
KNOWLEDGE THAT WILL LAST
LONG AFTER COLLEGE.
IT'S ANOTHER YEAR OF COLLEGE.
WE LOVE THE STRESS AND STRAIN.
SOMETHING WE DON'T KNOW
WILL FIND ITS WAY INTO OUR BRAINS.

STUDENT ONE
I HOPE THIS COURSE IS EASY.

STEPHEN
I HOPE THIS COURSE IS FUN.

HENRY
WILL EACH OF YOU PLEASE FIND
A SEAT? CLASS HAS NOW BEGUN.

Henry sets his briefcase on the desk.

(CONTINUED)

HENRY
MY NAME IS HENRY JACOBS.
PROFESSOR JACOBS, IF YOU PLEASE.
I'VE STUDIED LONG AND HARD,
AND I HAVE EARNED A FEW DEGREES.
I HAVE A MASTERS IN PHILOSOPHY,
AND A Ph.D. IN HISTORY.
I'M THE YOUNGEST PROFESSOR
EVER HIRED BY YOUR SCHOOL.
I WANT YOU ALL TO DO YOUR BEST,
AND THAT'S MY ONLY RULE.

He opens his briefcase.

HENRY (continuing)
I know I'm going to do my best to
make this the best year ever.

He takes out a stack of papers.

HENRY (continuing)
This is the course outline.
It contains the required
reading list, of which I see
at least one of you has
already become aware.

He sets the stack of papers on the desk as The Students voice their unenthusiastic opinion with a collective groan. He takes another stack of papers from his briefcase.

HENRY (continuing)
And this is your first exam,
due next week.

The Students show their disapproval with a louder groan.

<MORE> (CONTINUED)

HENRY (CONT'D)
Hey! It's a take home. All of the answers are on the Internet!
IT'S ANOTHER YEAR OF COLLEGE,
AND IT WON'T BE IN VAIN.
SOME THINGS YOU DIDN'T KNOW
WILL FIND THEIR WAY INTO YOUR BRAINS.

STEPHEN
IT'S ANOTHER YEAR AT FAIRMOUNT.

KATE
ANOTHER YEAR TO LEARN.

JASON AND KELLY
ANOTHER YEAR OF KNOWLEDGE.

ALL STUDENTS
IT'S ANOTHER YEAR OF COLLEGE.
ANOTHER YEAR OF COLLEGE
AND IT WON'T BE IN VAIN.
SOMETHING NEW WILL CERTAINLY
ILLUMINATE OUR BRAINS.
IT'S ANOTHER YEAR AT FAIRMOUNT.
ANOTHER YEAR TO LEARN
THE THINGS THAT PASS FOR KNOWLEDGE
THAT WILL LAST LONG AFTER WE ARE
FREED FROM ANOTHER YEAR OF COLLEGE.
IT'S ANOTHER YEAR OF COLLEGE!

**SONG:** **ANOTHER YEAR OF COLLEGE** ends

DISSOLVE TO:

EXT. HENRY'S HOUSE - DAY

A box of cereal falls to the ground.

(CONTINUED)

Henry struggles to get three bags of groceries from the trunk of his car. More items spill from the bags as he tries to close the trunk.

DAVID (O.S.)
Here, let me give you a hand.

David picks up the dropped items, takes two bags from Henry, and deftly closes the trunk with his left foot.

HENRY
Thanks.

DAVID
Don't mention it.

David follows Henry toward the house.

HENRY
I'm Henry Jacobs.

DAVID
Jacobs you say? So, Professor
Jacobs is your father?

Henry chuckles as he takes the key from the mailbox, and taps it on his nameplate.

HENRY
Actually, I'm Professor
Jacobs.

DAVID
No! You're pulling my leg!
You certainly don't look like
a professor.

(CONTINUED)

HENRY
I know, because I'm so young.

He opens the door, and they go inside.

DAVID
No, you just don't look smart enough to be a professor. No offense.

CUT TO:

INT. HENRY'S HOUSE - DAY

The hallway and living room are in worse shape than when Henry left this morning. The small side table by the stairs is overturned, the desk chair is upside down, all the couch cushions are on the floor, and the once tidy bookcase is in disarray. Hawthorn's ball bounces toward them.

DAVID
Hey, nice place.

HENRY
Hawthorn! You come here this instant!

DAVID
Hawthorn's your wife?

HENRY
My dog.

David sets the grocery bags by the staircase, and follows Henry into the living room.

(CONTINUED)

DAVID
He must not like being left alone. Or he hates living here, and wants to go back where he came from.

Henry sets down his bag, and extends his hand to David.

HENRY
I don't know. I'm sorry, I've forgotten my manners. Thank you so much for your help, Mister...?

DAVID
Just call me David.

HENRY
It's nice to meet you, David.

They shake hands. Henry begins to straighten the mess.

HENRY
So, David, what courses are you taking?

DAVID
Boring academic stuff. History, philosophy; useless crap like that. What do you teach?

HENRY
History. American History.

(CONTINUED)

DAVID
Ah, the easy one. You only have to deal with a few hundred years.

The doorbell rings.

DAVID
You want me to get that?

HENRY
Sure. Thanks.

DAVID
Don't mention it.

As David walks past the mirror, he feels an icy breeze blow across the back of his neck. He turns, looks around, decides it was nothing, and continues his way to the front door. He opens the door to find Sara standing on the porch.

DAVID
What's a nice girl like you...?

SARA
Oh, perfect!

She pushes her way past him, and enters the hallway.

HENRY
Hi, honey. David, I'd like you to meet my fiancée, Sara.

SARA
I've met David, Henry.

(CONTINUED)

DAVID
Yes, and on more than several memorable occasions.

HENRY
Really?

DAVID
Well, I'd better run along. I've got an exciting lecture to attend on the disintegration of modern romance. I don't want to miss that one. Anyone care to join me?

He steps out onto the porch.

HENRY
No, but thank you for the invitation, David. Maybe another time.

DAVID
How about you, Sara?

SARA
Good-bye, David.

She closes the door in his face.

HENRY
He seems like a pleasant guy.

SARA
Henry, that was David! Harvard David!

(CONTINUED)

HENRY
Oh. I didn't recognize him.

Sara exhales sharply, and they walk into the living room where they share a moment of uncomfortable silence. Henry returns to straightening up the mess.

SARA
This place is a pigsty.

HENRY
Why, thank you. I hadn't noticed. I thought Harvard David was rather nice.

SARA
Nice like a rash. What happened here?

She joins him in picking things up.

HENRY
It's Hawthorn. (PAUSE) What do you think he's doing?

SARA
He's obviously having trouble adjusting to the new house.

HENRY
I meant David.

SARA
He followed me here.

HENRY
That is so romantic.

(CONTINUED)

Sara hits him with a couch pillow.

SARA
I don't find it the least bit romantic or amusing.

Henry places the pillow on the couch. There is an uncomfortable beat of silence as they continue to straighten the mess.

HENRY
I don't have to worry about him do I?

SARA
Of course not. I'm sure Hawthorn will adjust.

HENRY
I was referring to David.

SARA
David who?

Hawthorn ambles down the stairs.

HENRY
There you are! We seem to be having a little problem here, Hawthorn.

Hawthorn barks, and then walks up to the mirror and growls.

HENRY
Hawthorn, are you listening to me?

(CONTINUED)

Hawthorn barks at the mirror.

HENRY
Hawthorn!

Hawthorn bears his teeth and snarls.

HENRY
What is wrong with you?

Hawthorn barks ferociously. Henry grabs him by the collar, and takes him to the front door.

HENRY
You are going outside until you learn to behave!

SARA
Don't be too angry with him. He's just displaying feelings of trauma and disorientation as he attempts to accustom himself to his new environment.

Henry and Hawthorn exit, and an unexpected gust of wind slams the door behind them.

SARA
That is, of course, only my educated opinion.

She starts to pick up a bag of groceries, but hesitates for a moment as she gets the eerie sensation someone is watching her. A book falls from the bookcase behind her. She turns toward the noise, and knocks over the grocery bag, spilling its contents.

CUT TO:

INT. HENRY'S KITCHEN - DAY

Sara enters, and sets a haphazardly repacked bag of groceries onto the counter. She hears footsteps in the hallway.

SARA

Henry? Could you bring me the other bags of groceries, please?

As she takes a few items from the bag she hears footsteps on the wooden staircase.

SARA

Henry?

She sets down the grocery items, and walks toward the kitchen door.

CUT TO:

INT. HENRY'S LIVING ROOM - DAY

Sara enters from the kitchen.

SARA

Henry?

She walks over to the staircase, and looks up.

SARA

Henry, are you upstairs?

(CONTINUED)

WE SEE Mister Moore in the mirror behind her. His hand reaches out for Sara's shoulder.

SARA

Okay, don't answer me!

Mister Moore's hand is almost to her shoulder. Sara senses something behind her, and she turns around. As she turns, Mister Moore's hand quickly retreats back into the mirror, and the mirror appears normal. Sara stares at her reflection, and casually fluffs her hair.

SARA

Men!

DISSOLVE TO:

INT. HENRY'S LIVING ROOM - NIGHT

Henry, Sara, and Dr. Armistice are seated at the round dining table.

DR. ARMISTICE

That was an excellent dinner. I always say if two people can cook together they'll have a happy marriage.

SARA

I've never heard you say that.

DR. ARMISTICE

Well then, I always say it from now on. Have you two set a date?

(CONTINUED)

SARA

Uncle!

HENRY

I think I'll clear the dishes.

SARA

I think I'll go home, and hit the books.

DR. ARMISTICE

Was it something I said?

Sara kisses her uncle on the cheek while Henry gets her coat.

SARA

Goodnight, Uncle Franklin.

DR. ARMISTICE

Goodnight, my dear. Sleep tight. Don't let the goblins bite.

SARA

It's bedbugs.

DR. ARMISTICE

My advice is to avoid them both.

Henry walks her to the door.

HENRY

(whispering)

I'll see you soon.

(CONTINUED)

Sara leaves. Henry walks back into the living room as Dr. Armistice pours two glasses of brandy.

DR. ARMISTICE
Now this is the life! Good food, good brandy; it's a pity my doctor made me give up good cigars.

HENRY
They're bad for your health.

DR. ARMISTICE
So are women, but does that stop us? And while I'm on the subject of women, I haven't altered any late night romantic arrangements have I?

HENRY
Oh, heavens no. Sara's got a psychology book begging for her attention. And she wanted to give you and I some time to talk.

Dr. Armistice hands Henry a brandy glass.

DR. ARMISTICE
Poppycock! We can talk whenever we want. (PAUSE) She'll be back in about an hour I presume?

HENRY
You presume correctly.

(CONTINUED)

Dr. Armistice raises his glass.

DR. ARMISTICE
Then I'll make my toast brief. To Henry Jacobs, whose character and principles honor the memory of his mother and father. I couldn't ask more for my niece.

CUT TO:

EXT. SARA'S ROOMING HOUSE - NIGHT

Sara walks up to the door, and inserts a key in the lock. She is startled when a hand reaches out and touches her on the shoulder.

DAVID
You weren't always so jumpy.

SARA
You didn't use to sneak up behind me!

DAVID
You used to love my touch.

SARA
Don't start! By the way, that wasn't a nice thing you did to Henry today. You could have introduced yourself.

DAVID
But I did.

(CONTINUED)

SARA
Don't play innocent! You know what I mean.

Sara's raised voice has earned the attention of one of her roommates, DIANE, who opens the door.

DIANE
Is there a problem here?

SARA
No, everything's fine, Diane.

DAVID
Hello, Diane. I'm David.

SARA
David's leaving.

DIANE
Then hello and goodbye, David.

Sara holds the door open as Diane retreats back into the house.

SARA
Stop following me! Is that clear enough for you?

DAVID
This mild hostility you're exhibiting could easily be interpreted as an affectionate form of foreplay.

(CONTINUED)

Sara exhales disgustedly, steps inside the
house, and slams the door in his face.

DAVID
No goodnight kiss?

DISSOLVE TO:

INT. HENRY'S HOUSE - NIGHT

Henry opens the front door, and Hawthorn enters. Dr. Armistice is standing at the mirror, putting on his coat. Hawthorn growls as he quickly passes the mirror and scurries into the kitchen.

DR. ARMISTICE
Was it something I said?

HENRY
He's been acting weird all day.

DR. ARMISTICE
Probably picked it up from you this morning.

HENRY
I could have sworn I was late.

DR. ARMISTICE
Now don't go getting defensive on me. You said it yourself that you hardly got a wink of sleep; all those crazy dreams. But you're a smart man, Henry, and a smart man's imagination can play some mighty elaborate tricks.

(CONTINUED)

HENRY
I suppose you're right.

DR. ARMISTICE
You suppose correctly.

He points to the two unusual markings on the upper left corner of the mirror's frame.

DR. ARMISTICE
Do you know what these are?

HENRY
No, but they look like oriental characters.

DR. ARMISTICE
If I'm not mistaken, they're Japanese.

HENRY
They don't seem to be part of the frame's original design.

DR. ARMISTICE
No, they don't.

HENRY
Asian graffiti, perhaps?

DR. ARMISTICE
Perhaps.

He takes a pen from his pocket, and copies the figures onto a scrap of paper.

DR. ARMISTICE (continuing)
But, I'm always intrigued by a mystery. How about you?

DISSOLVE TO:

INT. HENRY'S LIVING ROOM - NIGHT

**SONG: <u>WILD ABOUT YOU</u>**

Henry and Sara are curled up on the couch. Hawthorn sleeps on the floor in front of them.

SARA
So what did you and Uncle Franklin talk about?

HENRY
You.

SARA
I'm sure.

HENRY
You were the only thing on my mind.

SARA
Then you must have bored my uncle to tears.

HENRY
No, your uncle loves hearing about you. Almost as much as I love talking about you.

SARA
You are so sweet, Henry Jacobs.

(CONTINUED)

HENRY
YOU MUST HAVE BEEN SENT HERE
FROM HEAVEN ABOVE.
SENT HERE TO SHOW
EVERYONE HOW TO LOVE.
YOU TRY TO HIDE IT,
BUT I'VE FELT YOUR KISS.
IF YOU'RE NOT AN ANGEL,
THEN THEY DON'T EXIST.
IT'S TRUE; I'M WILD ABOUT YOU.

He picks Sara up, and carries her toward the stairs.

*(song "WILD ABOUT YOU" continues)*

DISSOLVE TO:

INT. HENRY'S BEDROOM - NIGHT

Henry and Sara have made love. Hawthorn comes into the room, and sits next to the bed.

SARA
LYING BESIDE YOU
IS ALL THAT I NEED.
HOLDING YOU CLOSELY,
HERE, NEXT TO ME.
I WANT TO TELL YOU
THE WORDS IN MY HEAD.
THERE ARE A FEW THINGS
THAT I'VE NEVER SAID.
LIKE, I LOVE YOUR LAUGH.
I LOVE YOUR TOUCH.
I CAN'T THINK OF ANYONE
THAT I'VE LOVED THIS MUCH.

(CONTINUED)

HENRY
YOU OVERWHELM ME
WITH EVERYTHING YOU DO.
STAY WITH ME ALWAYS;
I'M WILD ABOUT YOU.

They kiss and cuddle. Hawthorn "woofs" softly, and leaves the room.

HENRY and SARA
NOTHING'S FOR CERTAIN;
ALL THINGS MUST CHANGE.
IF I HAD ONE WISH,
WITH YOU I'D REMAIN.
GRANT ME MY ONE WISH;
MAKE IT COME TRUE.
ALLOW ME TO SPEND
ALL MY LIFE LOVING YOU.
I'M WILD ABOUT YOU.
IT'S TRUE; I'M WILD ABOUT YOU.

**SONG:** **WILD ABOUT YOU** ends

Henry and Sara drift off to sleep.

**SONG:** **WILD ABOUT LOVE**

*(song "WILD ABOUT LOVE" continues)*

DISSOLVE TO:

INT. HENRY'S BEDROOM - NIGHT

Sara sleeps peacefully while Henry tosses and turns. He is dreaming again.

*(song "WILD ABOUT LOVE" continues)*

DISSOLVE TO:

EXT. BARREN DESERT - DAY

Henry's dream: Henry sits up in his bed to see Mister Moore dressed in a tuxedo and top hat, carrying a silver cane, and dancing with Sara and a group of SEVEN SEXY WOMEN. Sara wears a very revealing white silk negligee. The Seven Sexy Women are dressed in provocative red lingerie. Mister Moore's mannerisms are erotically suggestive as he taunts and teases Sara. The Seven Sexy Women keep Henry at bay, thwarting his attempts to intervene.

MISTER MOORE

I'M WILD ABOUT LOVE;
CRAZY WITH PASSION.
I'M A MAN OF DESIRE
ITCHING FOR SOME ACTION.
I CAN TWIST YOU AROUND MY
FINGER, SO GIVE ME WHAT I NEED.
IF YOU'RE LOOKING FOR EXCITEMENT
YOU'D BETTER COME TO ME.
BECAUSE I'M WILD ABOUT LOVE.
I'M INSANE WITH PASSION.
LET'S GET IT DOWN TO BASICS;
IT'S AN ANIMAL ATTRACTION.
I CAN WALK ON YOUR EMOTIONS,
AND NEVER GIVE A DAMN.
IF YOU GET YOUR LITTLE FEELINGS HURT,
AT LEAST YOU'LL UNDERSTAND,
THAT I'M WILD ABOUT LOVE.

He "draws" a cartoon doorway with the tip of his cane.

<MORE> (CONTINUED)

MISTER MOORE (CONT'D)
YES, I'M WILD ABOUT LOVE.

He pushes the cartoon door open with his cane. The Seven Sexy Women drag Henry through the opening.

MISTER MOORE (continuing)
OH, I'M WILD ABOUT LOVE.

He pushes Sara through the doorway.

MISTER MOORE (continuing)
I'M WILD ABOUT LOVE.

He leaps through the doorway to follow everyone. The door closes and disappears.

*(song "WILD ABOUT LOVE" continues)*

CUT TO:

INT. A LARGE CATHEDRAL - DAY

The dream continues: Mister Moore's leap from the previous scene ends as he lands in the narthex of an enormous cathedral. He races up the aisle to the altar.

MISTER MOORE
Sorry I'm late.

He takes the position of priest. Bride Sara, dressed in a beautiful white gown that hints its origin as the negligee from the previous scene, stands beside groom Henry. David and Dr. Armistice are Henry's groomsmen, and the Seven Sexy Women are Sara's bridesmaids.

(CONTINUED)

MISTER MOORE
Dearly beloved. Ladies,

He gives a leering look toward the Seven Sexy Women that makes them swoon and fall at his feet.

MISTER MOORE (continuing)
and everybody else. We are gathered here. Blah, blah, blah, blah, blah; and so on; and so forth, and whatever and whatnot; forever and ever, amen.

As Mister Moore speaks, Henry attempts to give Sara a gold wedding band. She extends her ring finger to accept it, but Mister Moore grabs the ring and puts it on his own ring finger.

MISTER MOORE (continuing)
I now pronounce that Henry and I will be the talk of the campus!
NOTHING'S FOR CERTAIN;
ALL THINGS MUST CHANGE.
IF I REMAIN HERE
THINGS WON'T BE THE SAME.

He roughly grabs Sara's arm. She protests, but is helpless in preventing him from dragging her down the aisle toward the cathedral doors. Henry tries to follow them, but David and Dr. Armistice stand in his way.

MISTER MOORE (continuing)
I MUST HAVE BEEN SENT HERE
FROM HEAVEN ABOVE
TO BE WILD ABOUT YOU,
<MORE> (CONTINUED)

MISTER MOORE (CONT'D)
AND TO BE WILD ABOUT LOVE.

The cathedral doors burst open, and outside WE SEE hundreds of STUDENTS dancing and partying on the lawn in front of Henry's house.

*(song "WILD ABOUT LOVE" continues)*

CUT TO:

EXT. HENRY'S FRONT LAWN - DAY

The dream continues: The Seven Sexy Women, David, and Dr. Armistice join the lawn party. Henry tries to stop Mister Moore from dragging Sara toward the house, but his movements are slow and thick like molasses.

MISTER MOORE (continuing)
I'M WILD ABOUT LOVE.
I'M CRAZY WITH PASSION.
I'M A MAN OF DESIRES, AND
I'M ITCHING FOR SOME ACTION.

A knife with a black handle and serpentine blade suddenly appears in Henry's hand. Just as suddenly his movements are not restricted.

MISTER MOORE (continuing)
I CAN TWIST YOU AROUND MY
FINGER, SO GIVE ME WHAT I NEED.

Henry rushes toward Mister Moore, and plunges the knife into his back. Blood spurts from the wound.

<MORE> (CONTINUED)

MISTER MOORE (CONT'D)
IF YOU'RE LOOKING FOR EXCITEMENT

He falls to the ground.

MISTER MOORE (continuing)
YOU'LL HAVE TO COME TO ME.

Henry looks up and sees Mister Moore is now on the roof of the house with Sara at his feet clinging to one of his legs. Sara screams, and points toward Henry. Henry looks down at the body on the ground in front of him. It is David.

*(song "WILD ABOUT LOVE" continues)*

CUT TO:

EXT. HENRY'S HOUSE - DAY

The dream continues: The Seven Sexy Women, Dr. Armistice, and the Students continue to dance and party while Henry attempts to climb up the side of the house to the roof.

MISTER MOORE (continuing)
BECAUSE I'M WILD ABOUT LOVE.
I'M INSANE WITH PASSION.
LET'S GET IT DOWN TO BASICS;
IT'S AN ANIMAL ATTRACTION.
I CAN WALK ON YOUR EMOTIONS,
AND NEVER GIVE A DAMN.
I LOVE HURTING YOUR FEELINGS;
IT'S THE KIND OF MAN I AM!

(CONTINUED)

Henry's attempt to reach Sara fails, and he falls to the ground as everyone on the front lawn vanishes. Mister Moore picks Sara up, and leaps off the roof toward the back of the house. Henry gets up, and sees his front door opening slowly.

**SONG:** **<u>WILD ABOUT LOVE</u>** ends

**SONG:** **<u>THE MIRROR OF MISTER MOORE - REPRISE</u>**

Henry climbs the front steps of his house, and sees the words "PROFESSOR MOORE" crudely scrawled in red lipstick on his brass nameplate. The two Japanese characters inscribed on the leather frame of the mirror appear as dozens of sulfur-smelling sizzling blisters in the painted wood around the front door frame.

*(song "THE MIRROR OF MISTER MOORE - REPRISE" continues)*

CUT TO:

INT. HENRY'S HOUSE - DAY

Henry enters his house, and walks down the hallway. The walls appear to be liquid. The floor feels spongy under his feet. He approaches the mirror, and is horrified to see the reflection of Mister Moore standing over Sara as she lays seductively on top of the desk. She is urging Mister Moore to have his way with her. Henry turns away from the reflection, but sees no one on or around his desk. He turns back to the mirror, and is startled to see Mister Moore's face protruding from the mirror's surface as if it is pushing against thin latex sheeting.

(CONTINUED)

MISTER MOORE

TOUCH ME, HENRY JACOBS.
WHAT IS IT YOU FEAR?
YOU THINK THAT YOU'VE IMAGINED
ME, AND YET YOU WON'T COME
NEAR MY MIRROR,
PROFESSOR JACOBS.
I DON'T UNDERSTAND.
PROVE TO YOU I DON'T EXIST;
TOUCH MY HAND, HENRY.

Henry watches Mister Moore's face sink back into the mirror. He lifts his hand and sees the reflection of his fingers. He touches the reflection, and slowly curls his fingers. His fingers pass through the surface of the mirror, and the reflection of his fingers curls out from the glass and clasps his hand.

MISTER MOORE

Henry. ... Henry. ... Henry.

**SONG:** **THE MIRROR OF MISTER MOORE - REPRISE** ends

DISSOLVE TO:

INT. HENRY'S HOUSE - STAIRCASE - DAY

Henry, dressed in his pajamas, sleeps at the foot of the stairs. Mister Moore's voice has faded into Sara's. She kneels over Henry, nudging him lightly.

SARA

Henry? ... Henry? ...

Hawthorn comes over, and sniffs Henry's right hand. He growls, and walks away.

DISSOLVE TO:

INT. HENRY'S HOUSE - LIVING ROOM - DAY

Sara and Henry sit at the dining table eating breakfast.

SARA
I never knew you walked in
your sleep.

HENRY
That makes two of us.

She gets up to clear the dishes.

SARA
You certainly have a vivid
imagination. If you want my
opinion, I think it's clear
that your dream is about
anxiety.

She takes the dishes into the kitchen.

SARA (O.S.)
The guy who abducts me probably
represents your fear that I'll
leave you if you're not a good
professor. By stabbing David
you're exhibiting a subconscious
desire that he hadn't followed
me here. Oh, and all those
women?

She comes back into the room, and notices that Henry is not paying much attention.

(CONTINUED)

SARA

Well, they just make a girl feel insecure. (PAUSE) Do you have a lot of dreams about women? (PAUSE) You can tell me if you do. (PAUSE) I dream about other men sometimes. (PAUSE) A lot of other men! (PAUSE) And the things I let them do to me are, shall we say, X-rated. (PAUSE) I think I'll stroll around campus naked today! Is that all right with you, honey? (PAUSE) Henry, is is that all right with you?

HENRY

Uh, yeah, sure, it's all right.

Sara raises an eyebrow.

HENRY

Okay, I don't know what I just agreed to.

Sara grabs her coat, and hurriedly puts it on.

SARA

Pardon me for being such a bore, Professor!

She exits through the kitchen and out the back door before Henry has a chance to apologize. Henry puts his head in his hands, and groans.

HENRY

I shouldn't have mentioned the women in the dream.

(CONTINUED)

There is a scratching sound in the hallway, and Henry looks up to see Hawthorn's ball bouncing toward him.

HENRY
Come here, Hawthorn. I know you still love me. (PAUSE) Hawthorn?

The scratching sound stops. He gets up, and goes into the hallway. He yells upstairs.

HENRY
Hawthorn? Come here, boy!

He glances at the mirror.

HENRY
What'd you do with my dog?

He cracks a smile, and picks up his briefcase.

HENRY
Okay, Hawthorn, I'm leaving now. See you after class.

He walks toward the front door.

MISTER MOORE (O.S.)
Never let a woman leave a room without telling her you love her.

Henry drops his briefcase.

HENRY
Who said that?

(CONTINUED)

MISTER MOORE (O.S.)
My lips are sealed.

Henry walks back to the mirror. The images in the mirror are the reflections of Henry's surroundings, except he isn't among them. Mister Moore is.

HENRY
You?

MISTER MOORE
Me!

HENRY
It's nothing, Henry. There's a perfectly logical explanation for this apparition, and I just have to take the time to figure out what it is.

He watches Mister Moore point a finger at the grandfather clock; the hands begin to spin.

MISTER MOORE
Take all the time you need.

Henry turns away from the mirror, and sees the hands on the clock in his living room are spinning, but Mister Moore isn't in the room.

MISTER MOORE (O.S.)
Yoo-hoo! I'm in here.

Henry turns back to face the mirror, and again sees a reflection of Mister Moore instead of his own.

(CONTINUED)

MISTER MOORE
Time means nothing on my side
of reality, Professor.

He flicks his wrist, and the grandfather clock crashes to the floor. Henry turns toward the crashing sound behind him, and sees his clock in pieces on the floor.

MISTER MOORE
It's also nothing on your
side, but that's another
discussion altogether. Oh,
where are my manners! You've
got to get to class, and I'm
chatting away like an old hen.
Perhaps you won't mind if I
just sit quietly at your desk
until you get back? Maybe
then we can get better
acquainted. What do you say?

Henry looks into the mirror, and sees Mister Moore sit down in the chair at his desk.

HENRY
This can't be happening.

He turns toward his desk, and sees his chair slowly rocking but no one is sitting in it.

MISTER MOORE (O.S.)
You're such a skeptic.

HENRY
I'm standing here listening to a
figment of my imagination make
light conversation.
<MORE> (CONTINUED)

HENRY (CONT'D)
It could be temporary insanity. An hallucination from too much stress or tension, I suppose.

He turns back to the mirror. Mister Moore gets up from the desk chair, and approaches him.

MISTER MOORE
You suppose? We have a perfectly pleasant conversation, and you want to suppose I don't exist. Well, talk about denial!

HENRY
You don't exist!

MISTER MOORE
Really? Well, I sure had me fooled. Henry, if I don't exist, then your responses to me acknowledge your plunge from the edge of normal everyday behavior into the dark abyss of neurotic psychosis. Is that what you want for yourself? I don't think so. If you're sane, which you are, I'm here; which I am.

HENRY
You can't be here!

MISTER MOORE
Well then, I stand corrected. And I was so sure. Are you sure I'm not here?

(CONTINUED)

HENRY
Of course I'm not sure!

MISTER MOORE
Now we're getting somewhere!

HENRY
You have to be some form of hallucination! Some illusion brought on by mental exhaustion or an over-active thyroid for all I know, but I know I'm not crazy! I'm simply imagining that I'm conversing with a person who lives inside a mirror. Okay, that sounds crazy. Does it sound crazy to you?

MISTER MOORE
How kind of you to ask for my opinion. It seems to me strange things happen all the time that people can't explain. However, the fact is, I'm here whether you're crazy or not.

Henry closes his eyes.

HENRY
There is no one in the mirror. There's just me. There is no one in the mirror. There's just me. No one is in the mirror.

MISTER MOORE
Oh, have it your way.

He snaps his fingers and instantly vanishes.

(CONTINUED)

Henry slowly opens his eyes, and sees his own reflection. Confused by his experience, he inspects the mirror's surface.

HENRY
It's just me. I can say with absolute certainty that if I'm losing my mind, at least I'm extremely creative.

DISSOLVE TO:

INT. CLASSROOM - GOODMAN HALL - DAY

Henry stands at the lectern next to the desk in front of the classroom. He appears deep in thought. His STUDENTS fidget.

**SONG: <u>ANOTHER YEAR OF COLLEGE - REPRISE</u>**

ALL STUDENTS
ON OUR SECOND DAY OF CLASS,
PROFESSOR JACOBS
APPEARS DISTRESSED.
HE'S ACTING QUEER
AND CURIOUS.
HE ISN'T AT HIS BEST.

FEMALE STUDENTS
MAYBE HE'S JUST NERVOUS.

MALE STUDENTS
HE LOOKS A LITTLE TENSE.

ALL STUDENTS
HE'S CERTAINLY PREOCCUPIED.

(CONTINUED)

Henry pounds his fist on the lectern.

HENRY
It just doesn't make sense!

**SONG: <u>ANOTHER YEAR OF COLLEGE - REPRISE</u>** ends

The Students look on with apprehension.

HENRY
It just doesn't make sense that on such a beautiful day we should have to be indoors.

CUT TO:

EXT. THE GREAT LAWN - GOODMAN HALL - DAY

The Students are seated around Henry on the lawn. Contrary to Henry's statement it is a gloomy, overcast day. A sudden crash of lightning, booming thunder, and a deluge of rain interrupt the lecture.

HENRY
...and started the Whig Party! Don't forget! Essays are due next week!

The Students make various disgruntled remarks as they gather their books and scurry for cover.

HENRY
Class dismissed!

He holds his briefcase over his head, and runs toward the Administration Building.

CUT TO:

INT. DOCTOR ARMISTICE'S OFFICE - DAY

Dr. Armistice sits behind his desk. There is clutter and disorder everywhere. The rain and thunder continue outside his window, which faces the Great Lawn and Goodman Hall. There is a knock on his door.

DR. ARMISTICE
It's open!

A rain-soaked Henry opens the door, and steps in.

DR. ARMISTICE
Someone forgot his umbrella.

HENRY
You busy?

DR. ARMISTICE
If you're reporting to the dean, I'm always busy.

HENRY
I need to talk to you.

DR. ARMISTICE
Sounds important.

HENRY
It might be nothing.

The telephone rings.

(CONTINUED)

DR. ARMISTICE
Might be, but we won't know
until you tell me. Excuse me.

He picks up the receiver.

DR. ARMISTICE (continuing)
This is Franklin Armistice.
(PAUSE) Hello, Ben.

He cups the mouthpiece with his hand, and speaks to Henry.

DR. ARMISTICE (continuing)
It's Professor Cranston. I
asked him about those two marks
on your mirror.

He resumes his conversation into the phone.

DR. ARMISTICE (continuing)
Yes, It's some rainstorm.
(PAUSE) No, I didn't expect it
either, but you know what they
say, what you don't expect is a
gift. (PAUSE) You don't say.
(PAUSE) Well, I guess that's as
good an explanation as any.
(PAUSE) No, it's not much of a
mystery after all. Thank you,
Ben. Good-bye.

He hangs up the phone, and looks at Henry.

DR. ARMISTICE
Nootacchi hada.

(CONTINUED)

HENRY
I beg your pardon?

DR. ARMISTICE
That's what's scratched on your mirror. Nootacchi hada. Translation: "Don't touch skin."

HENRY
Don't touch skin?

DR. ARMISTICE
Ben says the symbol 'hada' taken literally means living skin, but since the frame is animal hide he figures the symbols mean, "Don't touch the frame."

Henry doesn't respond.

DR. ARMISTICE
Don't touch the frame. That's a bit odd, don't you think?

HENRY
Yeah, odd. Do you know who's lived in that house?

DR. ARMISTICE
No one of Japanese descent that I can recall.

HENRY
Someone who knew Japanese must have seen him.

(CONTINUED)

DR. ARMISTICE
Seen who?

HENRY
Why did he let a warning get scratched onto the frame?

DR. ARMISTICE
Who are you talking about, Henry. Nobody said anything about a warning.

HENRY
It might be a warning.

DR. ARMISTICE
Poppycock! How the devil would you move the mirror if you weren't supposed to touch it?

HENRY
Maybe I wasn't supposed to move it.

DR. ARMISTICE
Are you feeling all right, Henry?

HENRY
Oh, I'm fine. I never felt better.

DR. ARMISTICE
Uh huh. And I'm the Queen of England.

He wants to pursue what is obviously bothering Henry, but he decides to let it go.

(CONTINUED)

HENRY
If I wanted to find out who's lived in the house where would I look?

DR. ARMISTICE
I trust you've heard of a library? Newspaper archive section's your best bet.

Henry starts to leave.

DR. ARMISTICE
Henry?

HENRY
Yes?

DR. ARMISTICE
You let me know if there's anything I can do to help.

CUT TO:

EXT. THE MAIN PATH - DAY

The rain has stopped. Henry is deep in thought as he walks past a sign posted on a tree that reads:

**FACULTY / STUDENT MIXER**
**WEDNESDAY 7:30 P.M.**
**THE STUDENT UNION**

He passes some STUDENTS, but doesn't return their greetings.

(CONTINUED)

Henry proceeds up his walkway, but instead of going to the front door he detours to a window. He cautiously peers through the window into his house, and nearly jumps out of his skin when he is tapped on his shoulder.

DAVID (O.S.)
Everything okay in there, Professor?

HENRY
Yes, everything's fine. How are you, David?

DAVID
Very well. Thank you for asking. Say, are you going to the mixer tonight?

HENRY
Yes, I suppose I will.

DAVID
I would think you would. I hear that new faculty members are the guests of honor.

HENRY
Yes. Well, if you'll excuse me I have a few things to take care of before the festivities get under way.

DAVID
I understand. I'll see you later. Don't work too hard.

(CONTINUED)

David walks away. Henry climbs the steps to the front door, and takes the key from the mailbox.

CUT TO:

INT. HENRY'S HOUSE - DAY

Henry enters, and closes the door. He walks up to the mirror, and cautiously looks at his reflection. He sees his own face. He taps on the glass and blinks his eyes; he sees only his own image. The grandfather clock, which was in pieces earlier in the day, is in perfect working order and shows no signs of damage. The room is neat and tidy. Hawthorn comes down the stairs, and barks.

HENRY
Well, I'm glad to see you too!

Henry reaches down, and lifts Hawthorn up on his hind legs to give him a big hug.

HENRY
It had to be just some weird dream; my eyes playing tricks on me; something of that nature.

Hawthorn barks again as Henry lets him down.

HENRY
You're right, Hawthorn. Everything's okay!

**SONG: <u>HENRY'S RESOLVE</u>**

(CONTINUED)

HENRY

HOW COULD I BE SO STUPID?
TO THINK IT WAS SOMEONE ELSE'S
FACE THAT I'D SEEN?
I COWERED IN FEAR OF THIS
MIRROR, AND LET MY MIND
PLAY TRICKS ON ME.
HOW COULD I BE SO SILLY?
WHY HAVE I BEEN ACTING SO DUMB?
WHAT I THINK I'VE BEEN SEEING'S
A FANTASY.
I SAW NOTHING AT ALL,
NOT SOMEONE.
I'VE SPENT SO MANY HOURS,
AND DEVOTED SO MUCH TIME
TO BECOME WHAT I'VE BECOME:
A PROFESSOR.
I FOLLOW IN THE FOOTSTEPS
OF A MAN I'VE LONG ADMIRED.
WOULD FRANKLIN SIMPLY FOLD
UNDER THE PRESSURE?

Henry sits on the stairs and talks to Hawthorn.

HENRY (continuing)

No, he would not! So, no more hallucinations for me, and that's my final word on the subject. Agreed?

Hawthorn barks.

HENRY

Good!

Henry stands, and starts up the staircase.

(CONTINUED)

HENRY
Now I'm going to relax, take a hot shower, and put all this silliness behind me.

Hawthorn barks.

HENRY
That's right! I'm going to a party where I hear I'm one of the guests of honor.

Hawthorn emits a low growl.

HENRY
You don't think I should be a guest of honor?

Hawthorn barks.

HENRY
Well, you don't have a vote.

*(song "HENRY'S RESOLVE" continues)*

DISSOLVE TO:

INT. HENRY'S BEDROOM - DAY

Henry is finishing getting dressed.

HENRY
WHY DID I BEHAVE SO FOOLISHLY
BELIEVING THAT A MIRROR COULD TALK?
I'M EMBARRASSED TO CONFESS
THAT IN ALL OF MY DISTRESS
I MIGHT HAVE TAKEN THE MIRROR,
INSTEAD OF HAWTHORN FOR A WALK.

*(song "HENRY'S RESOLVE" continues)*

CUT TO:

INT. HENRY'S HOUSE - THE STAIRCASE - DAY

Henry bounds down the stairs. He walks up to the mirror and straightens his tie.

HENRY
SO, I KNOW THAT I
DON'T WANT TO BE IRRATIONAL.
SIMPLE REASON
AND LOGIC ARE THE KEYS.
I MUST STAY CALM AND CLEAR;
THIS IS NOTHING BUT A MIRROR.
NOT A SOUL LIVES IN
THIS MIRROR!
NOTHING HIDES INSIDE
THIS MIRROR!
THERE IS NO ONE IN
THIS MIRROR!
NO ONE!
JUST ME!

**SONG: HENRY'S RESOLVE** ends

He studies his reflection for a moment, then walks over to his desk. He picks up a small, heavy, heart-shaped paperweight.

HENRY
I'm glad I'm not
superstitious.

He hurls the paperweight at the mirror expecting to break the glass, but there is no impact. It passes through the surface of the mirror as if through an open doorway.

(CONTINUED)

The hurled paperweight hits the reflection of a bookcase, and a few books fall to the floor. A flabbergasted Henry looks into the mirror, and sees the paperweight on the floor by the bookcase. He turns toward the bookcase, and sees books on the floor but no paperweight. Stunned, he picks up a piece of fruit from the bowl on the side table by the stairs, and casually tosses it at the mirror. The fruit passes through the surface. He tosses another piece, and the same thing happens. He touches the mirror, and as he presses his fingers against the surface they disappear into it. He pulls his fingers out, and seeing nothing wrong he puts them through the surface of the mirror again.

DISSOLVE TO:

EXT. HENRY'S HOUSE - NIGHT

Just as Sara is about to ring the doorbell, the door flies open, and a very agitated Henry pulls her inside.

CUT TO:

INT. HENRY'S HOUSE - NIGHT

Henry quickly escorts Sara over to the mirror.

HENRY

You're not going to believe this, so just listen. This mirror?

<MORE> (CONTINUED)

HENRY (CONT'D)
I think there's something kind of, I don't know, magical about it; evil maybe. Maybe both! Magical and evil! You see these two symbols? Your uncle told me about these symbols today. Nootacchi hada. You know what that means? That's Japanese for "Don't touch the skin." Your uncle thought maybe it meant don't touch the leather frame, because leather is skin, right? Right. But wait a minute, how do you move something if you're not supposed to touch it, huh? How do you do that?

SARA
Why don't you tell me?

HENRY
I don't know, but it doesn't matter. You can move it all you want, because the symbols aren't referring to the frame.

SARA
They're not?

HENRY
No, but they are referring to skin!

SARA
They are?

(CONTINUED)

HENRY
Oh, yes they are! It's skin all right, and that's what the warning is all about.

SARA
The warning?

HENRY
The symbols are a warning!

SARA
Oh.

Henry points to the second symbol.

HENRY
This symbol 'hada'? It refers to living skin, and since the frame is leather, and leather is dead skin, it can't be the frame. And it's not the frame; believe me it's not the frame.

SARA
Have you joined a cult?

HENRY
Sara, be serious. Okay, now this is the really hard part. You remember that guy I told you about in my dream?

SARA
Uh huh. The dream with all the women.

(CONTINUED)

HENRY
Right, but they're not important. The guy? He's important. He's inside the mirror, and it's his skin that I wasn't supposed to touch.

SARA
You touched the skin of a man who's inside your mirror?

HENRY
I believe I did.

SARA
That's what this whole magic and evil thing is about?

HENRY
I believe it is.

SARA
Are you taking drugs?

HENRY
Do I look like the kind of guy who takes drugs?

SARA
I was just asking. Sometimes it's a person you least suspect.

HENRY
There's a man in this mirror, and I think he's trying to get out!

SARA
Okay.

(CONTINUED)

HENRY
I have to say, in all honesty, that it sounds like something I'm making up, but I swear I'm telling you the truth! There is a man living inside this mirror!

SARA
You said that.

HENRY
And he wants to get out!

SARA
You said that too.

HENRY
And you don't believe me!

SARA
I believe that you believe it.

HENRY
Go ahead. Be as condescending as you want.

He grabs a large book from his desk, and waves it in front of her.

HENRY
You don't believe me? Then believe this!

He confidently hurls the book at the mirror, thinking the book will pass through the surface, but to his surprise the mirror shatters. The book, and the fragments of glass crash to the floor.

(CONTINUED)

All that's left on the wall is the leather and wood frame. Henry is bewildered.

SARA
Okay. There was a man living inside your mirror. Now he's homeless.

HENRY
I don't understand.

SARA
Then it's unanimous. I'm going to head over to the Student Union. Do you want to come?

HENRY
I really should, you know, clean this up. Sara, am I going crazy?

SARA
Of course not, Henry. I think you're a bit confused and overly tired, but I'm sure there's a perfectly rational explanation for whatever it is that just happened. We'll talk about it later, okay? Don't be long.

She leaves. Hawthorn slinks up behind Henry, and growls.

HENRY
I know. I'm crazy.

(CONTINUED)

Henry sees the chair at his desk start to slowly rock back and forth. Hawthorn growls again, then whimpers and runs upstairs. The chair slowly pivots 180 degrees, and there sits Mister Moore.

MISTER MOORE
Oh, stop sniveling, Henry.
You're perfectly sane. It's
the world that's gone mad.

He rises, and walks slowly toward Henry.

**SONG: <u>MISTER MOORE'S TRIUMPH</u>**

MISTER MOORE (continuing)
But tell me,
for my own edification.
JUST WHAT DID YOU ASSUME
THAT YOU'D ACCOMPLISH?
THAT YOU'D PURGE YOURSELF
OF THE DEMON ON THE WALL?
WELL, GET READY FOR TODAY'S
HALLUCINATION.
YOU MERELY SHATTERED GLASS;
THAT'S ALL.
Two mirrors in three days?
Tch, tch, tch. So sloppy.
THINK OF ME AS SOMETHING
FROM A NIGHTMARE.
KEEP WISHING YOU HAD
NEVER SEEN MY FACE.
RACK YOUR BRAIN
IN SEARCH OF SOME SOLUTION
TO INDUCE MY DISAPPEARANCE
FROM THIS PLACE.

(CONTINUED)

He vanishes into thin air, instantly reappears behind Henry, and taps him on the shoulder.

MISTER MOORE

WHY IS THIS SO DIFFICULT,
PROFESSOR?
WHY DON'T YOU CONCEDE
TO WHAT IS TRUE?
YOUR MIND VOICED
ITS OBJECTIONS
BECAUSE YOUR REFLECTION
WAS SOMEBODY OTHER THAN YOU.
SO, YOU ARE NEITHER MAD,
INSANE, NOR CRAZY.
THERE'S NO ERROR,
NO MISTAKE IN WHAT YOU SEE.
NOTHING YOU EVER PREPARED FOR
COULD HAVE PREPARED YOU FOR ME.

**SONG: <u>MISTER MOORE'S TRIUMPH</u>** ends

Mister Moore walks around the room touching and smelling things. He regards a framed picture of Sara with much interest, and puts it in his pocket.

MISTER MOORE

Are you scared? You needn't be. In spite of the absurd little decorative efforts of a silly houseboy, you are my liberator, Professor; the very foundation of my freedom. No touchy hada, indeed! Henry, you must look for the triumph in what you imagine as adversity. As sure as there are two sides to every coin, there is always a silver lining.

<MORE> (CONTINUED)

MISTER MOORE (CONT'D)
For example, you now know with absolute certainty that your elevator goes all the way to the top floor, don't you? After all, here I stand; living proof, more or less.

HENRY
Who are you?

MISTER MOORE
Edwin Horatio, but-you-can-call-me-Mister Moore at your service, Professor. By the way, your question is a lie. You don't want to know who I am. You want to know what I am.

HENRY
All right. What are you?

MISTER MOORE
I just am.

HENRY
That's not an answer.

MISTER MOORE
It is to an existentialist. Oh, you'd better hurry. You're going to be late for your little date. Mustn't keep the scrumptious little morsel waiting.

(CONTINUED)

HENRY
You say I released you. How did you get in there?

MISTER MOORE
I live in there. Now I live here. It's really all up to you.

HENRY
What do you mean?

MISTER MOORE
This interrogation is tiresome.

**SONG: <u>MISTER MOORE'S TRIUMPH - REPRISE</u>**

MISTER MOORE
You can THINK OF ME
AS JUST A SMALL ANNOYANCE,
BUT DON'T EXPECT
THAT I'LL JUST GO AWAY.
FOR HOW COULD YOU CONCEIVE
THAT I WOULD EVER LEAVE?
YOU'RE THE ONLY REASON
THAT I STAY.

**SONG: <u>MISTER MOORE'S TRIUMPH - REPRISE</u>** ends

MISTER MOORE
You like parlor tricks, Professor?

Mister Moore stands in the center of the sharp fragments of the mirror, and extends his arms crucificially outward. He closes his eyes, and falls forward onto the fragments. His body is absorbed by the pieces of glass.

(CONTINUED)

In a swirling burst of energy the pieces rise, re-assembling the mirror in mid-air. The reconstructed mirror zaps back into the frame with a flash. Henry is astonished and exasperated. He grabs the bowl of fruit from the side table by the staircase, and throws it at the mirror.

HENRY

Damn this stupid mirror!

The bowl of fruit passes through the surface, and WE HEAR it crash to the floor. Henry grabs his coat, and bolts out the door. Hawthorn slinks down the stairs as the bowl, the paperweight, and the pieces of fruit are tossed from the mirror. The frame that held Sara's picture is the last item thrown out. It is bent, and the picture is missing.

DISSOLVE TO:

EXT. STUDENT UNION BUILDING - NIGHT

STUDENTS are strolling around. Some enter the building, some leave. A chilly wind swirls the fallen leaves and the light mist of fog that is settling over the ground.

CUT TO:

INT. STUDENT UNION BUILDING - NIGHT

STUDENTS and FACULTY mingle as a HIRED BAND finishes a popular tune.

(CONTINUED)

The GLEE CLUB assembles in front of the stage. David inches his way, unnoticed, toward Sara who is talking to Dr. Armistice.

SARA
I don't know where he is.

DR. ARMISTICE
I'm seventy-three years old, young lady. I know the difference between "I don't know" and "I've got a problem." What's going on?

**SONG: <u>FAIRMOUNT ALMA MATER</u>**

David notices Sara is upset, and moves closer to hear the conversation. The crowd quiets as the GLEE CLUB begins.

THE GLEE CLUB
I PLEDGE TO THEE
MY NOBLEST DEEDS.
TO HONOR TRUTH
ABOVE ALL ELSE.
AND TO THAT END I VOW TO BE
HONEST WITH MYSELF.

*(song "FAIRMOUNT ALMA MATER" continues)*

DISSOLVE TO:

EXT. STUDENT UNION BUILDING - NIGHT

The fog thickens. WE SEE an overhead view of the Student Union. Our attention is drawn to the edge of the campus grounds, and WE SEE the close proximity of the town of Fairmount.

(CONTINUED)

THE GLEE CLUB (V.O.)
AND WHEN I LEAVE
I WON'T FORSAKE
THIS SOLEMN OATH
I MAKE TO YOU:

WE SEE a small bar just off campus.

*(song "FAIRMOUNT ALMA MATER" continues)*

DISSOLVE TO:

EXT. THE FUNHOUSE BAR AND GRILL - NIGHT

Establish exterior. The fog makes the setting appear mysterious and foreboding.

THE GLEE CLUB (V.O.)
I WILL STRIVE FOR DECENCY
IN EVERYTHING I DO.

**SONG: <u>FAIRMOUNT ALMA MATER</u>** ends

Mirrored letters spelling "FUNHOUSE" are suspended unevenly over the entrance. The door is a curved, wavy mirror (like a funhouse mirror at a carnival). To the right of the door in red, white, and blue neon lights are the words: "BAR - FOOD - POOL." A few cars drive past. PEOPLE enter, and exit.

CUT TO:

INT. THE FUNHOUSE BAR AND GRILL - NIGHT

The bar has fifteen stools, ten small tables, numerous chairs, and four pool tables.

(CONTINUED)

The walls are covered with curved mirrors so reflections appear either squashed or stretched. TWO HUSKY STUDENTS are playing pool. Henry sits nearby at one of the small tables sipping a soda.

HENRY
Mirror, mirror on the wall. Was a demon in my hall?

Henry doesn't notice the blurred flashes of movement in the mirrors to his left and right.

HENRY
On second thought don't answer me.

Mister Moore plops down in the chair across from him.

MISTER MOORE
Miss me?

Henry gets up, and moves to another table.

MISTER MOORE
Oh, we're feeling antisocial tonight. You neglect your guest-of-honor duties, and now you neglect me.

He gets up, and joins Henry at the new table.

MISTER MOORE
How about a game of pool to take a bit of the edge off? What do you say?

(CONTINUED)

Henry ignores him. Mister Moore positions his chair so that Henry and he are face to face.

MISTER MOORE
Now we mustn't be impolite.
Winner gets a pretty picture.

He snaps his fingers, and the photograph of Sara he took from Henry's desk appears in his hand. Henry turns away as a WAITRESS comes over to the table. Mister Moore gets up, and then sits down in another chair to again face Henry.

WAITRESS
You boys gonna play musical
chairs all night?

HENRY
You see him?

WAITRESS
You don't?

MISTER MOORE
Pay no attention to my sour-faced
friend, madam. He's had a rough
day.

CUT TO:

INT. THE STUDENT UNION - NIGHT

The Hired Band plays as David continues to eavesdrop on Dr. Armistice and Sara's conversation.

(CONTINUED)

SARA
He said there was a man living in
his hallway mirror.

DR. ARMISTICE
And you're sure you heard him
correctly?

SARA
That isn't something I'd make
up, Uncle.

CUT TO:

INT. THE FUNHOUSE BAR AND GRILL - NIGHT

Mister Moore leers up and down the Waitress's well-endowed body.

WAITRESS
So, what'll you have?

MISTER MOORE
I will have something, but I'll
have it later.

She smiles at his presumption.

WAITRESS
You let me know when you're
ready.

MISTER MOORE
Oh, you'll be the first, I
assure you.

She walks away.

(CONTINUED)

HENRY
She saw you!

MISTER MOORE
Get a grip, Henry. I think you'd be more unsettled if she didn't see me.

CUT TO:

INT. THE STUDENT UNION - NIGHT

David continues to eavesdrop on Dr. Armistice and Sara's conversation.

DR. ARMISTICE
Did Henry say anything about clocks?

SARA
No.

DR. ARMISTICE
Anything about being late? Incorrect time?

SARA
No. Why?

DR. ARMISTICE
Nothing. Look, my dear, I'm sure he has a perfectly logical explanation.

SARA
And that would be what?

(CONTINUED)

DR. ARMISTICE
I have no idea. Conjecture is a fool's game.

CUT TO:

INT. THE FUNHOUSE BAR AND GRILL - NIGHT

Mister Moore saunters over to a pool table to observe the Two Husky Student Pool Players. Henry watches the scene from his table while sipping his soda. Pool Player One is lining up his shot. Pool Player Two stands next to Mister Moore.

MISTER MOORE
And how much longer do you gentlemen intend to play?

POOL PLAYER ONE
Keep your shirt on, Pops.

MISTER MOORE
Pops? Oh, that is rich! Did you hear that, Henry? He called me Pops.

Henry turns away from them.

POOL PLAYER TWO
You can have the table as soon as we sink the rest of the balls.

POOL PLAYER ONE
Of course, the way I shoot that could take all night.

(CONTINUED)

MISTER MOORE

Really?

He looks at Pool Player One's distorted reflection in one of the mirrors. The mirror's surface suddenly becomes flat and smooth under his glare. Pool Player One's reflection is normal as he shoots. The cue ball strikes and sinks the ball he was aiming at, and then it continues to bank around the table, striking and sinking the remaining balls one by one in numerical order. The Husky Pool Players are dumbfounded by this display.

**SONG: PLAY A GAME OF POOL WITH ME**

Mister Moore takes the pool cues from their hands, and thanks them for their participation. Two chairs magically slide up behind the Husky Pool Players, and they obediently sit down. Mister Moore points a cue in Henry's direction.

MISTER MOORE

PROFESSOR JACOBS,
YOU'VE GOT SUCH A SAD EXPRESSION.
OR IS IT ANGER,
I CAN'T REALLY TELL WITH YOU?
BUT YOU'RE ACTING VERY BADLY
FOR A PERSON OF YOUR STATURE.
SO, I THINK THERE'S ONLY ONE THING
YOU SHOULD DO.
And it won't even hurt.
You have my word on that.

(CONTINUED)

Mister Moore snaps his fingers at the pool table. The balls jump out of the pockets, and roll around the table until they are in the familiar triangular "break" position.

MISTER MOORE
PLAY A GAME OF POOL WITH ME,
AND YOU WILL DEFINITELY SEE
HOW UTTERLY RELAXING
A GAME OF POOL CAN BE.
WHEN YOU LEAN OVER THE TABLE
AND LINE UP YOUR SHOT,
YOU FORGET ABOUT
ALL OF THE TROUBLES YOU'VE GOT;
COME ON AND PLAY
A GAME OF POOL WITH ME.
JUST PICK UP A STICK,
RUB ON SOME CHALK,
HIT A FEW BALLS;
IT'S BETTER THAN SULKING.
YOU'RE SO MOROSE,
YOU'RE ACTING LIKE A FOOL.
Get over yourself!
THE LIFE YOU HAD WILL NEVER BE.
AND YOU CAN BLAME IT ALL ON ME.
COME ON, PROFESSOR JACOBS,
PLAY SOME POOL.

Mister Moore whistles while executing some fancy pool shots.

MISTER MOORE
Oh, this is so easy.

He makes a series of fantastic, and by all the laws of physics, impossible trick shots much to the delight of the patrons who are watching.

(CONTINUED)

MISTER MOORE

I feel so relaxed. Let me see now, the solid-colored balls will drop into the side pockets, but to make it a little more difficult the striped balls will try to stop them. No, that's too easy. I've got it! I'll do it with my eyes closed.

The balls dutifully roll into the triangle "break" configuration. Mister Moore closes his eyes, and strikes the cue ball. Just as he declared, the striped balls roll around the table in every direction trying to interfere with the progress of the solid-colored balls. After a flurry of activity, the solid-colored balls have deposited themselves in the side pockets, and the striped balls form a circle in the center of the table where they disappear in a burst of flame.

MISTER MOORE

Splendid! Come on, Professor! A little fun never killed anyone.
PICK UP A STICK,
LINE UP A SHOT;
YOU'LL FORGET
ALL OF THE TROUBLES YOU'VE GOT.
IT'S SO SOOTHING;
YOU'LL BE CALM AND COOL.
YOU'LL NEVER KNOW UNLESS YOU TRY.
TRUST ME JUST THIS ONE MORE TIME.
DON'T BE A FOOL, PROFESSOR.
PLAY SOME POOL,
AND YOU'LL FEEL BETTER.

<MORE> (CONTINUED)

MISTER MOORE (CONT'D)
LIFE IS MUCH TOO SHORT
TO PLAY THE FOOL.
COME ON, PROFESSOR JACOBS,
PLAY SOME POOL.

**SONG: PLAY A GAME OF POOL WITH ME** ends

MISTER MOORE
I'm beginning to think you don't like me. Nonetheless, I do believe you'll enjoy this game. Really I do, Professor. What do you say?

**SONG: PLAY A GAME OF POOL WITH ME - REPRISE**

MISTER MOORE
IF YOU'LL JUST PICK UP A STICK,
AND LINE UP A SHOT,
I'M SURE YOU'LL FORGET
ALL OF THE TROUBLES YOU'VE GOT.
It's extremely relaxing;
YOU'LL FEEL SO CALM AND COOL.
Give it a chance!
EXPERIENCE THE FUN OF IT.
TRUST ME JUST A TEENSY BIT.
DON'T BE A FOOL, PROFESSOR.
PLAY SOME POOL, PROFESSOR.
COME ON, PROFESSOR JACOBS,
PLAY SOME POOL.
COME ON, PROFESSOR JACOBS!
I CAN TAKE IT IF YOU FAKE IT!
I DON'T MEAN TO NAG, PROFESSOR,
BUT YOU'RE BEING A DRAG, PROFESSOR!
HAVE A LITTLE FUN AWAY FROM SCHOOL!
COME ON, PROFESSOR JACOBS,
PLAY SOME POOL.

(CONTINUED)

**SONG: <u>PLAY A GAME OF POOL WITH ME - REPRISE</u>** ends

Henry grabs the cue from Mister Moore.

HENRY
I want you to leave me alone!

MISTER MOORE
Ooh, temper, temper.

Henry lifts the cue into the air, accidentally hits a light fixture, and breaks the bulb. All the lights in the bar flicker, and Mister Moore vanishes.

BARTENDER
Hey! What do you think you're doing!

The BARTENDER comes out from behind the bar to confront Henry.

HENRY
I'm sorry, sir. It was an accident.

BARTENDER
Well, see that it doesn't happen again. Give me that stick.

HENRY
Yes, sir. I'm really very sorry.

As he presents the cue stick to the Bartender it flies out of his hand, and crashes into and cracks one of the mirrors.

(CONTINUED)

BARTENDER
Oh, so you wanna be a wise guy?

HENRY
I didn't throw it, I swear.

BARTENDER
Yeah, right! You're outta here.

He moves to grab Henry's arm to escort him from the premises. When Henry raises his arms in surrender, the Bartender is thrown backward as if hit by a great force. It appears to everyone in the bar that Henry has punched the Bartender, and knocked him out.

HENRY
That wasn't me. Honest.

He walks toward the front door. His path is blocked by the Two Husky Pool Players.

POOL PLAYER ONE
Where's your friend now, tough guy?

Pool Player Two grabs Henry's arms from behind. Pool Player One prepares to hit Henry in the stomach.

HENRY
You guys don't understand. I just want to get out of here.

Henry suddenly back-flips over Pool Player Two, and Pool Player One punches his friend's belly with great force.

(CONTINUED)

Pool Player Two crumples to the floor. Pool Player One picks up a chair to hit Henry, but the chair is pulled from his hands by an unseen force and it flies straight up to the ceiling. Henry quickly ducks behind a table to shield himself from harm. The table suddenly careens across the floor, falsely implying that Henry has thrown it, and it hits Pool Player One in the mid-section at the same instant that the chair, which was hovering overhead, smashes down on his head.

CUT TO:

EXT. THE FUNHOUSE BAR AND GRILL - NIGHT

Henry runs out the door into the thick fog. The Waitress comes to the doorway waving Henry's bar bill.

WAITRESS

Hey! Your bill!

She takes a few steps outside the bar, but Henry has disappeared into the fog. She turns to go back into the bar and sees Mister Moore standing to one side of the doorway.

WAITRESS

Your friend left without paying.

MISTER MOORE

I'll take care of it. Bring it to me.

(CONTINUED)

As the Waitress walks toward him, a sudden gust of wind swirls the thickening fog, which obscures her vision.

WAITRESS
Where'd you go?

MISTER MOORE (O.S.)
I'm right here.

She turns around, and sees he is standing in the roadway behind her.

WAITRESS
How did you get over there so fast?

MISTER MOORE
Magic.

The Waitress starts to walk toward him, but the fog covers him again.

WAITRESS
I like magic. Do you know any more tricks?

MISTER MOORE (O.S.)
That's for me to know, and you to find out.

She turns toward the sound of his voice, and sees a flicker of shadow by the lamppost.

WAITRESS
That's impossible. You were just over there.

(CONTINUED)

MISTER MOORE (O.S.)
Your mind's playing tricks on you.

WAITRESS
I hear you, but I can't see you.

MISTER MOORE (O.S.)
I'm over here by the door.

She hesitates for a second, then walks toward the neon-signed entrance. The air sizzles with lightning and rumbles with thunder.

WAITRESS
This is spooky, mister. I'm going back inside. You come in and settle your tab.

The Waitress bumps into Mister Moore, and she is frozen in her tracks. Lightning crackles overhead.

MISTER MOORE
Or we select option number two where I dictate policy.

Mister Moore extracts his bar bill from the Waitress's trembling hand, crumples it, and tosses it aside.

CUT TO:

EXT. THE STUDENT UNION - NIGHT

**SONG: <u>SARA'S QUANDARY</u>**

(CONTINUED)

Sara exits the Student Union, saying goodnight to some of the last STUDENTS to leave the mixer. She pulls her coat collar tight around her neck to deflect the chill of the wind that swirls the fog, which grows denser by the second. Flashes of lightning illuminate the dark gray air.

SARA
YOU'RE MAKING THIS QUITE
DIFFICULT, PROFESSOR.
I THINK YOU'RE ASKING
QUITE A LOT OF ME.
I KNOW I SHOULD BELIEVE YOU,
BUT WHAT YOU SAY JUST CAN'T BE TRUE.
SO, I'M NOT SURE EXACTLY
WHAT TO DO WITH YOU AND ME.
CAN'T YOU SEE MY PROBLEM,
HENRY JACOBS?
WHAT YOU'RE SAYING'S
OVERWHELMINGLY PREPOSTEROUS,
MY DEAR.
THE MORE I THINK ABOUT IT,
THE MORE I SIMPLY DOUBT IT.
THERE CANNOT BE A LIVING,
BREATHING PERSON IN THAT MIRROR.

**SONG: <u>SARA'S QUANDARY</u>** ends

CUT TO:

EXT. HENRY'S HOUSE - NIGHT

**SONG: <u>QUARTET OF DESIRES</u>**

A low roar of thunder follows a flash of lightning. Henry runs up the path to his house, opens the door, and Hawthorn runs out.

(CONTINUED)

HENRY
I'VE GOT TO FIND OUT WHO HE IS.
WHAT HE WANTS,
AND WHAT HE'S DOING.
WHAT HIS FULL INTENTIONS ARE.
IS THERE SOMETHING EVIL BREWING?

Henry and Hawthorn run down the campus pathway toward Sara's house. The fog swirls at their feet, and the pathway lights flicker in synch with the lightning.

HENRY
HAS HE GOT A MASTER PLAN
NOW THAT HE'S OUTSIDE THE MIRROR?
I DON'T REALLY UNDERSTAND, BUT
I HAVE GOT TO SEE THINGS CLEARER.
I'VE GOT TO SEE THINGS CLEARER!
NOW THAT HE'S OUTSIDE THE MIRROR!

*(song "QUARTET OF DESIRES" continues)*

CUT TO:

EXT. CAMPUS PATHWAY / GOODMAN HALL - NIGHT

Hawthorn runs ahead as Henry slows his pace.

HENRY
HE'S MAKING SUCH A FOOL OF ME.
I'LL BE
THE LAUGHING STOCK OF SCHOOL.
BEING THAT, I COULD ENDURE.
BUT I HATE LOOKING FOOLISH
TO HER.

*(song "QUARTET OF DESIRES" continues)*

CUT TO:

EXT. THE STUDENT UNION - NIGHT

David stands behind a tree watching Sara walk down the steps of the building with tears in her eyes.

SARA

HENRY JACOBS, TAKE A BOW.
I HOPE YOU'RE PROUD
OF YOURSELF NOW.
I WISH I MAY FIND SOMEWAY OUT
OF THIS NIGHTMARE YOU STARTED.

DAVID

I SEE SOMEONE,
SOMEONE WHO NEEDS ME NOW
TO MAKE THINGS BETTER.
YOU'VE LOST, PROFESSOR!
YOU ARE NOT HER FRIEND.
YOU AND SHE WILL END,
AND I'LL WIN HER HEART AGAIN.

*(song "QUARTET OF DESIRES" continues)*

CUT TO:

EXT. CAMPUS PATHWAY - NIGHT

Henry catches up with Hawthorn and grabs his collar. Mister Moore hides behind a tree watching Henry and Hawthorn.

MISTER MOORE

FACE IT, HENRY JACOBS.
YOU DON'T HAVE A CLUE.

<MORE> (CONTINUED)

MISTER MOORE (CONT'D)
YOU MIGHT FIND OUT
JUST WHO I AM,
BUT THAT KNOWLEDGE
WILL NOT DO YOU ANY GOOD,
MY DEAR FRIEND, HENRY,
AND I WON'T TELL YOU WHY.
IT'S MY LITTLE SECRET.
I'LL SHARE IT JUST BEFORE YOU DIE.

*(song "QUARTET OF DESIRES" continues)*

CUT TO:

EXT. CAMPUS PATHWAY / STUDENT UNION - NIGHT

Sara sits on a bench. The surrounding fog obscures anything more than a few feet away. She doesn't see David watching her from behind a bush.

SARA
DAMN YOU, HENRY JACOBS!
YOU REALLY MAKE ME MAD!

DAVID
WAY TO GO, PROFESSOR!
YOU'RE LOOKING REALLY BAD!

Henry and Hawthorn march up the granite steps. He does not see Sara or David, and they are not aware of his presence. No one notices Mister Moore sitting in a tree surveying the scene.

HENRY
DAMN YOU MISTER MOORE!
AND DAMN YOUR STUPID MIRROR!
<MORE> (CONTINUED)

HENRY (CONT'D)
I MAY NOT HAVE
THE SLIGHTEST NOTION
WHY YOU'RE EVEN HERE,
BUT I'LL DISCOVER IT,
I PROMISE YOU!
IF IT'S THE LAST THING
THAT I DO I'LL DEFEAT YOU!

MISTER MOORE
BRAVO, HENRY JACOBS!
GOOD FOR YOU!

HENRY
THOUGH IT ISN'T
VERY LIKELY, MY
CHOICE IS VERY
CLEAR.  I HAVE TO
FIND A WAY TO GET
HIM BACK INSIDE
HIS MIRROR.

MISTER MOORE
THOUGH IT ISN'T
VERY LIKELY THAT
YOUR WISHES WILL
COME TRUE,
BRAVO, HENRY
JACOBS,
GOOD FOR YOU!

MISTER MOORE
THE MIRROR MIGHT
HAVE BEEN MY PRISON,
BUT IT WILL NOT BE AGAIN.
BY THE TIME THE SUN HAS RISEN
YOUR LIFE WON'T BE THE SAME
MY FRIEND.

SARA
THERE MUST BE A REASON WHY.
HENRY, WOULDN'T TELL A LIE.
BUT WHAT HE SAID
JUST CAN'T BE TRUE.
WHAT'S THE ANSWER?
I'M CONFUSED.

(CONTINUED)

DAVID
CONFUSION'S GOOD;
IT LEADS TO DOUBT.
I'LL BE BACK IN THE PICTURE
WHEN HENRY'S OUT.

MISTER MOORE
OH, NO, IT ISN'T VERY LIKELY,
BUT HE'S MADE HIS CHOICE,
IT'S CLEAR.

SARA
THERE MUST BE A REASON WHY.
HENRY, WOULDN'T TELL A LIE.

DAVID
CONFUSION'S GOOD;
IT LEADS TO DOUBT.
I'LL BE BACK IN THE PICTURE
WHEN HENRY'S OUT.

MISTER MOORE
OH, NO, IT ISN'T VERY LIKELY,
BUT HENRY'S MADE HIS CHOICE,
IT'S CLEAR.

HENRY
I WILL FIND
THE WAY TO GET HIM
BACK INSIDE HIS MIRROR!

**SONG: QUARTET OF DESIRES** ends

**SONG: DANGER! (TONIGHT IS THE NIGHT)**

Mister Moore jumps from the tree, and stands in the pathway out of David's view. Sara gets up from the bench, and begins her walk home.

(CONTINUED)

David watches Sara disappear into the fog. Henry runs down the granite steps with Hawthorn, and up the path in the direction of his house.

MISTER MOORE

THERE'S A CHILL IN THE AIR TONIGHT;
A SINISTER STILLNESS
THAT CUTS LIKE A KNIFE.
IT MOVES WITH THE WIND,
AND HIDES IN THE DARKNESS.
IT PUTS LOCKS ON YOUR HOUSES,
AND FEAR IN YOUR SOUL.
IT'S OUT OF YOUR HANDS,
SO IT'S OUT OF CONTROL.
YOU TRY TO IGNORE IT,
THEN IT KNOCKS ON YOUR DOOR; DANGER!

He creeps down the pathway in the direction taken by Sara. He drops the small black apron that belonged to the Waitress onto the ground as he passes David. David sees a swirl of darkness move past him, and then notices the apron at his feet. He picks it up to investigate, decides it's not important, and tosses it aside.

*(song "DANGER! (TONIGHT IS THE NIGHT)" continues)*

CUT TO:

EXT. THE CAMPUS PATHWAY - NIGHT

Sara hesitates, thinking she hears someone walking behind her. She turns, sees no one due to the fog, but continues walking at a much brisker pace. She doesn't see Mister Moore leaning against a tree to her left.

(CONTINUED)

MISTER MOORE
TONIGHT IS THE NIGHT.
TONIGHT IS THE NIGHT FOR DANGER!

*(song "DANGER! (TONIGHT IS THE NIGHT)" continues)*

CUT TO:

EXT. THE CAMPUS PATHWAY - NIGHT

Lightning cracks. David's attention on Sara is distracted by something he thinks he sees ducking behind a tree. David goes over to investigate while Sara continues to walk to her rooming house. Thunder booms, and the now pea-soup thick fog swirls around her. She senses someone close to her, but all she can hear is the sound of the trees and bushes moving with the wind.

MISTER MOORE (O.S.)
IS THAT THE SOUND
OF THE RUSTLING LEAVES,
OR THE VIBRATING TREMBLE
YOU FEEL IN YOUR KNEES?
QUICKEN YOUR PACE, AND HEAR
HOW YOUR RACING HEART BEATS.
YOUR FEET START TO RUN,
AND YOUR HANDS START TO SWEAT.
YOU BEGIN TO GET DIZZY
WITH A SHORTNESS OF BREATH.
WHAT DO YOU FEAR?
YOU FEAR YOU'RE NEAR DANGER!
DANGER!
WELL, TONIGHT IS THE NIGHT.
TONIGHT IS THE NIGHT FOR DANGER!

*(song "DANGER! (TONIGHT IS THE NIGHT)" continues)*

CUT TO:

EXT. GROVE OF TREES - CAMPUS PATHWAY - NIGHT

David follows the dark form that is always just out of his reach. He thinks he sees it duck behind a bush, and he bats at the fog in an attempt to improve his line of sight. He carefully looks behind the bush, disturbing a bird that flies out and startles him.

MISTER MOORE
TONIGHT IS THE NIGHT FOR DANGER!

*(song "DANGER! (TONIGHT IS THE NIGHT)" continues)*

CUT TO:

EXT. THE CAMPUS LIBRARY - NIGHT

Henry and Hawthorn are in the bushes at a side window. Henry climbs up to the windowsill.

*(song "DANGER! (TONIGHT IS THE NIGHT)" continues)*

CUT TO:

INT. THE LIBRARY - NIGHT

There is a sound of breaking glass. A hand opens the broken window, and Hawthorn jumps into the room followed by Henry. Henry turns on a flashlight.

MISTER MOORE (V.O.)
TONIGHT IS THE NIGHT; DANGER!

*(song "DANGER! (TONIGHT IS THE NIGHT)" continues)*

CUT TO:

EXT. SARA'S ROOMING HOUSE - NIGHT

The house is dark. Sara runs up to the door.

MISTER MOORE (O.S.)
DANGER!

Sara fumbles through her purse looking for her keys. She can't locate them, so she dumps the contents of the purse onto the ground. She sifts through the pile and finds her key chain.

MISTER MOORE (O.S.)
THE AIR'S GETTING THICKER!
YOU CAN'T EVEN THINK!
THE SIDEWALK'S AN EGGSHELL!
YOU'RE OVER THE BRINK!
THERE'S MADNESS AND DEATH
IN THE DARKNESS OF THE SHADOWS.

*(song "DANGER! (TONIGHT IS THE NIGHT)" continues)*

CUT TO:

INT. THE LIBRARY - NIGHT

Henry is at the index card file, flashlight in his mouth, looking through the cards. He finds one titled "Fairmount University - History of."

MISTER MOORE (cont'd - V.O.)
WHY DON'T YOU RUN TO YOUR LOVER?

<MORE> (CONTINUED)

MISTER MOORE (CONT'D - V.O.)
I'M SURE HE'LL PROTECT
EVERY HAIR STANDING UP
ON THE BACK OF YOUR NECK.
BUT WHAT WILL HE DO
WHEN THIS NIGHT TOUCHES YOU
WITH DANGER? DANGER!

*(song "DANGER! (TONIGHT IS THE NIGHT)" continues)*

CUT TO:

EXT. A TREE NEAR SARA'S HOUSE - NIGHT

David sees Mister Moore leaning against a tree.

MISTER MOORE
DANGER! DANGER!

David moves slowly to the far side of the tree to get behind Mister Moore.

MISTER MOORE
TONIGHT IS THE NIGHT.
TONIGHT IS THE NIGHT FOR DANGER!

*(song "DANGER! (TONIGHT IS THE NIGHT)" continues)*

CUT TO:

EXT. SARA'S ROOMING HOUSE - NIGHT

Sara can't get her keys to work, and pounds her fists on the door.

SARA
Diane! Diane, open the door!

(CONTINUED)

MISTER MOORE (O.S.)
TONIGHT IS THE NIGHT.
TONIGHT IS THE NIGHT; DANGER!

*(song "DANGER! (TONIGHT IS THE NIGHT)" continues)*

CUT TO:

INT. THE LIBRARY - NIGHT

Henry sits at a microfilm viewer scanning a newspaper from the early 1900's. He stops at the headline "NEW HOUSING FOR FAIRMOUNT FACULTY." He studies the photograph of four well-dressed men standing in an empty lot surrounded by a throng of people. He magnifies the picture. Each man holds a shovel with a name imprinted on the handle. "GRANT," "PEARSON," "BATES," and "WEBSTER." Standing next to the man holding the "GRANT" shovel is an ORIENTAL BOY dressed in servant whites.

MISTER MOORE (V.O.)
TONIGHT IS THE NIGHT.
TONIGHT IS THE NIGHT. DANGER!

*(song "DANGER! (TONIGHT IS THE NIGHT)" continues)*

CUT TO:

EXT. A TREE NEAR SARA'S HOUSE - NIGHT

The fog is losing its intensity. David circles to the front of the tree, but the dark form he saw is gone. He turns to see Diane open the door and Sara rush inside. Diane looks around for a moment.

(CONTINUED)

MISTER MOORE (O.S.)
DANGER! DANGER!

Diane closes the door as the dark form appears to David's left. David turns, but it disappears again. He turns back toward the tree, takes a step, and walks into Mister Moore.

MISTER MOORE
TONIGHT IS THE NIGHT!
Hello, David.

**SONG: <u>DANGER! (TONIGHT IS THE NIGHT)</u>** ends

David makes a gurgling sound, and takes a step backward. He looks down to see that he has impaled himself on a knife.

MISTER MOORE
Good-bye, David.

David crumples to the ground. Mister Moore holds the knife from Henry's dream in his hand. He laughs as lightning cracks across the sky.

CUT TO:

INT. THE LIBRARY - NIGHT

Thunder booms as Henry stares at the microfilm viewer, and the headline: "FAIRMOUNT SLASHER DEAD." He magnifies a photograph of Professor Grant and the Oriental Houseboy. The Houseboy holds a tray with a glass of wine.

(CONTINUED)

Hanging on the wall behind them is the mirror of Mister Moore. The caption reads: "PROFESSOR GRANT IS THE FAIRMOUNT SLASHER."

HENRY
Hawthorn, listen to this! "The search for the Fairmount Slasher ended this morning when police discovered the bodies of Professor Harrison Grant and his houseboy, Satamoto. Investigators believe the professor stabbed Satamoto, and then took his own life by drinking wine laced with poison. Close friends confirmed that the professor had been acting strangely since the first slasher victims were discovered, and on several occasions had insisted he was communicating with a demon."

Hawthorn barks.

HENRY
You can say that again!

CUT TO:

INT. DOCTOR ARMISTICES' OFFICE - NIGHT

Lightning and thunder continue to punctuate the night as Dr. Armistice sits at his desk amid a clutter of books.

(CONTINUED)

Dr. Armistice is looking at an old yearbook; open to the same picture Henry was viewing. Using a magnifying glass, Dr. Armistice focuses on the Houseboy, then the mirror, then the tray and wine glass, then abruptly back to the mirror. His attention is on the mirror's reflection of the tray. There is only one glass on the tray, but two glasses appear in the reflection.

CUT TO:

EXT. THE LIBRARY - NIGHT

Henry climbs out the broken window. Hawthorn leaps after him, starts barking, and runs off toward the back of the building.

CUT TO:

EXT. THE BACK OF THE LIBRARY - NIGHT

A crackle of lightning briefly illuminates Hawthorn sniffing David's lifeless body. There is a crash of thunder, and another flash of lightning as Henry comes around from the side of the building.

HENRY

Hawthorn! Come back here!

Henry sees David's body just as a branch of a tree, cut loose by a gust of wind, falls and strikes him on the side of his head.

CUT TO:

EXT. HENRY'S HOUSE - NIGHT

As Dr. Armistice prepares to knock with his cane, the front door slowly opens.

DR. ARMISTICE
Henry?

A flicker of lightning brightens the hallway as he steps inside.

CUT TO:

INT. HENRY JACOB'S HOUSE - NIGHT

The floor creaks as Dr. Armistice walks cautiously up to the mirror. The reflection reveals someone behind him on the staircase.

DR. ARMISTICE
Henry?

He turns around, but sees no one there. He turns back to the mirror, and Mister Moore stares back at him.

MISTER MOORE
Doctor Franklin Armistice, I presume.

DR. ARMISTICE
I knew Henry was telling the truth.

(CONTINUED)

MISTER MOORE

Well, aren't you just the true believer. Very impressive that Henry has a supporter as distinguished as you.

Another flash of lightning illuminates the staircase, and WE SEE the reflection of the Waitress lying on the stairs. Her body is limp; her clothes are torn and bloody. Dr. Armistice turns toward the staircase to investigate, but there is no body there. Dr. Armistice turns back to the mirror, and sees the body of the Waitress draped over the banister in the reflection.

DR. ARMISTICE

My God!

MISTER MOORE

Your God had nothing to do with it!

With a menacing smile, he punches himself in the middle of his chest. Dr. Armistice reels from the sensation of being struck. He drops his cane, and falls to his knees, grabbing his chest and gasping for air.

DR. ARMISTICE

Henry!

MISTER MOORE

Dear Henry has his own problems, Doctor. I assure you; his hands are quite full.

DISSOLVE TO:

EXT. THE BACK OF THE LIBRARY - DAY

A POLICE PHOTOGRAPHER photographs David's body as THREE POLICE OFFICERS search the area for clues. Henry leans against LIEUTENANT FERGUSON'S car as a MEDIC puts antiseptic on his cut and bruised forehead. Lt. Ferguson is taking notes.

HENRY
Ouch!

MEDIC
Sorry.

HENRY
Look, Lieutenant...

LT. FERGUSON
...Ferguson.

HENRY
Lieutenant Ferguson. I told you; there was a flash of lightning, I saw the body, and then I blacked out. That's all.

LT. FERGUSON
Yeah, that's what you said, and that's just the way I wrote it down. Of course, it could be that this guy catches you breaking into the library; you get mad, and you chase him.

<MORE> (CONTINUED)

LT. FERGUSON (CONT'D)
Then you stab him, and he dies.

HENRY
That's ridiculous. I don't even own a knife.

LT. FERGUSON
So you say. I'm just saying how it could have been another way.

HENRY
Are you going to arrest me or can I go? I'm late for my class.

LT. FERGUSON
I've got just a few more questions, if you don't mind.

CUT TO:

INT. CLASSROOM - GOODMAN HALL - DAY

**SONG: ODE ON AN AX MURDERER**

Henry's Students stare at Mister Moore who stands behind the lectern next to Professor Jacobs' desk. He has his hands behind his back as he addresses the class.

MISTER MOORE
Our beloved Professor Jacobs has been somewhat unexpectedly, yet unavoidably detained.

<MORE> (CONTINUED)

MISTER MOORE (CONT'D)
Though no substitute teacher could ever hope to properly pay him the respect he is due, I, Edwin Horatio, but-you-can-call-me-Mister Moore, will do my best to make him proud. Now then, the lesson for today will be... Hmm, let me see... Ah! I have it! The lesson will be one of my favorite subjects: "The Misuse of Poetic License in Historical Events."

He clears his throat, and produces a large ax from behind his back.

MISTER MOORE
ELIZABETH BORDEN TOOK AN AX!

He wields the axe mightily into the center of the desk. The desk splits in half.

MISTER MOORE (continuing)
AND SHE GAVE HER MOTHER
FORTY WHACKS.
WHEN THAT EVIL DEED WAS DONE,
SHE GAVE HER FATHER FORTY-ONE.
ELIZABETH SAW WHAT SHE COULD DO,
SO SHE OFFERED HER AUNTIE
FORTY-TWO.
SINCE NO ONE STOPPED
HER DEADLY DEEDS,
SHE PROVIDED HER SISTER
WITH FORTY-THREE.
AS SIS LAY BLEEDING ON THE FLOOR,
SHE DELIVERED THE POSTMAN
FORTY-FOUR.
<MORE> (CONTINUED)

MISTER MOORE (CONT'D)

WHEN THE POSTMAN
CEASED TO BE ALIVE,
SHE DISPENSED THE MILKMAN
FORTY-FIVE.
ELIZABETH BORDEN
WAS GETTING HER KICKS.
THERE WERE BODIES IN PILES
LIKE PICK-UP STICKS.
THEN HER SWEET LITTLE DOGGIE
WALKED INTO THE MIX.
SAY GOODNIGHT, FIDO! FORTY-SIX!

**SONG:** **ODE ON AN AX MURDERER** ends

Henry's Students are bewildered and uncomfortable.

MISTER MOORE

That was an example of poetic license. It's a deception of the first order; pure and simple. I mean don't you think forty blows are a bit excessive? Think of the mess! Three or four would have easily done the trick. Elizabeth Borden took an ax, and gave her mother three or four whacks. Now, that seems a sufficient amount, don't you agree? Well, of course you do. But it has no grit! No substance! No thrust! And thus, poetic license comes into play. I make you believe that sweet, young Elizabeth Borden swung an ax more than three hundred times during her little foray, and not once did she sit and rest?

<MORE> (CONTINUED)

MISTER MOORE (CONT'D)
That's poppycock, as a friend of a friend of mine would say! Poetic license is merely a convenient way for the literati to lie to you, and justify it at the same time. Trust me on this! It's downright ubiquitous!

**SONG: <u>THE HISTORY LESSON</u>**

MISTER MOORE
THERE ARE PEOPLE WHO WOULD PULL
THE VERY WOOL OVER YOUR EYES;
EXPECTING YOU TO LIVE
BY ALL THEIR RULES.
THEY THINK THAT YOU'RE SO STUPID,
AND YOU WILL NOT
DEFY THEM, FOR YOU'VE BECOME
CONTENTED LITTLE FOOLS.
THEY PROCESS YOU LIKE CATTLE.
YOU'VE BEEN BRANDED WITH THE
NUMBERS OF YOUR BANK ACCOUNTS,
AND YOUR CREDIT CARDS, AND SUCH.
WHAT'S YOUR SOCIAL SECURITY NUMBER?
WHAT'S THE DATE WHEN YOU WERE BORN?
WHAT'S YOUR GRADE POINT AVERAGE?
IT'S JUST TOO MUCH.
I've never been one to answer questions of a personal nature. Some people use information in ways that can affect an individual in an adverse manner. My simple rule of thumb: Don't trust anyone!
SO WHEN SOMEONE WANTS TO KNOW
SOMETHING ABOUT YOU.
INQUIRING FOR SOME INFORMATION,
PLEASE.

<MORE> (CONTINUED)

MISTER MOORE (CONT'D)
AND YOU FEEL THAT WHAT THEY WANT
IS NONE OF THEIR BUSINESS;
YOU DON'T GIVE THEM THE FACTS!
YOU GIVE THEM THE AX!

He pulls the embedded ax from the splintered wood of the desk, and hurls it into the wall.

MISTER MOORE
THAT'S THE WAY TO HANDLE THAT.
It's a trifle extreme, a bit unpopular, but immensely effective. Just take a look at your history. It's full of examples of people who went about their affairs with eyes that didn't see, and ears that couldn't hear what was actually taking place behind their backs. And that, my unenlightened friends, will always lead to a person's downfall. Take a guy like Socrates. We all know that
SOCRATES MADE ENEMIES
BY THINKING DIFFERENTLY
THAN OTHER PEOPLE THOUGHT.
HIS FOES WERE NOT SO FOND
OF HIS CONCEPTIONS.
SO WHAT DID THEY DO?
THEY GAVE HIM A BREW!
HEMLOCK HAS A CERTAIN
POINT OF VIEW.

He produces a goblet of bubbling, vaporous liquid. He drinks from the goblet, licks his lips, and hands it to Kelly.

<MORE> (CONTINUED)

MISTER MOORE (CONT'D)
Here, my dear. You finish this.

With a wave of his hand the goblet vanishes from Kelly's hand. Six stringless marionettes dressed as Shakespearean actors appear over the front desk. They act out the next verse.

MISTER MOORE
JULIUS CAESAR WAS THE LEADER
OF AN EMPIRE.
CAREFULLY HE HAND PICKED
ALL HIS FRIENDS.
THE BUNCH HE CHOSE WAS
JUST A BAND OF SCOUNDRELS.
ONE NIGHT THEY GRABBED HIM,
AND THEY BRUTALLY STABBED HIM!
ALL BECAUSE THEY WERE
A LITTLE MAD AT HIM.

A geyser of blood squirts from the Julius Caesar puppet onto Two Students in the front row. They run from the room in revulsion.

MISTER MOORE
I would remind the rest of you that college is not for the squeamish.

Kate begins to levitate in her chair. Thick rope spins around her tying her arms and legs. As the verse continues, a large wooden washing bucket materializes above her head. The bucket tilts 90 degrees, and a deluge of water drenches her and floods the floor.

<MORE> (CONTINUED)

MISTER MOORE (CONT'D)
IN SALEM, MASSACHUSETTS,
THERE WERE WOMEN ACCUSED OF
BEING WITCHES CASTING SPELLS.
THE ELDERS OF THE TOWN SWORE
A WITCH COULD NOT BE DROWNED.
SO, THE ELDERS HELD THE WOMEN
UNDERWATER, AND THEY FOUND
THAT THERE WAS NOT
A SINGLE WITCH AROUND!

The ropes disappear, and a soaked Kate descends rapidly, but lands softly onto the wet floor. Mister Moore walks proudly down the aisle toward the doorway. As he passes Kate he swirls his cape around her, and she is instantly dry.

MISTER MOORE
Don't let anyone say that I'm
not a nice man!
NOW THE MORAL OF MY LECTURE IS
QUITE SIMPLE.
IF YOU WANT TO GIVE SOMEONE
THE UPPER HAND,

He extends his hand to Stephen who reluctantly accepts. Mister Moore's "hand" comes off at the wrist, and Stephen is left holding a gooey mess.

MISTER MOORE
MAKE SURE YOU KNOW
WHAT MIGHT BE HIDDEN IN IT;
ALWAYS KNOW WHAT SOMEONE ELSE
HAS PLANNED.

<MORE> (CONTINUED)

MISTER MOORE (CONT'D)
FOR IF YOUR EYES
SEE EVERYTHING BEHIND YOU,
AND YOUR EARS CAN HEAR
WHAT ISN'T BEING SAID,
YOU WILL HAVE THE CHANCE
TO BE IMMORTAL!
Just like me.
FOREVER YOU'LL EXIST!
CLASS DISMISSED!

Mister Moore triumphantly exits the classroom.

**SONG: THE HISTORY LESSON** ends

CUT TO:

EXT. THE BACK OF THE LIBRARY - DAY

Lt. Ferguson observes as Henry watches David being zipped into a body bag. Hawthorn barks as a patrol car drives up to the scene, and the body bag is lifted onto a gurney.

LT. FERGUSON
So, if I have any more questions for you, Professor Jacobs, I'll stop by your house.

SERGEANT ROZNER gets out of the patrol car, walks over to Lt. Ferguson, and whispers a short message in his ear.

LT. FERGUSON
Professor, do you know a Doctor Franklin Armistice?

DISSOLVE TO:

EXT. FAIRMOUNT HOSPITAL - DAY

Henry gets out of a police car, and rushes toward the entrance.

CUT TO:

EXT. HENRY'S HOUSE - DAY

Lt. Ferguson pulls up in front of the house. Hawthorn jumps out of the open car window, barks, and runs up to the open front door.

CUT TO:

INT. FAIRMOUNT HOSPITAL - DAY

Henry and a DOCTOR walk through the Emergency Room.

DOCTOR

I want to keep him here for a few days, but he says it's impossible. Maybe you can talk some sense into him.

CUT TO:

INT. HENRY'S HOUSE - DAY

Lt. Ferguson enters the house as Hawthorn runs up the staircase.

(CONTINUED)

LT. FERGUSON
Hello? Is anybody here?

He is vigilant as he walks down the hall. His police sense prompts him to unsnap his holster.

LT. FERGUSON
I brought the dog home!

He hears a sharp thud, withdraws his gun, and continues down the hall past the mirror. He looks into the living room, and sees a bloodstained knife imbedded in the desk.

LT. FERGUSON
Well, what do I have here?

He re-holsters his gun, goes to the desk, and wraps a handkerchief around the knife handle. He pulls the knife out of the wood, and studies the curved blade for a moment. Hawthorn comes down the staircase, and barks.

LT. FERGUSON
It seems our Professor may know a bit more than he says.

He gingerly puts the knife into an evidence bag, and deposits the bag in his pocket. Hawthorn growls, and runs into the kitchen.

MISTER MOORE (O.S.)
Not wanting to be counted among those who go around casting aspersions mind you, but the Professor knows very little about anything.

(CONTINUED)

Lt. Ferguson withdraws his gun quickly, spins around, and aims it at Mister Moore who stands in the hallway.

LT. FERGUSON
Put your hands up where I can see them!

MISTER MOORE
Little boys who play with pistols wet the bed at night. Or is it matches?

LT. FERGUSON
I said get your hands up!

MISTER MOORE
Actually, you said put your hands up. If you're going to repeat yourself, the least you could be is accurate.

LT. FERGUSON
I'm going to count to three!

MISTER MOORE
Well now, there's a formidable task.

Mister Moore raises his arms. Lt. Ferguson's hand begins to shake. He tries to speak, but no sound comes from his mouth.

MISTER MOORE
I do believe the proverbial cat has gotten hold of your tongue. Perhaps I should assist you.

(CONTINUED)

Mister Moore points at the pocket where Lt. Ferguson has put the plastic bag.

MISTER MOORE
One! Stealing is against the law.

The bag with the knife rises from the Lieutenant's pocket.

MISTER MOORE
Two! You will have to be punished.

The bag floats through the air toward Mister Moore's outstretched hand.

MISTER MOORE
Three! Oh, I don't think you're going to like number three.

CUT TO:

INT. THE DOCTOR'S OFFICE - DAY

Dr. Armistice is seated behind a desk finishing a telephone call as Henry and the Doctor enter.

DR. ARMISTICE
No. No message. Thank you, Diane. Good-bye.

He hangs up the phone.

(CONTINUED)

DR. ARMISTICE
Let's go, Henry. We've got a lot to talk about.

DOCTOR
Now just a minute, Doctor.

DR. ARMISTICE
I haven't got a minute, Doctor.

He ushers Henry out the door.

CUT TO:

INT. FAIRMOUNT HOSPITAL - HALLWAY - DAY

Henry and Dr. Armistice walk quickly down the hall.

HENRY
David was murdered last night, and the police think I'm a suspect.

DR. ARMISTICE
Did you say anything about the mirror?

HENRY
No. I wasn't quite ready to be put into a straight jacket.

DR. ARMISTICE
How's Sara taking all this?

(CONTINUED)

HENRY
I don't know. I haven't had a chance to talk with her since last night.

Dr. Armistice grabs Henry's arm and stops abruptly.

DR. ARMISTICE
Diane just told me you called Sara and asked her to meet you at your house.

CUT TO:

INT. HENRY'S HOUSE - DAY

Sara walks up to the open front door.

SARA
Henry?

She steps inside.

SARA
Henry, are you in here?

She walks to the staircase, and sees a flash of movement reflected in the mirror. She is startled to see the mirror in one piece, and raises her hand to examine the glass.

SGT. ROZNER (O.S.)
Excuse me, ma'am?

Sara jumps, and turns to the open doorway.

(CONTINUED)

SGT. ROZNER
Sorry I scared you, ma'am. I'm looking for Lieutenant Ferguson. Have you seen him?

SARA
No, I haven't, but then this is Professor Henry Jacob's house.

SGT. ROZNER
Yes, ma'am, I know that. The Lieutenant came here about a half hour ago, and his car's still sitting out front.

CUT TO:

EXT. HENRY'S HOUSE - DAY

Sgt. Rozner and Sara get into his car. WE SEE Mister Moore standing in the open front doorway flipping his knife as he watches them drive away. Mister Moore walks down the steps, and the front door slams shut with such force that all of the front windowpanes crack; broken glass falls to the ground. He disappears into the trees as Henry and Dr. Armistice pull up in a cab. Henry jumps out, and races up the steps. He opens the front door, runs inside, and then quickly runs back out with Hawthorn following.

HENRY
She's not here.

Dr. Armistice considers the broken windows.

(CONTINUED)

DR. ARMISTICE
That is probably a good thing.

HENRY
Do me a favor. Find Sara, and let her know what's going on.

DR. ARMISTICE
Of course I will, but Henry?

HENRY
Yes?

DR. ARMISTICE
What's going on?

HENRY
Just keep her away from here until you hear from me.

CUT TO:

INT. HENRY'S HOUSE - DAY

Henry enters. Hawthorn picks up his ball, and drops it; letting it bounce toward Henry.

HENRY
I can't play right now.

Henry slowly approaches the mirror.

DISSOLVE TO:

EXT. HENRY'S HOUSE - DAY

(CONTINUED)

Sgt. Rozner's car pulls up, and Sara gets out. She walks up the steps as he drives away. She is quite upset.

SARA
This is absolutely, positively,

CUT TO:

INT. HENRY'S HOUSE - DAY

Sara stomps in, and marches down the hall.

SARA (continuing)
the most maddening,
exasperating situation!

As she passes the mirror, she sees a reflection of Henry standing in the living room with a finger to his lips shushing her, and his other hand waving her away.

SARA
Henry, if you think for one
minute I'm going to keep quiet,

She turns toward the living room, but Henry isn't there.

SARA (continuing)
or just leave you alone, you...

She turns back to the mirror, and Henry isn't there either.

SARA (continuing)
Henry, what is going on?

(CONTINUED)

She hears footsteps on the staircase, and turns toward the stairs expecting to see Henry, but it is Mister Moore who approaches her.

SARA
Who are you? Where's Henry?

MISTER MOORE
You must be the young lady Henry's told me so much about.

He circles around her; his voice oozing with graceful menace.

MISTER MOORE
Why you're just as pretty as a picture. You're Sara Wagner, aren't you?

SARA
Yes, and you are?

MISTER MOORE
A very old and dear friend of the family.

SARA
And your name is?

MISTER MOORE
Edwin Horatio but-you-can-call-me-Mister Moore.

SARA
I see.

(CONTINUED)

MISTER MOORE
Do you?

Sara backs up slowly toward the front door.

SARA
Yes. Well, Henry doesn't seem to be home right now, so I think I'll just come back later. You be sure to tell him I stopped by, okay? It was very nice meeting you, Mister Moore.

She reaches for the doorknob, but her hand freezes in mid-motion.

MISTER MOORE
Leaving? So soon? We haven't even had a chance to chat. I must insist you stay!

He extends his arms toward her. Sara feels herself being pulled away from the door. She tries to resist, but she is no match against the invisible force that pulls her back down the hallway toward Mister Moore.

MISTER MOORE
Come here, my dear.

Sara tries to scream, but no sound comes from her mouth.

MISTER MOORE
Yes, please be afraid. Fear is quite the aphrodisiac.

A tear runs down Sara's cheek.

(CONTINUED)

Though Sara's back is toward Mister Moore, she can feel his hands are inches from her body.

MISTER MOORE
You will be mine before the night is through.

Sara doesn't see Henry leap out from inside the mirror onto Mister Moore's back.

HENRY
Run, Sara!

As Mister Moore bends and twists to throw Henry off, Sara feels a release from the force that was controlling her. She turns around to face them.

SARA
Henry!

HENRY
Get out of here, now!

Sara turns, and runs for the door. Mister Moore falls backward slamming Henry against the wall by the stairs.

MISTER MOORE
How dare you interfere!

Sara opens the door to escape, but Mister Moore nods his head, and the door slams shut. She screams for help, tugging and pushing on the doorknob. Henry tackles Mister Moore, and the door flies open. Sara runs out just as the door explodes into pieces.

(CONTINUED)

MISTER MOORE

Damn you!

He throws Henry violently from his back, but quickly regains his composure and flicks his wrist just before Henry careens into a bookcase. Henry's momentum ceases, and he hangs in mid-air.

MISTER MOORE

I mean, for heavens sake, I wasn't going to hurt the little darling.

He points at Henry, and Henry slowly and softly descends to the floor.

MISTER MOORE

You take away all my fun.

As soon as Henry's feet touch the floor he rushes to attack Mister Moore, but Mister Moore points his finger at him, and Henry is frozen in his tracks.

MISTER MOORE

Such hostility.

HENRY

Hostility? You kill people!

MISTER MOORE

So what's your point? A lesson on proper social behavior?

The telephone rings breaking Mister Moore's concentration. This lapse allows Henry's interrupted charge to be completed.

(CONTINUED)

Henry slams into Mister Moore, and they crash headlong into a bookcase, and fall to the floor. Mister Moore twitches his eyebrows, which causes Henry to be hurled into the air and suspended over the couch. Mister Moore gets up, and dusts himself. The telephone continues to ring. He looks over at the phone, and melts it with a wrathful glare.

MISTER MOORE
Odious modern convenience.

**SONG: <u>WHY HAVEN'T YOU KILLED ME?</u>**

MISTER MOORE
Any more shenanigans, Professor, and you're liable to meet the same fate.

With a slight twist of his finger he gingerly drops Henry onto the couch.

HENRY
You don't scare me. If you wanted to kill me, you've had plenty of opportunities.

He gets up, and rushes toward Mister Moore again; this time to be flung like a rag doll in the direction of the hallway. His forward motion stops just as he is about to slam into the staircase banister, and he is deposited gently on his feet.

MISTER MOORE
I like you, Professor, but you're starting to get on my nerves.

<MORE> (CONTINUED)

MISTER MOORE (CONT'D)
You would be wise to remember
I CAN CRUSH YOU LIKE A WORM!
I CAN SWAT YOU LIKE A FLY!
I CAN SQUASH AND PULVERIZE YOU
IN THE BLINK OF AN EYE.
I CAN MASH, OR BASH,
OR FLATTEN YOU;
I'M MULTI-TALENTED!
I CAN MAKE YOU WISH
THAT YOU WERE DEAD!

HENRY
SO WHY HAVEN'T YOU KILLED ME?
IT'D BE THE SIMPLEST THING TO DO.
WHY HAVEN'T YOU KILLED ME?
IT SHOULDN'T BE HARD FOR YOU.
YOU COULD STAB ME
LIKE THE OTHERS,
OR I COULD BE POISONED
JUST LIKE GRANT,
BUT YOU HAVEN'T KILLED ME.
MAYBE YOU CAN'T.

MISTER MOORE
Don't be silly, Professor.

Mister Moore picks up the heart-shaped paperweight, and crushes it.

MISTER MOORE
I CAN GRIND YOU INTO DUST!
DO YOU WANT IT ANY CLEARER?
SHALL I SHATTER YOU TO PIECES
LIKE YOU TRIED TO SMASH MY MIRROR?

<MORE> (CONTINUED)

The screen of the television set, and the glass in all the picture frames around the room shatter in unison.

MISTER MOORE (CONT'D)
I WOULDN'T WAIT OR HESITATE
TO HELP WITH YOUR DEMISE,
AND YOU SHOULD NOT BE THINKING
OTHERWISE.

HENRY
SO WHY HAVEN'T YOU KILLED ME?
I HAVEN'T GOT A CLUE
WHY YOU HAVEN'T KILLED ME?
I WOULD IF I WERE YOU.
THERE MUST BE SOMETHING
YOU'RE NOT TELLING ME.
I'VE GOT TO UNDERSTAND
WHY YOU HAVEN'T KILLED ME,
AND WHY I DON'T THINK YOU CAN.

Mister Moore produces his knife, and holds it against Henry's throat.

MISTER MOORE
I'm warning you, Professor.
I'll peel you like a cucumber.

HENRY
Go ahead. I let you out of
the mirror. I deserve to die.

Mister Moore pushes the blade of the knife more firmly against Henry's throat.

MISTER MOORE
Yes, the world loves a martyr.

(CONTINUED)

HENRY
So, what are you waiting for?

MISTER MOORE
Inspiration.

HENRY
Get it over with.

MISTER MOORE
I don't want to.

He lowers the knife.

MISTER MOORE (continuing)
I'm much too fond of you.

HENRY
You're lying.

MISTER MOORE
It's what I do best.

HENRY
I think you don't kill me
because you need me alive.

MISTER MOORE
That's the riddle isn't it?
Will I or won't I. Maybe I do;
maybe I don't. Hmmm, what a
puzzle!

Henry discovers he is no longer being held frozen by Mister Moore's power. He grabs the knife, and backs away.

(CONTINUED)

MISTER MOORE
Be careful, Professor. That is not a toy.

HENRY
Are you afraid I'll hurt myself?

He playfully pokes his shirt with the tip of the blade to demonstrate to Mister Moore that he is considering stabbing himself in the heart. Mister Moore displays concern with this scenario.

MISTER MOORE
Henry, I don't want you to do something we'll both regret.

HENRY
Why am I so important that you can't kill me?

MISTER MOORE
I can kill you. I just happen to like you. It's a moral dilemma.

HENRY
You have no morals.

MISTER MOORE
Sticks and stones, Henry. Give me the knife.

HENRY
Why don't you just take it away from me?

(CONTINUED)

MISTER MOORE

I'm trying to be civil. Besides, force is so proletarian

HENRY

Do you need me alive because I let you out of the mirror?

MISTER MOORE

If I tell you will you put down the knife?

HENRY

I make no promises.

MISTER MOORE

Then I'll just have to trust you. The answer to your question, my dear Professor Jacobs, is yes. If any harm comes to you, I'll perish. There, I've said it. That's my deepest secret. If you kill yourself, I die too. So let's be sensible. Give me that knife!

HENRY

No!

He makes a motion implying he is about to plunge the knife into his chest.

MISTER MOORE

Henry, I beg you, please don't do that! You're scaring me.

(CONTINUED)

HENRY
If any harm comes to me, you perish? I'd call that an acceptable tradeoff.

He thrusts the knife toward his chest.

MISTER MOORE
No, Henry! Don't!

Henry stops just as the tip of the knife touches his shirt.

HENRY
Wait a minute.

He lowers the knife to his side.

HENRY (continuing)
You can toss me across the room with a glance. You suspend me in mid-air with the flick of your wrist, but when I'm about to kill myself you don't lift a finger?

MISTER MOORE
I would have stopped you.

HENRY
With, 'No, Henry, don't?'

MISTER MOORE
I admit it sounds a trifle limp, but I was in a temporary state of shock.

(CONTINUED)

HENRY
You're hiding something.

MISTER MOORE
Your accusation cuts me to the quick.

HENRY
Grant drank poison, and you didn't stop him.

MISTER MOORE
I didn't know he was drinking poison. Anyway, I can see the knife, so I promise I'll be more forceful when I try to stop you the next time you try. Cross my heart.

HENRY
You don't have a heart.

MISTER MOORE
Touché.

Henry paces around the room as he begins to put two and two together.

HENRY
You say you'll perish if any harm comes to me.

MISTER MOORE
Yes.

HENRY
But you were going to let me kill myself.

(CONTINUED)

MISTER MOORE
No, I would have intervened.

HENRY
You need me alive, but you
want me dead.

MISTER MOORE
You're making this sound much
more confusing than it is.

HENRY
You want me dead, but you
won't kill me, so there must
be a reason you need me to
kill myself.

MISTER MOORE
You're overanalyzing the
entire situation.

HENRY
Hah!

MISTER MOORE
I'm sorry? Hah what?

Henry triumphantly hurls the knife into the mirror.

HENRY
YOU WON'T KILL ME!
YOU WON'T BECAUSE YOU CAN'T!
YOU DON'T WANT TO KILL ME.
YOU DIDN'T WANT TO KILL
PROFESSOR GRANT.
YOU MUST HAVE POISONED HIM
BY ACCIDENT!
<MORE> (CONTINUED)

HENRY (CONT'D)
I'M SAFE, AND I KNOW WHY
YOU WON'T KILL ME.
IF YOU DO YOU WILL BE
ONCE AGAIN A PRISONER
ON THE OTHER SIDE OF HERE.
IF YOU HARM A HAIR UPON MY HEAD
YOUR FUTURE'S VERY CLEAR.
IF YOU KILL ME
YOU'LL BE DOOMED; FOREVER
TRAPPED INSIDE YOUR MIRROR.
I'LL MAKE YOU KILL ME,
MISTER MOORE!
I'LL RID THE WORLD
OF MISTER MOORE!
I'LL BE DEAD,
BUT THERE'LL BE NO MORE
MISTER MOORE!
MISTER MOORE!

**SONG: <u>WHY HAVEN'T YOU KILLED ME?</u>** ends

MISTER MOORE
Or!

**SONG: <u>MISTER MOORE'S TRIUMPH - REPRISE #2</u>**

MISTER MOORE (continuing)
YOU'RE WRONG,
PROFESSOR JACOBS, RECONSIDER
BEFORE YOU ASK
TO PERISH BY MY HAND.
ARE YOU REALLY SO SECURE
IN YOUR BELIEF?
ARE YOU SURE
THAT I WON'T END YOUR LIFE
WITH A QUICK THRUST
OF MY KNIFE?

(CONTINUED)

HENRY
YOU COULD ABSOLUTELY,
POSITIVELY, THOROUGHLY,
MOST DEFINITELY KILL ME,
BUT YOU DON'T!
AND YOU WON'T!

**SONG: MISTER MOORE'S TRIUMPH - REPRISE #2** ends

MISTER MOORE
Congratulations, Professor. You're right, of course. I should have realized you were much too smart for me.

HENRY
Save your Edwin Horatio, but-I-can-call-you-Mister Moore, flattery. I have to figure out how to get you to kill me, and that's not going to be easy. I don't suppose you'll help me out, and just slice my throat.

MISTER MOORE
Oh, that's not very likely. You know, none of this would be happening if Professor Grant's little Oriental houseboy hadn't screwed everything up. The professor was all set to do himself in with some arsenic-laced wine. Satamoto, the Oriental houseboy in question, switched the glasses, and gave me the one with the poison.

<MORE> (CONTINUED)

MISTER MOORE (CONT'D)
I inadvertently exchanged glasses with Professor Grant; that was my mistake. When I handed him that poisoned glass of wine I became responsible for his death on a technicality. You can imagine how upset I was. I rushed out of the house to get an antidote. There wasn't a minute to lose.

DISSOLVE TO:

INT. HENRY'S HOUSE IN THE EARLY 1900'S - DAY

PROFESSOR GRANT is slumped in a chair, dying. A wine glass rests on its side on the floor next to him. SATAMOTO is on his knees working feverishly to finish crating the mirror of Mister Moore. Using Mister Moore's knife, he scratches the symbols "Nootacchi" and "Hada" on the upper left corner of the frame. Mister Moore rushes in.

MISTER MOORE (V.O.)
I got back as quickly as I could, but alas, nothing could be done to save the professor.

He wrestles the knife from Satamoto and stabs him in the back.

MISTER MOORE (V.O.)
I remember being very angry.

Professor Grant falls dead to the floor.

<MORE> (CONTINUED)

MISTER MOORE (V.O.)
Then I remember nothing.

He begins to evaporate as he's pulled toward the mirror by an unseen force. He becomes a wisp of smoke that is sucked into the small section of mirror that remains uncovered. Satamoto, though mortally wounded, nails the last piece of wood in place, and drags the crated mirror toward the basement.

DISSOLVE TO:

INT. HENRY'S HOUSE - DAY

Mister Moore and Henry stand close to the mirror at the edge of the living room by the hallway.

MISTER MOORE
And then I remember you. I promise you, Professor, I will not have a hand in your death.

Hawthorn walks in from the kitchen with his ball. He drops it, and it rolls across the floor as he growls and snarls at Mister Moore.

MISTER MOORE
I can, however, kill your dog.

HENRY
Don't you hurt Hawthorn!

MISTER MOORE
I said I can. I didn't say I would.

(CONTINUED)

He waves his hand at Hawthorn who stops growling, and obediently sits. Dr. Armistice appears in the front doorway.

MISTER MOORE
Well, hello, Doctor. Feeling better are we?

Mister Moore points his finger at Dr. Armistice, who grabs his chest, and falls to one knee. Sara, who was standing outside, runs to his aid.

SARA
Uncle Franklin!

MISTER MOORE
Well, isn't this the family gathering. Hello, my little love.

He waves his hand again, and everyone is frozen in place. He takes a menacing step toward Sara.

HENRY
I'm warning you, leave her alone!

MISTER MOORE
Or you'll do what? Your bravado is touching, Professor, but utterly pointless.

He takes another step, and accidentally steps on Hawthorn's ball. This causes him to lose both his balance and his control over the others.

(CONTINUED)

Henry seizes this opportunity, and jumps on Mister Moore's back. They tumble to the floor. Mister Moore staggers to his feet with Henry tenaciously clinging to him.

MISTER MOORE
Stop fidgeting!

HENRY
I'm not fidgeting!

Mister Moore lifts his arms to throw Henry off, but Henry frantically shifts his weight, which causes them both to fall sideways into the mirror.

MISTER MOORE
That felt like a fidget.

Sara and Dr. Armistice are horrified seeing Mister Moore's shoulder and Henry's head pass through the mirror's surface.

DR. ARMISTICE
Incredible!

Henry shifts his weight further into the mirror. He calls out to his friends.

HENRY
I've got to get him into the mirror!

Mister Moore (half in and half out of the mirror) holds onto the edge of the frame.

MISTER MOORE
Easier said than done.

(CONTINUED)

As Henry struggles to pull Mister Moore in, Sara rushes up and slaps Mister Moore's hand. Startled, he releases his grip from the frame and falls headlong into the mirror.

MISTER MOORE (O.S.)
It seems I was mistaken.

Looking into the mirror Sara sees Henry and Mister Moore fall against the staircase, but when she turns toward the stairs there is no one there. The side table and bowl of fruit crash to the floor.

MISTER MOORE (O.S.)
Excuse us.

Sara is jostled and pushed backward by invisible hands. She falls to the floor.

HENRY (O.S.)
Sorry, honey.

SARA
It's okay. I'm okay. Are you okay?

Dr. Armistice helps her to her feet. They look into the mirror, and see Mister Moore throw Henry against a bookcase.

SARA
Henry!

She and Dr. Armistice turn toward the living room as books and bric-a-brac tumble off the shelves from the impact, but they see no physical presence of Mister Moore or Henry.

(CONTINUED)

MISTER MOORE (O.S.)
Henry this! Henry that! I'm sick of hearing his name!

Sara and Dr. Armistice look back into the mirror, and see Mister Moore approaching them with his knife.

MISTER MOORE
You are both going to wish you'd never heard mine!

He throws the knife at them, but it misses because Henry has grabbed him at the same instant and shoved him behind the living room wall. This puts them both out of the angle of what the mirror can reflect.

HENRY (O.S.)
Don't look in the mirror!

SARA
I can't see you if I don't look in the mirror.

Dr. Armistice grabs Sara's arm, and pulls her down against the wall under the mirror.

DR. ARMISTICE
Henry's right. We must avoid being reflected in the mirror.

They peer into the living room and see Henry's desk topple to its side from an invisible impact.

CUT TO:

INT. HENRY'S HOUSE / INSIDE THE MIRROR - DAY

POV - The mirror's reflection of the living room. Henry and Mister Moore get up from behind the desk. They are out of breath.

MISTER MOORE
You can't win, you know.

HENRY
I don't know that.

MISTER MOORE
Then you're not as smart as you look!

HENRY
That's part of my charm.

Mister Moore gestures at the table lamp by the couch, and it hurtles across the room toward Henry. Henry lifts his hands to protect himself from the impending blow, and the lamp changes course, hitting Mister Moore in the back of the head.

MISTER MOORE
Ouch!

Henry wiggles his index finger at the bookcase, and a book flies off the shelf. Henry frantically waves his arms, and every object in the living room reacts. The couch starts to bounce across the floor; a table crashes through the window.

(CONTINUED)

Mister Moore ducks as a chair flies over his head, then he calmly holds up his little finger, and the careening objects begin to fly around the room in a figure eight pattern.

MISTER MOORE
Rookie.

CUT TO:

INT. HENRY'S HOUSE - DAY

Dr. Armistice and Sara press against the wall under the mirror as they watch the swirling figure eight of objects in the living room.

SARA
We've got to get Henry out of there.

DR. ARMISTICE
And keep Mister Moore in.
I've got an idea.

He stands up on his side of the mirror, and jiggles the frame. All the objects in the swirling figure eight crash to the floor.

MISTER MOORE (O.S.)
Hey, who's rocking the boat?

A book flies from the mirror whizzing past Dr. Armistice's head.

SARA
Uncle, be careful.

(CONTINUED)

DR. ARMISTICE
Careful has already left the premises. Help me carry this thing outside.

As they tilt the mirror slightly upward to lift it from its hook, everything in the area that is reflected (except fixed objects) slides in the direction of the mirror, and collides against the walls.

CUT TO:

INT. HENRY'S HOUSE / INSIDE THE MIRROR - DAY

As the mirror is being lifted from the wall everything (except fixed objects) bumps into and slides past Henry and Mister Moore, and crashes against the mirror's side of the room.
*[The view (reflection) of the real world from inside the mirror is right/left reversed. Over the next few scenes, Dr. Armistice and Sara carry the mirror down the hallway, and outside of the house. This movement causes Henry and Mister Moore's reflected environment to move under, over, behind, in front, around, and against them. - The environment moves like a solid liquid while Henry and Mister Moore are stationary objects.]*

CUT TO:

INT. HENRY'S HOUSE - DAY

Dr. Armistice and Sara balance the mirror between them, and carry it toward the open front door. An invisible force cracks the wooden banister as they pass.

CUT TO:

INT. HENRY'S HOUSE / INSIDE THE MIRROR - DAY

The banister has cracked from its collision with Henry, and it breaks when it slams into Mister Moore. The hallway walls and floor continue to move past them.

CUT TO:

INT. HENRY'S HOUSE - DAY

Dr. Armistice and Sara continue toward the door. WE HEAR loud scraping sounds along the hallway walls. Mister Moore's head comes out of the mirror.

MISTER MOORE
Who's driving this thing?

His sudden appearance scares Sara, and she loses her grip. The jolt of the mirror dropping to the floor causes Mister Moore to fall back inside. Henry pops his head out.

HENRY
Don't let him get to you.

SARA
I'll try not to. I love you.

HENRY
I love you too. Gotta go.

He disappears back into the mirror.

CUT TO:

EXT. HENRY'S HOUSE - DAY

Dr. Armistice and Sara carry the mirror out the door, and down the front steps.

DR. ARMISTICE

Just a little farther.

They carry the mirror across the lawn toward the campus pathway. Hawthorn follows, and barks as the wind howls.

DR. ARMISTICE

Henry, do you remember when I told you that the ability to read a clock was overrated?

There are flashes of lightning and rumbles of thunder in the colorless sky. CURIOUS STUDENTS gather to see what's going on.

CUT TO:

EXT. CAMPUS PATHWAY / INSIDE THE MIRROR - DAY

Henry and Mister Moore grapple as the front lawn, the pathway, and then the grassy field across from Henry's house rolls under them.

DR. ARMISTICE (O.S.)

Remember that a quarter to three when reflected in a mirror looks like nine-fifteen!

(CONTINUED)

The environment around Henry and Mister Moore abruptly stops moving.

DR. ARMISTICE (O.S.)
Get ready, Henry!

CUT TO:

EXT. GRASSY FIELD ACROSS FROM HENRY'S - DAY

Sara and Dr. Armistice have set the mirror down on the grass. He tilts it forward.

DR. ARMISTICE
When does six-thirty look like twelve o'clock?

MISTER MOORE (O.S.)
When it's upside down! But that won't make any difference to me!

Dr. Armistice tilts the mirror backward, then forward again.

DR. ARMISTICE
We shall see. Now, Henry!

He tilts the mirror backward, and lets it go.

CUT TO:

EXT. GRASSY FIELD / INSIDE THE MIRROR - DAY

As the mirror begins its fall backward, Henry pushes Mister Moore against a tree, and then grabs hold of the frame.

(CONTINUED)

The mirror's environment rapidly shifts from ground and grass to trees and clouds. As Henry dangles from the edge of the frame, Mister Moore scrambles to avoid falling into the oblivion of the sky.

CUT TO:

EXT. GRASSY FIELD ACROSS FROM HENRY'S - DAY

The crowd is shocked to see Henry's hands gripping the frame. Then, as the mirror completes its fall to the ground, the crowd is amazed when Henry bursts through the surface. He is half in, half out, and he clutches the frame to avoid falling back in. Sara and some Students rush forward to help.

HENRY
Get back!

As he starts to lift himself out, another hand reaches out from the surface and grabs hold of the edge of the frame opposite him. Mister Moore pulls himself up.

MISTER MOORE
Did you think I'd let you get away so easily? Not on your life, Professor! Actually? You are my life! As for the rest of you, say your prayers!

There is a loud crash of thunder.

HENRY
I released him, Sara!
<MORE> (CONTINUED)

HENRY (CONT'D)
I'm responsible! I love you.

SARA
I love you too, Henry!

MISTER MOORE
Are you two quite through!

HENRY
You're through, Mister Moore!

He leaps across the mirror onto Mister Moore. Together they fall and disappear into the mirror. Sara drops to her knees in tears.

SARA
Oh, Henry!

There is a sudden stillness, then a low rumble of thunder. Hawthorn walks over to the mirror's edge, and growls. Dr. Armistice carefully leans over to have a look into the mirror. Inside the mirror WE SEE Henry and Mister Moore dangling precariously upside down from the branches of a reflected tree. Dr. Armistice backs away from the mirror, and points to THREE STUDENTS.

DR. ARMISTICE
You three! Over here; quickly!

He beckons the Three Students to a birch tree, and points to a low hanging branch.

DR. ARMISTICE
Pull this branch down toward the mirror!

(CONTINUED)

The Three Students comply with the request.

DR. ARMISTICE
Careful now. Slowly...

The branch bows downward to the mirror and touches the surface. When Henry's hand reaches out and grabs it, the crowd exhales a sigh of relief.

DR. ARMISTICE
Bring him up! There's not a second to lose!

The lightning and thunder intensifies as the Three Students raise the branch, with Henry hanging on, away from the mirror.

SARA
Hold on, Henry!

Henry is almost out of the mirror. The crowd gasps when Mister Moore's hand bursts from the mirror and grabs hold of one of Henry's legs. Henry tries to shake him off, but Mister Moore reaches up and grabs the branch.

MISTER MOORE
You are all making me very angry!

Mister Moore's eyes bulge with rage as he puts his foot up on the edge of the frame for balance while holding tightly to Henry and the branch. Hawthorn snarls.

MISTER MOORE
Nice doggie. Now go away!

(CONTINUED)

Hawthorn barks, and bites Mister Moore's foot.

MISTER MOORE

Ow! Bad dog!

His eyes turn blood red. He moves his foot from the frame, and releases his hand from Henry so he can strike Hawthorn.

MISTER MOORE

I've had just about enough of you!

SARA

And we've all had more than enough of you!

She grabs her uncle's cane, and slams it against Mister Moore's hand that holds onto the branch. He lets go of the branch with a furious roar, and falls backward into the mirror. The Three Students pull the branch and Henry away from the mirror. There is a final deafening crash of lightning and thunder that comes from both the sky and the mirror. The clouds dissipate revealing a splendid early fall sunset. Sara gives the cane back to her uncle, and rushes to Henry, smothering him with kisses.

SARA

Oh, Henry! Henry! I'm so sorry I didn't believe you.

HENRY

That's all right. I wouldn't have believed me either.

(CONTINUED)

Dr. Armistice joins them, and hands Henry his cane.

DR. ARMISTICE
Would you like to do the honors?

HENRY
With pleasure!

He steps close to the mirror, and see the reflection of the sunset. He taps the glass with the cane. The surface is hard and firm. He raises the cane in the air preparing to destroy the mirror.

STEPHEN
Careful, Professor. That's seven years of bad luck.

HENRY
Poppycock!

Henry shatters the mirror with a powerful blow of the cane.

HENRY (continuing)
I'm not superstitious.

DR. ARMISTICE
Henry, my boy, when I told the dean I thought you'd make an extraordinary addition to the faculty I didn't know how true my words would be.

**SONG: <u>ANOTHER YEAR OF COLLEGE - FINALE</u>**

(CONTINUED)

The crowd cheers. Henry and Sara embrace and kiss. TWO STUDENTS roll a trash barrel over to the shattered mirror. The crowd begins depositing fragments of broken glass and frame into the barrel.

FEMALE STUDENTS
IT'S ANOTHER YEAR OF COLLEGE.
FILLED WITH STRESS AND STRAIN.

MALE STUDENTS
WE HOPE THAT SOMETHING USEFUL
FINDS IT'S WAY INTO OUR BRAINS.

ALL
IT'S ANOTHER YEAR AT FAIRMOUNT.
ANOTHER YEAR TO LEARN THE THINGS
THAT PASS FOR KNOWLEDGE THAT WILL
LAST LONG AFTER WE ARE FREE
OF ANOTHER YEAR OF COLLEGE.
IT'S ANOTHER YEAR OF COLLEGE!

Police cars pull up to the scene as Henry, Sara, and Hawthorn walk back toward the house. Dr. Armistice begins a conversation with Sgt. Rozner. A few POLICE OFFICERS question some Students.

ZOOM-IN next to Sgt. Rozner's foot. A small fragment of glass has been left in the grass.

EXTREME CLOSE-UP of the fragment reveals one of Mister Moore's eyes. It looks very angry.

**SONG: ANOTHER YEAR OF COLLEGE - FINALE ends**

The eye blinks.

BLACKOUT:

HEARTLESS
(The 3rd Movement from SYMPHONY #1 (THINK) IN G Major)
(Lyrics by Amanda George)


DEKE'S THEME - (YOU WONDER)


THINK
(The 1st and 4th Movements from SYMPHONY #1 (THINK) IN G Major)
MUSIQUE DE LA FEMME ANTOINETTE
(The 2nd Movement from SYMPHONY #1 (THINK) IN G Major)
MUSKETEER'S THEME
(The 2nd Movement from SYMPHONY #2 (WHISPER) IN $E^b$ Minor)
COMPLETELY NUDE
THAT'S WHAT I CALL LOVE
HARD HEADED, COLD-BLOODED, EVIL, HEARTLESS BITCH
CHOCOLATE TAPIOCA PUDDING
BLESSED VICTORY
THE ORPHAN STOMP
MOONLIGHT
MOB SONG
SANTA CLAUS LOVES LAS VEGAS
DO YOU EVER THINK OF ME AT ALL?
I GOT BAD TASTE
THE OVERTURE OF THE MIRROR
LUCKIEST GUY IN THE WORLD
I FOUND SOMEONE
THE MIRROR OF MISTER MOORE
ANOTHER YEAR OF COLLEGE
WILD ABOUT YOU
WILD ABOUT LOVE
THE MIRROR OF MISTER MOORE – REPRISE
ANOTHER YEAR OF COLLEGE – REPRISE
HENRY'S RESOLVE
MISTER MOORE'S TRIUMPH
MISTER MOORE'S TRIUMPH – REPRISE
FAIRMOUNT ALMA MATER
PLAY A GAME OF POOL WITH ME
PLAY A GAME OF POOL WITH ME – REPRISE
SARA'S QUANDARY
QUARTET OF DESIRES
DANGER! (TONIGHT IS THE NIGHT)
ODE ON AN AX MURDERER
THE HISTORY LESSON
WHY HAVEN'T YOU KILLED ME?
MISTER MOORE'S TRIUMPH – REPRISE #2
ANOTHER YEAR OF COLLEGE – FINALE

## about the authors

*TUXEDO BOB*, was born from a two-page fictional biography that Rob wrote in 1997 about a quirky singer/songwriter. Susan thought Tuxedo Bob was an interesting character, and suggested they use the bio as the basis for a novel. Rob thought she was kidding. Five years and many reams of paper later he realized that she wasn't.

They live in Southern California with their four cats, and are currently discussing the theme of their second novel.

Rob's songwriting credits include "JUST AS I AM" for AIR SUPPLY, "(LET'S) DO IT FOR OUR COUNTRY" for the movie *GREASE 2*, "SINNER MAN" for SARAH DASH, and a number of songs for short-lived television shows. His recordings include the cult classic "TOMMY, JUDY & ME" for RCA Records, and an instrumental dance version of "IN A GADDA DA VIDA" for Kama Sutra Records.

Printed in the United States
1090200001B/31